The House-Warming

The House-Warming

A Novel

Kristin Offiler

THOMAS & MERCER

Published by Thomas & Mercer, Seattle

www.apub.com

Amazon, the Amazon logo, and Thomas & Mercer are trademarks of Amazon.com, Inc., or its affiliates.

EU product safety contact:
Amazon Media EU S. à r.l.
38, avenue John F. Kennedy, L-1855 Luxembourg
amazonpublishing-gpsr@amazon.com

ISBN-13: 9781662530920 (paperback)
ISBN-13: 9781662530913 (digital)

Cover design by Kimberly Glyder
Cover image: © MonaMakela / Getty

Printed in the United States of America

For Matt, my love

Prologue

PATRICIA

August 2014

A soaking rain fell for three days straight, so heavy it seeped through waterproof jackets and rubber boots. Swells crashed on the jetty, the ocean visibly angry as it thrashed the island. Discarded ferry tickets and crumpled paper coffee cups swirled in puddles at the feet of search-party volunteers, who, like a pack of hunting dogs, shook the rainwater off their backs as they looked for her.

Zoe Gilbert, a young local jeweler from the mainland, was missing after a weeklong vacation with friends. The details were scarce: She'd stayed behind after the rest of her group boarded the ferry to leave Block Island on Sunday morning, telling them she wanted one more day on the beach. She hadn't been seen or heard from since. Calls to her cell phone went straight to voicemail. Her bank account appeared untouched. Even her parents, with whom she was close, hadn't heard from her.

There was no evidence she'd left the island, and none that she was still there, either.

On Monday night, the day after she was last seen, her roommate realized Zoe had never returned home. Zoe's parents reported her missing, and by Tuesday afternoon, a search was organized on the island. The group trudged through the rain, asking vacationers and locals if they'd seen Zoe Gilbert, checking with businesses and private residences near the ferry landing for video footage. And mostly, hoping they would find her alive and well in some remote corner of the tiny island, with nothing worse than a broken ankle and a mild case of dehydration.

Tuesday ended. They found nothing. The rain fell in sheets all night. They repeated the search on Wednesday, and again, no sign of her, no witnesses who recalled seeing her.

But on Thursday, once the sun rose and the storm finally blew out to sea, a pair of red heart-shaped sunglasses washed up on a stony beach at the base of the two-hundred-foot-tall Mohegan Bluffs. The lenses, scuffed and filmy with salt, reflected the morning sunlight and caught the eye of search-party volunteer Patricia Adele.

She pushed her own sunglasses up and crouched in a tidal pool to get a closer look at the glinting red hearts. Then she unfolded Zoe Gilbert's Missing poster, which she kept tucked inside the pocket of her shorts alongside a small notebook, and compared the sunglasses in Zoe's photo to the pair in front of her.

"I think I've got something here!"

She waved to the other volunteers searching this particular beach, accessible only by a 141-step wooden staircase nestled into the cliffside. She had volunteered to search here because she was fit enough for the trek—and because Zoe Gilbert's four friends were in the group.

Patricia had trailed them during the previous day's search, hopeful they'd talk to her about Zoe, but they hadn't noticed her. Patricia had hundreds of blog readers who would drop everything to read the inside scoop on an ongoing missing person case if she could get someone to talk.

The friends jogged over to Patricia.

"Oh, shit," the moody one said, her gaze landing hard on the sunglasses. The crooked name tag stuck to her tank top read *Lindsey*, and her dark hair was fixed in an unruly bun with a claw clip atop her head. Patricia had seen her quietly sucking back the small bottles of alcohol she kept in her bag when she thought no one was looking. "Could they be Zoe's?"

"Maybe. But this style is so common, right?" the quiet one, Meg, said. This was the first time in days Patricia hadn't seen Meg in tears. She cried as if she wanted everyone to know she missed Zoe the most.

"Yeah, they sort of look like the ones she was wearing last week," Callie, the rich friend, said with a downturn in her voice. "But it's hard to tell."

It was clear Callie had money, given her diamond-stud earrings and indestructible blowout, the soft twists of her blond ponytail bouncy and defiant against the elements. She carried a seemingly inexhaustible stack of Missing posters printed in full color on nice-quality cardstock. Whether it had to do with her wealth or her good looks or some long-ago established hierarchy, she was clearly in charge.

Callie bent down and lifted the glasses out of the sand.

"Cal, no—don't touch them," Tess said in a loud whisper. She wore a threadbare Ives Art Camp T-shirt and frayed jean shorts, her short hair pulled into a stubby ponytail. Patricia sensed something about Tess was stuck in the past. She'd heard the girls met as teenagers at the now-defunct Ives Art Camp, but why a twentysomething-year-old woman would still be wearing a shirt from her teenage days was beyond her. Unless Tess was clinging so tightly to the past, she couldn't even let go of something as simple as a shirt.

"Who wants to call this in?" Patricia asked. Surely this discovery would earn her their trust. It could give her access to pose the questions she'd been dying to ask and tell Zoe's story to her readers in a way that felt more human than the dry local news reports.

But instead, they looked at Patricia as if she had been made of ocean mist until that very second and were just registering her existence for the first time. Their collective attention dredged up a prickly memory for her: a pack of girls in the high school locker room cornering her because she'd snitched on them for smoking behind the gymnasium. The ringleader had shoved Patricia hard against the cool metal lockers and bruised the side of her face, hissing at her to mind her own business next time. And when the volleyball coach asked what happened to Patricia's cheek, the girls lied.

She tripped over her own feet, one girl said before Patricia could answer.

You should really watch where you're going, another said to her.

Those girls had protected each other the moment someone sought the truth.

"I'm sorry, I don't think we've met," Callie said. Her brows knit together above her dark designer frames. "Do you live on the island? Or know Zoe?"

"No," Patricia said. "But I saw the story on the news and wanted to help. I'm a bit of a reporter. I mean, I have a blog where I write about missing people, but I've never had a chance to join a search firsthand like this. My readers are really interested in the details."

"Oh," Callie said. "Well, thank you for helping."

"You're going to call the detective, right?" Patricia asked. She gestured at Tess. "And she's right. You shouldn't touch the glasses. They could be evidence."

"We'll bring them to the detective ourselves," Lindsey said. "We're about to head back up."

"That's not how it works," Patricia said, coarser than she intended. "I'm sorry, I know you must all be so worried about Zoe. But look, I'm working on a blog post; maybe I can ask you some questions while we wait for the detective. Get some details about your trip. Hear from your perspective what happened."

"You can talk to the police if you have questions," Callie said. "We aren't giving interviews."

Patricia tilted her head. "Why not? You were the last people seen with her, and you just spent the entire week with her on the island.

You're the best ones to speak about Zoe. I can send you the link to my blog if you want to see the kinds of cases I—"

Callie cut her off. "What part of 'we aren't giving interviews' wasn't clear?"

Then she turned, and the others followed as if pulled by invisible marionette strings, definitively slicing Patricia out of the group.

Patricia watched from a distance as they stood in a tight circle and passed the sunglasses back and forth, inspecting them. Except for Tess. She held her hands away, refusing.

Their voices were drowned out by the waves crashing on the rocky beach. Patricia wished she could hear the conversation clearly. What were they saying? Why was Tess the only one unwilling to touch the sunglasses? Were they discussing what to do with those red frames? Did they need to make them disappear?

And, if their conversation was innocent, why not include Patricia herself, the only other volunteer on this beach—a twentysomething, like them—who was giving up her time to look for *their* friend? Why didn't they want her help spreading the word of their friend's disappearance?

Then she remembered cold metal against her cheek, the ringing silence in the locker room once she was alone, eyes burning with tears. The feeling of being punished for trying to do the right thing.

Her sense of justice ran too deep to sit this out.

"I'm calling the detective," she yelled over to them. "I'm sorry, but you're tampering with potential evidence. I know a thing or two about this stuff."

"We'll take care of it, thank you," Callie called back in a tight voice.

Patricia pulled her cell phone from her pocket and made the call. A distinct thrill filled her when the detective answered and she explained what she'd found.

"I'll be down shortly," he said. "For now, just leave them where you found them."

"I tried to," Patricia said.

She hung up and began planning what she would write about this discovery. *Her* discovery. Then she thought better of it. This deserved to be documented. She'd show her audience and let them feel like part of the action.

Patricia started recording with her phone and aimed it at Zoe's friends. She zoomed in on the red sunglasses in Callie's perfectly manicured hands. A cloudy tapestry of fingerprints covered the sunglasses now. They continued to discuss something Patricia could not hear, but with her phone, she captured the shape of the words on their mouths. Maybe later she could decipher them.

Lindsey noticed Patricia recording them and glared at her.

"Stop," Lindsey mouthed slowly and pointedly.

Patricia shook her head and kept recording. She wouldn't be pushed so easily into minding her own business. Especially when her instincts told her not to look away.

Twenty minutes later, the detective climbed down the cliffside staircase and lumbered over the rocky beach to Patricia.

Zoe's friends made their way over when they saw him arrive.

Patricia tried to catch their gazes, but they wouldn't look at her. The detective mopped his red, sweat-drenched face with a wilting stack of brown paper napkins, then shoved them into the pocket of his khakis.

"This humidity is killing me," he muttered, taking the sunglasses from Callie. "Okay. So, who found these, exactly?"

Patricia raised her hand. "I did. The glasses were right over there, sitting by that boulder in the sand."

"Well, don't get so excited," he said as he whipped open an evidence bag and dropped them inside. "It's an interesting find, but it's not a person. They're sending another group down this way to help you grid-search the beach. Hang tight."

Patricia knew she should leave it at that if she wanted to salvage a chance at connecting with Zoe's friends, but she couldn't help herself. What they'd done was wrong.

"How will we know if this is evidence of a crime if they touched the sunglasses? Isn't that contamination?"

"Ma'am," the detective said, a trace of irritation in his voice, "there's no reason to jump to foul play just yet. Sure, I'd prefer if no one touched these before I got here, but it isn't going to make or break anything. We're looking for a person right now. Not signs of a crime."

"I know how important evidence preservation is," Patricia said. "If it's a clue, it's now compromised."

"You sound like you hope she's dead and there's a killer to catch," Lindsey said. "And why were you recording us? What the hell is your deal?"

"Just let it go," Meg murmured to Lindsey.

"No. I want to know," Lindsey said. "Sir, she was recording us on her phone. I want that video deleted."

"Lindsey," Callie said. "Chill."

Patricia didn't want to delete it. Especially if they wanted her to. What were they so worried about?

"Actually, I was trying to get service, not recording you. Paranoid much?"

"Tell you what," the detective said to Patricia, "since you found the glasses, why don't you come with me to log it back at home base. You can help me out, okay?"

She nodded and followed him slowly back up the rambling wooden staircase, casting a final glance at Zoe's friends. They stood near the water's edge, watching her. Happy to see her go, no doubt.

The detective struggled up each of the nearly 150 steps, giving her plenty of time to think.

He must have kids, Patricia thought. *Probably daughters.* He'd probably sensed the charge between her and them, and knew from experience how quickly tension could devolve into ugliness. Smart of him to pull her away, even though she would've preferred staying with the group and trying a little harder to crack them open. Even if they didn't like her, she had struck a nerve with them.

Sometimes a struck nerve was more telling than the words a person said out loud.

And that was fine. So they didn't like her. What did it matter? They were never going to befriend her. In fact, she had the distinct feeling these people were not Zoe Gilbert's friends, either. They were the worst kind of girls: phony, disloyal liars.

The kind of girls who'd keep each other's secrets.

A week later, Patricia Adele removed the skeleton of a tent from its protective bag and began feeding poles through nylon loops until it sprang to life. She staked the tent in a grassy corner of a public park that shared a property line with Meg's mother's house. From there, Patricia could keep an eye on the girls but technically wasn't trespassing. Inside her tent, she unrolled a sleeping bag and arranged her notebook, a handheld camera, and spare batteries on the ground. She opened her laptop and skimmed the flood of new comments on her most recent video with Zoe Gilbert's boyfriend. She let the video play while she read. Every time it played, she made another few cents. And if an ad ran on the video, a few dollars.

"People say when a woman goes missing, it's always the husband or boyfriend who did it," Patricia had said to Blake, her camera recording their interview from the sidewalk outside Meg's mother's house.

"I've heard that," he said. His tattooed arms were crossed tight across his chest. "It's not true now, though."

"Why should people believe that?"

"Because I'm out here trying to help. I wouldn't be helping if I was hiding something. Plus, I already talked to the cops. They didn't arrest me, did they? And I'm talking to you, aren't I?"

"You're right. It does say something that you're willing to speak out. Unlike Zoe's friends, who won't talk to me," Patricia said. "Not since I started asking questions they don't want me asking. Do you know them well?"

Blake's eyes darted to the camera lens for a split second. Patricia caught an air of nervousness in his body language, but he corrected it quickly.

"I don't really know her friends at all," he said.

"So tell us where you were on the Sunday Zoe reportedly went missing."

"At home, all day and night. My roommate has already vouched for me. I haven't seen Zoe since the day she left for Block Island, a week before she went missing. Now it's been over two weeks. I can't believe she hasn't tried to call or text me or anything. We didn't always talk every day, but almost." He paused, blinked rapidly, then cleared his throat. "But I wasn't the last one to see her. A lot of people saw her after the last time I did."

Blake was similar to the guys Patricia had liked in college: overly confident, slightly unkempt, happy to remind you he could do better if you turned him down. Probably allergic to real commitment but pissed if the girl they wouldn't commit to dated anyone else. She could read him. He was withholding something—but she didn't think he knew where Zoe was.

"Were things with you and Zoe serious?"

"Serious enough." He looked straight into the camera. "Zoe, baby, I miss you. Come home. At least call me if you see this. Let me know you're okay."

This is where Patricia had cut the footage. It was powerful to end on a hopeful note, to show Zoe's boyfriend pleading for her safe return. Something her friends hadn't done once.

New comments appeared on the video every few minutes. Patricia loved seeing her work gain traction.

I always say the husband/boyfriend did it but her BF is clearly innocent!!

Why aren't those girls being arrested right now? Silence = guilt.

My bro's friend went to school w/ Lindsey. DM me if you want to know more.

We all know how this goes: the last people to see a missing person are guilty. This isn't rocket science. BF didn't see her but friends did. HELLO??

Thank u, Patricia, 4 being Zoe's voice. Keep reporting what u find. Some1 will crack eventually and then we'll know the TRUTH.

Patricia peered out the mesh window of her tent at the sound of voices approaching. Her local blog readers gathered on the street, signs in hand. One person knelt to prop a teddy bear and a bouquet of flowers against the mailbox's wooden post. Another passed around battery-operated candles. They aimed their chanting at the house where Callie, Lindsey, Tess, and Meg were hiding.

Patricia stepped out of the tent to join them. She planted her feet just at the edge of the property, held up her camera with one hand, and spoke into the lens.

"Thank you all for your support as I cover Zoe Gilbert's case. We're having a great conversation in the comments section of my last video, the interview with Zoe's boyfriend, Blake. Join us there and share your thoughts. I'm also happy to see so many of you still commenting on my first video from last week. I know the footage is a little grainy, but it's been incredible to read the comments from body-language and lip-reading experts. Some of the interpretations of what Zoe's friends were saying in that footage—and what their bodies were saying—are truly fascinating. And so many of you were upset to see Zoe's friends handling the sunglasses, just like I was!

"But so far, the police haven't been able to say with certainty if they're Zoe's sunglasses or not. My gut tells me they are, and that something happened to her on that secluded beach. There's more to this story than meets the eye, and if you're as determined as I am to find the truth, I encourage you to keep interacting with my videos and blog posts. Keep telling Zoe's friends that the world wants the truth.

"None of this work would be possible without your generous contributions. So, if you like what I'm doing and want to play a part in getting justice for Zoe, click the link below this video and donate to my virtual tip jar. The highest contributor each day receives a special shout-out in my next video. Today we have Rita, with a two-hundred-dollar contribution! Thank you, Rita."

Patricia stopped recording and turned to the house. The girls watched from an upstairs window, their mouths moving as they spoke to each other behind the glass. Patricia waved, and the curtain fell sharply in front of them.

The people on the street chanted in a steady cadence. *"Where is Zoe? Where is Zoe?"* Patricia slipped back inside her tent and uploaded her next video.

The speed with which it was liked and shared was dizzying. Intoxicating. People clamored to hear about missing women. It almost didn't matter who she was, so long as her story had some meat for the public to chew on, some mystery for them to pick apart.

The truth of the mystery, Patricia believed, was locked away inside the walls of the girls' impenetrable friendship. But even the most solid of friendships had fault lines that could fail given the right pressure. That's all she was doing—testing for weak spots. Eventually, the fortress would crack and she'd know what happened to Zoe.

As Patricia fell asleep that night in her tent outside Meg's mother's house, she thought of the sunglasses. The cherry-red frames, the faint cracks in the lenses. The way the ocean had delivered them at her feet like a sign that Zoe Gilbert was out there somewhere, just waiting for the right person to uncover the truth and set her free from whatever hell those girls had caused her.

Chapter One

CALLIE

Five years later

Callie Sutter never expected to set foot back on Block Island after all it had taken from her. Some people and places simply belonged in the past.

But her husband, Nathan, had been talking for months about finding an oasis outside New York City, a soft place to land after selling MindBalm, their successful mindfulness app. Somewhere they could take a break from the city.

"It might be nice to be closer to my parents," Callie said when he asked where she wanted to live.

With that, Nathan found listings of available houses in New England, specifically around Rhode Island, for them to consider.

One of the listings—by far the most beautiful—was for a breathtaking three-story house with gray, weathered shingles; a shimmering saltwater pool; and towering oaks lining a long, curving driveway. It came with a guesthouse. It was nestled in a quiet neighborhood with picturesque water views. Callie fell in love with everything about the property before she realized its location: Block Island.

"I'm sorry, I didn't even notice," Nathan said when she pointed it out. "Forget about that one."

"No, hold on," Callie said, scrolling through the photos of the house again. She could picture them preparing dinners of kale salad and salmon in the spacious, sunny kitchen and swimming laps in the pool under the warm glow of bistro lights. She knew where she'd put the Christmas tree.

And the parties—the house was practically made for hosting.

"Maybe it's perfect?" she said.

"Or maybe living out there will dredge up too many bad memories," he countered.

The truth—which had been buried for years but began resurfacing lately—was that she'd never truly processed what had happened. The time after Zoe's disappearance had splintered her life, leaving her friendless and with so much grief, it was easier to ignore her feelings than face them. Then she met Nathan, and the almost-nonstop work on MindBalm had been the perfect distraction, filling her calendar and life with meetings, decisions, late-night work for years. Now that all of it was gone, she would have to reckon with her past. There was no getting around it.

"What if that's what I need right now?" she asked, mostly to herself. "It's been five years. Maybe I need to dredge."

Nathan considered this. Callie could see his interest growing as he skimmed the listing photos, too.

"It would be a huge change of pace for us," he said. "There's additional effort getting back and forth between the island and mainland on the ferry. There's winter—that'll be an experience, for sure. And then there's . . . your history."

Callie's logical side told her to put it out of her mind. Be realistic. Her husband made some very good points about the impracticality of this idea.

But another side of her—the side she'd dubbed her maternal voice, a voice very much *not* like her actual mother—said something else. It reminded her that her memories weren't all bad. That there were many, many more good ones tied to the island; the bad ones were just larger and louder. It said this was a story she could rewrite.

"Let's just ask about it," she said. "We don't have to buy it. We can just inquire."

Nathan raised a brow. "I know that look. That's the look you get when you're determined. Is this something you really want to do?"

She held up her hands. "You sent me the listing! Let's just ask if anyone else is interested. See if there's wiggle room in the price."

The asking price was three million dollars. High, but not out of their budget after selling MindBalm. They could afford it, and then some. If they wanted, they could spend a few quiet years doing no work at all.

After that, everything happened quickly.

Their inquiry turned into an offer, which was accepted right away by the seller. Four weeks later, they were sitting in an attorney's office in Rhode Island, signing what felt like a thousand sheets of paper, officially making the house theirs. The fluorescent lights overhead hummed as their Realtor handed Callie a ring of gleaming keys.

"Block Island," the Realtor said with smile and a small shake of her head. "You two are really living the dream."

Afterward, in the car, Nathan took a long sip from his iced matcha. The plastic cup was beaded with condensation.

"Can't believe we just did that," he said.

"We might be out of our minds."

He set the cup down and shook his head. "Our wild ideas always turn into our best ones. This will, too." He nodded toward the phone in Callie's hands. "Posting about the move already?"

"Not yet," she said. "I need to tell Tess, Meg, and Lindsey first. I don't want to blindside them with an Instagram post. They'll probably have questions. And I want to feel them out. See if anyone has softened, you know?"

"Good call," he said.

"Here's what I have so far," she went on. "'This is Callie, in case you don't have my number anymore. Nathan and I just purchased a beautiful property on Block Island, and I wanted you to be the first ones to know. On August tenth, we're throwing a housewarming party, and it would mean the world to me if you three would come. We'll hold a memorial for Zoe at the party. We never had a proper one together, but now is the time. I hope to see you there.'"

Nathan stopped at a red light and looked over at Callie.

"August tenth?" he asked.

"I told you I was working on the housewarming," she said, skirting around his question.

"But you didn't tell me we're throwing a housewarming party on the fifth anniversary of your friend's disappearance," he said, more of a statement than question. The light turned green and Nathan turned the car toward the harbor.

"I'm telling you now!" she said, nudging his arm. "You always say to trust the process. Try trusting *my* process. I promise it'll be great."

"But August tenth?"

"It has to be the tenth," Callie said, her voice firm. There wasn't room for negotiation.

With that, she hit send on her message before she could change her mind. Her stomach swooped. It was done. An olive branch extended to the friends who hadn't spoken to her in five years. All she could do now was hope they'd accept it.

Nathan cut the air-conditioning and rolled down the windows as they pulled in line for the ferry. The stink of low tide and idling cars was a portal into the past—to those golden summers at art camp and, later, tipsy vacations in a rented cottage with her friends. All of it in another lifetime.

Dozens of people at the ticket booth were lined up with coolers and overnight bags, leashed dogs in tow. Parents wrangled babies in floppy sun hats, and big kids carried boogie boards. While they idled in the car line, Callie lifted her phone and snapped a few photos to share with her one hundred thousand Instagram followers. They loved moments like this, little peeks into her polished life.

But first, she shared a glimpse of the house, just a fraction of the stone patio and an expanse of spring-green grass rolling down to the saltwater pool. Nothing too identifiable—she'd learned her lesson the hard way years earlier when it came to strangers on the internet and their proclivity for sleuthing. She captioned it: *Surprise! Leaving NYC behind for a little place called Block Island. I have stories to tell about the many summers I spent here and the dear friends it gave me, but that's for another day. Right now, I'm soaking up this new beginning and feeling serene. Must be the negative ions from the ocean. Remember, when it comes to ions, negative means good, and my favorite air ionizer is linked in my bio. Use my code for $200 off.*

Soon, they parked the car in the belly of the boat, climbed the steel stairs up to the open-air top deck, and found a seat at the end of a crowded bench. A stranger rubbed her sunscreen-greased forearm against Callie's expensive blazer by mistake. Was there a dry cleaner on the island? She'd have to check on that.

A horn sounded and the ferry began to move. Callie felt briefly disoriented: a forward tug of her static body coupled with the surreal sensation of going back. If she imagined hard enough, she could pretend the stranger's arm next to her belonged to Zoe, that they were all together on the way to another annual trip, where Zoe would spend the hour-long ride creating absurd names and backstories for the other passengers just to make her friends laugh.

But Callie wasn't going to play those games with herself. It wasn't healthy to dwell in the past, especially when the past was such a minefield of secrets and loss.

Whitecaps and boats dotted the rippled ocean below. Soon, the island in the distance became a visible crease, flat and insignificant at first but quickly unfolding into land. There was a magical quality to how the island appeared and disappeared into the contour of the horizon. How many times had Callie stood on the deck of this ferry with Zoe and the others, watching the land shrink into itself over the course of an hour as the ferry pulled them back to the mainland? The island shrank and shrank until it was a flat line in the distance, and then nothing at all. A wisp of something real before vanishing.

American flags slapped the wind, each one occupying a pole along the front porch of the historic hotel opposite the harbor. Dozens of buoys in shades of blue and red hung on the sides of shingled buildings. Day drinkers in damp bathing suits walked along the slick rock jetty, plastic cups in hand, raised high to prevent their beverages from sloshing out. Callie could almost taste the too-sweet drinks and feel the jetty underfoot.

She and Nathan followed the crowd down to the bottom of the boat and found their car. When it was their turn, they rolled off the boat ramp and turned onto Water Street, where pedestrians darted into the road and mopeds zipped around idling traffic. The hot air was scented with salt water, fried food, beach roses. Most buildings along the main drag were a hundred years old, a mix of New England saltbox and Victorian architecture. As they passed quick-bite shacks and shops selling Block Island souvenirs and coastal home decor, Callie swallowed the lump climbing the back of her throat.

Five years. So much was unchanged, yet nothing was the same.

"This is exactly the oasis I was picturing for us," Nathan said once they'd cleared the congestion of the ferry terminal and Water Street and were cruising up Spring. The ocean stretched endlessly to their left, a shimmering blue eternity.

The house sat a few minutes down the road, not far from the Mohegan Bluffs, at the end of a long driveway in a quiet neighborhood. As the trees thinned, the house came into view, roof peaks at various heights and a circular turret at the front center piercing through the third floor. A copper whale-shaped weather vane protruded from one of the peaks, its directionals spinning lazily in the breeze.

Nathan parked in front of the three-car garage. They got out and Callie looked up, one hand shielding her face and the other clutching the key ring.

"You should do the honors," Nathan asked.

She walked up the steps, slid the key into the lock, and gave it a turn. They stood silent in the entryway, then Callie turned to Nathan as her vision blurred.

"I don't know why I'm about to cry," she said with a laugh-sob.

"You okay?" Nathan squeezed her hand, and she nodded. "Be right back; I'll grab the bags."

Callie stepped inside, her watery gaze skimming the space. The house felt different in person, but not in any obvious or terrible way. She knew all the stats: 5,017 square feet, five bedrooms and seven bathrooms, two acres of land, a guesthouse out back. The polished hardwood floors, stone fireplace, gleaming marble countertops all looked how she'd expected. But there were aspects she couldn't have known until now, like the laundry-detergent smell of the previous occupants, the long angle of late-morning light through the windows, how it would feel to finally return to the island, to set foot back in the place where the best and worst things had happened to her.

She started opening windows and doors—first in the sitting room, then the dining room, and through the kitchen and breakfast nook—eager to get new air into this place. Down the hall was a half bath, a mudroom off the garage, and a large family room with another fireplace, built-in shelves for books, and a wall of tall windows.

Callie noticed an older man in a wide-brimmed hat tending a raised-bed garden next door, the two yards separated by a sprawling stone wall. The man halted at the triple beep of Nathan locking the SUV and eyeballed their house. She pictured inviting the neighbors over for chilled organic wine on the patio, making new friends, gently revealing her connection to Zoe and the island once she knew she could trust them. Rewriting her relationship to this place so it could truly feel like home.

Callie went back down the hall where Nathan was lugging two suitcases over the threshold. He nodded to the French doors off the kitchen that led out to the backyard.

"I'm dying to see the guesthouse in person," he said. "You're sure your parents will be comfortable out there when they visit? It's on the small side."

Callie followed him out the back door and eyed the guesthouse. It was plenty large enough for two people visiting their daughter and son-in-law for a night or two at a time, even if it was minuscule compared to her parents' estate in Jamestown.

"They'll survive," she said.

Nathan scoffed. "Have you ever met your parents?"

Callie laughed, always grateful for how well he knew her and her sometimes-complex family dynamics. When she'd first told her parents about Nathan, they were confused. He wasn't from a wealthy family and didn't have an impressive job. He meditated every morning and rarely drank alcohol. He was practically an alien to her parents.

But those were the aspects Callie loved about him. And together they'd turned his appreciation of mindfulness and meditation into the MindBalm app, surprising the investors with how popular it was right out of the gate. She'd left her job in social media management to go all in with Nathan, leveraging the connections her last name and family reputation afforded her. And then, selling MindBalm just a few years after building it had given them a financial windfall and the time to slow down and decide what to do next, as well as the chance to live close to her parents. With her father showing symptoms of memory decline the last few years, Callie had felt she should be closer to home. She just didn't want them constantly on her doorstep.

"What do you think?" she asked as they passed through the main room of the guesthouse. It was homey, a bit dated, nothing special.

"I think it's great they left the furniture. Imagine shipping two houses worth of stuff out here," Nathan said.

Callie smiled, though her first thought upon seeing the floral-upholstered couch was that she'd need to find a replacement ASAP. Her mother had *opinions* when it came to interiors, especially fabrics. Callie's childhood bedroom had been decorated in a specific sage-green palette to match the custom curtains her mother had designed. The family boat had been outfitted with cushions and quilts in what her mother claimed was a one-of-a-kind textile. She was sure her mother would be allergic to the mass-produced floral couch and the white linen window treatments in the guesthouse.

"You hate it?" Nathan asked. He leaned against the back of the couch, eyeing the pillows. "Or you're thinking your mother will hate it."

Callie crossed the room and wrapped her arms around his waist.

"You know me too well. It doesn't matter if she likes it, though. What matters is if we're happy here," she said, surprised by the crack in her voice. "We'll be happy here, right?"

Nathan smoothed his hand along her back and kissed the top of her head.

"Of course we will. I can feel it," he said.

Callie ran out for groceries later in the day while Nathan unpacked. The general store was just as she remembered: compact, well organized, clean. It carried a smaller selection than a grocery store on the mainland, but it was still well stocked with her essentials, like oat milk creamer and kombucha.

She made her way around the store, filling the cart with veggies, gluten-free bread, organic coffee beans, tofu, sparkling water. When her cart was sufficiently packed, Callie got in line behind a teenage couple evidently on their way to the beach. Flip-flops, a cooler sitting at their feet, striped towels rolled up under their arms.

A familiar faded logo spread across the back of the girl's T-shirt, shoulder to shoulder, and Callie's heart hitched. IVES ART CAMP EST. 1986. MAKE ART + MEMORIES!

It was the same style shirt Callie had worn several summers in a row as a teenager. The same one she remembered Tess wearing while they searched for Zoe.

Tess had also worn it before Zoe disappeared, while they were on the island during their last trip. Callie was slapped with a memory from that week that she hadn't thought about in years. The five of them on the beach one afternoon, the August sun high and strong in a clear sky. Tess toweled off and pulled the T-shirt over her bathing suit, and Lindsey dryly asked why she still wore it, why she clung to old stuff like that.

Zoe, her new heart sunglasses covering her eyes, dark hair wavy and damp after a swim in the ocean, had swatted at Lindsey for the critique.

"No one judges you for clinging to the same Forever 21 dress you've had since college," she'd said to Lindsey. "You look great in it, don't get me wrong. As good as Tess looks in a shirt she wore at sixteen. Leave her and her Ives shirt alone."

"I do judge her for that dress, actually," Tess had said.

They'd all laughed and moved on before it turned into anything more. Hurt feelings, a spat. Zoe could always read the group like that. She had radar for incoming trouble and could head it off before it arrived better than the rest of them.

Callie couldn't remember what happened next, but she could still *feel* that trip. It felt like grains of sand all over the cottage's tile floors, cold drinks at the bar, scratchy sheets on flimsy mattresses. The last moments of that life as she knew it.

"I went there," Callie said to the girl's back. She didn't know why; she just needed to say it out loud.

The girl turned, confused.

"Sorry," Callie said. "Your Ives Art Camp shirt—I went there. Back when it existed, I mean. What is it now? A wedding venue or something?"

"I guess so. This was my mom's," the girl said, plucking at the fabric. "I found it in her closet. It's vintage."

"*Vintage.* Ha. That's so funny."

The girl smiled, barely suppressing an eye roll. "Yeah. But like, technically stuff that's twenty years and older is vintage, so. This qualifies."

Which meant Callie's teenage years at that camp would soon be vintage, too. Time marched forward, and she was powerless to slow it. The thought made her head swim. Wasn't she just there? Crying on the steps of the cabin, Zoe's calm presence the first thing that made her think she might survive the summer?

The boy and girl paid, collected their cooler, and left without another look at her. Callie loaded her items onto the conveyor belt, then went to the end to bag. The cashier, another teenager, glanced over as she scanned.

"This looks like a rental haul. Here for the week?"

"No, actually, my husband and I just moved here."

"For the summer?"

"Permanently."

"Wow. Brave. I can't wait to graduate next year and go to school in Boston," she said with a grin. "I need to get outta here."

"I get that," Callie said. Sometimes getting out was the only option. "But I'm looking forward to living here for a while. I used to visit in the summer, growing up. I've always wanted to come back."

She had just bagged a few more items when she felt a tap on her shoulder. A woman with short, brown hair swept behind her ears squinted at Callie, a delicate fan of wrinkles creasing around her eyes. She wore a white polo shirt and white skirt, everything about her crisp and tidy.

"Excuse me, are you . . . ?"

Callie smiled. She figured eventually she'd run into a fan, but she didn't expect it would happen so quickly.

"Callie Sutter? Yes, I am. Are you a MindBalm user?"

"A what balm?"

"Sorry, I forget some of my Instagram followers don't use the app."

"I'm not on any app," she said, her expression cooling. "I just wanted to say you have some nerve showing your face here. It takes a lot of gall."

The cashier recited the total, and Callie slid her credit card into the reader, keeping her eyes on the screen. Hoping the woman would realize she'd made a mistake and leave her alone. But a creeping sense of unease worked its way up the back of her neck.

"I saw the flyer, you know," the woman went on. "The one of you and your little friends. It's audacious to waltz around like you have any right to be here."

"What flyer?" Callie looked up. "We haven't circulated any flyers about Zoe in ages."

The original Missing poster had only shown a picture of Zoe. Unless someone was circulating new ones ahead of the anniversary. The detective? No, he would've called her about it first. One of her friends? But who would've done that on their own? They all had their strengths, but it was no secret she and Zoe had been the self-starters of the group. The others did best when Callie or Zoe led the charge.

Callie pulled her credit card from the reader. "I'm sorry, but I don't know what you're talking about."

"Of course you'd say that. But there are a lot of people on this island who remember the whole Zoe Gilbert debacle. You aren't fooling anyone."

Callie's voice failed her. The stranger walked off briskly, disappearing with a shopping cart into the produce section.

Callie took the receipt from the cashier. "That was so bizarre."

"You knew Zoe Gilbert? Her poster is still on the bulletin board out front, you know."

"Really?"

"I see it every time I rearrange the board. It seems, like, really mean to throw it away, so I just leave her up there."

Callie barely managed to thank the cashier before taking her groceries and pushing her cart into the vestibule. She flipped through the papers on a corkboard littered with ads for rental houses and community events until she found it, buried under a notice for an au pair job.

The Missing poster was faded and tattered, and Callie gingerly took it down. She traced a finger over Zoe's name, her photo, the description of what she'd been wearing the last time she was seen. Callie had been the one to give that description to the authorities. *Blue-and-white tie-dyed tank top, jean shorts, black bikini. Leather sandals. Tan bag. Red heart-shaped sunglasses.*

Callie smoothed the corners of the poster, her throat tightening. She hadn't run to the store expecting to confront Zoe's Missing poster. It was like an artifact, a piece of the past that realistically shouldn't even exist anymore. Yet the poster had been waiting patiently all these years for the precise moment when someone would find it. Callie's eyes burned hot with impending tears. She blinked them away and slipped the Missing poster into her purse.

Before she left the parking lot, she checked her phone. No response to her reunion text. Callie tossed her phone into the passenger seat. How long would they punish her? Wasn't five years long enough? Was it such a crime that she'd taken action while the rest of them floundered in the sea of accusations Patricia had thrown them into?

The interview hadn't been her idea. To this day, the details of how it came to be were murky.

"We got a call about setting up an interview," her mother had said over the phone.

Callie was still holed up at Meg's mother's house at the time, the four of them trying to figure out how to exist in the world now that they were recognizable and distrusted by the general public. Patricia was still showing up outside daily to make videos for her ever-growing group of conspiracy theorists. The weight of Patricia's accusations grew heavier each day Zoe was still missing.

"But they only want you, sweetheart," her mother went on. "I think it's a good idea."

Callie remembered looking over her shoulder at Lindsey, Meg, and Tess. They sat around the kitchen table, useless. Something in Callie gave out, no longer able to helplessly tread water with them. Patricia had spent two weeks obsessing over a pair of sunglasses and a grainy cell phone video, convincing strangers it was enough evidence to prove the friends were hiding something. Strangers who knew their faces had figured out where they lived and worked and who they'd dated. Strangers who went feral over the idea of lifelong friends killing each other.

Callie couldn't stand the thought of letting it continue unchecked.

"Tell them I'll do it," she'd said to her mother.

The next day, stepping onto the local morning-show set, Callie had second thoughts. She regretted not telling her friends, not giving them the chance to speak, too. For lying when she left the house, saying she was going to see her parents.

"Excuse me," she asked a producer holding a clipboard at the door to the greenroom. "If my friends want to give interviews, who can they call? Who organized this?"

The producer paused. "I guess they can call me. But I thought your assistant set this up?"

Callie was confused. "I don't have an assistant. Did you talk to my mother?"

"Maybe?" the producer shook her head. "You're here, that's all that matters. And we only need your interview, unless they have a different story to tell."

Callie thanked the producer but immediately wondered if her friends had told her everything. It was a thought she hadn't allowed herself to have while in their constant presence for two weeks, a thought that was easier to contemplate in the quiet of the greenroom. For two weeks, Callie had pushed away any suspicions that wormed into her mind. Suspicions that someone was lying, that the growing awkwardness between them all was a result of something more than just Zoe's disappearance. But suspicions weren't facts, and without proof, they were nothing more than empty imaginings.

She was soon whisked out to the set and was live on the air with a reporter.

"We've all seen the video of you and your friends with the sunglasses. Tell us what you were thinking at that moment," the interviewer said.

Callie froze. She wanted to talk about Zoe. She had the police tip line number memorized and was ready to share it. She wanted to speak about the harassment they'd been receiving, to condemn the public's obsession with true crime as entertainment, to defend her friends.

"We were thinking . . . I don't remember, exactly," Callie said. The lights on set were bright. Sweat beaded on her scalp. "It was an overwhelming moment."

"Some people believe that in the video circulating of you and your friends, you were discussing a plan to hide evidence. Is that the case?"

"No, of course not."

"The internet is abuzz right now with discussions on Zoe's case. What is it about you and your friends that people seem fascinated by?"

"Fascinated? They're obsessed. Obsessed with the idea of a crime that never happened instead of finding Zoe. We have to all do our part to reject sensationalized theories in favor of real facts."

The reporter leaned back in her chair. "Where do you think Zoe is?"

"I don't know. We're desperate to find her, though. There's a tip line anyone can call if they saw or heard anything that might help the search."

"We'll share that number with all of you watching at home," the reporter said. "Just one final question, Ms. Sutter: Are you positive none of you were involved in Zoe Gilbert's disappearance?"

Callie hesitated. The voice of her public relations consultant came to her mind: *Just speak for yourself. You can only vouch for your actions, your thoughts, your whereabouts. Giving people the benefit of the doubt might mean being inadvertently tangled up in their lies later on.*

Callie spoke carefully. "In my heart, I believe we're all innocent of any wrongdoing. But I can only speak for myself. I just know we left the island together, without Zoe, and then I went home to New York by myself. Zoe was fine when I last saw her on Block Island. I have no idea what happened after that. If she saw someone on the island—or even back on the mainland, for example—I don't know about it."

The reporter raised a single eyebrow. "You think it's possible Zoe went back to the mainland? Back to her apartment, the one she shares with your friend Lindsey Sherman?"

"There's no evidence of that," Callie said.

"But it's possible, isn't it?" the reporter asked. "As you just said, someone—such as Lindsey Sherman, Meghan Bradley, or Tess Winters—could've seen Zoe after you left and never told you."

Callie felt cold all over, her hands clammy. "That's not what happened."

"You know this for certain?"

"There's no evidence of what you're suggesting," Callie said. "But no. I don't know for certain who—if anyone—saw Zoe after I left."

But as soon as the words left her mouth, she knew she'd said too much, that in tiptoeing around the question, she had stomped directly on her friends. A sour taste had filled her mouth. She wanted to cut and redo her answer, but the show was live. She swallowed hard.

"Unfortunately, there's not much evidence of anything in this case," the reporter said. She turned to the camera. "Thank you to our viewers for tuning in, and thank you to Callie Sutter for joining us. If anyone watching has information about the disappearance of Zoe Gilbert, please call the number on your screen."

Afterward, back at Meg's mother's house, Callie pushed through Patricia's curbside mob and tried to explain herself to Tess, Meg, and Lindsey.

"She backed me into a corner with that question," Callie pleaded. "I was trying to say that there's no way for me—or *any* of us—to know anything for sure if we weren't there. I didn't say any of you *did* anything to Zoe."

"No, but you sure left plenty of room for it to sound that way," Meg said. "What are people supposed to think now? You're on-air, suggesting Zoe came home and one of us, what? Killed her? Is that what you want people to think so they don't look at you too closely or something?" Meg's voice shook with rage. "Leave. Now."

They sliced Callie out so quickly, it was as if they had all vanished with Zoe. Her four closest, lifelong friends, all gone in one fell swoop.

Now she started the car and backed out of the parking lot to drive back to the house, no GPS needed. The roads were as familiar as they'd ever been, each turn proving that no matter how much time passed, there were some things that could never be forgotten.

Chapter Two

MEG

Meg Bradley's office at the Stallard Literary Agency was technically a closet, but it was wide enough for a small desk and had a door that closed. She needed to angle her hips to wedge herself around the chair, and the office heating and air-conditioning didn't vent into that room directly, and sometimes it smelled like egg salad. But besides that, it was completely fine, and it was hers.

As usual, Meg arrived in the morning before her boss, the agency's founder, Lydia Stallard, and senior agent Tina Wincomb. She flicked on the office lights, illuminating two sleek leather couches on either side of a minimalist glass table in the reception area, then started the coffeepot brewing in the break room. She listened to voicemails, jotted down messages for her colleagues, sorted the stack of mail, and finally turned the thermostat to sixty-seven, Lydia's preferred temperature.

When Meg joined their team as office manager a couple of years earlier, her plan was to learn the ropes and become an agent as soon as she could. And while she still spent most of her time taking notes during meetings and restocking the snack pantry, Meg was proud of her recent promotion to associate agent—a title change that made her feel more like an equal.

Once she finished with her morning rounds, she set up her laptop in the conference room and checked her reflection in the large windows that overlooked a Boston side street. She straightened the collar of her cream blouse, ran her fingers through her air-dried hair to smooth away some of the frizz, and wiped a smudge of lipstick off her incisor. Meg sometimes wondered when Lydia and Tina would realize she was an impostor and ask her to leave. Surely her previous work experience shelving books at Barnes & Noble and sweeping hair clippings at an upscale salon did not a literary agent make.

Or maybe it did, and instead of doubting herself all the time, she should try having some confidence. Like Callie, who clearly still possessed an unshakable nerve. All morning Meg's thoughts had entertained one cynical question: What was Callie planning this time?

Before Meg could get too tangled in thoughts, though, Tina's and Lydia's voices drifted into the office. Tina breezed into the conference room first, all striking white teeth and terra-cotta lips, her deep-brown hair parted down the middle, sleek as a sheet of paper.

"Morning, Meg," Tina said.

Lydia took her seat at the head of the table before peeling off a printed silk neck scarf and using it to tie her hair into a low ponytail. She opened a Moleskine notebook and uncapped her fountain pen.

"Good morning, team. Just a few things to go over today." She picked up her phone and skimmed a fingertip over the screen. "We've got a cookbook proposal from Chef Miller out of Portland, Maine. He does all that wacky stuff with seafood. But he has three agents requesting meetings, so if we're interested we need to hop on it. Cookbook, anyone?"

She looked at them over the top of her square, black-framed glasses.

"I just worked on that vegan dessert cookbook. Pass," Tina said.

Meg shook her head. "Not my jam."

"Pun intended, I assume," Lydia said with a slight smile as she wrote in her notebook. "What do you two have for me?"

Tina tapped on her laptop keyboard. "I'm considering a true crime proposal, but it just came in yesterday, so I don't know much." She swept her glossy hair behind her ear as she read from the computer. "It's about the case of a missing woman named Zoe Gilbert."

Meg's arms went numb first. The feeling swiftly spread into her legs. Her lungs felt empty. But she kept her face neutral, as though her past hadn't wormed its way into the safe confines of her workplace. A past she had never told her colleagues about.

"It happened five years ago," Tina went on. "She disappeared on vacation, but the case eventually languished. The author says that since then, she's helped locate several missing people by covering their stories on her blog and podcast. With her experience and track record, she wants to reopen her files on Zoe's case and solve it this time." Tina looked up. "She has about seventy-five thousand followers on Instagram, twice that on Twitter. Half a million unique hits monthly on her blog. Her podcast consistently ranks in the top fifty true crime shows on Apple. This could be good."

"Interesting," Lydia said, drumming her pen on the table lightly. "You don't think the market's too saturated?"

Tina shrugged. "Hardly. Do the producers of *Dateline* ever worry about saturation? Why shouldn't we take advantage of the market, too?"

Lydia and Tina looked at Meg. For once, she wished she was still the invisible note-taking assistant in the background rather than someone who held decision-making power.

"I don't know." Meg forced a doubtful tone. "Like Lydia said, the market is incredibly saturated. This book would probably get lost in the mix."

"There's always room for more," Tina countered. "It wouldn't be such a hot market otherwise."

"What's the author's name?" Meg asked, bracing herself even though she already knew.

"Patricia Adele," Tina said. She looked up from the screen. "Like I said, it just came in, and I haven't done a deep dive yet, so I can't say if everything will check out. But she seems legit enough. Her podcast is award winning. Have either of you listened to it?"

Lydia laughed. "If only I had time for podcasts."

"I wonder if this is really the type of book we want to represent," Meg went on, her nerves tensing as she pictured Tina researching Patricia's work and finding Meg's face attached to Zoe's case. "Is it ethical to profit off the trauma people experience when someone they love is missing? Whether or not these people are ever found, she still receives advertisement money and sponsorship deals and who knows what else. It's exploitative."

Meg heard the shaking in her voice but hoped they didn't. She shrugged as if it didn't matter to her either way.

But it mattered more than anything that this pitch died. And maybe they would happily quash it if she told them her connection to this case, but she'd managed to build a good reputation for herself over the last few years at the agency. She'd worked hard to carve out a new life for herself in Boston, to blend in with the rest of the city instead of sticking out as the girl around town known for maybe, possibly, making her friend disappear. She wasn't prepared to explain what happened five years earlier and why she'd never mentioned it to Tina or Lydia.

She also knew the omission would make her look like a liar, at best.

"Valid points," Lydia said. "But let's take a look at the proposal, shall we? I never like to pass until we've seen everything. Could you send it over to us, Tina?"

"Already sent," she said as she clicked the track pad on her laptop. "And listen, I hear you, Meg. There are real people behind every story like this one. But from a business perspective, there's money to be made here. Possibly a lot of money. And if this author helps find a missing person in the process, that's a win-win for everyone, right?"

The meeting wrapped up, and they each went into their respective offices to work. Meg squeezed herself behind her desk and stared at a crack in the wall. In the back of her mind, she'd known this day would come at one point or another. Eventually, the true crime machine would need to be fed another story, and Zoe's had the makings of a great one: a beautiful woman gone without a trace, the friends who swore they knew nothing yet were caught seemingly conspiring over the single piece of potential evidence that had turned up, a small island full of day-trippers who could've done anything before slipping away on the ferry.

Meg couldn't blame Tina for her interest. In another world, Meg also would've been interested. But Zoe's memory deserved to be protected. And Meg had to protect herself, too.

She could still smell the interview room at the police station—burned coffee and citrus air freshener—and feel the chill of the metal chair. Meg had nearly told the detectives about her final conversation with Zoe, the strange way she'd been behaving all week, and the argument that ended the final night of their trip.

But instead, she'd managed to creatively talk *around* certain details, leaving out specifics that would have drawn too much attention to her. Even her friends didn't know everything she'd held back, though she would've eventually told them if they hadn't stopped speaking.

Meg stretched her neck side to side and exhaled. She hated revisiting that time. In general, she tried not to think about Callie Sutter if she didn't have to. What was the point? To upset herself?

Meg remembered holding Lindsey back as she lunged for Callie, ready to grab whatever she could: a fistful of blond hair, the collar of her designer top. But almost instantly, Lindsey had slackened, her rage quickly shifting to heartbreak as she'd asked, *How could you do that to us? How?*

"We're done with Callie Sutter," Meg had said as they watched Callie drive away. She'd felt like she was declaring Callie dead. And she was—dead to them. Meg would've never done an interview without the rest of them, let alone say anything that left room for the public to wonder.

But Meg couldn't have anticipated how losing another friend would alter the dynamic between the remaining three. Without Zoe and Callie around—not only their collective glue, apparently, but also, more importantly, their leaders—Meg, Tess, and Lindsey were unable to recalibrate as a trio and fell apart, too.

They retreated back to their individual lives only a few days after Callie left. Lindsey went first, saying she was out of vacation days and work wouldn't let her take any more time off. Meg always suspected Lindsey preferred being alone in her apartment with Zoe's silent bedroom to being with her and Tess.

Another couple of days passed before Tess hugged Meg and promised to call soon. She got into her sister's car and left, and then it was just Meg inside her mother's house with Patricia and her mob on the sidewalk.

Left holding the bag for four people all on her own.

They spoke less and less as the months wore on, and eventually, they stopped checking in with each other entirely, even after Patricia backed off, her fans losing interest and needing a new mystery they could obsess over. The slow death of a long friendship.

Meg opened her laptop and typed Patricia Adele's name into a search browser, skimmed the first page of results, and clicked over to her website. There was a post at the top announcing a new season of her podcast, *Missing and Unforgotten*. Along the top bar of the site was a drop-down menu of "Infamous Cases." Zoe was the first one listed. Meg clicked it.

Up popped a grid of video thumbnails, each one a snapshot of Patricia's reporting outside Meg's mother's raised ranch five years earlier. Meg clicked the first video, titled "What Do the 'Friends' Really Know?"

The video quality was poor, out of focus at first. Patricia held the camera in her hand and aimed the lens at her face. The shot was unsteady, the work of someone still figuring out how to use a new camcorder. The footage was almost embarrassing compared to her more recent videos, all shot professionally in a studio with lighting that erased pores and blurred wrinkles.

"First, a massive thank-you to those of you who have helped our investigation so far. Whether you've come here in person to show your solidarity, or you've provided support online by sharing my videos or sending in your tips and theories or financially contributing to my work, I couldn't do any of this without you. But it's not over until we know where Zoe Gilbert is. I read every comment and take every tip seriously. Now, onto your update for this morning. A detective was here briefly about an hour ago, and when I asked why, he said they were just 'ironing out some details.' Could this mean they were sorting out some inconsistencies in the friends' stories? Why would there be any details to sort out if they've already given the police their official, *truthful* statements? I'll let you ponder that in the comments."

Meg pushed her laptop away. She remembered that day. A week and a half after Zoe had disappeared, just days before Callie's interview. The detective had stopped by to share that his office was sifting through the incoming tips and discovering many of them were from Patricia's fans. And they weren't really tips but rather works of fiction—theories, if he was being generous—spun under her influence.

"It's becoming a problem," he said.

"You're right. This whole thing is a huge problem," Meg's mother, Lucy, said to the detective while she divided up a pan of scrambled eggs onto four plates. "Their phones keep ringing and ringing. This is harassment—you should hear the messages people are leaving them. Death threats, promises to hunt them down. It's out of hand."

"I know. Believe me, we're trying to deal with it," the detective said. Meg remembered how weary he looked that day. Patricia was draining his resources and energy, too.

They sat around the kitchen table, the food going cold in front of them. No one had any appetite.

"Let me go out there," Lindsey said. Meg looked at her across the table and saw in her eyes that she meant it. "Let me deal with her."

"Honey, no," Lucy said. "That's exactly what she wants. She's provoking you. Best to not engage."

"She's right," the detective said. "I'll talk to her again. Please don't escalate things."

They had dumped their uneaten breakfast into the trash methodically, one after the other before piling into the bathroom to brush their teeth, apply deodorant, dry-shampoo their hair. Just like a decade earlier at camp, crammed around a single mirror, someone peeing while telling the others not to look, someone else pulling a comb through unruly bangs. Just like the final day at the cottage with Zoe, scrambling to pack up and get out the door after they overslept.

Later, Patricia trailed them to the car, firing questions.

"Do you trust each other? How do we know one of you isn't responsible for Zoe's disappearance and you're all covering something up? How can you sleep at night?"

"How can *you* sleep at night? You're in the way, bitch," Lindsey snapped, shoving past her.

Meg and Tess pulled Lindsey into the back seat of the car as Callie turned on the engine.

"He told you not to escalate things," Tess muttered once they were on the road.

"She was in my way," Lindsey said.

Meg closed her laptop, but Patricia's words from the past persisted. *Do you trust each other?*

They'd kept countless secrets for one another over the years, as friends do. They kept quiet about Callie's binge drinking that first summer at camp. Lindsey's abortion freshman year of college. Tess's one-night fling with an ex when she had a long-term boyfriend. Meg's ill-fated visit to see her estranged father at seventeen even though her mother forbade it. But Zoe, she never asked anyone to carry secrets for her.

Except once.

Chapter Three

TESS

Emmy was three weeks old and the size of a loaf of bread when Tess first brought her to the beach. Prior to that day, she'd barely managed one trip down the block, making it only a couple of houses before Emmy blew through her diaper and forced Tess home to clean slick baby poop off them both.

But five weeks postpartum, despite her brain feeling like a husk of itself, Tess made it all the way to the cove with Emmy. It was a tiny victory, but a victory nonetheless.

Tess had just set Emmy down on a muslin blanket and opened a small bag of popcorn when her attention was caught by a woman walking down the beach. The woman's long, dark hair had the same easy wave as Zoe's. Her brisk gait, the tie-dyed shirt and black baseball cap—familiar, all of it.

Tess took six or seven steps and yelled, "Zoe!" The woman looked over her shoulder. Of course it wasn't Zoe. Tess was fantasizing again.

And then she realized, with a drop in her stomach, that Emmy was still on the blanket, alone. As if reading her mind, the seagulls swarmed for the unattended food, screeching and diving toward the baby. Tess ran back and grabbed the bag, throwing it as far from the blanket as she could. But it was too light and just wheeled in the air. She curled over Emmy, blocking her from the birds. One of the seagulls snagged the popcorn bag in its beak and flew off, the rest of the flock cawing behind it.

She'd been thinking about that day constantly, ruminating over what she'd done wrong and what it possibly said about her as a mother. It confirmed for her that she was someone who could turn her back on a person she loved.

"That was a fluke," James said when Tess brought it up again. He poured coffee into a travel mug, pressed the top in place, and looked over at her. "You're not a bad mom just because the seagulls around here are fearless monsters."

"It's not about the seagulls," Tess said.

She sliced an avocado in half, dragging the knife through the bumpy skin, pushing deep enough to hit the core. Then she twisted both halves in opposite directions and pulled until it gave way from itself.

"It sounds like it's about the seagulls," James said.

Tess spread the avocado on a slice of toast and dropped the knife into the mountain of dishes in the sink. How could she explain to James what had actually scared her?

When she told him about the incident, she left out the fact that a Zoe look-alike had been enough to make her walk away from her infant on a public beach. Even now, weeks later, it made her sick to think of what she was capable of doing. She wasn't sure what he would think of her if he knew the whole story.

To confess it out loud would mean admitting she might be losing herself in this whole motherhood thing. That she wasn't sure she could trust her own brain anymore. That she desperately needed a village—had been *promised* a village by society at large—but was feeling more alone and lost than ever.

James slipped on his work boots by the door. He was a practical thinker, firmly rooted in logic. See a problem, fix it.

"All I'm saying," he went on, "is that you don't have to dwell."

"Me? Dwell?"

James walked over and pulled her in for a hug. She pressed her face into the front of his shirt as he kissed the top of her head.

For a few seconds, she felt like old Tess. Tess who slept through the night and whose nipples didn't leak like a drippy faucet. Tess with a busy job that kept her pleasantly distracted from spiraling into loneliness and provided her with coworkers to grab happy hour drinks with, at least giving her a semblance of a social life.

A cry came then from the baby monitor, and Tess reached for it reflexively. She'd once tried to explain to James that her nerve endings felt exposed and on fire when Emmy cried. His face had clouded with worry when she told him this, and since then, she'd felt his attentiveness more than ever. But still, it wasn't quite enough.

"I should stay," he said, eyes on the monitor.

"No, go. We'll be fine."

She hated to be alone, but even when James was home, there was always something missing. There'd been something missing for a while, but Tess had been able to compartmentalize it until she became a mother. Her loneliness, packed up and tucked away for years, roared to life the day she had Emmy. She didn't have the power to ignore it anymore.

James hesitated at the door but then left with the promise to be back soon. Tess headed upstairs.

In the nursery, Tess scooped Emmy into her arms. The baby quieted and softened, her small mouth searching. Tess sat on the sand-colored rocker, a comfortable chair they'd spent too much on at Pottery Barn, and nursed until Emmy lazed and calmed. Her bald little head lolled to the side, lips parted. Tess put her boob away and let Emmy sleep on her as they rocked, even though she'd heard that "contact naps" could ruin a child.

Motherhood was an endless bombardment of advice and second-guessing. Every time she opened a baby app or scrolled through a mommy group or texted her mother, she learned something else she was doing wrong. Put the baby down. Wear the baby all the time. Let the baby self-soothe. Pick up the baby when she cries. Feed on demand. Keep her on a schedule. Bed share. Put her in a crib. Set her down *drowsy but awake.*

Never before in her life had she felt so inundated by the opinions of others, aside from when Zoe went missing and the entire world weighed in on Tess's character.

And never before had she wished so desperately to have friends she could lean on through this phase of life. Not just friends but *her* friends. She could've used the comfort of their presence a million times already in the eight weeks she'd been a mother.

They were supposed to be here. That had always been the plan. They'd promised to do life together, to someday push strollers and eventually walkers together. But maybe she'd been stupid to bank on that, hopelessly lost in her nostalgia. Maybe she was just so tired and far from herself that she was longing for something that never really existed.

She shut her eyes, lulled by the white-noise machine's rhythmic sound of waves. *Had* she made it all up? The closeness between herself and her friends? It was possible they'd meant more to her than she did to them. But she remembered one night the year before Zoe went missing, a memory she was sure she could trust.

They'd missed the last ferry waiting for Meg to get off work at the bookstore, and the next boat wasn't until the following morning. Standing at the ferry terminal as the sun set and their ride to Block Island was nothing but a speck on the horizon, they worked out a plan.

"You're all coming back to our place," Zoe had said, always one to take the lead. Between her and Callie, the group was never without direction. "We're having an old-school sleepover tonight. I'll even pay for the pizza."

"No, I'm buying," Meg said. "I made us miss the ferry, so dinner's on me."

Lindsey and Zoe lived in a small apartment in Newport, about half an hour from the Point Judith ferry terminal. They piled into Callie's Lexus, sneaking the other cars into the overnight lot and affixing small notes on the windshields promising to pay the parking fee in the morning.

"If my car gets towed, they can just keep it," Lindsey said as she buckled into the passenger seat beside Callie.

"You'd miss that old beater," Zoe said from the back seat. "Think of all the memories."

"Oh, yes," Lindsey said. "There was the time it broke down on ninety-five north in Providence during rush hour. Or what about the winter when a family of mice built a home in the engine?"

"And you killed them all," Zoe said with faux somberness. "But we still love you, murderess."

Back at their apartment, Lindsey and Zoe had pulled out every pillow, blanket, and cushion they owned and tossed them all into the center of their small living room. Tess offered to walk with Meg down the block to pick up the pizza while the rest of them built what Zoe called "a nest of cozy." Once they were back with dinner, they changed into pajamas, poured wine into water glasses, and piled into the nest. The pizza box sat open on the coffee table for easy access.

Tess remembered the night because it was so unusual. For years, they'd habitually spent a week together on Block Island every summer— but never one-off nights. Not in a long time, at least.

"I feel bad for our future spouses," Zoe had said after the pizza was gone and they'd found a channel playing a true crime documentary. "Not only are they statistically the most likely people to kill us, but they have to deal with *this*." She gestured at their bodies sprawled around the nest. "You kind of have to marry all of us when you marry one of us."

"I'm not getting married," Lindsey had said. "Men don't wash dishes."

"*You* don't wash dishes," Zoe said, tossing a throw pillow at Lindsey.

"Neither do you!" Lindsey shot back, laughing.

They settled deeper into the nest as the documentary played on. A familiar, sad story about a woman dying at the hands of a jealous ex-husband. Tess wondered why they were watching it, until Zoe finally changed the channel unprompted.

"This is so depressing," she muttered, clicking the channel over to *The Office*. "Maybe we should all skip marriage and go straight to building a commune in the woods together."

"I'm in," Callie said drowsily, her eyes half lidded, lips red from the wine. "Let's grow our own food. And can we get goats? I've always wanted goats."

"Oh, sweetie. I can't imagine you doing hard labor," Zoe said as she smoothed a hand over Callie's head. "It would ruin your hair. But yes. Whatever Callie wants, Callie gets."

Tess remembered nearly asking if they could find a way to go off the grid and exist in their own bubble. But then Meg chimed in.

"Communes always fall apart eventually," she said. "We're better off like this. I'll even babysit your kids when some of you inevitably do get married."

"Kids," Zoe had said wistfully. "We should at least make a pregnancy pact or two someday. I wouldn't want to do that alone. I don't think I *could* do that alone."

Emmy murmured in her sleep, and Tess opened her eyes. What was she supposed to do with her memories? They were useless, nothing but bombs that exploded when she least expected it.

She reached for her phone in her pocket and welcomed its thought-deadening blue glow.

Tess opened Callie's text message. It was alone in the thread like a boat adrift in a big sea. Who would be the first to reply? Or to point out the strangeness of the invitation, the new house, the date? The message was so out of the blue, Tess was wary of it. But she couldn't deny she was intrigued by the prospect of speaking to her old friends. Even if there was no guarantee they'd reconnect, it would be enough to know them again, however briefly.

Then she clicked over to Callie's Instagram page. They may have stopped speaking, but Tess never stopped keeping tabs on Callie, Meg, and Lindsey. Watching their lives play out without her was a bittersweet hobby. And maybe a creepy one, but she had to know they were okay, happy. More than once, she imagined them sitting on her porch, taking turns holding Emmy, talking about work and love and everything else going on in their lives, the things Tess wanted to know so badly but was too spineless to reach out and ask. It felt like too much ground to cover, too many years to make up for.

Callie, the brave one. The only one willing to break the wall of silence.

Tess scrolled back through Callie's entire feed, reaching into the past as far as she was allowed to go until she hit the first post. Callie at brunch in the city, holding a mimosa in her hand, head tilted back in open-mouthed laughter. The post was dated four years earlier, less than a year after Zoe disappeared. The caption said *Life is good.*

What had Tess been doing back then? Isolating herself, trimming her world down to almost nothing after Zoe was gone. Unemployed, she had lived in a spare room at her sister's house, grieving the friends she had thought would always be there, the privacy she'd never thought twice about until it was stripped away by Patricia Adele. She was decidedly not living a life that felt *good.*

She scrolled back up to Callie's most recent posts. The comments on a filtered photo of deep-blue hydrangeas in a square vase all said some version of the same sentiment: *I want your life!*

Tess pinch-zoomed on the photos Callie shared of her new house. She was being secretive about it, only posting bits of grass or the corner of a sunny room or ripples in the pool. Shards of truth, but it was plenty for Tess to compose a bigger picture.

She opened Zillow, searched for properties recently sold on the island, and scoured them until she found a listing that matched Callie's house fragments. Tess read the description of the property and learned when it was built; was stunned by how much the taxes cost annually, how many rooms it contained. She scanned the photos and viewed the aerial blueprint layout of all three floors plus the guesthouse. The address was at the top of the listing. If anything, Callie was living with only an illusion of privacy and safety. Maybe they all were.

An unpleasant sensation crept through Tess. She closed the listing and then Instagram and slid her phone into the pocket of her shorts.

She was no better than Patricia Adele, combing through Callie's online life in search of meaning. But Tess was different. She'd never stalk her old friends with the intention of hurting them.

No. Patricia's fixation was one of malice. Tess's only crime was caring too much.

Chapter Four

LINDSEY

Lindsey had a few rules: no sex, no hand holding, and no googling each other. That was, by far, the most important rule. It gave her a clean slate and an air of mystery, reducing her to someone who might look vaguely familiar but without any concrete baggage attached.

She leaned over the bathroom sink in her apartment above a noisy Newport bar and lined her brown eyes, brushed dark mascara onto her long lashes, and smoothed a berry lipstick on her lips. Tonight was her second date with Fred, and she was going into it with her upcoming credit card payment in mind. A decade earlier, fresh out of college and brimming with feminism, Lindsey would've balked at herself. Now she was drowning in too much debt to care what it meant to take money in exchange for her time and company.

Lindsey wiped away a few flecks of dried mascara from under her eye and fluffed her hair. She flicked off the bathroom light and went to her bedroom to change into a strappy black dress from Forever 21 that she'd had since her days of dorm room pregames, and she slipped on the only pair of heels she owned. Whenever she wore them, she was reminded of nights out with Zoe a lifetime ago. *You're a giraffe in those things,* she told Lindsey once inside a dark nightclub. It was true; barefoot, Lindsey had towered over Zoe, and the heels gave her another few inches, enough to rest her forearm on the top of Zoe's head. Once, too drunk to think better of it, she'd hoisted Zoe up onto her shoulders and walked them home on those trusty heels, Lindsey's legs wobbly stilts underneath the two of them.

Now she stuffed the lipstick and her license into a small handbag and went to the kitchen to pour a tequila shot. She rinsed out the shot glass and returned the bottle to the cupboard above the sink exactly as she found it. Her roommate, Madison, was a student at nearby Salve Regina University, but Madison's lacrosse-playing boyfriend rented a room in a converted mansion on Bellevue Avenue, so Lindsey almost never saw her. Madison did, however, occasionally measure the alcohol levels in her bottles and accuse Lindsey of stealing from her stash.

"Maddy, I'm a grown-ass woman," Lindsey had told her. "I wouldn't steal booze from a college kid."

Going out with Fred had actually been her roommate's idea. Maddy's parents paid her portion of the rent, and early on she got tired of hearing Lindsey harp about money woes every month. On a rare night when they were both in the apartment splitting a pizza, Maddy had suggested Lindsey find an older guy to go out with if she needed extra cash.

"I know some girls at school who do it casually. Dinners here and there when they need some money," Maddy said indifferently. She draped the end of a slice of pizza into her mouth, chewed, swallowed. "I mean, I know you're a lot older than me. But you still look super young."

"Gee, thanks," Lindsey had said.

"Or you could drive for Uber, I guess."

"My car could never," Lindsey said. "I think a friend of mine might've done that, though. Dated guys with money. Or something along those lines."

"See?" Maddy had said, her lips glossy with pizza grease. "Everyone knows someone who does it. It's not a big deal."

So Lindsey decided she would do it, too. Temporarily. Casually. Just long enough to pull herself out of her debt hole and breathe a little easier. Student loans and the credit card bills she'd racked up when Zoe was no longer around to pay her half of the rent were the biggest problem. They'd snowballed with interest over the years, a constantly growing monster Lindsey could never tame on her own. And, even though she knew Callie would never collect on it, Lindsey did technically still owe her share for the cottage they'd vacationed in five years earlier.

Not that Callie seemed to need that thousand dollars, by the looks of her current life. A life Lindsey had tried her hardest to ignore. But Maddy, obsessed with MindBalm and all things Callie Sutter, talked about her to Lindsey all the time.

"I can't believe you have two famous friends," Maddy had said when Lindsey moved in, referring not only to Callie but to Zoe, too.

"Had," Lindsey corrected her. "I don't have either of them in my life anymore."

Lindsey locked the apartment door behind her. Outside, the bar below her apartment was packed, music seeping through the walls, college kids spilling onto the sidewalk. She waited on the outskirts of the chaos for Fred's car to roll down the one-way street. A pair of tipsy girls stumbled past her, one of them bumping Lindsey. They apologized and kept moving, then broke into hysterical laughter just moments later. Lindsey watched them for a second. It was almost like looking into the past, seeing herself and Zoe, arms entwined as they stumbled home. She turned away, struck by how much it stung to see other people living her old life.

Fred pulled up in his black BMW, giving her no time to dwell. He parked at the curb, climbed out of the car, and opened her door.

"It's great to see you again," he said as she slid past him into the car.

"You too," she said.

Their first date had been a week earlier. They'd chatted about expectations while sipping overpriced lattes and walking Bowen's Wharf.

"For me, this is about connection," Fred had said when they stopped to look out at the cluster of boats bobbing in the water. "I've made a few good friends this way. Had a few women ghost me entirely, which is fine. But at the end of the day, it's about meeting people. I've never liked the pressure of dating, but I'm always interested in connecting with people."

"I'm not looking for a relationship," Lindsey had said. "Nothing physical. But I know I'm good company, and I know you're willing, for some reason, to pay me for my time."

She was still feeling him—and the possible arrangement—out after Maddy's friend had put her in touch with him, promising that Fred was one of the good ones.

"Shouldn't you be paid for your time?" he'd asked.

"For eating dinner? And going on coffee dates? Most people go out for free."

"Maybe we're not most people," Fred said. "And in my experience, sometimes the free dates come with more of a cost."

Lindsey hadn't thought of it like that. And he wasn't wrong; she'd been with one person in the past who had cost her more than she ever thought possible.

He'd studied her face for a few seconds. "You think I'll pull a bait and switch on you."

"No," Lindsey had said. "I don't fall for tricks or let myself look like a fool anymore. Once was more than enough. And I have rules."

"That's fair. How about if we have dinner and see if we get along? No pressure on either end. We'll keep it light."

Now he eased the car down a side street off Thames toward an expensive French place. The street was crowded with antique houses that gave the illusion of tipping forward on their foundations, cars parked bumper to bumper along the curb. Fred found a spot, and they walked down a block to dinner.

As he held the restaurant door open for her, Lindsey caught a whiff of his cologne; it smelled expensive. The small lobby was dim, wood paneled, the walls covered in black-and-white pictures. They were seated immediately; Fred, friendly with the chef, had scored a reservation that allowed them to jump the three-month wait list. The waitress served wine and the first course of the tasting menu minutes after their arrival.

"I've walked by this place a million times," Lindsey said as she smoothed a cloth napkin over her lap. "Not exactly my usual scene."

"What's your usual scene?"

"Honestly, I don't really have much of one anymore," she said.

"Well, maybe this is the start of finding one. But if you hate the food, we'll pretend it wasn't my idea to come here," Fred said. "Cheers."

Lindsey tapped her glass against his. She sipped her wine and looked at him, taking in his softly square face, slightly pouting mouth, hooded eyes, the light scruff on his face. There was a perpetual touch of amusement at the corners of his mouth like he was always on the verge of making a joke. His dark hair was laced with gray and combed neatly to the side. Overall, he was an objectively good-looking man, and she didn't mind looking at him. There were worse ways to make a couple hundred dollars.

Their waitress appeared again after a few minutes to refill their glasses and serve the next course. Once she was gone, Lindsey asked him what they were about to eat.

"Duck foie gras," he said. "I can have them bring you something else if you don't like it."

"I had Taco Bell for dinner last night. I'm not skipping duck," she said.

"And what, exactly, is wrong with Taco Bell?"

Lindsey took a bite. The foie gras was tender and tasted better than anything she'd eaten in years.

"Absolutely nothing," she said, eyes closed. "But this is an *experience*."

They ate and talked for the next hour, easily finding their common interests. They talked about movies they'd seen lately, what they did on the weekends, music they enjoyed.

Lindsey was careful to keep the topics generic, but after Fred told her he'd bailed on college right before his graduation for a woman who broke his heart, Lindsey felt emboldened by the endless flow of wine to tell him a similar story.

"It was forever ago, but I skipped a semester of college to tag along on tour with a local band," she said. "We were in a different city every day, partying with new people every night. I could barely keep up." She smiled. "My parents were absolutely furious."

She left out key details: how the whole thing had been Zoe's idea because she was dating the drummer, Blake, and had begged Lindsey to go with her. Or how Lindsey had been interested in Blake first, a crush she downplayed when Zoe asked for permission to go after him. *You don't mind, right? He's not really your type.* Lindsey had agreed, saying it was fine for Zoe to date the charismatic drummer with tattoos up and down his arms. Zoe always took what she wanted in a way Lindsey only dreamed about. So she stifled her feelings and pretended to be happy for Zoe and thrilled to join the band on tour.

"So what happened? You didn't like groupie life?" Fred asked.

Lindsey laughed. "The novelty wore off. Too many hangovers. The bus bathroom was vile. And eventually, I needed to sleep in my own bed again and get back to school so my parents wouldn't disown me."

It ended the night Zoe and Blake ended. A loud and messy breakup in the alley behind a club, Lindsey eavesdropping from around the corner. She rented a car in the middle of the night for herself and Zoe, and drove them the seven hours back to Rhode Island from Buffalo, New York, in one straight shot while Zoe slept off her sadness in the passenger seat. Lindsey remembered looking over at Zoe while stopped at a red light and feeling a confusing mix of love and resentment for her best friend.

"Impressive," Fred said. "I couldn't live on a bus. My boat, yes. But not a tour bus."

"You'd hate all the girls, too," Lindsey said. "Way too many girls."

Fred snickered. "Sounds like a nightmare."

They were served crème brûlée and espresso for dessert, and soon after, they left the restaurant. Outside, the air had cooled and the sky darkened, but the shops and bars and restaurants still buzzed with people. Lindsey was enjoyably drunk, the kind of drunk that didn't yet feel sour. It was a degree of drunkenness that let her feel some hope for herself, that maybe she'd just stumbled into an unusual but beneficial situation and, for once, she was doing something right.

"I had a great time," she said when they reached Fred's car. "I'm going to walk home, though. I'm only a few minutes away, and it's such a nice night. But thank you for dinner. Let's do it again?"

"You sure you don't want a lift?" he asked. She said she was sure and then watched as he peeled open his wallet and removed a few crisp hundred-dollar bills. He put them into her palm and held her hand for a second. "I agree, we should do this again. Call me when you're free."

He let go of her hand, and she put the money in her purse. "Keep an eye on your phone. I'll definitely call."

The walk back was short, but by the time she was on her street, her feelings had changed course. She questioned everything she'd said over dinner, wondering if she should've shared less. Had she been too specific? Would he be able to look her up based on something she'd said? And if he did, would that send him and his wallet running? Would her opportunity for quick, easy money vanish once he saw that Lindsey had a murky past tied to a missing woman?

She could've walked upstairs to her apartment and called it a night. But instead, she pulled open the door of the bar, wove through the maze of college kids packed inside, and ordered herself a drink.

Lindsey woke to sun pouring through her bedroom window, an assault on her eyeballs. Her mouth tasted like she'd licked a sewer grate. She groaned as she sat up, still wearing the dress from the night before.

She stopped to pee and stare at her face in the bathroom mirror, rubbing at the eyeliner smeared around her eyes in dark rings. In the kitchen, she started the coffee maker and dropped a bagel into the toaster. While she waited for both to finish, she plugged in her nearly dead phone and scrolled through her unread messages. There were two from her manager, Hayden, asking Lindsey to log on to work over the weekend to answer customer emails, a request she planned to ignore.

Below that was one from Meg in the group chat Callie had started a few days earlier. Lindsey froze. Someone had finally broken the stalemate. She'd been determined to ignore Callie's text and forget it had even been sent, expecting Meg and Tess to do the same. That had been their agreement five years earlier, and she didn't see why it should change now. Lindsey clicked open the message.

Meg: I'm sorry to tell you this in a text, but Patricia Adele is working on a book about Zoe's case. She pitched it to someone I work with. Don't have a lot of details, just what she included in her proposal, which I'm still wading through. We should talk ASAP.

Lindsey read Meg's message again before her hungover brain caught up.

She read on.

Tess: Wait. A book??

Callie: I'll talk to my lawyer and have him draft a cease and desist. She can shop an idea but it doesn't mean anything will come of it.

Meg: Well, my colleagues are interested.

Tess: Even with the history you have with Patricia?

Meg: I didn't exactly tell them about that. Just trying to get them to pass so it'll go away. She's working on a podcast about Zoe, too. I'm sure we'll probably feature prominently in both.

Lindsey pressed the heels of her palms into her eyelids, thinking. The anger was hot and sudden in her stomach. She picked up her phone and typed back.

What a shameless leech. She really wants to do this again? Fine, bitch. Let's go.

Callie: Take a deep breath. She only has the power to upset you if you let her. Also, curious if you guys saw my text about the party? Seems even more important that we're together on the anniversary now.

Lindsey let out a harsh laugh and clicked her phone off and went back to bed. The fitted sheet was half pulled off the mattress and still warm. Her mind swam, her stomach went queasy. She wished she had something to take, remembering the time she and Zoe had walked back to their apartment at dawn after accepting mystery pills from a girl in a bar bathroom. They woke up the next afternoon on their living room floor, impressions from the carpet pressed into their cheeks. Zoe had retrieved candied ginger from the kitchen, and they shared the entire container until they felt better. Zoe was always picking up Lindsey's pieces, even when she felt rough herself. Even when Lindsey didn't deserve the love.

The interview with the police. She hated thinking about it, but it rushed into her mind now.

You live with Zoe, the officer had said. They wanted to know if Lindsey had heard her come home. Had Zoe made it to the mainland? Were they even looking in the right place? *You're basically the only one who can say for certain if she made it back here or not.*

She'd said she had no idea. That she'd gone to bed early and Zoe's bedroom door was shut the next morning.

Did you check if she was in bed? You didn't notice if her light was on?

Lindsey said they respected one another's privacy, and she had so much to catch up on at work after a week off that she'd left early and didn't think to check on Zoe.

But it wasn't even close to the truth about what happened that night.

Now her phone pinged a few times from the kitchen. She pulled herself out of bed to turn it off; she couldn't handle any more talk of Patricia Adele today. Didn't feel like processing the fact that the very person to break them was now, in a twisted way, forcing them back together.

But when she picked up the phone, the notification was from Fred.

Feeling a little green after all that wine last night. Going for a beach walk to get fresh air if you want to join me. You can say no, but wanted to offer.

No part of her should've said yes, but she needed the distraction.

I could use some fresh air. Where are you?

She changed out of her dress from the night before and washed her face while she waited to hear back. No makeup for this outing, her hair thrown up into a quick bun. Just leggings and sneakers with her keys and phone thrown into a tote bag.

Walking down your way now, he texted back.

She went outside and paced the sidewalk while she waited for him, her mind twisting with thoughts. The sun was high and unfiltered by cloud cover. Lindsey started to sweat instantly.

When Fred appeared from around the corner, he was holding a tube of antacid chewables.

"Figured you might be feeling the same this morning," he said, handing them to her. She dropped a few into her mouth and chewed the chalky tabs. They settled the churning in her stomach, though it was unrelated to the wine they'd had over dinner. She'd done this to herself.

"Does this count as a date?" she asked as they started walking down the street.

"I'm taking up your time," he said.

Lindsey tried to calculate how long she might have before Patricia exploded her life again. How many times she'd be able to go out with Fred before everyone in her orbit turned on her again.

And then it hit her. She likely didn't have long at all. Just like another opportunist, Callie Sutter, Patricia must be planning something for Zoe's anniversary. Some new theory to reinvigorate her fan club. Or worse, something true she'd managed to uncover.

"Is today the thirteenth?" Lindsey asked.

Fred said it was. "Why?"

"Just can't keep the days straight anymore," Lindsey said.

Less than a month until August tenth, the worst day of the year. A day that was already bad enough without Callie and Patricia making it worse. All Lindsey wanted to do was forget, forget, forget all of it.

Chapter Five

CALLIE

"How are you going to maintain the lawn? And keep the house tidy? Are you hiring help?" Elizabeth Sutter asked.

Callie pressed the portafilter into the espresso machine, triggering the grinder's deep rumble. It drowned out her mother for a few blissful seconds.

"Why not just buy a nice boat and come and go to Block Island as you please?" Elizabeth adjusted the strand of pearls around her neck and tilted her head. "You two have money for a boat, don't you?"

Callie pressed a button on the espresso machine. "You want foam in this?"

"You're not using full-fat milk, are you?"

"Two percent. Or oat milk."

"Sweetheart, no. Don't pretend that's a real thing. Two percent is fine."

Callie frothed the milk, poured foam over the espresso, and handed it to her mother, who was settled on the white settee in the sitting room off the kitchen. Elizabeth pressed a palm into the cushion next to her.

"This sofa is too firm. And this fabric? You could get some beautiful Italian material to reupholster this whole thing." She took the coffee cup and sipped, looking over the rim at Callie. "Hmm. And you could hire a chef who also knows their way around an espresso machine."

"Maybe someday," Callie said, suppressing her annoyance. "Right now, I'm focused on settling in and planning the housewarming and memorial for Zoe."

"Well, just a word of advice," Elizabeth said as she tapped a manicured nail on the side of the mug. "Some people find mixed events distasteful. Hold a memorial another day."

"No one will think that," Callie said.

"I've organized enough parties to know what I'm talking about. I'm happy to help you plan it. I'm sure Nathan is busy with meditating."

Callie ignored the dig.

While her mother did have experience in event planning, Callie didn't need or want help. This party would be nothing like the ones her mother used to organize. This one had an important purpose, but for now, Callie was keeping that purpose to herself.

Elizabeth took another sip of coffee as her eyes roved over the room.

"Let's go over what you have so far. Party planning is a little like spinning plates: easy to drop one and make a mess unintentionally."

This was an apt metaphor, given how many times Callie witnessed the waitstaff and even guests literally break plates and glasses at the parties her parents used to throw at their estate. The flocks of adults in summer linen suits and silk dresses, colossal diamonds on their jewelry, flutes of champagne twirling in their hands while a string quartet played off to the side, everyone drunk and clumsy. Occasionally, she would catch some foul behavior in action, like the woman who pushed a waiter into the pool for offering a vegan appetizer. Or her own father, the time she saw him slinking behind the barn to kiss someone who was not his wife. But that was water under the bridge now. Her parents had moved past the indiscretion, having shipped Callie off to camp on Block Island the summer it happened so they could fix their marriage. Although Callie believed her mother had banished her to Block Island for sharing what she witnessed, as if the real crime had been the revelation of the truth. And because of that, Callie felt responsible for her parents' rough patch that summer; if she hadn't been spying, they could've kept pretending they were a perfectly happy family.

"Let's take a walk and see what Dad and Nathan are up to," Callie said, suddenly needing to get out of the house and into the fresh air. Even as a grown woman, she still felt anxious when she reflected on the summer of her banishment.

"They were swimming laps last time I checked," Elizabeth said.

"It's so nice out. Come on."

Elizabeth sighed and set her coffee down. Outside, they crossed the yard, the grass warm under Callie's bare feet. They walked the long way around to the guesthouse, following the stone wall that bordered their yard. Callie noticed her neighbor in the next yard tending an overflowing vegetable garden.

"We should say hi," she said with a nod in his direction. "It'll only take a minute."

The neighbor approached the divide between the two yards with a garden hose kinked in his hand. He was stocky and short, tufts of white hair poking out around his gardening visor.

"Hi there," Callie called. "That's a beautiful garden."

"You the new folks?" the man asked.

"Yes," Callie said. "Well, my husband, Nathan, and I are the new folks. I'm Callie. This is my mother, Elizabeth."

He sniffed. "And you're renting out that spare house?"

Callie smiled, surprised at his gruffness. "The guesthouse? No. Not renting anything."

"There are rules about rentals," he went on. "You can't just do whatever you want."

Elizabeth sighed. Callie could read the impatience and boredom in her mother's body language, could practically feel it vibrating in the air.

"You must be on the board of the homeowners' association," Elizabeth said.

"We don't have one here," Callie said through a smile. "I'm sure he's just a concerned neighbor. Maybe you'd like to swing by later for drinks on the patio to meet my husband and father?"

He stared at them for a moment, then said, "What's going on with the missing girl?"

Callie tensed. "Sorry?"

"I moved out here right before the place was swarmed with people looking for her. It was a mess. Zoe something, right? And then for months, everyone was talking about her friends. We all wondered why the last people to see the missing girl never had to answer for her disappearance." He stared at her for a few seconds. "That was you, wasn't it? And now here you are. Living next door to me."

Callie looked at her mother, unsure what to say as a feeling of powerlessness washed over her. Elizabeth wore a disinterested expression. Then she sighed deeply again.

"Do you feel better getting that off your chest?" she asked. "Yes, my daughter's friend went missing years ago. And it seems you heard—and believed—all the abhorrent rumors that were spread about her and her friends. But what you're not going to do is make her uncomfortable in her new home just because you decided to believe the worst of a perfect stranger. You're an adult, aren't you? Act like it."

Callie grasped her mother's forearm as she watched the neighbor scowl. Her mother could be direct in a way that read as rude, and Callie worried that rudeness would kill any chance she had of getting on her neighbor's good side. Clearly, she was already at a disadvantage without her mother's help. Callie forced another smile.

"It's okay, it's just a misunderstanding. What's your name, sir? I didn't catch it."

"Because I didn't say." He released the bend in the hose and sprayed his garden, turning his back to them.

"Let's go, sweetheart," Elizabeth said to Callie. "You're not making any friends here."

She followed her mother, bewildered by the interaction.

"Some woman recognized me in the store the day we moved in." Callie recounted the run-in, and taking Zoe's Missing poster off the board, for her mother. "I thought it was just a coincidence."

"Well, you moved to the small town where your friend vanished. You were one of the faces of her disappearance. And you went on television to talk about it. Of course people around here will recognize you." Elizabeth gave a small shake of her head. "I truly don't understand why you chose this island, of all the places in the world to live."

Callie stopped walking. "Because I like it here and wanted to be closer to you and Dad. I shouldn't have to avoid Block Island forever when I did nothing wrong in the first place."

"This isn't exactly close to us," Elizabeth said, crossing her arms. "We have to drive from Jamestown to the ferry and then sit on a boat for an hour to get to you. If you wanted to be close, you could've bought property on Aquidneck Island. Honestly, anywhere on the mainland would've been more convenient. Don't pretend you moved here for us. At least be honest with yourself."

Callie shook her head, defensiveness squeezing her chest tight.

"I am honest with myself. But I don't deserve to be treated like that by a neighbor, do I? He doesn't even know me."

"Regardless," Elizabeth said, "you live next to someone who's wary of you. That's simply a consequence of your choice to move here. I'm sorry, but that's your situation now."

They walked behind the guesthouse and toward the pool. Her mother trailed behind, silent. Logically, Callie understood her mother had a point. She'd expected the move would unearth the past. She just thought it would look different.

They reached the pool and found her father reclining on a lounge chair, eyes closed. In the shade of the umbrella above him, his face looked more weathered than usual, his limbs skinnier and frailer. His hands were clasped on his belly, his knuckles thick knots of bone. Nathan was still in the pool, doing the backstroke from one end to the other.

"Napping, are we?" Elizabeth asked as she sat beside her husband.

"I'm awake," Ben said, not opening his eyes.

"He got a cramp," Nathan said as he pushed himself out of the water and retrieved a navy-and-white-striped towel from one of the teak chairs. Callie had received a seemingly endless supply of these towels from a sponsorship deal she'd done with a brand earlier in the year.

"How do you feel?" Callie asked her father.

Ben kneaded his forehead. "Fine. Cramp's gone now. It's very relaxing out here, you know. I used to rock you to sleep when you were a baby and doze off myself. Reminds me of that."

Callie paused. "That's sweet."

"I just handled things at night so your mother could sleep. Like when you had a nightmare or wet the bed."

"I remember," Callie said. "You even put one of your shirts into my suitcase before I left for my first summer at camp."

"So you would sleep okay," he said with a shrug. "My father did the same for me when I went off to boarding school. It's nothing special."

Callie met Nathan's eyes. She felt a flicker of hope whenever her father spoke of the past; maybe the decline of his memory wasn't as severe as her mother claimed. Maybe he would get better. She knew Nathan clocked those moments, too. He knew how important they were to Callie.

"You're snoring, Ben," Callie's mother said a few moments later. "Let's go inside if you're going to sleep."

He grumbled his agreement and slowly brought his body to the edge of the teak lounge chair. Nathan offered him a hand, and Ben hoisted himself to his feet. Elizabeth took his arm, and they walked up the stone steps toward the guesthouse.

"We'll be by for dinner later," Elizabeth said over her shoulder. "Unless that horrible neighbor takes you up on your offer, Callie. Then I'm staying in."

Nathan tilted his head. "Horrible neighbor?"

"It's nothing," Callie said. "The guy next door gave me an earful about Zoe."

Nathan's eyebrows drew together. "What happened? What did he say?"

"Just the usual garbage I've heard a million times. I promise I'm fine. He's just a curmudgeon."

Nathan watched her skeptically for a few seconds. "Fine. But if you want me to try and talk to him, I will."

"I can handle people like him. He's nothing special."

This seemed to convince Nathan, but Callie felt a ripple of unease. Two stranger confrontations in less than a week of living on the island. Would there be more? Had she made a grave mistake putting down roots in a town that possibly hated her?

Back at the main house, Nathan went upstairs to shower while Callie stood at the back door, eyes on the neighbor's yard. As if sensing her, the neighbor looked up and stared at the house for a few long seconds. Callie wasn't sure if he saw her, but she turned the dead bolt and stepped out of view anyway.

It didn't erase the feeling of being watched. A feeling she had come to know all too well.

Chapter Six

MEG

The office lights were already on when Meg arrived at her usual time. She stood in the entryway and scanned the lobby and the conference room. No computer keys clacking, no smell of coffee brewing, not even the purr of the air-conditioning breezing through the vents, but all the lights were turned on.

"Hello?" she called out, positive she'd shut them off before leaving the night before.

Tina's office door opened.

"I see why you like to get here so early," she said as she propped a hip against the doorframe. "The silence is just divine for thinking. I'm already halfway through my inbox."

"Right?" Meg said as she adjusted the thermostat. "It's nice to get a jump on the day."

"Would you mind starting the coffee? I'm useless with that thing."

Tina followed Meg down the hall. Meg dropped her workbag at her office door, then went to the kitchen, Tina just a few steps behind her.

"So," Meg said as she opened the bag of ground coffee, "what brought you in early?"

She scooped a few tablespoons into a fresh filter and set it into the machine, then poured the water into the reservoir.

"You know that proposal from the other day?" Tina asked.

Meg paused. "The one I didn't like?"

"I know you weren't interested, but I couldn't stop thinking about it. I spent last night looking at the sales of comparable titles. The numbers are there, Meg. Yes, we need to know more before we could take her on, but as far as the market goes . . ." Tina shrugged. "So I emailed the author and asked her to come in today for a meeting. She's local."

"She's coming here? Today?" Meg asked. Dread sank in her gut like a heavy stone dropped into water.

"I came in early because I have to finish reading the proposal, to be honest. I got distracted doing market research. Did you read it?"

Meg shook her head.

She had tried, but the file was seventy pages long, much of it about Patricia herself. Her perspective on Zoe, the good fortune of her being the person to find those sunglasses, the impressive size of her social platforms, and the other missing people she'd helped find over the years. Meg couldn't stomach reading it in full, so she'd searched the document specifically for any mention of her name instead. But, to keep her process and leads confidential while she shopped her project, the identities of the people Patricia hoped to interview and write about were redacted. Meg was relieved that all four of their names were missing from the pages.

Tina and Lydia wouldn't immediately connect Meg to the case unless they did extra research on Zoe. And Patricia hadn't volunteered her connection to Meg when she first emailed Tina, likely to play mind games with Meg or weasel her way into the agency undetected. Meg might've been able to kill any interest in the project without revealing why, exactly, she hated it so much.

But now, with Patricia coming into the office? Meg would look like a liar—the very thing Patricia had always accused her of being.

The coffee maker gurgled and spit. A creeping feeling of claustrophobia came over Meg in the stuffy, windowless kitchen. She grabbed a cold bottled water from the refrigerator and skirted around

Tina. Meg crossed the hall and wrenched her office door open. She stepped inside and pressed the cool bottle to her neck and cheeks.

"Are you upset?" Tina asked, following her. "Usually, you're happy to take meetings with potential clients."

Meg stared at Tina, in her expertly tailored plaid blazer and black designer jeans. Dressed to impress her potential client. She wanted this book.

"I just . . ." Meg started, unsure how to explain all of it. "I know her personally. And this author isn't someone you should attach your good name to, Tina. I'm looking out for you."

Tina studied Meg's face longer than was comfortable. Meg hoped her word was a sufficient enough reason to cancel the meeting.

"Why didn't you tell me the other day? Now that I've got a meeting on the books, you share that it's not the project you dislike, but the writer?" Tina asked.

"Because there's too much to tell—you just have to trust me."

Tina's eyes narrowed. "Where is this coming from? How do you know the author?"

"You didn't look into Zoe's case at all?" Meg said. A wave of heat rippled through her body. "Not a single search of her name? You didn't see?"

"See *what*?"

"That I was friends with Zoe Gilbert. I was one of the last people to see her before she disappeared. I'm one of the people Patricia believed did something to Zoe."

Meg could hardly believe she'd gotten the words out. Tina closed her eyes for a few seconds, dipping her head. She took a long breath before looking back up at Meg.

"Okay, listen. This is a lot for me to process. I hear you and I'm sorry you have a complicated history with this person. But you should've told me sooner. I want to have your back, Meg. But I also want to make that judgment call for myself. She's coming in at nine, and I think you should join us. Maybe we can iron out your differences and work together."

"They're not *differences*. It's nothing we can mediate," Meg said.

Something inside her caved. Would anyone ever believe her over Patricia?

"She's just a person like you or me," Tina said. "You don't have to be so scared of her."

"She's probably going to accuse me of a crime in that book. Wouldn't that scare you?"

"Did she *say* she was going to accuse you of a crime?"

Meg massaged her neck. Defending herself against Patricia Adele was supposed to be behind her. Ancient history. Buried in the past, where she'd left it with everything else she wanted to forget.

"No, but I'm telling you. She's going to write about me."

"Come to the meeting," Tina said with finality. "We'll hear her out before deciding anything. There's just no way she pitched our agency if she wants to attack you in her book."

"I'm not paranoid," Meg said, so defensive she didn't even believe herself. She was nothing but paranoid about what Patricia might do.

"I never said you were. I'm just asking you to have an open mind," Tina said. "Can you do that? For me?"

The coffee maker beeped from the kitchen, slicing the air. They stared at each other. Meg had no leverage; she'd spent it all confessing her ties to Zoe and Patricia, and it hadn't been nearly enough for Tina to take her side.

Meg would face Patricia, then. Because she had to. There was no other choice.

Their voices echoed down the hall, Lydia and Tina laughing at something Patricia said. Meg stood at the door to her office, hands clammy, willing herself to be strong as she listened to their chatter. She couldn't hide from this forever, so she took a breath and walked to the conference room, shoulders pulled back.

"There she is," Lydia said as Meg entered the meeting and took a seat opposite Patricia. Meg couldn't bring herself to look at Patricia as Lydia passed her a printed copy of the proposal. "Patricia, this is Meg, our newest agent. She's been an incredible addition to our team."

"No introduction needed," Patricia said, her voice cool, silky. "Great to see you, Meg."

"Actually, yes," Tina cut in, addressing Lydia. "There's something we should get out in the open before we start. Earlier this morning, Meg shared with me that she knew Zoe Gilbert before her disappearance, and in turn, she knows Ms. Adele, too."

Lydia seemed to be trying to smile, to keep some kind of semblance of normalcy. Meg felt a weight on her chest at the thought of all the trust she'd established with Lydia—gone so easily.

"That's an interesting development," Lydia said. "Meg?"

At this, Meg lifted her gaze. Patricia's eyes were edged with creases that hadn't been there five years before, and her face seemed chalky up close, like she'd overdone it with setting powder. Her blond hair was slicked back in a low ponytail that draped over her shoulder like a snake, resting on her crisp white blouse.

"We have a history," Meg said to Lydia. "It's a complicated one, which is why I didn't tell you right away. I was caught off guard when I heard about the book. The book that will falsely name me as someone who harmed Zoe."

Patricia lifted her chin ever so slightly. A challenge.

"I don't remember writing that in my proposal," she said.

Meg thought of running out of the conference room, pushing through the front doors of the office, and sprinting down the street. But no, running had never worked before.

"Well, you redacted our names. You don't say exactly that, but—"

Patricia cut Meg off. "Then you just assume you *should* be named as someone who harmed Zoe?"

The energy in the room shifted in the silence that followed this question. Lydia set down the pen she'd been holding, which had been poised over her Moleskine notebook, ready to document her thoughts on what should've been a standard meeting. She seemed to be measuring her words before speaking. Meg braced herself.

"Forgive me, I'm trying to catch up here," Lydia said. "Patricia, do you plan to include Meg in your book about Zoe Gilbert's disappearance?"

"She'll have to be in the book to an extent because she's a part of the story, yes," Patricia said.

"What, exactly, are you planning to write about her?" Lydia asked. "I'm sure you can understand the awkward position it puts us all in if we're representing a client who's writing a book that defames one of our agents."

"I won't defame anyone. I've only ever sought the truth," Patricia said. "And all I'll do with this book is seek the truth. At the end of the day, what I write about Meg depends on what I uncover in my investigation. If I find something concrete that needs to be in the book, I'm going to put it in the book."

"In theory, your pitch sounds excellent," Tina said. "I'm eager to work on a true crime project, but we can only work together if you can guarantee Meg will be kept out of it."

Patricia folded her hands on the stack of papers in front of her. "I understand what you're saying, but she's too closely tied to Zoe to be excluded completely."

"Then we can't have you writing anything negative about her," Tina said.

Meg hated that her name was being bargained right in front of her, yet she felt like she had no say in the terms.

"And what if my investigation leads to something negative?" Patricia asked.

Tina shot Lydia a glance. Meg shrank in her chair. She knew that kind of glance, had seen it many times before. It was a look of mistrust and reservation. *What if?* was the question Meg saw pass between her colleagues. *What if she never told us before now because she's hiding something?*

"I'm not saying I'll be *looking* for anything negative to write about you. And there's the option for us to work together," Patricia said to Meg. "You've always maintained your innocence, so why not help me with my research and investigation? That might ease your worries about what I'm writing and allow me to work with Tina. And, of course, give me access to your firsthand source about the disappearance."

Sitting across from Patricia was unbearable. Meg pushed to her feet. Her head swam. She gripped the back of the chair to steady herself.

"You were grasping at straws back then, and there's no reason to think your book will be anything but a work of fiction," Meg said.

Lydia put up a hand signaling Meg to slow down.

"Patricia," Lydia said. "You must've seen on our website that Meg works here. Did you hope to upset her?"

"I want to work with Tina," Patricia said, her expression neutral. "She'd be a great fit for this project. And yes, I knew Meg was one of your agents, but I'm not asking to be her client. Do I think there's space for us to collaborate on this book? Of course. To be honest, I wasn't sure what to expect when Meg and I saw each other today. A part of me wondered if we might see past our differences. But I can see now that I was wrong. That's always been the case, hasn't it, Meg? When I ask questions, you push back. I find evidence, and you four snatch it up before the police can examine it."

"What?" Tina asked, her gaze locking on Meg.

"It's all on my website," Patricia said. "I'll send you some links to look at."

Meg stepped backward toward the door, shame burning in her throat. She had to get out.

"That won't be necessary," Lydia said to Patricia. "It seems like our wires were crossed—you shouldn't have pitched us knowing Meg worked here, Meg should've told us her connection to you as soon as we received your proposal, and Tina should've canceled this meeting before you came all the way down here. Why don't we end things and all try to salvage the rest of our day?"

Patricia gave Lydia a small, resigned nod. "I understand. This was a long shot, I suppose. I'll walk myself out. But I'd like one more minute with Meg, if that's okay."

"Meg?" Lydia asked.

"It's fine," Meg said. It wasn't fine, but it might be her last chance to set Patricia straight.

The conference room door sealed shut behind Lydia and Tina after they exited. Patricia nudged her stack of papers across the table to Meg.

"The top pages there, you should read them."

Meg swiped her hand clean through the pile before she was even aware of lifting her arm. Paper scattered everywhere, sheets flying into the air before fluttering lazily to the ground and across the table. Meg blinked at the mess, surprised at her impulsivity.

"Wow," Patricia said. "Big feelings."

Meg got on her knees and began scooping up the papers, mortified that she couldn't keep herself in check. That she was letting old feelings flare up.

Patricia gathered pages from the opposite side of the table.

"Maybe it was wishful thinking," Patricia said, "but I thought you and I would find common ground today. I thought there might be a chance you'd want to help with a book about Zoe."

Meg reached for a sheet by one of the table's legs. "You thought I would want to help you? After what you did to us?"

She scanned the words on the paper; it was a list of names, but the list wasn't redacted like the proposal had been. Meg crumpled the paper and shoved it into her pocket. She stood up and placed the rest on the table.

"I didn't expect that kind of outburst from you," Patricia said as she sorted out a few pages and set them aside. "That's more of a Lindsey move. How's she doing, anyway? All of the girls—everyone still chummy?"

"Everyone's fine."

"Look, there's still time to switch sides." Patricia held a smaller pile of paper out to Meg. Gave it a little shake. "Read this and see if it changes anything for you."

"Whatever it is, I don't want it."

Patricia angled her chin down. "Meg. Can you drop the stubborn act for a second? I'm trying to throw you a life preserver here. Help yourself while you can."

"What are you talking about?"

"You want nothing to do with me, but I have a soft spot for you. And my instinct tells me you got in way over your head five years ago. That maybe other people were responsible for Zoe's disappearance, but you were tangled up in the mess by association. Read this and call me when you're ready to stop taking the fall for your friends. Are they even still your friends? I know it'll take a lot to convince you to talk to me for this book, but I have a feeling you'll be much better off if you do."

Meg was paralyzed. Patricia dropped the papers and shrugged, then picked up the rest of her proposal and slid it into her bag.

"Read it. No one else has seen this yet. You're the only one I'm sharing this with." She slung her bag onto her shoulder. "No need to walk me out; I can manage."

But Meg followed her out to reception, needing to see Patricia leave with her own eyes. Patricia pulled the heavy glass door open and shot one more glance over her shoulder.

"Zoe's story isn't going away," she said. "Call me."

And then she left, the door swinging shut behind her.

Meg's hand went straight to the wadded-up list of names in her pocket. The impulse to keep it had been so decisive and swift, it reminded her of the last time she'd been with Zoe. How sometimes a decision could be catalyzed into action with an unwavering sense of surety. And how sometimes that impulse could be wrong.

She went to her office and smoothed out the list of names on her desk. Both familiar and unfamiliar names filled the page. She took her phone from her bag and typed a text to the others.

Patricia just left my office. I think she's working the story from a different angle this time.

Callie wrote back first, and quickly.

We can handle her. Let's discuss it at the party. Everyone on board??

A minute passed with no response. Meg tapped her foot against the side of her desk, restless. She wondered about the handful of papers sitting on the conference room table and Patricia's insistence that Meg read them.

Then, finally, more messages pinged on her phone.

Lindsey: Patricia was IN your office? Stop. I would die.

Meg: Here in the flesh.

Tess: Wow . . .

Callie: We'll get on the same page when we're together.

Together.

Now Callie wanted to be a united front, to make sure they had the same story before Patricia wrote them into a book?

Patricia's words rattled around in Meg's mind.

Call me when you're ready to stop taking the fall for your friends.

Had Meg imagined it, or had there been a touch of something genuine in the offer? No, of course not. Hell would freeze over before Patricia would try to help Meg.

But still. What if?

Meg went back to the conference room. The papers were sitting where Patricia had left them. She snatched them off the table, turned her cell phone on silent, and locked her office door so she could read without interruption.

Chapter Seven

Tess

Before Emmy, the middle of the night was not a place Tess liked to visit.

It was where her mind spiraled around itself with an endless catalog of what-ifs. What if she'd been a better friend? What if she'd stayed longer on the island? What if she went the rest of her life never again feeling like she belonged anywhere?

But now, the middle of the night had a purpose. Tess would guide herself down the dark hallway into the nursery by touch, her fingertips dragging along the wall until she found the doorknob. She'd locate Emmy as if by instinct, some primal, animal part of herself she'd never had access to before. She'd nurse until Emmy was asleep again, before finding her way back into her own bed. James would stir, ask if she needed anything, and drop back into sleep effortlessly.

Tonight, though, James snored by her left ear, the fan overhead made a clicking noise every few rotations, Emmy's squeaky sleep sounds intermittently chirped over the baby monitor. Tess was bone tired but wide awake, aware of every sound. Restless, she quietly peeled herself from bed, grabbed her phone in one hand and the monitor in the other, and crept downstairs.

The house took on a different quality at night. In the dark, the clutter and disarray of baby toys and dirty laundry and empty coffee cups were concealed, the half-done house projects were smoothed over by shadow. Even Tess's own reflection was hard to read as she passed the hall mirror.

She settled into the couch and, on her phone, pulled up Callie's Instagram page. The move was automatic. Even when Callie hadn't updated, Tess still clicked the old posts, read the same comments again, watched the Stories she had already seen. Callie was a familiar stranger. Her expressions were the same ones Tess remembered. Callie still fiddled with her earlobe when she spoke, still smiled with a slightly puckered mouth. Yet Tess couldn't decipher Callie's true motivation for calling them back to Block Island.

Tess didn't know this Callie; this wasn't the girl who blew into Ives Art Camp on a random summer breeze eighteen years earlier, stomping into the cabin with tears on her face. Callie, who had clung to Zoe like a barnacle that first summer and, years later, took charge the minute they realized Zoe was missing, supplying the Missing posters and food for the search party. But was it the same Callie who'd sat on that television set with perfect makeup and hair, professing her innocence to the world while Tess sat inside Meg's house listening to the chanting voices of an angry mob clogging the street outside? Or had she changed?

Tess looked at the time. Almost three in the morning, forty-five minutes of potential sleep sacrificed to watching Callie Sutter from afar. She closed out the app, deciding it wasn't fair to judge Callie like this. People changed. No one was meant to remain the same forever. But what she'd give to slip back in time for a single day, to be back in that camp cabin with the girls just one more time and be a little wilder, a little less worn down. And much less alone.

She checked her email, skimming the digital clutter to tire her eyes. Nothing but junk newsletters she should unsubscribe from and promotions for stores she no longer shopped at.

But before she selected "All" and hit delete on the whole page, a subject line she hadn't noticed stopped her cold.

My Book Needs Your Perspective

She clicked it open as the ceiling above her creaked.

"You okay?" James whispered from the top of the stairs.

"Just a little insomnia," she responded. "Go back to bed. I'll be right there."

"Want some company?" He started down the first few steps.

"I was just on my way up," she said. "One sec."

He retreated, the floorboards plotting his track back to their room. Tess returned to the email.

> Hi, Tess. I'm working on a book about Zoe's disappearance and keep thinking about you. Could we talk, just us? You seemed the most concerned, the most haunted when she went missing. I'd love to ask you some questions. I hope you'll consider speaking to me for the book—this could be huge. Let me know. –Patricia

Tess scrolled back to the top of the email to read it again. The ache in her chest pressed hard against her ribs, and she blinked her eyes up at the ceiling to quell the tears. *The most haunted.* She'd felt that way, too. But then again, they had all been haunted back then. There was no measuring or comparing it.

Tess closed her email and clicked her phone off. She would delete the message tomorrow.

She sat in the dark a while longer, her eyes fixed on the shadows draped over the walls. She told herself to go to bed and then found herself halfway up the stairs before she realized she'd even moved from the couch, as if time had skipped ahead without her.

At the pediatrician's office the next morning, a nurse weighed, measured, and prodded Emmy before leaving them in the exam room to wait for the doctor.

Emmy, wearing only her diaper, was irritated by all of it. Tess paced the small, warm room, bouncing Emmy to keep her from dissolving into tears, but each time Tess stopped moving and leaned her head against the cold wall for a few seconds, Emmy would start to grunt and fuss. Tess walked the short path back and forth, wall to door, for what seemed like hours.

Eventually, she fished her phone out of the diaper bag to check the time. They'd been waiting for thirty minutes already. Not an eternity, but far too long to leave a mother and baby trapped in an exam room with no end in sight.

Tess forced a deep breath into her lungs and exhaled it through the tight O of her lips. She opened Instagram out of blind habit and scrolled, skimming with her free hand while she continued to walk with Emmy.

Her thumb paused over a post of Callie donning a crisp white bikini, her sun-kissed body trim and toned, not an imperfection in sight. Tess stared at the picture, assessing every detail. Callie, mid-laugh, a wave crashing into her back. Her straight white teeth looked as if they'd never been touched by coffee or wine. Water droplets sprayed out from around her in a crystalized aura. The sun was low in the background—golden hour. The ocean around Callie carried a dewy, gilded tint.

Tess noted the location tag on the photo and was flooded with the memory of being on that same Block Island beach with her friends. The first day of their final trip. They'd spent the afternoon settling into the cottage, biking the island, and shopping. At a small souvenir shop on Water Street, Zoe had put on the heart sunglasses and puckered her lips as she looked in a mirror.

"Are they me, or what?" she'd asked the others, posing. Tess hadn't liked them, thought they were silly and juvenile, but she didn't say so.

"They're . . . bold," Callie said.

"By that, she means yes. They're you," Meg said.

"Oh good, another pair of plastic sunglasses for you to eventually stuff in the kitchen junk drawer," Lindsey said, punctuating the comment with a wink.

"Is there even room in the drawer with all your unpaid parking tickets?" Zoe had asked. "I might have to actually wear these forever."

That day, they were all in good spirits, happy to be together and off work for a week. Later, they brought take-out clam cakes and chowder to the beach for dinner to watch the sun set. Conversation flitted easily between subjects.

"Oh, Zoe," Tess had said, tearing a clam cake in half and dipping it into the chowder. "I keep meaning to ask, are you still moving Zoe Gilbert Designs into a studio in Newport?"

Zoe had been wearing jean shorts and a cropped T-shirt, the strings of her bikini top tied around her neck. The heart sunglasses were perched on the top of her head. She blinked but held her eyes shut for an extra second, as if willing herself to have patience. Tess backpedaled, so attuned to her friends' body language that she knew right away she'd hit a nerve.

"Sorry. Do you not want to talk about it?"

"No, it's just . . . Do you know how hard it is to find a good studio space, let alone one in a town like Newport? With Newport rent?" Zoe asked. A twinge of irritation in her voice, something that made no sense, given how pleasant the day had been.

"Which reminds me," Lindsey said, "our rent is going up next month by two hundred dollars."

Zoe groaned. "They can't keep doing that every year."

"You guys should buy," Callie said. She sipped soda from a Styrofoam cup and shrugged. "It would be cheaper in the long run."

Zoe made eye contact with Tess. "I'm sorry, I didn't mean to snap like that. I'll find a new studio soon. There are a lot of moving pieces when you run a business."

But that conversation had been enough to set off Tess's radar. She watched Zoe with a keen eye the rest of that week, noting when she seemed detached or when she took off for a walk without telling anyone first.

They'd stayed on the beach well after the sun went down and their food was gone, leaving only once Zoe started to feel uneasy about how dark it was.

"Someone could rush us," she'd said, "and we wouldn't see it coming."

Now Tess was about to type a comment on Callie's post—something about the last time they'd been on that beach together—when the exam room door swung open and the doctor rushed in.

"*So* sorry about the wait," she said, flicking on the faucet and scrubbing her hands with soap. Over a shoulder, she said, "And how are we doing, Miss Emmy?"

Tess forced a smile. She still wasn't used to the way people talked to her as a new mother, addressing the baby directly and forcing Tess into a kind of ventriloquist role.

"Sleep is still iffy, but she's eating well and we're doing tummy time daily," Tess said.

The doctor nodded approvingly and dried her hands with a paper towel. She performed a basic exam, which took no more than three minutes, and on her way out the door, paused.

"By the way, we have a new-mom group starting up soon, if you're interested. It's never too early for babies to make some friends! And grown-ups need to socialize, too, right? I found it nearly impossible to make new friends as an adult once I had my kids." She tugged a piece of paper off her clipboard and put it on top of Tess's diaper bag. "Call us if you want to sign up. It meets weekly, and you might just find some lifelong pals in the other moms."

Tess thanked her, but once she was gone, she crumpled the paper and tossed it in the trash.

Later, once Emmy was asleep, Tess escaped for an overdue shower.

"I need a long one," she told James as she walked upstairs. "I feel like I need to unzip my skin and scrub my brain."

While the water warmed, she sat on the closed lid of the toilet and looked again at the photo of Callie illuminated by the sunset. Tess studied it as if she could read the answers to all her questions in Callie's face, questions about how Callie's life had turned out luminous and full after everything they'd suffered, or if Callie ever thought back to their last days with Zoe with regret. If Callie ached to have a second chance with the past the way Tess did.

Steam filled the bathroom as Tess pulled up her email and reread the message from Patricia. She'd thought Tess was the most haunted by the disappearance. Was that true? How could she know for sure without talking about it with anyone? Maybe Tess was more open-minded now than she had been before. Maybe this version of herself might actually be able to tolerate sitting down with Patricia Adele to talk about Zoe. That didn't mean she had to tell Patricia everything.

Tess hit reply on the email and typed a response.

When are you free? I guess I can at least hear you out.

She set her phone down on the edge of the sink after sending the email and climbed into the shower, exhaling as hot water pelted her scalp and back. She could feel her skin turning pink like a sunburn, and she loved it. Sunburns always reminded her of the deliberate carelessness of being young and "forgetting" the tube of sunscreen so she could get a little color. She'd burned badly one summer; her shoulders blistered, and Zoe laid into her about being irresponsible. *Don't be careless with yourself,* Zoe had said. *If you keep doing that, you'll be a wrinkled old handbag by forty.*

Tess scrubbed shampoo into her scalp, remembering how Zoe's speech had scared her into wearing sunscreen every time she left the house. Tess hadn't wanted to be a wrinkled old handbag of a woman by forty. Zoe would never see forty, never even saw thirty. Tess would have done so many things differently if she'd known how short their time together would've been. She would have visited Zoe's studio more often just to watch her weld silver bangles and gemstone-embedded rings. Just to see her long, thin fingers carefully nestle the jewelry she'd made into boxes for her customers. Most importantly, she would have been kinder to Zoe on that last night.

Tess shut off the water and stepped out. With a towel wrapped around her body, she checked her phone. Patricia's reply was already waiting. Tess's wet hair dripped onto the floor around her feet as she read the email.

> How about in a couple of days at the café near your house? I've been working there when in town. I'm glad you're willing to talk with me. Let's meet around noon. See you then!

She set the phone down and dropped her towel to sop up the puddle at her feet. Patricia had been closer than she realized, literally around the corner for days? Weeks? And how did she even know where Tess and James lived?

A wash of goose bumps swept over her. She looked up at her reflection in the mirror, at her damp brown hair hanging long over her shoulders; at her breasts, those taut, milk-filled, foreign parts of herself; at the shadows under her eyes and the paleness of her narrow face. Who was this person who had just made plans to meet with Patricia? She'd crossed some kind of invisible threshold after having her daughter, everything from her body to her mind broken apart and reassembled into someone strange and unfamiliar.

Chapter Eight

LINDSEY

Lindsey's desk mate, PJ, had a bushy beard and wore bulky noise-canceling headphones from the moment he sat down at his desk each morning to the minute he clocked out. He'd been sitting across from her for a couple of months and, to date, they hadn't interacted more than a handful of times.

While Lindsey's computer booted up, she watched his eyes flit back and forth across his own screen as his fingers tapped the keyboard. She wished he'd look up for a second to say good morning or, better yet, commiserate with her about some of the emails that had landed in their work queue. *These customers are ridiculous,* they might say. *But at least we're just answering emails and not dealing with people in person.*

His eyes never left his screen, though, so Lindsey opened her inbox and waded through the grievances. One customer's rope bracelet had arrived slightly frayed, and they wanted a replacement. Another complained a hand-painted candleholder came with a chip on the bottom, where no one would see. A third customer was unhappy her nautical bookends were smaller in person than they appeared online, despite the measurements being listed in the description. Lindsey cleared her queue quickly, writing short replies just to get them done. In the beginning, nearly eight years earlier, she gave each message her full attention and thought through the best resolution. Now she issued refunds left and right. Whatever it took to get through the work.

Once she'd cleared out a few dozen emails, she left her desk to refill her water bottle. Hayden, Lindsey's manager, leaned out of her glass-walled office and motioned for her to come over.

"Hey," she said to Lindsey. "You have a minute?"

She followed Hayden into her office. Hayden was a few years out of college, with silver-dyed hair and thick-rimmed glasses, which Lindsey was pretty sure contained nonprescription lenses. An attempt at being someone she was not.

"You know," Lindsey said as she took a seat, "I might have to head out early today. I'm starting to feel a migraine coming on."

Hayden looked at her skeptically, then dug through her purse.

"Would Tylenol help? I have essential oils, too." She held up a small amber bottle. "Peppermint."

Lindsey forced a smile. "No thanks."

She'd only ever experienced two migraines in her life: one after a particularly crazy night while tagging along with the band on tour, the other after Callie's interview had aired. Lindsey knew what to say and how to behave in order to convincingly fake a migraine to skip out of work early.

Hayden set her bag down and toyed with the strap. "By the way, we need to review your sick leave usage soon. But that's not what I wanted to talk about."

"Okay," Lindsey said.

"I asked you in here because that reporter we had an issue with years ago has been making contact again. She called the front desk this morning and asked to be patched through to you, but you weren't here yet. She emailed corporate, and they forwarded it to me because she said your personal email and cell weren't working. Anyway, legal asked me to go over this agreement with you and have you sign it."

Lindsey had the urge to scratch at her skin, or maybe crawl out of it.

Hayden handed her a sheet of paper. "Basically, it says the employee—you—acknowledges that personal legal matters must be kept out of the workplace, and if they're not, corporate has the right to terminate your employment." Hayden sighed. "Whatever is going on with you and this person, they don't want it to mess with company culture or distract you during work."

A faint headache began to throb in Lindsey's temple, as if she'd manifested it.

"This woman is a lunatic, Hayden. I didn't do anything."

"I didn't say you did. But I do need you to be fully present when you're at work, regardless of your personal life. New relationships or friend drama included."

"What are you talking about?" Lindsey asked. She'd never mentioned her personal life—especially not Fred—to Hayden.

"In the email, Patricia said you were wrapped up in some messy legal stuff with your friends again and that you were dating someone new. I don't need to know any of the details. I mean, technically I can't even ask. But we just want to protect you, so let's get this document signed, and you can go back to work."

How would Patricia even know about Fred? There were only a few ways Lindsey could imagine Patricia learning about him, and all of them made her skin crawl.

Lindsey's tongue felt like cotton. She held her empty water bottle, desperate for a drink. But her stomach tightened, threatening to reject even a small sip.

"Hayden, come on. I'm not signing this thing. You can't be serious."

"Listen," Hayden said, lowering her voice, "they remember the last time she harassed the company about you. You have to sign it. This is out of both of our hands."

Lindsey toyed with the water bottle cap, embarrassed to remember the last time. When Lindsey returned to work after they'd stopped looking for Zoe, the higher-ups had immediately lassoed her into a meeting. Patricia had been calling and emailing nonstop, seeking

Lindsey's employee file and records of any disciplinary action taken against her at work. They refused, but it had thinned their patience.

"We've spoken with our lawyers, and so far, there's no reason to act," the company president had said. He was usually a relaxed leader, always dressed casually and unbothered by typical corporate matters. This time, though, he was serious. "Here's the thing, Lindsey: Whether or not it's true, it just isn't a good look to have one of our employees go viral because the internet thinks she might be responsible for a missing person. We're getting flooded with emails. Some customers want us to fire you. It's causing a massive distraction for our team and putting us in an awkward position."

She hadn't said much in that meeting, still reeling from the previous weeks. She figured they let her keep her job only because they felt sorry for her—but would they do that twice?

"I'm sorry, I'm really starting to feel that migraine," Lindsey said to Hayden.

Hayden's expression deflated. "You're out of sick days. Try to do some work remotely if you can. And off the record? I think you should get representation."

Lindsey tried to wet her lips. Her voice cracked as she said, "I don't need a lawyer."

"Are you sure? Just hire an attorney and have them shut her down. She doesn't seem like the type to stop until she gets what she wants," Hayden said.

The only lawyer Lindsey had ever had access to was Callie's family's attorney, an emotionless old man who had told Callie over speakerphone five years earlier that he would contact Patricia on their collective behalf and tell her to back off, but that anything more would require a retainer fee. Now Lindsey felt breathless at the thought of needing a lawyer. The expense alone would leave her homeless, carless, more adrift than she was currently.

"Go get some rest," Hayden said. "You don't look like you feel well at all."

Lindsey left Hayden's office with the unsigned agreement in hand. At her desk, she shoved the paper deep into one of the drawers, looped her bag over her shoulder, and left.

In her car, she opened all the windows to vent the stale heat and rooted around in her bag for her phone. She skimmed through her personal-email inbox, something she did maybe once a quarter. She had tens of thousands of unread emails, nearly all of them spam. But when she searched for the keywords "Patricia Adele," she found the messages Hayden had mentioned. Two weeks old and sandwiched between student loan statements and a reminder from her dentist that she was overdue for a cleaning.

Lindsey read all four of them. They were the same message each time: She wanted to chat, wanted to give Lindsey a chance to answer some questions, and her phone number was at the bottom of the email. Lindsey stared at it. She should call and quash this mess now. Maybe lightly threaten Patricia, tell her exactly where she could go.

She couldn't do it, though. At least, not here in the office parking lot, where coworkers could see or hear. And not without a little added courage first.

It was only lunchtime, but Lindsey parked outside her apartment and went straight into the bar instead of upstairs. The place was empty except for the bartender, a girl with light-brown hair pulled up in a tight bun, and a scruffy middle-aged guy nursing a beer. They both glanced at her as she pushed the door open and deposited herself at the far end of the counter.

"What can I get you?" the bartender asked.

She wanted a shot but was embarrassed to ask for one this early in the day.

"How about a Bloody Mary," she said instead. "A double, please."

The bartender gave Lindsey a nod and turned to make the drink. The man at the other end of the bar stared up at the television in the corner, watching the midday local news while absently tipping the beer bottle into his mouth. Lindsey had avoided this particular news channel for years; they'd replayed Callie's interview for days after it first aired, coining her the "grieving friend of a local missing woman." Lindsey had always wondered what that made the rest of them.

"Hungry?" the bartender asked when she returned with the glass. She held a laminated menu in her other hand.

Lindsey said no; she had food in the apartment, and it wasn't like she was getting paid for work today. No frivolous spending.

She took a sip and let the taste distract her for a few seconds. The bite of the horseradish and the burn of the vodka swirled with tomato in her mouth. She closed her eyes and let it be the only thing in her world for a moment.

But when she opened them, she was back in her life, in the crappy bar below her apartment, drinking alone in the middle of the day because of Patricia Adele. She took another sip. A bigger sip. One that would help her be brave enough to dial Patricia's number. She plucked the skewered olive from the glass and ate it. Took another sip. And another. The bartender gave her a sidelong glance before returning to her job of emptying a bucket of ice into the cooler. Lindsey drank the rest of the Bloody Mary and pushed the glass across the bar.

"Could I get another when you have a second? I'm going to step out and make a quick call."

The bartender said yes. Lindsey slid off the barstool with her phone, a relaxing buzz already taking hold of her limbs, and went outside. She dialed the first three digits of Patricia's phone number but quickly chickened out.

She texted Fred first just to say hi, and hoped it didn't come across as clingy. But when he didn't respond right away, she considered saving face by following up with another text saying she'd meant to send the message to someone else. She didn't want him to think of her as desperate, not that it would be the first time a man had lobbed that word at her like a grenade, imploding her sense of self.

Lindsey glanced inside the bar and saw her refilled drink waiting. Now she had some motivation. She dialed Patricia's number and hit the call button before she could think better of it.

She paced the sidewalk. The line rang a few times.

"Patricia Adele speaking."

"This is Lindsey. I hear you've been trying to reach me."

"Lindsey," Patricia said, a touch of surprise in her voice. "You're hard to track down. Did you change your number?"

Lindsey leaned against the door to her apartment stairs. The pressure of her molars compressing together rippled through her jaw.

"Funny story," she said. "Someone convinced thousands of unhinged people online to harass me after my friend went missing, so I had to keep changing my number. Might be why you had trouble getting ahold of me. I only give the new one to people I trust."

"You didn't block it just now before you called," Patricia said.

Lindsey blinked, furious at herself. How stupid was she?

"I want you to leave me alone. Stop contacting my workplace. You're upsetting people and causing problems. Do you understand? No more calls to my work. Don't email me, don't call me. Forget that I exist. Forget this phone number."

Patricia sighed. "I'm happy to know you're still a firecracker."

"Don't patronize me."

"I'm not. You were the only one ever willing to call me out. I respect that. I probably needed to be called out even more back then, to be honest. I think if you'd actually taken the time to listen to me, though, you would've learned how much I value that about you."

Lindsey felt momentarily disarmed by this. But it passed quickly.

"I don't care what you think about me, Patricia."

"You must care a little bit, if you're this upset."

Lindsey pulled the phone away from her ear. She could hang it up and block Patricia's number. Go inside the bar, finish her next drink, and forget.

"I know you care," Patricia said, her voice small and distant. Lindsey put the phone back to her ear. "I feel like you all really care about how you're perceived. Callie certainly did. You can control how you're perceived, if you'll sit down with me. Have a conversation."

"You're obsessed. I'm hanging up now. We aren't going to talk today or ever about Zoe or anything else. She was a good person, and you don't get to be in charge of her story."

"I'm going to tell her story even if you disagree. You don't want to be a part of that? To help?"

"Goodbye, stop contacting me. Get a real job."

Before Lindsey could disconnect the call, Patricia asked one more question.

"How's your love life these days? Getting out there and meeting new people?"

Lindsey froze. Was she imagining it, or did the question carry a hint of warning? Not only did she know what Lindsey did with her free time, but she could reach into her life and wrench away the one decent thing about it—Fred.

Lindsey was done letting Patricia get into her head like this. She mashed the "End" button and pressed her hand against her chest. Her heart thumped against her warm skin.

The sound of an incoming text message made her jump. She expected Patricia, was ready to block her number, but saw it was Fred responding, finally.

Lunch with a client right now. Meet up later?

Lindsey typed yes and went back into the bar to down her second drink. It was watery, but she drained it anyway and paid her tab. Upstairs, the apartment was empty, so she pulled Maddy's tequila bottle from the shelf, poured a shot, and carefully measured enough water to replace what she'd stolen. Then she put everything back where she found it, rubbing the glass bottles with the cuff of her shirtsleeve to erase her fingerprints. As if she could erase her tracks that easily.

When Fred came by hours later, Lindsey was so drunk that she was stumbling in her heels. *Just like old times,* she thought as she tripped outside, Fred catching her by the elbow as they walked down the street from her apartment to a different bar.

"Maybe we should take it easy tonight," Fred said as they slid into a corner table with drinks in hand. Lindsey cackled when he raised his brows at her.

"You okay?" he asked.

"No, no, I'm fine." She felt herself blink too slowly. She tried again, faster. "Just a rough day."

"What happened?"

She laughed again. "We don't do that."

"We don't do what? Ask about a bad day? Why can't I do that?"

Lindsey thought she heard a twinge of disappointment in his voice and hated that it made her sad. But this was only their fourth date, far too soon to relax the rules about getting personal.

"You don't need to, like, care," she said. "About me."

He looked down into his glass and swirled the drink around a few times.

"I mean," she went on, "at some point you're going to realize I'm not all that great. Might as well get started now."

"I really don't think it's going to happen."

"Someone once told me I was desperate," she said. "Like, right after we slept together. Do you think I'm desperate?"

He flinched. "I'll walk you home when you finish that drink. By the looks of it, you could probably use some water and sleep."

"I shouldn't have told you that," she said. Tears pricked at the corners of her eyes. "I can be so stupid. Forget everything I just said, okay?"

Lindsey pushed out of her chair and bumped into a cluster of people standing next to the table. She muttered an apology as she grabbed her bag, then wove through the bar, pushing bodies out of the way with her shoulders.

Fred called her name, but she didn't stop or look back at him. She had to get out.

On the sidewalk, Lindsey turned in the direction of her apartment, her ankles boneless in her cheap heels. She made it only a few steps before tripping. Someone grabbed her to stop her from face-planting, and when she turned, expecting to find Fred, her vision swam. It was a stranger, some man with his hand gripped tight around her arm. Too tight. She wrenched herself free, her pulse thudding like wind in her ears.

"Don't touch me," she said, jerking her arm away.

"Jesus. Sorry for helping," he said, a look of disgust on his face.

"Lindsey?" Fred said from behind the stranger.

She burst into tears. He set an arm over her shoulders, pulling her into his torso as they walked. She sniffed and wiped her nose against the back of her hand. Fred didn't ask what was going on, didn't offer any unsolicited advice. He simply walked her up to her apartment, helped her onto the couch, and asked where she kept the Tylenol.

"I'm sorry," she said as he dropped a couple of pills into the palm of her hand.

"I've been worse off, believe me," he said. "Take these so you don't wake up feeling dead."

He left a few minutes later with the promise to check on her in the morning. She lay in the dark living room, listening to the sounds from the bar below and replaying every hazy, embarrassing detail of the night. She pictured Patricia recording her like she had five years before. Lindsey's stomach turned at the thought, and she ran to the bathroom to get it all out.

Chapter Nine

CALLIE

Callie stood on the tufted seat of a dining room chair, angling her body to snap photos of the tabletop below. A careful arrangement of crisp white envelopes and pale-blue invitations for the party were scattered across the gray oak surface. She'd also fanned out several dozen wallet-size photos of Zoe. Each snippet of party planning she shared with her followers ginned up curiosity on their end; without fail, the questions and comments rolled in as soon as a post went live. They said things like *Can't wait to see it all come together!!* and *The girl in that pic is so pretty, what does she ask for at the salon?*

Callie would've been annoyed people were paying attention to the wrong things, like how Zoe looked or where an item could be purchased, but she didn't care *what* drew eyes to her content as long as they were looking. As long as she could string her posts like beads on a thread and lead her audience where she wanted them to go.

Nathan walked into the kitchen, sweaty from a run, and dropped a stack of mail onto the counter. Callie stepped off the chair and began swiping through her pictures while he splashed his face with water at the kitchen sink and patted it dry with a hand towel.

"How was your run?" she asked as she selected the most striking photo in the bunch, added a preset, and typed out a caption: *Our housewarming is soon. Stay tuned for some surprises . . .*

"Great," he said. "I found a little wooded trail today. Nice and quiet and isolated."

He replaced the towel and pulled the refrigerator door open.

"Oh," Callie said. It was surreal to picture her husband jogging the trails she used to haunt long before she ever met him. Her new life merging with the old. "The island has lots of secret spots."

They'd been masters at sneaking away from camp without being seen. One edge of the campground abutted the woods, and together the five of them would explore the trails, getting lost while smoking and drinking and talking about their lives, someone swinging a cheap plastic flashlight that gave off an anemic glow. It was usually enough light, until one night when it died completely. Zoe had been holding it as she led them through the woods, then stopped abruptly when it flickered out and the path went dark. She hit the flashlight against the palm of her hand, willing the batteries to have just a little more juice left in them, but it was to no avail.

"I think we're only a few minutes from the end of the trail," Zoe had said over her shoulder. Callie could still remember the uncertainty she'd heard in her friend's voice. It was subtle, camouflaged by the nonchalance she was trying to convey. But Callie knew Zoe hated the dark. Hated when she couldn't see what was right in front of her.

"I'll take over the lead," Callie had said, slipping in front of Zoe. "I have a little penlight on my keychain, anyway."

"Thank you," Zoe whispered as they started off again, this time with Callie guiding them down the trail. She had no idea where she was going, but on Block Island, all roads eventually led to a familiar place.

How strange to think that all these years later, her husband was now jogging the same trails. It almost made her dizzy trying to reconcile these two different periods in her life.

Callie pushed it from her mind and flipped through the mail instead, finding mostly junk. But at the bottom was an envelope with her and Nathan's names handwritten on the front.

"Our first piece of real mail?" she asked, holding it up. Nathan glanced at her over the Vitamix he'd filled with spinach, coconut milk, and berries.

"No stamp," he noted before powering on the blender.

She peeled the envelope open and removed the folded paper inside. Once the blender was off, she read it out loud to him.

"To our new neighbors: As you settle into our community, there are some concerns we wish to address."

"Is this some kind of homeowners' association thing?" Nathan asked, pouring the smoothie into a glass. "I hate HOAs. Bad energy."

"There's no HOA here. I triple-checked." Callie kept reading. "We understand you're familiar with the missing person case of Zoe Gilbert. While we believe that everyone is innocent until proven guilty, we're concerned your presence could disturb our peaceful neighborhood. We respectfully ask you minimize the impact of your presence on your neighbors and cooperate with any investigations into the disappearance."

Callie looked up from the letter. Nathan frowned.

"The hell is that about?" he asked. "Who's it from?"

"No name," she said, flipping the paper over and back. "And no return address. I bet it's from my buddy next door."

Nathan took a long sip of his smoothie. Then he set it down on the counter and nodded.

"I know you said you could handle it," he said. "But let's go over there together and see what his deal is."

Callie opened the pantry, removed a box of store-bought gluten-free chocolate chip cookies, and dumped them onto a white plate. She covered them with a clean tea towel while Nathan watched.

"It's harder to hate someone who brings you cookies," she said.

The house next door was nearly the same size as theirs, with two floors instead of three and a white-shingled exterior. The front lawn was cut with military precision, but the plants around the walkway were lush and overgrown. Wildflowers and ornamental grasses swayed from the flower beds, and rogue vines climbed the brick chimney.

Callie knocked. When the door opened, they were greeted by a woman with brown hair cut in a short bob and tortoiseshell glasses. She wore a white-and-navy-striped shirt tucked into dark jeans.

"Hi," Callie said brightly. She held out the plate and introduced herself and Nathan. "We live next door. I made these for you and . . . your husband? Is that who's always working in that incredible garden out back?"

"Oh, you're so sweet." She took the plate from Callie and set it down on a table in the entryway. "Walt isn't home right now, but I'm Rose. Would you like to come in for some iced tea?"

"We don't want to impose," Nathan said. "Just wanted to say hello."

Callie lowered her voice, charming yet conspiratorial. "I feel like I might've gotten off on the wrong foot with your husband the other day. He seemed pretty upset about my missing friend. And then today we got this anonymous letter in our mail . . ."

Rose fidgeted with the cuff of her sleeve. "Oh?"

"Do you know if he sent it?" Callie asked.

Rose cleared her throat. "No. And Walt's on the mainland right now, otherwise I'd have him talk to you himself."

Callie's jaw tensed. "Right. It's just, he seemed aware of who I was before I told him my name. Then the letter arrived, and it seems pretty obvious he sent it." She paused. "Maybe when he gets home you could remind him the detectives cleared me—all of us—of any involvement. We didn't do anything wrong."

Nathan pressed the palm of his hand gently against Callie's back. She took a breath.

"It could've been anyone," Rose said, gesturing toward the road and the other houses nearby. "When that reporter came around, she was asking so many questions, it stirred everyone up. Not just Walt."

"That was five years ago," Callie said. "Why won't they let it go?"

"No," Rose said. "When she was here recently. Just before you moved in, she came right up to our front window and tapped on it while we were eating dinner. Actually, hang on." Rose disappeared inside, then came back with something in hand. "She was handing these out. Everyone around here got one."

At the top of the paper was a large color photograph of Callie, Zoe, and the others taken a few days before Zoe disappeared. It was one of

Callie's photos, but she had no idea how Patricia got a hold of it. Callie had long since deleted everything online that didn't directly relate to her life in New York and MindBalm. Unless Patricia had saved copies of her pictures before Callie had done that purge.

Underneath the picture was a short description of Zoe above Patricia Adele's contact information. One bolded line read **You could be featured in a book! Contact me today.**

Callie pulled her eyes from the flyer. "You talked to her? What did she say?"

"She wanted to set up an interview with Walt, but he turned her away. He never agreed with how she covered the story. She once made a video suggesting that an island resident could've done something to that girl. And then, because of her video, someone else compiled a list of every male homeowner out here and posted it online. That got messy."

"She made a lot of messes back then," Callie said.

"We got married two years ago, so I wasn't here for all of that," Rose said with a shrug. "But I've heard other people express concerns about you living here, too. They still talk about the canceled vacations and lost business because some tourists thought it wasn't safe to come here. Then there was the nagging from that reporter." Rose studied them for a moment. "I'll be honest. As nice as you two seem, some of the neighbors think you living here means our street will become a hot spot for the true crime folks. That disappearance left a mark."

Callie folded and unfolded a corner of the flyer as she read it again, a feeling of injustice blooming in her chest. She understood what Rose meant, but she doubted it was Zoe's disappearance that had left a mark on the community. How many of these people would be able to accurately describe Zoe? To say one factual thing about her? No, it wasn't her vanishing that people remembered or cared about. It was her story and the frenzy around it. The way it felt when the hungry eyes of the true crime monster roved too close to home. The way it had to feed, truth be damned. Everyone knew this. People simply preferred when it feasted on someone else, in another quiet neighborhood somewhere far away.

"We plan to stay here for a while," Callie said, looking up from the flyer. "And I guess now's a good time to tell you about the housewarming party we're having on August tenth. I hope you and Walt will stop over and see for yourselves how normal we are."

Rose reached out to squeeze Callie's arm. "That's kind of you to invite us. I'll pass it along to Walt."

"We shouldn't take up any more of your time," Nathan said. "It was great meeting you, and I hope the four of us can have dinner together sometime soon."

"Oh, how thoughtful. It was nice meeting you both," Rose said.

They walked home hand in hand. Callie felt Nathan's concern through his palm but hoped he couldn't sense hers, too. Patricia was farther along than Callie had realized, walking her neighborhood streets before she'd even had the chance to do it herself. Maybe even creeping around the property before Callie ever set foot through the front door. If she'd been in the area and knew where Callie was going to live, Patricia could've taken pictures of the house, maybe even the inside through the windows and doors, too. What might she do with those images? Callie had been careful to post only vague images of the house, and this potential violation of her privacy chilled her.

When they were back in their own yard, Nathan turned to her.

"How did Patricia know we were moving here?"

Callie shook her head. "I have no idea. No one knew until we closed on the house. Maybe she didn't know we'd be here, exactly. Maybe it's just a coincidence."

"A coincidence that she handed out flyers to our future neighbors right before we moved in?"

"Maybe she handed them out all over the island. Or she got a tip from someone at our Realtor's office, maybe? I don't know."

Nathan rubbed his forehead. "So what do we do about it?"

Callie could usually troubleshoot problems, solutions materializing in her mind with little effort. But not now. She shook her head again.

"Maybe the lawyer can talk to her like last time," Callie said.

"But she hasn't made contact or harassed you directly," Nathan said. "It's like she's circumventing you completely. Targeting people around you instead of going right for you."

She felt short of breath. Like she was trapped in a too-small room with limited air.

"I hadn't thought of it like that," Callie said. "She's circling me. I might not have even noticed if Meg hadn't told us about Patricia's book and if I hadn't tried talking to Walt the other day. Maybe she thinks I'm oblivious."

"But to what end?" Nathan asked. "She wasn't successful last time."

Callie thought back. The first time around, Patricia had been undeniably green. Just a true crime blogger with a meager following who'd lucked herself into the middle of Zoe's case. And even then, being in the right place at the right time hadn't given her skills. All she'd known how to do was cling to her version of the story and repeat it with enough conviction that her followers believed her. But now, Callie worried there was a strategy behind Patricia's actions. More resources, more know-how. And that might mean more eyes on her work this time. She wasn't a detective, and therefore wasn't bound by any rules. She could still say whatever she felt justified in saying about Zoe's disappearance, and people would listen.

"Maybe she'll drop it when she realizes there's nothing here," Nathan went on.

But doubt sank heavy in Callie's stomach. She knew better than to hope for the impossible.

Back in their house, Nathan retrieved his meditation cushion and Tibetan singing bowl and invited Callie to sit with him outside.

"It'll take your mind off things to meditate awhile," he said.

"I really should work on the party," she said. "We have a few days without my parents around; I might as well take advantage of the extra time."

Once he was outside, Callie went to the garage. It was filled with yet-unpacked boxes and remnants of the house's previous inhabitants.

A physician couple, they'd left behind not only the furnishings inside the house but also odds and ends in the garage, such as an enormous first aid kit, two sets of crutches, a wheelchair, and an industrial-size box of gauze and bandages.

But Callie was there for the boxes in the farthest corner of the garage. She opened the first one and rummaged through the topmost layer of MindBalm-branded memorabilia. Pens, lanyards, squishy stress-relief balls still packaged in plastic bags. A few photos of Callie and Nathan with MindBalm employees on a team retreat in Hawaii just before the company sold. Underneath were two of Callie's old journals, duct-taped shut as a deterrent for prying eyes. Next, the handbook for her social media management job before MindBalm, a life she hardly remembered anymore. A life she lived in the immediate wake of Zoe's disappearance.

At the bottom of the box, she found what she was looking for. An old Kate Spade shoebox with the words "Ives Art Camp 2002" scrawled across the top in black Sharpie. She pulled off the cover and rummaged through the items young Callie had deemed important enough to keep. Loose sketches, a tattered rope bracelet, various shells and hunks of sea glass picked off the beach, notes written on colored paper in contrasting gel-pen shades. Grains of sand swished around the bottom as she shifted the contents.

And then, the photos.

Tess had brought her mother's Polaroid to their second summer at camp, and the five of them had quickly burned through several packs of film. The photos in the shoebox showed them in their various spots around the island: crammed together in their cabin, their arms slung over one another's shoulders while a counselor snapped the shot; on the beach, their skin damp and coated in sand; in the art studio, working on their summer projects. That year, Callie had worked on a watercolor self-portrait, painting her own distorted image on a large canvas. Lindsey had made her first matching earthenware set of mugs and plates. Tess's project was a series of black-and-white photos she took on film and developed in the darkroom, while Meg spent the summer weaving a large macramé wall hanging.

Zoe had them all beat that year, though. The Polaroid that showed her project was on the bottom of the pile. She'd made her first cohesive jewelry collection using sea glass she'd collected from the beach. She'd bent twists of wire around smooth lumps of milky glass and hung them from earring hooks and chains. She only used unusual and rarer colors—cobalt blues and pale pinks, the occasional shock of turquoise.

On the last day of camp, she'd slipped one of her necklaces into Callie's hand, and now it rattled around inside the shoebox with the rest of the memories from those summers.

She pulled the tarnished necklace from the box and clipped it around her neck, then rolled the deep-blue glass pendant in her fingers. In another world, Callie could imagine Zoe re-creating a series of sea glass–inspired pieces for her jewelry line but casting the glass in real gold and silver this time. A more mature take on her youthful vision.

Callie took a deep breath and refocused her attention on what was in front of her. She lifted an envelope of pictures out of the box and flipped it open. The photo at the top of the stack was her favorite. She made a mental note to order an enlarged version to display at the party. In it, Zoe stood at the top of the Mohegan Bluffs staircase. She was mid-laugh as she reached to brush hair out of her face, fingernails painted bright white. The steps behind her descended down to the rocky beach where it met the hazy, white-capped ocean. A hand was at the edge of the shot, pointing into the distance. Callie tried to remember the day this was taken, but the specific moment in time was lost to her. The hand could've been anyone's. But then Callie saw the rope bracelet on the wrist and knew it was her own hand. Pointing at what, she didn't know.

She repacked the box and brought the pictures and journals into the house with her.

Their home office was on the first floor opposite a bathroom. The walls were lined with floor-to-ceiling bookshelves, and a compact writing desk sat by the window overlooking the yard. Callie had scanned the shelves when they'd first moved in, deciding which books left by the previous owners could stay and which would be donated. Nathan had appreciated the self-help books the most. His most recent read sat open, face down on the desk—*From Husk to Human: The Wild Man's Guide to Mindfulness.*

Callie nudged it aside and set her box down. For a moment, she stared out the window at the backyard, picturing the green lawn filled with her guests, her friends learning she had kept something else from them. The past whispered in her ear, but she ignored it. This time, they would understand.

She pulled her cell phone from the back pocket of her shorts and sent off one text message.

Everything's coming together nicely. Can't wait to watch their faces when they see you.

She set her phone down on the desk. The photo of Zoe at the top of the bluffs stared back at Callie. She pulled the Missing poster from inside one of the desk drawers and smoothed it out on the desktop. It was a timeline, before and after. But there were missing pieces: the present and the future. And those pieces mattered just as much, if not more.

The only way Callie could change the future was by taking control of the present and bending it the way she wanted it to bend. Like Zoe, spiraling thick-gauge wire around glass to make the pendant in her imagination come to life in her hands.

Then, she typed a text to the group. Please tell me you'll all come for the party. You have no idea how important it is that we're together for this.

Without waiting for a response, Callie carried her old duct-taped journals to the kitchen and dropped them into the deep sink, lit one of her artisanal matches, and let the past burn away. The flames took hold instantly. The paper quickly shriveled into nothing. She opened the window to let the smoke out and ran the faucet, washing away any trace of what had been.

Chapter Ten

LINDSEY

Lindsey rinsed out the coffeepot and set it on the drying rack next to the sink. Behind her, Fred tapped his spoon a few times on the rim of his mug. She picked up her own mug, took a breath, and turned around to face him. He was wearing a crisp white shirt, a blue plaid tie, and tailored navy trousers. Fred had walked into the apartment that morning smelling like clean laundry and looking pristine, while Lindsey wore a pair of gym shorts from college and an old Cape Cod tank top.

She took a quick sip of coffee and got on with it already.

"I'm really sorry about the other night," she said, her free hand falling open in front of her. "I don't have an excuse. I just drank too much."

"You don't have to apologize."

"No, I do. I'm not some out-of-control party girl. I used to be, but I'm too old for that now. It was just a really bad day."

"Don't beat yourself up," he said. "Nobody's perfect."

Lindsey considered giving him some context, maybe telling him about the call with Patricia in a veiled way that wasn't too specific but just enough to help him understand. She didn't have the chance before he spoke again.

"You can say no," Fred said after a quick clearing of his throat. He scraped a hand through his hair. "But I'm going out of town this weekend. If you're free, maybe you'd like to come?"

"Oh," she said, surprised by the turn in conversation.

Her first instinct was to say no. Going away together already? Especially after she'd been a disaster the last time he saw her? She'd be so focused on how she behaved and what she said, she'd never fully relax and enjoy herself. But on the other hand, it would be nice to escape her real life for a few days.

Fred cleared his throat again when she didn't respond. "It's all good, I understand."

"No, I didn't—" she started to say when another voice said her name.

Maddy stood in an oversize T-shirt, eyeing them curiously from the hallway.

"Maddy, hey. I had no idea you were here," Lindsey said.

"I came home last night to study for my summer class," she said. Then, gesturing at the kitchen: "Can I . . . ?"

"Of course," Lindsey said. "I'm sorry I didn't save you any coffee. This is Fred, by the way. Fred, this is my roommate, Maddy."

"Sorry," Maddy said as she skirted between them. She started another pot with the ground coffee she kept in her cupboard—coffee from an imported organic brand she'd seen on Callie's Instagram. Once it was brewing, she eyed Lindsey and Fred curiously. "I'll be out of your hair in a minute."

"I should actually hit the road myself," Fred said with a glance at his watch. "But thank you for the coffee, and sorry if we woke you, Maddy."

Maddy waved a hand. "The walls are thick."

Lindsey shot her a look. Fred laughed and drained the last of his coffee, then said bye to Maddy. Lindsey followed him outside, hoping he'd mention the trip one more time and give her another chance to accept.

"Your roommate is funny," he said. "But she definitely thinks I'm a creep."

"She's the one who told me to start seeing a creep. In fact, her friends are the ones who told me *this* creep was a nice guy."

Fred laughed again and opened his car door. "See you next week?"

Lindsey felt herself deflate. She couldn't tell whether he was giving her the chance to backpedal and ask to join him or if he'd already moved on.

"See you next week," she said, not wanting to seem desperate. She watched his car disappear up a one-way street and went back inside. Maddy was filling her bag with textbooks at the kitchen table.

"Hey, so, next time give me a heads-up if your sugar daddy is going to be here," Maddy said.

"He's not . . ." Lindsey started to say. "It's more nuanced than that."

"Sure," Maddy said. "Does he know about Zoe?"

"We're keeping it casual. That subject isn't exactly light conversation," Lindsey said.

Maddy paused with her hands clasping the strap of her bag. "The reporter hasn't called him yet?"

"What do you mean?"

"That reporter lady who was obsessed with you. She left me messages three days in a row. I just figured if she knows how to reach me, then she'll definitely contact your sugar daddy."

"Stop saying that," Lindsey said. "Did you talk to her?"

"Only for a minute." Maddy smirked. "I said the way she covered Zoe's case was so cringey, I'd be embarrassed to do it again if I were her. I believe I called her 'the epitome of a pick-me girl.' She was literally speechless. Pretty sure I hurt her feelings, but it felt great." She hitched her bag on her shoulder and checked her phone. "I gotta run to campus. You should probably tell him about Zoe, though. Or at least ask if he's gotten a call. Put it out in the open. Might as well come from you before he hears it from her."

Later, at the office, PJ wore his usual headphones. On his desk was some crumpled tinfoil, the remnants of his breakfast. A few errant white crumbs were nestled in his beard.

Lindsey tapped the top of his computer to get his attention. He looked at her, lifted one headphone off his ear.

"You know you can take a real break, right?"

He brushed a palm over his beard. The crumbs dropped away. "Yeah, I know."

"Like, by law, you're supposed to walk away from the computer. Get some fresh air, eat in at the break room. You don't have to give this place every second of your life."

"Sure, yeah. I know how important it is to do things by the law."

He readjusted his headphones and went back to typing. Lindsey stared at him for a second, puzzled by his response. She sat in her chair and jiggled the mouse to wake up her computer and tried to put it from her mind. But as she stared into the void of the inbox, PJ's words nagged at her. She answered a few emails, trying to forget about the deliberate way he'd said *by the law* so pointedly.

She answered another half dozen emails, and had finally fallen into a groove when PJ tapped the top of her computer, for once seeking her attention.

"Yeah?" she asked.

He pointed behind her toward the office lobby. Lindsey looked over her shoulder, saw Patricia's tightly pulled ponytail before anything else, and turned back to her computer. Her body froze. She willed herself to run to the bathroom and hide in a stall, but her legs wouldn't move. Maybe if she stayed with her back turned, Patricia wouldn't see her. Maybe security would kick her out once they realized who she was.

"Sorry I didn't tell you before," PJ said, prying Lindsey out of her own head. "That woman stopped me when I was getting into my car after work the other day. I think it was the day you went home sick. She wanted me to talk to her about you. I mean, I didn't, but she asked me if I respected justice and the rule of law. It was bizarre. I thought she was a scammer."

"She is," Lindsey said. Sensation slowly returned to her body. "And thank you for not talking to her."

Hayden opened her office door and pointed at Lindsey. *Come here,* she mouthed to her.

"What's she doing here?" Hayden asked. She shut the office door behind Lindsey. "Sue just buzzed me that Patricia's lingering around the front desk and won't leave until I talk to her. What am I supposed to say?"

"Don't look at me; I told her to drop it," Lindsey said. "I can't control her."

"Lindsey," Hayden said. She sat behind her desk, dropped her head into her hands. "This is so above my pay grade. If I say the wrong thing, she'll blast us online. And you know how much people love to boycott businesses for doing the wrong thing. I can't be responsible for that."

"Send her away. You don't have to talk to her."

Hayden looked up. "Come with me." Lindsey started to refuse, but Hayden narrowed her eyes. "You're coming. Let's get this over with."

Lindsey followed Hayden to the lobby. Patricia stood at the large floor-to-ceiling windows that lined the front of the old mill building, taking in the harbor views. She turned when Hayden's and Lindsey's footsteps announced their arrival.

"Can I help you with something?" Hayden asked.

Patricia smiled and held out her hand. Hayden didn't take it. Patricia dropped her arm.

"I've been reaching out, but no one has gotten back to me," Patricia said.

"Because I don't want to talk to you," Lindsey said. Hayden held up a hand, motioning for her to stop.

"With all due respect, you can't be here," Hayden said. "I'm sure you know this is inappropriate. We're at work. If you need to reach

Lindsey, there are ways to do it without involving her employer. And if she doesn't want to talk, she doesn't have to."

"That's valid," Patricia said. "It's not my first choice to show up unannounced, believe me. But I also have to do my due diligence as a reporter and ask some questions that need to be asked. This is the only place I know for sure that I'll find her."

"You're stalking me again." Lindsey's hands shook, adrenaline coursing fast through her. "What don't you understand? No one wants you telling Zoe's story. If I say it louder, will you get it then? Is that better?"

Lindsey's composure shrank as her volume increased. Her breath went ragged. She was aware of Hayden and the receptionist watching her but not stepping in. Just letting her spin out in the middle of the office.

Patricia held up her hands. "Have you ever thought about downloading MindBalm? Callie has some great meditations on there that might help you with . . . this."

Lindsey drew a slow breath. "This? *This* is because of you. I don't need meditation; I need you to go find a bridge and jump off."

"Okay, that's enough. We're done here. You have to go," Hayden said.

She slid an arm into the space between Patricia and Lindsey and gestured toward the exit. Patricia turned and walked with her. She handed Hayden a sheet of paper and looked over her shoulder at Lindsey.

"I know you weren't where you said you were the day Zoe disappeared," Patricia said. "All I want to do is ask you about that. But I guess you'd rather I figure it out for myself."

Lindsey's ears rang and a cold numbness spread through her body. How could Patricia know that? How could she call Lindsey's bluff in such a chilling, specific way?

Hayden opened one of the doors and gestured for Patricia to go.

"Wow," Hayden muttered as she rejoined Lindsey. "You weren't kidding about her. And what is this?"

The flyer in Hayden's hands featured a photo, with text underneath that read IF YOU KNOW ANYTHING ABOUT ZOE GILBERT'S DISAPPEARANCE ON AUGUST 10, 2014, OR THE OTHER WOMEN IN THIS PHOTO, CONTACT ME TODAY. YOU COULD BE FEATURED IN A BOOK!

"This is garbage," Lindsey said, crumpling it and tossing it into the trash.

She followed Hayden back to her office.

"Listen, what happened out there wasn't professional," Hayden said. "Word's going to travel up the ladder. They're going to ask me if you signed the legal agreement yet. Let's just take care of it now so it doesn't bite us later."

"No," Lindsey said, shaking her head. "I shouldn't have to sign it. I'm the victim here. You just saw for yourself that she's obsessed with me. How is any of that my fault?"

Hayden pushed her glasses up onto her head and studied Lindsey.

"Why did she say that?" she asked. "Why does she care so much about you not being where you said you were?"

Pain shot through Lindsey's jaw. She was clenching her teeth, her shoulders, her entire body. She watched as Hayden, normally a logical person, fell under the familiar veil of skepticism created by Patricia's accusations.

"Please don't pay any attention to her," Lindsey said. "She made a big deal out of it because it's the only thing she knows how to do."

"Regardless," Hayden said, "you have to sign that agreement. Your job's worth it, isn't it?"

"No," Lindsey said before she realized what was coming out of her mouth. Her eyes went wide. "No, I didn't mean that. I just—"

Hayden pressed her palms against the desk and stood up.

"I think you did mean it, and I think you don't care about this job at all. I've cut you *so* much slack since I started managing your department. Did you know they wanted to let you go two years ago because your customer response ratings were so low? Let's be real. You don't want to be here. I think this is where we should part ways permanently so you can look for something that's a better fit. Your final check will be available next week in payroll, or I can have it mailed to you."

"Wait," Lindsey started to say, words failing her completely now. She stood up, too, but went dizzy as soon as she was on her feet. "Hayden, wait, okay? I didn't mean it. Can we slow down for a second? I'm not thinking clearly right now."

"Do you want to work here? Be honest."

Lindsey hesitated. She knew she could lie. She'd been doing it for years.

"I need an income and health insurance."

"You can find that anywhere," Hayden said. "This hasn't been a good match for a while, and you know it."

Rent, food, student loans. A sick heat rose up the back of Lindsey's throat. She swallowed, but it persisted.

"I wish you the best," Hayden said as she walked to her office door and held it open for Lindsey, as she had for Patricia in the lobby.

There was nothing more for Lindsey to say. Wordlessly, she returned to her desk, threw all her personal items into her bag, and left without even attempting to say goodbye to PJ.

Lindsey drove home in a daze, her mind tangled in worry. When she parked in her usual spot and turned off the engine, she realized she had no recollection of the trip home. No memory of how she had gotten from there to here. It was a small miracle she hadn't gone off the road.

The bar wasn't open yet, another small miracle. She couldn't imagine going up to her empty apartment, either. What would she do with herself? She didn't trust that she'd be able to keep her hands off the bottles in Maddy's cabinet.

She'd walk and think, clear her head a little bit. Figure out her next move. It wasn't the end of the world yet.

Lindsey walked briskly down to the wharf, where rows of shops and restaurants were opening for the day, some already filled with tourists and brave locals. The sun beat down hard, and Lindsey felt the top of her head growing hot. She stopped at a gift shop to buy a hat, but not a single one cost less than forty dollars. She left empty-handed.

Outside the shop, she sat on a metal bench so hot that it burned her legs through her pants. She fished her phone out of her bag and opened her text exchange with Fred. Was it too late to ask if she could tag along on his trip after all? The extra money wouldn't hurt. She couldn't bring herself to type the words, though. Every sentence she wrote sounded more pathetic than the last.

She thumbed over to her group text with Tess, Meg, and Callie. Their last exchange—Patricia showing up at Meg's office, Callie again pushing her party. Lindsey still hadn't decided one way or another if she'd go. But if anyone in the world could understand what she was dealing with right now, it was them.

Got fired thanks to Patricia. Hasn't really sunk in yet. No idea what I'm going to do.

She sent the text and leaned back against the bench, letting the warmth permeate her from every angle. Should she tell Fred she'd been fired? That admission would open the door for questions she didn't want to answer. But maybe Maddy was right and Lindsey was just avoiding the inevitable. Her phone pinged in her hand. Then pinged again. And again.

Meg: Oh, Lindsey. What did she do? Are you okay?

Tess: They FIRED you?? I'm so sorry. That's awful.

Callie: This is getting out of hand. Can you come out here? We'll strategize.

Lindsey wasn't sure what kind of response she'd expected from her old friends—a part of her hadn't expected anything. She wasn't sure she would've written back if the shoe had been on the other foot and, say, Meg had been fired because of Patricia. What did they owe each other anymore?

But their replies to Lindsey were immediate and full of concern. An ache bloomed in her chest, and she started to cry on that bench in the middle of the busy wharf. People looked at her strangely as she sobbed by herself in the sun.

"Are you okay?" one woman asked, crouching next to Lindsey. "Do you need help?"

"I'm fine," Lindsey said through hitching breaths. "I lost my job today. But my old friends were nice about it."

The woman patted Lindsey's knee, a confused look passing across her face, and told her to hang in there. Then Lindsey was alone again, her phone pinging once more in her lap. She looked down. Another text from Callie, this one sent solely to Lindsey.

She's never going to stop. Let me help you. My lawyer can take a look at your situation. Maybe you have a wrongful termination case on your hands.

Lindsey wiped her eyes and considered how to answer. Callie, ever the problem-solver, once again using her resources to make sure things turned out just right. It reminded Lindsey of camp, how she was the poor one who'd only gotten in because of a scholarship. How, the following year, when she didn't get the scholarship, Callie pulled some strings to make sure her parents' endowment went toward Lindsey's tuition. It was a kind gesture, which Lindsey didn't think much about at the time, too ecstatic about another summer on the island with her friends to care how the money had materialized in her name. But later, once she was an adult, Lindsey realized her friend's privilege was the only reason she'd been able to return to camp. Pure luck. If Lindsey had befriended a different cabin of girls her first year, she would've been at home that next summer, working a part-time job at an ice-cream shop. How was this any different, Callie using another arm of her privilege to fix a problem?

Why do you want to help me? Lindsey texted. Within a few seconds, her phone rang. Callie. Lindsey answered it.

"I'm not going to go back and forth over text about this," Callie said. "I want to help you because I care about you. Whether or not you believe that, it's the truth."

Lindsey made a faint sound in the back of her throat. Neither one of agreement nor disagreement, but acknowledgment.

"I'm not sure I trust you," Lindsey said.

"Then don't trust me," Callie said. "But let me help you, okay? We'll handle this together."

More people filtered into the wharf as she sat on the bench, thinking. A voice in the back of her mind told her not to forget Callie's last attempt at fixing the problem of Patricia. How there had been no *together* in that solution.

"You told us we weren't doing interviews, then you went and gave one," Lindsey said.

"I told you not to do an interview?"

"On the beach, yes. Remember? When Patricia started asking us to tell her about Zoe. You said we weren't doing interviews."

Callie took a breath. "Wait, what? I only said that to get her off our backs. It wasn't a command, Lindsey. I said it because I could feel her grabby energy right away. She was practically salivating at the thought of getting us to talk, and I had a bad feeling about it. Rightfully so. She was calling it true crime, complaining about us putting fingerprints on the glasses. You're kidding, right? You thought I meant we should never give interviews?"

Lindsey thought back. She'd never questioned Callie before that day on the beach, especially when it came to making big decisions for the collective, so when she heard that they weren't giving interviews, Lindsey had assumed it meant Callie knew the best course of action was to close ranks, stay quiet.

"Of course we thought that. You were in charge," Lindsey said, feeling pathetic to admit it out loud. "You took control of the situation, and we followed your lead. Don't you remember what you said when we took the sunglasses away from Patricia?"

A sound of shifting fabric came through the line, like Callie was moving to a more secluded spot to have this conversation.

"I remember. And I regret it all the time," she said in a low voice. "But we were all panicking at the sight of those glasses. Not just me. We were all trying to figure out what to do."

The sun beat the back of Lindsey's neck as she sat on the bench by the wharf. Same as that day on the beach, the distinct feeling of her skin burning, her mind was in a million other places while she examined the red sunglasses. Callie taking them from her hands.

"These are probably hers," she'd said with a sigh of resignation.

Then the glasses were in Meg's hands, her eyes spilling with tears.

"What the hell, what the hell," Meg murmured as she turned them over. "What the *hell*?"

"Calm down. Listen, now is the time to say if anyone knows why these are here," Callie said. "Say it, and we'll figure out what to do about it."

Lindsey remembered the shock of that statement, the way it had slapped her with the realization that there might be mistrust between the four of them. But, in a strange way, how it also spoke to their unity.

"What are you implying?" Tess had asked, holding her hands up in surrender. She would not touch the sunglasses.

"I'm not implying anything; I'm just opening up space for . . . whatever anyone needs to say."

"Are you serious? You think one of us is the reason Zoe's missing and her sunglasses are here?" Lindsey asked, the boldness of a few tiny bottles of raspberry Smirnoff coursing through her veins. "Why don't *you* tell us why the glasses are here?"

"I have no idea. Look, the last night we were all together was tense," Callie said. "I'm just . . . I want to make sure no one needs to get anything off their chest."

"The other night was nothing," Lindsey said. "Right, Tess? It was just some bickering. It was nothing."

"It was nothing," Tess repeated.

"So no one knows why these are here?" Callie asked, meeting each of their gazes. "Fine. Good. That keeps it easy."

"Easy?" Meg sputtered. "Oh my God, Callie. Nothing about this is easy."

"I just meant—"

"That we don't have to cover for anyone," Tess had finished for Callie, her voice flat.

Lindsey might've told them about her lie, that she was not actually where she'd claimed to be once she returned home from the trip. But she couldn't do that after Callie gave them permission to wonder who might be keeping secrets.

"That girl is recording us," Callie had said. "Right now. She's pointing her phone over here."

Lindsey turned in Patricia's direction and mouthed for her to stop. Shot her a glare made of daggers.

She'd always wondered if her reaction in that moment had been part of the catalyst for Patricia's behavior. If telling Patricia to turn away had only made her more interested in watching.

"So, what do you think?" Callie's voice asked now from the phone. "Come out here?"

Lindsey stood up from the bench and walked in the direction of her apartment. She pushed against a tide of incoming pedestrians and skirted around people on bikes and scooters.

"I'll see if I can get on a ferry this afternoon," she said. "I need to get out of town for a little while. I feel like I'm suffocating."

"Great. You can breathe out here," Callie said before they hung up.

But Lindsey wasn't so sure. Sometimes the past smothered her even more than the present, like a pair of invisible hands wrapped around her neck.

Chapter Eleven

PATRICIA

Draft one of introduction for book in progress

When a missing person case goes unsolved, it's natural for people to wonder. After all, our minds are impressive machines that prefer certainty, and an unresolved disappearance is about as far from "certain" as it gets. But our brains are also able to recognize patterns and make connections between two seemingly unrelated details long before we're consciously aware of it. Sometimes we're solving mysteries without even knowing it.

It's no wonder that a case like Zoe Gilbert's would baffle and intrigue the true crime community. Thousands of us have spent years pondering where she went, reviewing the facts, and spinning our own tales about what might've happened based on the patterns and connections we've observed. Our minds are conditioned to seek answers.

Zoe Gilbert vanished without a trace on August 10, 2014. I didn't know her personally before she disappeared, but the day I heard that a search party was being organized to look for a local missing woman, I boarded the Block Island ferry to assist however I could. I was in the early days of writing my blog at the time, and my readers were ready for me to give them something more than retellings of old cases. This was my chance to tell a new story from my own perspective and give a voice to someone who had been silenced.

I'd long been interested in missing person cases. Drawn in by the mystery, I would read or watch as much as possible about each case. And then my mind would play out dozens upon dozens of scenarios to help explain the ambiguity of a disappearance. I consider the people involved, the known facts, and my own instincts, and then craft narratives to possibly explain why a person has disappeared and where they might've gone.

The narratives are just speculation, but they're always rooted in reality.

In the years since I started doing this work, I've helped authorities solve several missing person cases with my own curiosity. I'm able to make connections, see patterns, think outside the box in a way some detectives can't. And Zoe Gilbert's disappearance is next.

As you read my book, you'll learn the key players, the facts investigators were able to confirm, and my own impressions about what happened to Zoe.

You may already have some familiarity with this case and my involvement in it. I was the only person to find any evidence during the search for Zoe, and soon after that, I began posing questions to my community of readers and viewers based on the connections my mind naturally drew. Those questions upset many people—namely, the people who were last seen with Zoe Gilbert before she vanished.

Those people were her friends: Callie Sutter, Tess Winters, Meghan Bradley, and Lindsey Sherman.

They were with me on that beach when I found sunglasses that most likely belonged to Zoe before her disappearance, but their behavior that day, and in the days and weeks that followed, set off alarm bells in my head. *There's something here; there's a pattern worth observing,* I told myself. So I observed. I made connections. I developed theories about Zoe Gilbert's fate.

In this book, I'll tell you more about those theories than I ever did in my past videos or on my blog. I'll share, in great detail, the facts about Zoe's disappearance: the damning reason why I think her sunglasses appeared on that beach, why I homed in on her friends so quickly, and why I think Zoe's final days with her friends were far from idyllic.

But most importantly, you'll meet real eyewitnesses overlooked by the investigators. Eyewitnesses who will talk only to me. They'll share firsthand how their accounts contradict what Callie Sutter and Lindsey Sherman, specifically, told police about Zoe's disappearance and their own whereabouts in the hours after she went missing. I'll explore what I think those inconsistencies really mean.

From there, you can draw conclusions of your own. Was Zoe the victim of toxic friendship? Did one or even all four of her friends have a hand in her disappearance and then try to cover up the only piece of evidence? Or did something else happen on that August day? And if so . . . what?

Chapter Twelve

MEG

Meg read the opening pages of Patricia's book at least twenty times over the course of a few days. She read on the train home, her shoulders pressed between other commuters. She read sprawled on her well-loved couch, with her mother on speakerphone talking about two warring squirrels in her backyard. She read at work, in the quiet of her office before anyone else arrived. For now, though, she kept the existence of those pages a secret from Tina and Lydia.

The office air-conditioning kicked on with a loud gust, but the cool air didn't reach Meg. Her office was like a warm tomb closed up tight with her inside. Just her and Patricia's words on a few pieces of printer paper, while the rest of the book—and whatever revelations it might hold—existed out of reach.

Meg pushed the chair out from her desk, both her legs and mind too restless to continue sitting and ruminating over Patricia's writing. She left the office, took the elevator down to street level, and walked out into the warm morning. But everyone outside moved too slowly, without any urgency. A sidewalk full of leisure, while Meg fought the urge to sprint. She darted around suits and moms pushing strollers, her restlessness silently screaming at them to *move*.

Even though she wanted to ignore it, Meg knew exactly what the anxious energy coursing through her was caused by—the fear she would make the wrong choice. Because when it came down to it, she had to choose: either talk to Patricia for the book or risk being culpable by association for whatever lies her friends might've told.

She walked faster. Her blouse grew damp under the arms and on the lower back, and her feet were starting to ache trekking the city in heels, but she kept going. Thinking. The more she moved, the more she could transmute her restlessness into strategy.

There was also a third option. An option Patricia likely wouldn't predict, even if she had a hidden agenda in leaving her manuscript's first pages in Meg's possession. Meg could run down the list of names she'd stolen from Patricia, talk to each person herself, and try to find the supposed witnesses who could refute Lindsey's and Callie's stories. Once she knew the information Patricia was working with, Meg could choose her allegiances wisely.

But it would be hard to do that alone from Boston. She was certain Patricia was on the ground in Rhode Island, talking about Zoe's case and scrounging up witnesses, whoever they were. Meg wasn't sure she should tell Callie and Lindsey any of this until she knew more—for their sakes and to protect herself, if it came down to that.

She could trust Tess, though. Always could. And she might even be willing to help.

Back at the agency, Meg stopped into Lydia's office to ask for permission to work remotely.

"I owe my mother a visit," she said, not a total lie. She hadn't gone home in a while. "I'm thinking of spending a couple of weeks with her."

"Of course. We'll patch you in for important meetings, but summers are always a bit slower. Go, enjoy some family time," Lydia said, waving Meg out of her office.

She packed up her work laptop, some drafts of novels she was reading for clients, and Patricia's list of names. To be safe, she fed the opening pages of Patricia's book to the office shredder. It didn't matter if the words were gone; they were already seared into Meg's mind.

The commuter rail took Meg from South Station down through Rhode Island, giving her two hours to listen to the slow rattle of the train on its tracks while she trawled Facebook and Instagram pages, blogs, and LinkedIn profiles for the people on Patricia's list.

Meg only recognized one of the eight names—Blake Connors. There had always been something about Blake that didn't sit right with her. She'd only met him a few times, and there was nothing special about him. Zoe could've done so much better.

Blake's digital footprint consisted of a Twitter account, which he hadn't used in over a year since last posting about his band breaking up, and a few random mentions of him on friends' social media accounts. His Facebook was open to the public but also appeared abandoned, the majority of his photos dating back a decade to 2009 and earlier when he was touring with his band. Zoe and Lindsey were even in a few of the photo albums, mostly in the background of shots. Except for one.

In it, Lindsey and Zoe were arm in arm, walking away from the camera down a dark sidewalk, both of them dressed for a night out in short black dresses with their hair flat-ironed within an inch of its life. Despite their height difference, they leaned their heads in toward one another while they walked. The surprise of finding an unexpected photo of Zoe squeezed Meg's ribs. She blinked away the sudden tears in her eyes. Zoe's absence never felt easier, never hurt less.

She closed out Blake's Facebook page and continued skimming through his extinct accounts. He wasn't a total dead end, though. His LinkedIn page showed his current workplace was a brewery in Rhode Island. If she caught him off guard, maybe he'd admit what he'd told Patricia.

Maybe Meg wouldn't have to do that alone.

She pulled her phone from her bag and called Tess. As soon as the line started to ring, Meg's throat tightened. A kind of homesickness wormed into her gut. But she could hardly remember the exact tone of Tess's voice and wasn't even sure if an unannounced call like this would be welcome. Before Meg could hang up, Tess answered.

"Meg?" she said. "What happened? Is everything okay?"

"Oh, hey," Meg said. "I'm sorry, everything's fine. I should have texted you."

"It's been so long," Tess said.

Meg understood what she meant. Once, unsolicited calls happened without second thought. Calls never signaled that something was wrong; they were simply a normal part of their relationship. But it had been so long that norm was dead. Now a random phone call could only mean something terrible.

"It's great to hear from you," Tess went on. "How are you?"

"Good, good. I'm on the train home right now," Meg said. "Going to stay with my mom for a while. I thought you and I could get together while I'm in town, if you're free. But I know with the baby . . ."

"With the baby, I'm somehow free and busy at the same time, all the time," Tess said, and she let out a flat laugh. "Come by the house this afternoon. I'll be around later."

This whole time, Meg had been picturing Tess at her old apartment. But there was no way she still lived there, not with a family now.

"This afternoon, yeah," Meg said. "I just . . . What's your address? I hate admitting I don't even know where you live."

"I don't know where you live, either," Tess said. "We bought a house in Wickford last year."

She gave Meg directions and the address. Meg jotted it down on the edge of the list of names and thanked her. Tess lived close to the brewery, probably no more than a ten-minute drive.

"Hey, listen," Meg said. "This is a weird question, but do you remember Blake?"

"Unfortunately," Tess said. "Why?"

"I'll explain when I see you," Meg said. "But if you're up for it, maybe we can take a drive to the brewery where he works. I want to ask him something."

"Cryptic," Tess said. "Way to leave me hanging."

"There's just a lot to it," Meg said. "Too much for me to get into right now. But I'll explain everything when I see you."

They hung up, and Meg went back to work on the list. The other seven names seemed so random and unconnected to Zoe, Meg had no idea what Patricia's thought process might be. She tapped her pen on the seat beside her. There were four people, including Blake, who had easily findable contact information online. Meg drafted an email to each of the other three—Angie Carlson, Cameron Oakes, and Miles Bell—and sent the messages off into cyberspace, hoping that soon she'd know who these strangers were to Zoe.

When she got off the train, she found her mother's car idling in the parking garage. Lucy threw open the car door and ran to hug Meg.

"What a treat this is," Lucy said, kissing Meg on both cheeks. She smelled like the rose-scented moisturizer she'd used since Meg was a little girl. Lucy pulled back and placed her palms on Meg's shoulders. "You look exhausted. Have you eaten?"

"Of course," Meg lied, not wanting her mother to worry about the meals Meg had been skipping lately—or the sleep she wasn't getting. She followed Lucy to the car and climbed in.

"Well, you could use a snack, I'm sure."

"Actually, Mom, I could use your car. Can I borrow it for a little while? I have plans with Tess."

She shot Meg a look as she steered out of the parking garage.

"*Tess* Tess? Really? Does this mean you're talking again?"

Meg shifted under the pressure of her seat belt. "I'm not really sure what it means."

"You haven't spoken in years, have you? Did she reach out to you?"

"We had to start speaking again. Patricia's writing a book about Zoe," Meg said. The silence that followed told Meg her mother didn't know yet. "She'll probably contact you and ask for an interview. You don't have to talk to her."

Meg watched her mother's hands tighten on the wheel. A tendon in her temple flexed.

"That woman," Lucy said, a catch in her voice. "She tortured you girls. She turned our home into a prison, but what she did to you four was unforgivable. Dragging your names through the mud like that."

"I know," Meg said. "Don't worry, I've got it under control."

"Turning a missing person case into a circus. At the *expense* of Zoe's best friends. And what she did was useless—it didn't even find Zoe. It helped no one except for *her*."

"Mom, I know. I remember."

"I'm sorry," Lucy exhaled. "Let's just get you home so you can eat something and go visit your friend. I'm sure it'll be nice to see Tess after all this time. Maybe you two can pick up where you left off. Sometimes that happens. It's like no time has passed at all, like nothing has changed."

For the rest of the short drive, Lucy told Meg about the latest neighborhood drama, but Meg was only half listening.

She thought back to where she and Tess had left off.

A tearful phone call in the middle of the night a few months after Callie's interview, once the rest of them had finally drifted apart. The last time they had spoken before now.

Meg had answered the call despite her desire to ignore the ringing of her phone for all eternity. What had she gotten when she answered it? Tess, sobbing on the line, barely able to catch her breath as she repeated the same thing over and over again.

"This is our fault, Meg. I'm never going to forgive myself. This is all our fault."

Chapter Thirteen

Tess

The day was overcast and warm. With the added weight and bulk of Emmy strapped to her, sweat immediately began to collect in the hollows of Tess's body: under the band of her nursing bra, in the curve of her lower back, behind her knees. She walked through the neighborhood briskly, already late for the meeting because of Meg's call, already second-guessing it entirely.

When Tess reached the café, she peered through the front window before entering. The space was crowded, and Patricia was sitting alone at the far end, face angled down at the phone in her hands as she typed on the screen. Her chair was positioned awkwardly away from the table and facing the door.

Tess entered the café to the sound of a blender whirring and music pouring from overhead speakers. Staff behind the counter called out orders to one another. As if sensing her presence, Patricia looked up and locked eyes with Tess. She raised a hand and motioned Tess over.

"Didn't want you sneaking up on me," Patricia said as she stood up and set her chair back in alignment with the table. "But it's probably hard to do that with a tiny alarm system attached to your body."

She studied Tess for a few seconds; Tess hoped she couldn't see the gleam of sweat on her forehead.

"How have you been?" Patricia asked.

"Busy," Tess said.

"I heard you didn't go back to work after you had the baby," Patricia said. "That must've been hard. It was, what? Your third job in six years?"

"If you want me to know you're still prying into my life, just say so. But I thought we were here to talk about Zoe."

"You're right," Patricia said, holding her hands up as if caught. "Just trying to make small talk. It's the podcaster in me making sure my interview subject is comfortable."

"Right," Tess said. "And I hear you're an aspiring author now, too."

"Yes, that, too. Just like all of you, I contain multitudes."

Tess gave her a steady look. "And you want me to talk about our multitudes, is that right?"

"I thought we were here to talk about Zoe. But if you want to tell me about your complexities, I'm all ears. I've always wanted to understand your world."

"You sure acted like you understood us," Tess said. "You even seem to think you know how *haunted* I am. What did you mean by that?"

Patricia glanced at the front counter, then back at Tess. "Can I buy you a coffee?"

"I can't stay long," Tess said. Her internal clock was already ticking toward Meg's arrival. The train ride from Boston was only a couple of hours, and Meg could've already been on it for a while when they talked. She could show up on Tess's doorstep any minute.

The café bustled around them, a mix of conversations and too-loud jazz atop the mechanical grinding and brewing of the coffee machines.

"It was just something I noticed from the beginning," Patricia said. "At the search, you wouldn't touch the evidence I found. You just seemed . . . apprehensive."

Tess bristled. "Because I was."

"Why didn't you want to hold the sunglasses? Your friends were so eager to get their hands on them, but not you."

Tess swallowed. She could remember the moment clearly. Not only because she'd lived it, but also because she'd watched Patricia's footage several times. She had the experience memorized from every angle, the grainy image of herself pulling away while her friends passed the glasses back and forth.

Tess knew how it appeared, but the shameful truth was that she'd fought with Zoe the night before she vanished. And in the heat of the argument, she'd insulted Zoe's taste, specifically calling her sunglasses tacky and juvenile. It was something Zoe would've never done to Tess. The expression on Zoe's face after Tess said it was proof enough that Tess had crossed an unspoken boundary. So the sight of those glasses in the wake of Zoe's disappearance brought the memory of Tess's cruelty back to the surface. Touching them was the last thing she wanted to do.

"You've always been good at seeing what you want to see," Tess said to Patricia, refusing to answer her question.

"Or, I see things others don't." Patricia shrugged. "I could be wrong, though. I'm human and imperfect, after all."

"This book," Tess said. "What are you trying to accomplish? Just let the police handle Zoe's case. They're the only ones who can solve it. You're not an investigator."

"But I am. And I need to finish what I started five years ago," Patricia said, leaning back in her chair. "You only know the intense and obsessive version of me, so you're not sure how to feel about me now. If I were you, I might be wary, too. I get it. But I like to think I'm more self-aware now. More conscious of staying grounded in my investigations."

This worried Tess more than the thought of Patricia merely having an axe to grind.

"Why write a book, though? At least with your blog, you could edit the posts when you learned new information. A book is forever. Whatever you write about us won't go away."

"Well, from a strategic standpoint, Zoe's case launched my career initially. It was the story that catapulted me from a blogger with fifty readers to a respected figure in true crime–podcasting circles. So it makes sense to use her story for my next platform jump from podcasting to writing books."

"You're using her—and us—all over again for your own benefit," Tess said.

"It benefits everyone when a case is solved. That's why I want your help." She folded her hands. "You should talk to me for the book. I never thought it was fair the world only heard from Callie. You deserve a chance to speak out, too."

Tess hated that she agreed with Patricia. But still, she refused to admit it out loud. Tess remembered the disbelief she'd felt watching Callie's interview air on television, how she knew right away things would never be the same. She thought of Meg's confusion and Lindsey's rage as Callie's disembodied voice carried through the room around them. How the three of them, already brimming with so many emotions, overflowed. There simply wasn't room in that house to hold their vast constellation of feelings.

Patricia rested her chin on her fist. "And how are you all doing now? Do you still speak?"

"Of course," Tess said. "You've never understood what we mean to each other."

Patricia tilted her head slightly to the side. "Or what you'd do to protect each other?"

Emmy squirmed in the carrier and let out a small whine. Tess rested a hand on her back.

"This is getting old," Tess said. "I thought if I heard you out, maybe you'd say something that justified what you did to us. But you're still spinning the same tired story."

Emmy began to whine more consistently, and Patricia noticed.

"I know you can't sit here all day, but you should do yourself—and that sweet baby—a favor and chat with me for the book. Imagine I make a big discovery in the course of my investigation, and you haven't explained yourself. You won't be able to blame me if that discovery turns out to be a bomb in the center of your life."

The café felt too small and too hot. Emmy opened her mouth to wail. Tess's nervous system electrified. Everything was too much.

"Is that some kind of threat?" Tess asked. "If I don't give you what you want, you'll make sure I look guilty?"

"No, absolutely not. I just think," Patricia said, leaning in, "that maybe it's time you started acting more like Callie Sutter. This is your chance to speak. You didn't have the chance to do that before. You have a child and her future to think about now. Aren't you tired of being entwined with those girls? Imagine your daughter was in your shoes. You can't possibly say you'd want her to side with three people she can't fully trust. You'd want her to have a backbone and defend herself, right?"

Emmy's cries intensified, and Tess felt the fire of the sound in every tiny corner of her body.

"You have nothing concrete in Zoe's case," Tess said, hoping she was right.

"And who, exactly, said that?"

Tess knew better than to take Patricia at her word, but there was something about the way she asked this that gave Tess pause. So confident and sure. Tess glanced at the downy top of Emmy's head, her little face scrunched up and red. What if Patricia did know something? What if?

"You never wondered why Callie was so quick to leave you in the dust and make sure the world knew she didn't trust *you* three?" Patricia went on. "But you're supposed to trust her until the end of time, at your own expense?"

Emmy screeched. Tess's resolve shattered.

"Fine," she said, her voice hoarse. She stood up and patted Emmy to quiet her, but it didn't help. She needed to get out of there.

"Great. Let's talk soon so you don't change your mind on me. I'm going to grab another coffee; you sure you don't want anything?"

Tess told her no and left the café. She moved quickly, adrenaline thrumming in her veins. She had to put as much space as possible between herself and Patricia. Had to get home before Meg arrived, change out of her sweaty clothes, splash cold water on her face, feed the baby, and calm down her own frazzled body.

And figure out how to justify agreeing to talk to Patricia.

Tess rounded the corner to her street and saw the car parked at the curb. She knew it on sight—that was Lucy's car. A pang of homesickness struck her. Lucy, like a second mother to Tess for so many years. The one who had sheltered the four of them when they needed it most. Losing her friends had meant losing their people, too.

Meg stood by the car, smiling awkwardly. She was wearing a simple navy-blue dress and heels, like she'd come from work. Her auburn hair, streaked with strands of gray, was twisted into a low bun at the nape of her neck. She looked so professional and polished. A more mature version of the Meg she once knew. Tess took a breath as she approached on the sidewalk, as nervous as if it were a first date.

"I just pulled up," Meg said. "I saw you leaving the café when I drove past, and I would've stopped to offer you a ride, but I don't have a car seat."

Tess wondered if Meg would feel her nervousness radiating off her like heat.

"You drove past the café?" Tess asked. Her empty hands suddenly felt conspicuous. "I'm so sleep deprived, I sucked my coffee down before I left."

"I almost stopped to grab something," Meg said as she followed Tess up the front steps. "But I've had two already today and haven't eaten a real meal yet. I'm on edge enough without adding fuel to the fire."

Tess shoved her key into the door lock. Meg could've walked in on her with Patricia. That news would've made it back to Callie and Lindsey immediately. Their resentment and anger would've been swift and final. She knew because she'd been on the other side of it once.

Tess pushed open the door, and Meg stepped into the living room. Tess and James had just started dating when Zoe went missing; Meg had only met him once or twice, and she'd never seen the house they eventually bought together. All moments stolen by years of separation.

"Your place is so cute," Meg said. "Exactly how I pictured you decorating a house."

"Really?" Tess was surprised. Flattered, even.

"Absolutely. I love those prints hanging up over there. They're very Tess. And of course you have a green velvet chair. Is it vintage?"

"It's very vintage," Tess said. "I don't think anyone has ever noticed my stuff. Or attributed it to my style."

Meg turned, surprised. "Really? This place is so you. It reminds me of that apartment you had right after college."

Her first apartment. She'd had two roommates, both hairstylists in training, and their collective decorating aesthetic consisted of cheap or free items. Tess had the time and desire to scour thrift shops and yard sales, often with Zoe tagging along and giving her opinion on how certain pieces would work together. The embroidered throw pillow on the green velvet chair had been one of Zoe's finds. Tess could still recall the way Zoe's face had lit up when she spotted it under a ratty wool blanket in the back of a secondhand shop. *Someone made this,* she'd said, tracing her fingers over the embroidered cluster of maroon roses and green, leafy vines winding along the edge. *Probably in the sixties. This is so special. It's made for your green chair. You have to get it.* And then she dropped it into Tess's cart, conversation over. Tess happily bought it and refused to ever let it go.

In the end, that apartment had looked like a thrift shop itself, but a stylized one thanks to Zoe and Tess's shared vision. Purposefully shabby, a little maximalist. How Meg could still see this part of Tess so clearly after years apart astounded her.

Tess removed Emmy from the carrier and settled on the couch to nurse her.

"Do you mind if I . . . ?" she asked Meg just before unsnapping her nursing bra.

"Of course not. Wouldn't be the first time I saw your boobs, would it?"

Tess laughed with a whisper of nervousness as she adjusted Emmy so she could latch. "I don't know what you're talking about."

"Right, right. You never went skinny-dipping ever. Definitely not."

"That was never my idea!" Tess said.

"Maybe not, but you always did it," Meg said, pointing at her.

"Who could say no to Zoe?"

But as soon as she'd invoked Zoe's name, she wished she could take it back. Meg's demeanor changed. The playfulness evaporated. Meg cleared her throat and pretended to be absorbed in the prints hanging on the wall.

"I'm sorry," Tess said.

Meg turned around. "Why should you apologize? It's me. I guess I should just get down to it and tell you why I'm here."

Tess was dreading it, whatever Meg had to say.

"This isn't something I'm comfortable sharing with Lindsey and Callie yet," Meg said, sitting on the edge of the couch. She pushed her heels off and nudged them away with her toes. Flexed her feet and took a breath. "I'm only telling you this because I know I can trust you. When Patricia came to my office, she left me with the first couple of pages of her manuscript."

Tess's stomach dipped. The sensation reminded her of the first few weeks of breastfeeding, when she'd feel a subtle, creeping sense of dread in the pit of her stomach when Emmy would start to feed. She googled it, fearing she was feeling that way because she was a terrible mother, only to find that it was a real condition no one had ever told her about. Now, though, this dread felt worse.

"What did she write?" Tess asked.

"That's the thing," Meg went on. "She claims she has witnesses who dispute Lindsey's and Callie's stories about where they were after we left

Zoe on the island. I don't know if it's true or if she's just screwing with me. It's probably that. She wants to interview me for her book, but I'm not doing that. Absolutely not."

Tess looked away so Meg wouldn't see the shame in her eyes.

"But that's not all," Meg said. "I sort of snapped and tossed a bunch of her papers everywhere in the heat of the moment. She had a list of names, and I took it."

Tess looked back. "Names of who?"

"I don't know. Maybe her eyewitnesses are on the list," Meg said. "Blake's on it. I'm going to contact as many of them as I can get a hold of and find out. I need to know who said what about Lindsey and Callie."

"This is why you came home and want to go to the brewery," Tess said.

"I want to know if he talked to her. Maybe it's dumb, but I was losing my mind up in Boston. I had to come home and do *something*."

"And you want my help," Tess said.

"Only if you want to help," Meg said. "But you're the only one I trust right now. What if they're hiding something from us? I mean, I hope that's not the case. But I just don't know."

Tess looked down at Emmy again. This was her moment to tell Meg what had just happened with Patricia in the café. Meg would understand the impossible position Tess had been put in, especially since she had her own skepticism now about their friends. Patricia was either playing them both or, in her own twisted way, trying to help.

"I trust you, too," Tess said. "In fact, I should tell you—"

But then Meg's phone rang, and she bolted to her bag to fish it out.

"I'm so sorry, this is for work. I need to take it," she said. "Just one sec."

Tess waved her on to answer the call, and Meg slipped outside to the porch.

The moment was gone, and Tess felt more relief than she should've. She trusted Meg, but she'd wait and see if anything serious materialized from the list of names Meg was investigating before admitting to taking a meeting with Patricia and promising to talk to her again.

Because if Tess knew one thing for sure, it was that she'd protect her daughter's world—and her own role in it—at all costs. Even if it meant betraying the people she had once thought she'd die for.

The Backwind Brewing Co. was only a short drive from Tess's house. She changed Emmy's diaper while Meg finished her call, clipped the baby into her car seat, and waited by the front door.

"Ready to go?" she asked Meg when she returned from the porch. "I'll drive."

Meg gave her a quick, conspiratorial smile. "I always knew one day you'd have a kid and we'd take her out for drinks."

"Me too," Tess said.

Reality pierced her like a dagger. They were only together now because of circumstances outside their control, not because they'd truly chosen it. But maybe in some alternate universe, they were still close, and Zoe was still with them. Maybe another version of Tess was living the correct life.

Tess lifted the car seat in the crook of her elbow and led Meg out to the small detached garage. She clicked the child seat into its base, gave it a good tug to make sure it was secure, and climbed in the front with Meg.

"How are you planning to do this?" she asked as she backed out of the driveway.

"I'm not sure," Meg said. "I'd like to take him by surprise, though."

Tess drove back roads to the brewery, which sat on a wooded plot of land by the water. She knew her husband and his college friends who were still local occasionally met here for weekend drinks, but she'd never tagged along. It never appealed to Tess, being the plus-one in an already established group and being on the outside of their shared history, their inside jokes, their group lore. She wanted that for herself or not at all.

She parked in the gravel lot and surveyed the scene.

"Seems kinda dead right now," she said to Meg.

Meg unbuckled and squinted out the window at the brewery. "Yeah, it's the middle of a weekday. But let's hope he's working."

Tess took Emmy from the back and strapped her into the baby carrier on her chest, hoping she'd sleep through this meeting, unlike earlier. Then she followed Meg up to the doors of the log cabin–style brewery.

Inside, a small gift shop sat to the left, and a bar counter stood to the right. Straight to the back of the building were huge glass barn doors that were open, leading to a seating and game area and beyond that, the ocean. Several high-top tables were scattered throughout the interior portion of the building.

"Should we order something?" Tess whispered to Meg, who was scanning the handful of customers and waitstaff milling around the place.

"Probably," Meg said. "Oh— Can you drink if you breastfeed?"

"Who knows," Tess said. "I've heard beer is good for milk production, but I've also heard it inhibits it. That's how parenting is. Every decision is right and wrong."

"Sounds confusing as hell," Meg muttered. "I don't know how you do it."

Tess gave her a quick nod and bit her lip. She didn't know how she did it, either, especially without the web of support she'd always expected would be there. But here Meg was, offering her a minuscule taste of what it would've been like.

"Grab a table, and I'll order us something to eat and scope out Blake," Meg said.

Tess chose a high-top by the back doors, giving them access to both spaces in case Blake was working one or the other. After a few minutes, Meg returned with two beers.

"Okay, so . . ." she said as she slid one glass across the table. "Yours is nonalcoholic. I ordered us some tacos. And Blake is definitely here."

"Wow," Tess said. "Where?"

"The girl at the counter said he's in the back," Meg said.

"Now what?" Tess asked. Emmy was awake but quiet, her eyes locked on the huge ceiling fan spinning above them.

"When he comes out, I'll talk to him. Do you want to come with me?" Meg asked, her eyes darting to Emmy. "Is it weird for you to do this with your baby here? Is this crazy?"

"I want to help you," Tess said. She did want to help, and she *needed* to help. For her own peace of mind.

Before they could plan anything, a man stepped out from a door behind the bar area with a plate of tacos in hand. Tess knew right away it was Blake. He'd changed little in the five years since she last saw him standing on Meg's front lawn, giving his interview to Patricia. The interview in which he begged for Zoe to come home, claimed they were so happy together. Meanwhile, Zoe had spent the previous week on Block Island telling Tess and the others how their relationship was a roller coaster.

"There," Tess said to Meg with a sharp jut of her chin in Blake's direction.

Meg turned her head. Blake was headed over with their food order. He noticed the two of them but at first showed no sign of recognition. Then his face changed. His steps slowed. He was only a few tables away, his eyes traveling from Tess to Meg and back again. Tess raised a hand to wave him over and realized her fingers were trembling.

"Need anything else over here?" he asked as he set the taco plate on the table.

"Blake, you talked to Patricia Adele again," Meg said. "What did you say to her this time?"

Tess wondered if he would've kept pretending not to know them if Meg hadn't spoken up.

"I don't know what you're talking about," he said.

"You do know."

Blake looked at Tess. "Didn't bring the whole group to harass me at work? Did you two draw the short straws or something?"

She blinked at him. "She's just asking you a question. It's weird you're avoiding answering it." Then Tess softened. Maybe it was her maternal side or just an empathetic streak, but she felt for Blake. "Or maybe we should be asking if Patricia threatened you. Did she say something that made you nervous?"

He flinched, ever so subtly, but she clocked it. "Why do you care?"

"Because you loved Zoe like the rest of us, and it's not fair if Patricia made you feel otherwise."

Meg shot Tess a questioning look.

"You were her golden interview subject last time," Meg said. "The innocent boyfriend. Is she not singing that tune anymore?"

"I told her I didn't want to be a part of the book," Blake said. "She said her investigation might go in an unexpected direction, and I could either help her with an interview or take the chance of being a bigger part of the book than I want."

"Okay," Tess said. "What did you do?"

"Nothing." He glanced over at the bar. "I have to get back to work. Do you need anything else, or are you good?"

"No, wait," Meg said. "Did you say something about Callie or Lindsey to Patricia? Did you tell her something you withheld before?"

His eyes went flinty. The short-lived cooperation Tess had earned from him was gone.

"All I said was that I never felt right about you four. I told her I thought some of you were just pretending to like Zoe."

"What the hell is that supposed to mean?" Meg asked, pushing off her stool.

"Meg," Tess said, reaching out. But Meg ignored her.

"We *pretended* to like her? You cheated on her. *You* were just pretending to like her."

134

Blake laughed dryly. "You can pay your bill at the front when you're done."

Then he walked away, disappearing back through the kitchen door.

The tacos looked soggy and old. The yeasty smell of the beer turned Tess's stomach. She touched Meg's arm. Meg heaved a deep sigh.

"Let's go," Meg said. "I'm not paying. They can deduct it from his paycheck, for all I care."

Tess climbed off her stool and walked out the front door with Meg, their food and drinks untouched on the table and an uncomfortable energy running between them. They drove back in silence, Meg's gaze aimed out the window the whole way.

Back at her house, Tess parked in the garage and shut off the car.

"Do you think that was something Zoe told him?" Meg asked, finally turning to Tess. Her eyes were dull. She fidgeted with a silver ring on her index finger using her thumb.

"That some of us were just pretending to like her? No. I think he said that to be cruel. I think we caught him off guard, and he was defensive."

Meg shook her head. "I can't shake the feeling that he meant it. That he said it specifically because he knew it was real and would hurt."

"I don't think Zoe would've said that about us."

But Tess was only hoping. She'd felt it, too, the weight of Blake's words and their sharp, truthful edges. The memory of their last night on the island and the tension between them all.

"I'll get out of your hair," Meg said as she unbuckled. "I'm sure you have a lot to do. Sorry for taking up your afternoon on something so pointless."

"It wasn't pointless. You're going to keep going with the list, right?"

"If I hear back from the others," Meg said. "But I'm not sure I want to know any more."

Tess tilted her head. "Blake's full of shit. Forget about him, okay?"

Meg gave a quick nod. She got out of the car and walked over to where she'd parked on the street. It was only a few moments until Meg's engine started and her car sped away. And once again, Tess was alone.

Chapter Fourteen

LINDSEY

The overnight parking lot down the street from the harbor was nearly full. After looping through the rows looking for a space, eating up the few precious minutes she had to board the ferry, Lindsey considered bailing on Callie. Maybe it was a sign, a firm *NO* from the universe. Do not go back to the island, do not spend the night with someone you aren't sure you trust.

But then a small hatchback pulled out of a spot. Lindsey glanced at the dashboard clock—four minutes to park and run to the ferry. Or she could pretend she never saw the spot, text Callie an apology for missing the boat, and wallow on her own at home. Alone.

She pulled in, killed the engine, and bolted for the harbor, her weekend bag slamming her hip as she ran. She was one of the last people to board and had to search to find an open seat on the upper deck. Passengers were crammed together, but a couple with a toddler offered Lindsey a spot on the edge of the bench. She thanked them, slipped earbuds into her ears, and tried not to think about where she was going.

An hour later, Lindsey got up from her seat and clung to the steel railing. A cool spray misted off the water. As she watched the island appear at the edge of the ocean, she felt a lurch of seasickness. She'd always assumed she would never set foot out here again, sealing off that portion of her life entirely. But a part of her knew it was only a matter of time before she was drawn back.

When she disembarked the boat, she spotted Callie across the harbor parking lot, idling in an expensive-looking black SUV. The last time Lindsey had seen Callie, she was backing her hand-me-down Lexus out of the driveway at Meg's mother's house after the interview. And then Callie had disappeared from her life.

Lindsey made her way over to the SUV and tapped on the passenger window, drawing Callie's attention from her phone. She unlocked the doors with a sharp click—even that sounded expensive.

Lindsey climbed into the passenger side and shoved her bag into the back seat. The car's leather interior was tan and smooth, and there wasn't a bit of trash in sight.

Callie flashed an apprehensive smile. "I wasn't sure you'd come."

"Me either," Lindsey said. She ran her hand over the leather console. "What happened to your Lexus?"

"You remember it?" Callie asked. "I think it's still sitting at my parents' house. I stopped driving it after . . ." She paused and flashed another smile. Out of the center cupholder, she picked up a glass bottle sloshing with reddish liquid. "Here, I brought you a kombucha. Figured you'd be thirsty, and I remember how the ferry used to make you sick. This might settle your stomach."

"Thanks," Lindsey said. She twisted the cap, and the drink bubbled gently. It had a sweet, vinegary tang, and Lindsey couldn't tell whether she liked it or not.

"It's locally sourced and small-batch," Callie said.

The way Callie watched her made Lindsey uneasy, like she was waiting for permission to bring up the past. But Lindsey didn't want to open the door for that yet. She set the bottle of kombucha down and nodded toward the street.

"Can't wait to see the house that got you to come back here."

"It's pretty special," Callie said.

She put the car into drive and pulled out of the parking lot. The two were quiet for the next few minutes of the ride; Lindsey wasn't sure how to talk to Callie Sutter anymore. This kombucha-drinking, multimillion-dollar-house-buying version of her.

Callie's driveway was long and lined with tall trees all the way to the end, where the view opened up and revealed the house. Lindsey leaned forward, taking it all in. The house was larger than she'd expected—and grander. The turret in the center was imposing, pointing at the sky like a huge finger. The landscaping was pristine, every bush overloaded with fat hydrangea blooms and the grass a vibrant green that looked fake.

"This is unreal," Lindsey said. The engine ticked as it cooled.

"You're sweet," Callie said, opening her door. "Come on, I want to show you around."

Lindsey followed her into the house. The entryway opened to a sitting room and dining room, and around the corner, a large sun-filled kitchen. Callie toured her through the ground floor, pointing out the refrigerator (camouflaged as a cabinet) and where she could find snacks in the pantry, all of which were organic and allergen-free. Next, they went up to the second floor, where Lindsey had the pick of four guest bedrooms, each with an adjoining bathroom.

"I'll go with this one," Lindsey said as she stepped into the butter-yellow room. The windows looked out over the trees and, in the distance, the ocean.

She dropped off her bag and followed Callie back downstairs. On their way outside, Callie plucked a bottle of wine and two glasses from the counter. She introduced Lindsey and Nathan and told him they'd be down by the pool.

"I'm going to grill dinner soon—you okay with grass-fed steak, Lindsey?"

"Sounds great. What can I help with? I make a mean bagged salad."

Nathan laughed and shooed them away. "No, I got it. You two go catch up."

Lindsey followed Callie to a shimmering saltwater rectangle nestled at the bottom of a slight hill. Teak lounge chairs draped with blue-and-white-striped towels lined the pool area, and bistro lights crisscrossed overhead. It was almost dark, and Callie set the wineglasses down on a small table to light several tall hurricane vases around the perimeter.

"So," she said once she was done, dropping the lighter and pulling a corkscrew seemingly out of thin air to open the wine. She poured two generous glasses and handed one to Lindsey.

"So," Lindsey said. They sat at the edge of the pool, their feet in the warm water.

"I've been thinking about what you can do about your job," Callie started.

Lindsey looked down at her feet, distorted under the surface.

"Could we maybe talk about that later?" Lindsey asked. "I'm still processing the fact that we're sitting here together, and that's about all I can handle right now."

Callie's finger tapped against the side of her glass.

"I shouldn't have done the interview," she said. "Let's just put that out in the open. I regret some of the choices I made back then."

"We all do." Lindsey drained her wineglass and reached for the bottle to refill it. "But you," she said with a laugh that held no amusement, "yours was epically bad."

Callie tilted her head back. Lindsey followed suit. The sky was dimming and stars were beginning to show themselves.

"I'm looking for forgiveness," Callie said. "For a fresh start."

Lindsey felt suddenly exhausted. The wine was hitting her fast, and she had no energy to think about *fresh starts* or what they entailed.

"God, this stuff is strong," Lindsey said, twirling her glass.

"It's organic," Callie said, as if that explained it.

"Locally sourced?" Lindsey asked, needling.

"Actually, yes," Callie said. Either she didn't pick up on the goading, or she had chosen to ignore it. Lindsey bet it was the latter. If she hadn't been trying so hard to patch things up with the three of them, the old Callie would've gone toe to toe with Lindsey in a heartbeat.

She let out a small laugh.

"What?" Callie asked with a sideward glance.

"Nothing. I was just thinking about how we used to bicker over, like, everything," Lindsey said.

Callie smiled. "But we were fast to forgive and forget, weren't we?"

She wondered then if Callie was angling for this visit to be like a card she could play in the event Meg and Tess did not want to reconcile. *Look, even Lindsey is over what happened.* But she didn't want to be anyone's pawn.

"I think I'm going to head inside and rest before dinner," Lindsey said. "Today has kicked my ass."

"Oh," Callie said. "Sure, yeah."

"Thanks," Lindsey said as she pulled her feet out of the pool. "I need to shut my eyes for a few minutes, that's all."

She left shadowy, wet footprints on the stone as she walked away.

Lindsey woke the next morning wrapped in cool linen sheets, sunlight filtering through the windows of her guest room. She pulled herself from the bed and showered using Callie's expensive soap; it left her smelling like eucalyptus and mint. A quick search online showed that the soap and lotion sold for seventy dollars a set. She laughed out loud at the price. Even at half off, the set would still be a luxury item for her.

Lindsey dressed and left her room, following the sounds of Callie's and Nathan's voices downstairs. They were sitting at their kitchen table, a spread of fresh-cut fruit between them. Lindsey joined them and scooped some fruit onto a plate. Callie made her a coffee on their industrial-looking espresso machine and then ran upstairs to change.

"I'm grateful to finally meet you. You all loom so large in Callie's past, it's like meeting a celebrity," Nathan said. He twisted the cap off a small glass bottle of chlorophyll and put a few green drops into his smoothie, then offered it to Lindsey.

"No thanks," Lindsey said.

Nathan wasn't the type of man Lindsey imagined Callie would marry. Callie had always gone for the country-club boys whose families had pockets as deep as the Sutters'.

"What are you doing for work now that you've sold MindBalm?" Lindsey asked.

"We're set for a while," he said. "But eventually, we'll start something new, I'm sure. Maybe create another app. I might write a book or start a podcast. We have endless options."

"That must be nice," Lindsey said. "To have options. And money."

Before Nathan could reply, Callie came bounding down the stairs ready for the beach. She carried a large tote bag stuffed with supplies. She wedged two stainless steel bottles of ice water into the bag alongside the towels and sunscreen.

"Shall we?"

They walked to the beach. Lindsey followed her onto the sand, where they found an empty patch and rolled out the blanket Callie had packed.

"It's from a Turkish brand," she said as she smoothed it out. "The sand doesn't stick to it. I worked with them last year; they gave my followers a forty percent discount code."

"And you get paid for that?" Lindsey asked. She stretched out beside Callie.

"Looking to switch careers?" she asked over her sunglasses. "You could totally do it. How many followers do you have?"

Lindsey propped herself up on her elbow and reached for the sunscreen Callie had packed.

"I'm not . . . influential," Lindsey said. "Not like you, anyway. My life isn't charmed."

"There's an audience for everyone," Callie said.

"What do you think I should do?" Lindsey asked as she slathered her shoulders. "I'm not going to be an influencer. Do I try to get my job back?"

"I think you need a lawyer," Callie said. "Have someone look into whether your firing was even legal. If not, have them put pressure on your employer to take you back or make it right with a decent severance package."

"I absolutely can't afford a lawyer, but go on."

"My lawyer can help you out, don't worry. I think you should also let everyone in your life know what's going on. Prep them with what to say when she reaches out," she said. "We can write up a script. Maybe you need a no-contact order, too? The fact that she showed up at your office uninvited might be enough ammo for that."

"That doesn't seem too far?"

"No. I think we've been underestimating her. Her focus seems different now. She isn't just trying to make us look questionable because she caught us on camera handling a pair of sunglasses. She's going deeper, using skills she didn't have before."

"That doesn't mean she'll find anything concrete," Lindsey said.

"But she also doesn't have to play by any rules," Callie said. "We know that. She's not bound to the same ethics as a typical reporter. She doesn't have to follow procedures like a detective. So what's stopping her from causing chaos for us while she writes this book?"

Lindsey hated that she had to even think like this, but she also knew there was truth in what Callie said. She shifted to her knees and looked toward the water, suddenly overheated.

"I'm going to take a dip."

"I'll come," Callie said, hopping to her feet.

They wound through the maze of beachgoers and waded into the ocean. With every wave that crashed, Callie gripped her sunglasses. They covered half her face, a designer name stamped in gold on the arm. They probably cost what Lindsey owed in rent every month.

"I don't want to inform every single person in my life about Patricia," Lindsey said, thinking of Fred.

"She's already out there talking to people," Callie said. "I mean, look at me. She somehow learned we were moving here and handed out flyers to the neighbors *before* we closed on the house. A few already dislike us because of her. And a stranger accosted me in the grocery store." She paused, her lips going thin. "They still had the Missing flyer hanging up at the store, you know."

Lindsey grounded her feet on the sandy ocean floor while the current jostled her. "You're kidding."

"It's at the house. I couldn't just leave it." She adjusted her glasses after another wave hit her body. "If I didn't take it, it would've been like abandoning her all over again."

Lindsey twisted her hair and wrung the salt water from it. "Is that how you see it? You think we abandoned her?"

"I guess I could just relate to the feeling of being left behind," Callie said.

"You were left behind? Or did you walk away?" Lindsey asked.

"I walked away when things got heated."

"And why did things get heated?"

Callie didn't say anything.

Lindsey trudged away from her, pushing against the suction of the outgoing tide. When another wave came in, she let it press her forward. She stumbled over a narrow stretch of stones and then found her balance back on the sand.

As she passed some beach chairs, she heard her name. A man. It took a second to place him out of context. Fred.

"Hey, you." He was shirtless, skin glowing with sweat. "What are you doing here?"

"What are *you* doing here?" Lindsey asked, face on fire.

"I told you I was going away. Just took the boat out here for a few days."

It was only then that Lindsey registered the young woman next to him, a pretty brunette in a small white bikini, and felt herself wither inside. Why had she assumed she was the only woman Fred was seeing? Why did she care?

"Have a nice time," she said, desperate to get away.

"Hang on," Fred said, reaching out a hand that didn't quite reach Lindsey's. "Are you staying the night? We could get dinner."

The woman next to Fred didn't seem concerned about him making plans with another woman while she was right there. In fact, she seemed fascinated with the arm of her chair, picking at something stuck to the metal.

"Are you going to introduce us?" Lindsey asked.

"This is my niece, Erin. Erin, this is Lindsey."

"Hey," Erin said before going back to ignoring Lindsey.

At first, Lindsey felt relief. She was just his niece. But Erin's body language said she didn't approve of her uncle speaking to Lindsey. She would not give Lindsey an ounce of attention, shaming her with the coldest of cold shoulders.

"If you're free later—" Fred started to say.

"I'm actually here visiting a friend," Lindsey said. She was embarrassed he was angling for a date in front of his niece. And she would be even more embarrassed to explain who he was to Callie.

"Okay, no problem," he said. He looked slightly wounded, and she felt even worse at the thought of hurting his feelings.

She darted away. Callie was close behind when she reached their blanket.

"Who were you just talking to?"

Lindsey ran a towel over her arms and legs. "No one."

"That older guy over there," Callie said gesturing. Lindsey couldn't decipher Callie's tone—long gone was her ability to discern whether she was teasing or just asking a genuine question—and Lindsey's irritation bubbled.

"Do I have to report my every move to you while I'm here?"

Callie froze with her towel half wrapped around her body. She opened her mouth to speak, but nothing came. She finished pulling the towel and sat down on the blanket.

"Cal, I'm sorry," Lindsey said.

"No, it's fine," she said. "I shouldn't be surprised you hit a boiling point when all I've done since you got here is talk about your job and pry into your life. You'll open up to me when you're ready. If you're ever ready. I know that's how you are, Linds. It's okay."

Lindsey glanced in Fred's direction, still feeling out of sorts but recognizing an unusual feeling that was clarifying for her. She wanted to be with Fred over Callie. A man she knew little about versus an old friend she'd known since she was sixteen. It was far less complicated to exist around him—he didn't know her past the way Callie did, and he wasn't allowed to ask. He didn't have any preconceived notions about her based on history, or know what was going on in her life outside the hours they spent together. She needed that level of simplicity.

"Do you want to head back?" Callie asked.

Lindsey's skin felt sensitive all over, taut and itchy from the salt water. She pulled at her bathing suit top, wanting to be out of it. Wanting to be out of her own body.

"Yeah, I'm ready to go back," Lindsey agreed.

They packed up their space and shook sand out of the blanket, thousands of tiny grains rolling right off the expensive weave just as Callie said they would.

Getting out of the house wasn't difficult; Lindsey slipped silently out the front door after Callie and Nathan went to bed and walked to the marina where Fred had his antique cruising yacht docked. After the beach, she'd spent a few hours in her room texting with him as if their awkward run-in never happened. Erin was gone, he'd said. Took the ferry back to the mainland. Gave him a bit of an earful about hitting on some girl while on family time.

Now Lindsey was sitting on the boat's bench with her feet on Fred's lap.

"Sorry for getting you into trouble with your niece," she said.

"She'll be fine," he said. "Who are you staying with? Friends?"

"Don't worry about that." She pulled her legs back and sat upright. "Let's go for a walk. I have so much restless energy right now."

It was late, and the island was quiet and closed down. Rental cottages dark for the night, hotels sleeping. The restaurants and bars locked up.

"For a few summers when I was a teenager, I came out here for an art camp," Lindsey told him as they passed a desolate beach.

"Art, huh? I didn't realize you had a creative streak."

They crossed the street and followed a trail along the edge of the water.

"I was mostly into pottery," she said. "But I stopped when it got to be too expensive of a hobby. I was good, though. I worked on a collection of mugs that won an award."

Fred's footsteps quieted behind her. Lindsey glanced back. He was shaking his head.

"Can I ask you more about your art? And yourself in general?"

"Nope. But I'll show you where I learned pottery, if that counts."

Lindsey led him to the camp property. The crisp nighttime air, the swish of ocean breeze through tree branches, the distant pop of sporadic fireworks—she was transported back to sixteen, seventeen. Blistered feet from running around barefoot. Clay and paint perpetually caked under her fingernails. The ghost scent of weed on her clothes. Hair crispy from swimming. Lindsey could still feel the hay-like texture of the end of her braid on her tongue, salt filling her mouth as she sucked on it.

She thought of Callie in her bed across the island, how perfect her life had turned out. But the day they'd met, she'd been anything but. Callie had sat on her cot and cried herself red. She hated her parents, she'd said. But to Lindsey, Callie had just sounded like a spoiled brat. Lindsey's own parents had borrowed money to pay their daughter's camp tuition that year.

They'd all huddled up out of Callie's earshot to discuss what to do with the sad girl in their cabin.

"Is she going to cry all summer?" Lindsey had asked.

"Maybe," Zoe said. "We should still be nice, though."

"Doesn't it feel cramped in there with five of us?" Meg asked.

"It's tight," Tess agreed. "But let's get ice cream and see if we can distract her."

"She needs more than ice cream," Zoe said. Lindsey's ears perked up. Zoe pulled a joint from her pocket, and it was clear to Lindsey they would be good friends.

Now Lindsey was struck that the camp still looked so much like she remembered, though it had been transformed into a wedding venue. On a slight hill sat the main hall, where campers could call home, see the nurse, sign up for classes. Down beyond the main hall were rows of cabins, ten in total, half for boys and half for girls. There was a dining hall, a recreation center, and—the star of the property—an old barn that served as the art studio.

"They still have the sign," Lindsey said, pointing at the main hall as they approached. The hand-painted sign—a large piece of driftwood hammered into the exterior of the building—hung above the double doors and boasted the name IVES ART CAMP in green script set atop a crashing wave.

"Did you like it here?" Fred asked, standing behind her.

"Sure. Some of the best days of my life happened here," she said.

He followed her around the hall and toward the cabins. Their exterior was unchanged. Up close, she saw the alligator-skin texture of chipped lead paint around the windows, still flaking all these years later.

Lindsey peered inside. The space was mostly empty except for a desk and a set of bunk beds. She remembered some things. The sound of the pipes in the bathroom clanking while the shower warmed up. How the summer lightning storms lit up the cabin and rattled the roof. The buoyant joy she'd felt when she said something to make her friends laugh, especially Zoe. But long gone was any trace of their five bodies crammed in that room. Long gone were their shrieks of laughter and their petty arguments, the hallmarks of girlhood.

"It's eerie," Fred said as he looked into the window.

"Three summers here, and so much of it's blurry now," she said. "I wish I could remember more of the boring day-to-day stuff."

"Time's a bitch," Fred muttered.

"Yeah," Lindsey said, her chest tightening. "Can we go?"

They retraced their steps to the main gate.

"Are you okay?" Fred asked as they started back up the street.

Maybe it was the darkness that made her feel safe, or maybe it was Fred. Or maybe being back on the island—seeing Callie, standing at their old cabin—highlighted the futility of trying to hold on to elusive things like privacy. Or the past.

"I lost my job," she said. She stopped walking.

Fred took her hand and squeezed it. "I'm sorry. That's awful news. What did you do for work? I know some people hiring. If you want, I can put some feelers out for you."

She took her hand out of his and kept walking.

"That's okay," she said. "You don't have to do that for me."

He laughed. She liked how it sounded, how light he could be. How unburdened he was by life.

"It's just a little help job hunting," he said. "Not a proposal."

She didn't respond right away. They walked back up the shadowy, quiet roads of the island until they were back at his boat.

"Stay?" he asked. But she could see the horizon threatening to brighten and didn't want to deal with Callie's questions about where she had been.

"Next time," Lindsey said, and kissed him. She felt his surprise before he kissed her back, pulling her close to his body. She was surprised, too. She was bending her own rules because a nice man had offered to help her? Because the night air on the island made her feel young again and impulsive? Was that all it took for her to abandon her boundaries, her better judgments?

"And that's not too personal?" he asked.

"Night, Fred," she said over her shoulder as she walked away. She could feel him watching her all the way to the corner, where she slipped into a building's long shadow and disappeared.

Chapter Fifteen

CALLIE

Callie woke early to the sound of footsteps on the stairs. She checked her phone: not quite five in the morning. The footsteps slowed and were followed by the sound of a bedroom door on the second floor closing. Lindsey.

Callie was too alert to go back to sleep. Ever since she saw Lindsey talking to those people on the beach, she'd been trying piece together the last five years. She didn't know Lindsey anymore. Didn't know who she lived with, who she hung out with, who she dated. Callie hadn't realized how enormous the chasm between them had become—or how unwilling Lindsey would be to let Callie know her again—until now.

Awake for the day, she pulled herself from bed and sat on the meditation cushion on the balcony while the sun rose. Her mind was more difficult to wrangle than usual, her thoughts overlapping like vines rather than drifting past like clouds. She continually returned her attention to her breath, but within seconds the vines were back. Thoughts of Patricia stalking around the island, whispering Callie's name to whoever would listen. Thoughts of Lindsey on the beach with those strangers. Thoughts of the housewarming and the many to-do-list items ahead of her still. Of her dad's declining health and the future she'd have to accept if the father she'd always known was suddenly gone.

She opened her eyes, quitting the useless session early. The rising sun was a wavering orange orb over the horizon, and though it burned, she looked straight at it.

"Want to join us this time?" Nathan asked Callie and Elizabeth as he held the door open for Ben. "The water's perfect."

"Oh, no. My hair's done. I won't be swimming," Elizabeth said. "And I need to chat with my daughter."

Nathan shot Callie a quick look before closing the door. Her father had gone to the doctor the day before—maybe it was bad. Worsening symptoms, decisions to be made as a family about his care, the future.

"What's going on?" Callie asked, bracing for the news.

"Well," Elizabeth said, crossing her legs and cupping her hands around her knee. "I can't help you with this party if you don't tell me what you need me to do."

Callie gave her mother a hard look. "I thought you needed to talk to me about something serious."

"This is serious. Where's your guest list? I'll check your guest-to-food ratio. You always need more than you think."

"The ratio is fine," Callie said, turning away from her mother to hide her annoyance.

She sealed up the leftover vegan casserole from breakfast with beeswax-paper wrap. Only she and Nathan had eaten it, her parents picking at the crust with their forks until they declared themselves full.

"Let's go sit by the pool," she said. Before her mother could argue, Callie walked out the back door. Elizabeth followed a few moments later.

"I'm just trying to help," she said. "At the very least, I can look over your plans and tell you where things might fall apart."

"My party," Callie said as they crossed the lawn, "is not going to fall apart."

"Do you trust yourself to do this properly?" her mother asked.

The question stopped Callie in her tracks and stirred every fear she'd had since the day she was exiled to Block Island for two months as a teenager. It ignited the anxiety she could never completely extinguish, no matter how many therapists told her it wasn't her fault her father had kissed someone else and she'd seen it. Even if her mother acted as if speaking an ugly truth out loud was a deeper betrayal than the act itself.

Do you really trust what you think you saw? her mother had asked back then.

Callie remembered the claustrophobic panic of being dropped off at the ferry by her housekeeper. The torment of having no contact with her parents all summer. Her only connection to them the shirt her father had tucked into her luggage to help her sleep. The darkness she felt returning home and realizing her mother resented her. The only thing that kept her going that summer were the girls. The humid, messy cabin had turned into her sanctuary.

And Zoe. Callie's secret keeper, the only one who knew why she'd been sent away from home so abruptly.

"You know what, you go down to the pool. I forgot something inside," she said, leaving her mother and returning to the house. She needed to put space between them and take a few breaths before she said something she'd regret.

Inside the house, Callie filled a glass with cold cucumber water from the pitcher in the fridge and drank it in one go.

"You good? You look pale," Lindsey said, coming into the kitchen as Callie put the glass down.

Callie eyed Lindsey's pajamas: shorts that nearly revealed her ass and a camisole without a bra.

"Just thirsty. It's hot out." She tried to smile, but it felt wooden. "I made a vegan casserole, if you're hungry."

"Thanks," Lindsey said as she slid onto a barstool at the counter and reached for an orange in the fruit bowl. "Where's Nathan?"

"Down at the pool with my parents," she said.

Lindsey paused peeling the orange. "I didn't realize you had company."

"It's just my parents," Callie said. She changed the subject. "Oh, I forgot yesterday, but you definitely need to send Patricia a cease and desist. How can I help you start informing your circle about how to handle Patricia? Do you want me to draft an email or make some calls?" Callie paused. "Your friends from the beach yesterday, should we start with them?"

Lindsey locked eyes with Callie, then cleared her throat and looked down at the orange peel she was twisting around her finger.

"No, we don't need to do that."

"By the way, did you go somewhere last night? I thought I heard you come in late."

"Weird," Lindsey said. "Maybe you have ghosts."

"I don't believe in ghosts."

The back door opened then and Nathan walked inside, followed by Callie's parents. Her father wore a damp T-shirt and had a towel wrapped around his waist. Lindsey startled, fidgeting with her pajama top.

"How was your swim?" Callie asked.

"He's sleepy," Elizabeth answered for him.

"No, I'm relaxed," Ben corrected.

"Your mom said you ran off on her. You okay?" Nathan asked Callie. She waved a hand and smiled. "I had to pee."

Elizabeth sidled up next to Lindsey at the counter. "Goodness, it feels like forever, darling. You haven't changed a bit. How's life treating you? Married? Any children? Own some property?"

Lindsey let out a sharp laugh. Elizabeth flinched.

"Not sure any of that is in the cards for me."

"Oh, you're still young. Give it time," Elizabeth said. She looked over at her husband, who was sitting at the kitchen table, sipping the water Nathan had given him. "I know you're *relaxed*, but don't be rude. Say hello, will you?"

"Sorry, sorry. Good to see you. Tess?" He paused. "Sorry. Zoe?"

Callie's face flushed. She gave Lindsey a swift glance and saw she was trying to muster a smile.

"That's Lindsey, Dad," Callie said. "Remember?"

"He gets mixed up sometimes," Elizabeth said. "It's been a long time, and his memory isn't what it used to be."

"Not that long," he said. "Only a year or two since you girls were in all that trouble."

Callie let out a nervous laugh. "It's been about five years, Dad. And we weren't in trouble."

"It was a mess," he said.

"It was," Elizabeth agreed. She turned to Lindsey. "How have you been doing since that vile woman started working on her book?"

"Hanging in there," Lindsey said. Callie heard the twinge of discomfort in her voice. "Lost my job the other day over it."

"You're kidding," Elizabeth said.

"It's all going to be fine," Callie said, mostly to Lindsey. "We're figuring it out."

Ben rapped the table with his knuckles. "That's right, I guess it was about five years ago that she called us. Not two years."

Everyone in the room paused.

"Who?" Callie asked.

Ben blinked at her. "The reporter. Right? Wasn't that five years ago she called and got you that interview?"

Callie's mind went blank, her limbs heavy. What was he saying? She looked at Nathan as if he could explain what she was hearing.

"Ben," he said. "Sometimes the mind creates false memories when it can't retrieve a certain piece of information. It's very normal."

"Well, Nathan dear, that did actually happen," Elizabeth said. "But we had no intention of sharing it. I guess the cat's out of the bag now, though."

"Wait, wait, wait," Callie said, pushing her body off the counter she was leaning against and walking over to the table. "How is Patricia

Adele the one who got me on-air for the interview? And why didn't you ever mention that minor detail to me?"

Elizabeth sighed and patted Lindsey's arm. "I'm sorry, this must be awkward for you to be in the middle of right now."

"Oh, I mean. No, it's just—" Lindsey started.

"I think she's just as invested in this revelation as I am," Callie said, her emotions surging in so many directions, she wasn't sure how to feel. She couldn't read Lindsey's face, and Nathan simply looked stunned.

"Explain," Callie said to her mother, low and firm.

"Darling, please take a breath," Elizabeth said. "In the grand scheme of life, it was insignificant."

"In the grand scheme of *my* life, it was quite significant," Callie sputtered.

A look of concentration filled her mother's face. "Well, let's see. She called us; she said she could get you on-air through a contact at the station and that it would be a good opportunity for you. We said sure," Elizabeth said breezily. "In our defense, you were barricaded up at that house, and we had no idea what was going on until after the fact. Maybe if you'd been more forthcoming with us, we would've been aware. But once we put the pieces together and realized she was the same reporter harassing you, we decided to keep the *how* of the interview to ourselves. It wouldn't have helped you to know."

Callie let out a breathy laugh. "Are you kidding? I would've said no to the interview! I would've made different choices if I'd known. You didn't have the right to lie about that."

Ben grunted. "Callie, calm down. It's not worth getting upset over now."

"We did what was best," Elizabeth said. "I'm sorry, Lindsey. I know the rest of you felt left out, but we were told the interview could only be with Callie, and she was our priority."

"Don't worry about it," Lindsey said tightly. She balled up the orange peel and napkin, then hopped off the stool. "Callie, I just remembered I promised my roommate I would help her with something today. Could you drop me off at the ferry in a little bit?"

Callie studied her face and tried to pry from it a clue about how Lindsey felt. But her expression was stoic.

"You sure?" Callie asked. She wanted—*needed*—Lindsey to stay. To process this admission with the one person in the room who could understand the gravity of it.

"Positive, thanks," Lindsey said. She tossed the napkin into the trash and dashed upstairs.

"She's a bit skittish," Elizabeth commented once Lindsey was gone.

"She just heard that Patricia Adele pulled the strings to get me on the interview that ended our friendship," Callie said. "Of course she's skittish."

"She didn't have to run off, though," Elizabeth said.

"And she was in her pajamas," Callie said, more to herself than anyone, guilt coursing through her for unknowingly putting Lindsey in such an awkward situation.

"Yes, I noticed the pajamas," Elizabeth said with a downturn in her voice. "And she wasn't even wearing any undergarments."

Callie idled in the harbor parking lot. Lindsey sat in the passenger seat, texting someone, her phone angled away so Callie couldn't see.

"Are you sure you want to go?" Callie asked. "You can stay another night. I could use it, honestly. I still don't know what to think about the interview and Patricia . . ."

"Really?" Lindsey asked. "It's so clear what happened. We refused to play nice with her, so she went around us completely. And in the end, she got what she wanted."

"She didn't get an interview with me," Callie said, not understanding. "It didn't benefit her at all."

Lindsey's voice went soft. "She wanted to turn us against each other more than she wanted an interview. Mission accomplished."

"But why?" Callie muttered. "There wasn't anything in it for her."

Lindsey sighed. "I'm sure she thought once we turned on you, we'd run to her to give our own interviews. She probably expected one of us to fold."

Callie rubbed her forehead. Pressure behind her eyes bled into her entire skull, a throbbing that would not quit. She was still confused and angry, but Lindsey seemed to be taking it in stride.

"Why aren't you more upset about this?" Callie asked.

Lindsey's phone pinged in her hand. She didn't break her eye contact with Callie, though.

"Because at the end of the day, it's less about the interview and how it came to be and more about your reluctance to defend us when you had the chance," Lindsey said. "Thank you again for your help and the hospitality. I had a nice time."

She opened her door and jumped out with her bag slung over her shoulder. Callie watched her jog to the line at the ticket counter, texting whoever was on the other end while she waited.

Callie backed out of her spot and turned onto the road. She made a loop instead of going the more direct route, bringing her car back up to the main drag on a side street a few minutes later.

She had braked at a stop sign when she saw, down at the corner, Lindsey walking away from the harbor. Away from the ferry she was supposed to be getting on.

Callie grabbed her phone and called Lindsey. Lindsey stopped walking and answered.

"Just wanted to see if you could use a snack or anything for the ride," Callie said, her eyes on her friend.

"No, thanks," Lindsey said. She kept walking. Callie inched her car forward. "They just started boarding us. I'll grab something to eat once I'm on the boat. I should go."

The call dropped, and Callie lost sight of Lindsey. She squeezed the steering wheel, torn between following Lindsey and going home. She wasn't sure why it mattered so much, why she needed to know what Lindsey was doing—besides the fact that this was exactly how Zoe had vanished, wandering off alone when she should have gotten on the ferry home.

Callie sat at the stop sign another few seconds before jerking the wheel in the direction of her house. Lindsey was an adult who could take care of herself. Just like Callie, despite how small and naive she felt.

Chapter Sixteen

MEG

Meg sat outside the café near Tess's house with a black coffee and slice of lemon loaf, trying to focus on the manuscript she was supposed to have already read for a client. But her attention fizzled after a few paragraphs. Her eyes glazed over, and she stared at the black marks on the screen of her laptop, her mind—once again—thinking only about Blake's words a couple of days earlier.

She couldn't remember Zoe ever saying she thought one or more of them were only pretending to like her. Never got the sense that there was anything fake about the way any of them felt. And Meg was sure she would've remembered if Zoe had said so. But then again, Meg feared that never hearing this from Zoe meant *she* was the one Zoe thought was pretending. And, in a way, that might've been true.

A man walked by then with a spry goldendoodle on a leash. Its shoulder bumped Meg's table as it passed, sloshing her coffee onto the track pad of her laptop and jolting her out of her mental spiral.

"Sorry!" the guy called as he trailed his dog down the sidewalk.

Meg pressed her molars together as she dabbed the coffee off her computer. Her patience was thin; an accident like that wouldn't usually bother her. But today, everything needled her. Everything felt personal. All she could think about was that asshole Blake and his asshole words.

Meg took a long sip of her coffee and returned to the manuscript, willing her brain to focus. She made it through two pages before she heard her name called out from across the street.

It was Tess, waving from the sidewalk opposite the café, Emmy tucked into the carrier like the last time. Tess jogged over.

"What are you doing here?" she asked Meg, sweeping hair out of her face. She wore an outfit reminiscent of the one she'd worn a couple of days earlier: leggings and a long, billowy top. Her hair was pulled back into a knot at the back of her head, some shorter pieces springing out around her temples.

"Needed to get out of my mom's house to do some work," Meg said. "I'm not having much luck, though. I can't stop thinking about our run-in with Blake."

"Ah," Tess said as she pulled out a chair and sat down. "I'm relieved to hear you say that."

"You too?"

Tess nodded. "Maybe Zoe thought I hated her."

"Zoe did not think that," Meg said. "She loved you."

"I think about her constantly," Tess said. She pinched the bridge of her nose. "I took Emmy to the beach one day and saw a woman I swore was Zoe. I actually thought it could be Zoe doing a normal everyday thing like taking a walk, and I forgot my baby was on the blanket behind me. I walked away from Emmy for a few seconds."

"You're human. We've all had moments like that."

"I was going to beg Zoe to forgive me. I was going to tell her I was sorry for not staying with her. For turning my back on her." Tess paused for a moment. "But it wasn't her. And then a bunch of seagulls swarmed Emmy. I felt so stupid."

Meg didn't know what to say. She remembered the night Tess called in tears, adamant that they were to blame. Meg hadn't known what to say then, either. Words had failed her, even though they were her profession.

"You're too hard on yourself," Meg finally said now.

"I just miss the way things used to be," Tess said, swallowing hard. "Anyway, are you thinking of going to Callie's housewarming? It might be nice to all be together. You and I could even take the same ferry over so we're not alone."

Meg bit her lip. "You don't think the timing is weird? Throwing her party on Zoe's five-year anniversary? And she hasn't asked us to help. We're part of this; we should be involved in the memorial. Right? Something is off."

"We can go to the party even if we have reservations about it."

"We *can*, but should we?"

"It's five years, Meg. Whether we like it or not, this is her memorial." Tess studied Meg's face for a moment, then smiled. "I should go so you can get back to work."

"Okay, listen," Meg said, her resolve crumbling. "Maybe you're right. But I'll only go if we do it together."

"That would be great," Tess said.

Tess started back for her house. Meg was even less able to focus on her work now, so she opened her email and clicked through her dozens of unread messages. She had a few updates from Lydia, a meeting request from Tina to go over an upcoming debut-novel release, and a dozen new query letters from prospective clients.

And a reply from Angie Carlson, one of the people on Patricia's list. Meg's stomach swooped. She clicked it open and read the message.

> Meg, thanks for reaching out. I did have a conversation with Patricia Adele and would be happy to tell you what we discussed. I don't think it's confidential or anything. Or maybe it is haha! Well, I never signed anything promising not to share what I said with anyone else, so if you want to talk, call me.

Her number was at the bottom of the email, and Meg dialed it immediately. It rang once before Angie answered.

"It's funny to be on the phone with you," Angie said, her voice slanted with a faint Boston accent. "After all the stuff I saw online, to actually talk to you is wild."

Meg shifted in the metal bistro chair. She hated when people referred to her notoriety but failed to acknowledge Patricia's harassment as the reason any of them were known figures.

"Thanks for taking my call," Meg said. "I'm just curious about the conversation between you and Patricia. Did you tell her anything about Callie Sutter or Lindsey Sherman?"

"Oh gosh, yeah. I told her about bartending at a place in Newport a million years ago."

"What about it?" Meg asked.

"I told her that I was pretty sure—not *positive*, but pretty sure—I saw one of the girls at my bar. One of you girls. Not you, but one of the other ones. I saw her at my job either the day they say Zoe disappeared or the day after. Around then."

Meg tapped her foot against the leg of the table, anxious energy coursing through her.

"Was it Lindsey?" Meg asked.

"How'd you know? I told Patricia I saw Lindsey at my bar. And she was there all night, let me tell you. With a guy."

Meg's foot stopped tapping. "What guy?"

"No idea. But Patricia said if I was right about when I saw Lindsey, then she was lying about something. Not sure how she'll confirm it, because there's no way any security footage goes back five years, but that's what I told her."

"How do you know it was Lindsey, though?" Meg asked. "How can you remember which night you possibly saw her that long ago?"

"Oh, I saw her a lot, that's how," Angie said. "She was in my bar all the time. But that night, she was there with a guy for the first time, at least in my memory. Usually, she was out with her roommate. And I know it was a Sunday or Monday. Back then I worked those nights at that bar because I was in school and also had a serving job the rest of the time." She laughed. "Like, it won't hold up in court, I bet. But it's fine for a book. That's what Patricia said."

"Thanks," Meg said. "I appreciate your time."

"Hey, you can be in that book, too, you know," Angie said. "She's looking for other people to weigh in. I bet you'd have a lot to say."

Meg compressed her teeth again. The involuntary tic sent a wave of tension into her face. She blew a stream of air out of her mouth to loosen everything up.

"You're not wrong," Meg said. "But I'm not willing to help that woman."

They hung up. Meg didn't want to believe Angie saw Lindsey out at a bar with a man instead of being at home like she'd always claimed, but what reason would Angie have to lie? And worse, what reason would Lindsey have to keep the truth from the others?

Meg went back to her inbox and saw she had another response waiting for her.

> Hello, Meghan. To be honest, I was barely acquainted with Zoe before she disappeared, but if it would give you some comfort, I'd be happy to chat. I don't know a Patricia but if she needs me to share information, I'm more than willing to speak with her, too.

He'd closed the email with an office address and the days and times he was available over the coming week. His signature graced the bottom of the message: Cameron Oakes.

Meg considered deleting his email and quitting while she was ahead, if she could even consider herself to be ahead. All she had to show for her poorly devised plan was a run-in with Zoe's ex, which had left a terrible taste in her mouth, and a conversation with a bartender that had left her with more questions than answers.

But Cameron Oakes had some kind of tie to Zoe, and Meg didn't know him. Her curiosity was piqued. Maybe he'd be able to tell her something useful, whoever he was.

> Mr. Oakes, thank you for getting back to me. I'll come
> by your office tomorrow at 2 p.m. – Meghan Bradley

She downed the rest of her coffee, packed up her laptop, and tossed the remainder of the lemon loaf into the trash, her appetite gone. On the drive back to her mother's house, Meg considered dropping by Tess's to fill her in about the call with Angie and the email from Cameron. But then she drove past without stopping, deciding to keep it to herself for now.

Chapter Seventeen

TESS

Patricia arrived wearing all white. Tailored white slacks, white mules with small gold buckles, and a white blouse under a creamy blazer. Slung over her shoulder was a black leather tote bag embossed with her initials in gold.

"This place is precious." Patricia's eyes skimmed over the living room. She removed her blazer and handed it to Tess. "A green chair. How fun."

Tess hung Patricia's blazer in the coat closet and snuck a peek at the label. A luxury brand, probably worth more than ten pairs of the maternity leggings Tess owned. True crime money had treated Patricia well.

Patricia sat on the couch and arranged a notepad, pen, and voice recorder on the coffee table.

"Can we talk without all that first?" Tess asked.

Patricia leaned back on the cushion and crossed her arms.

"Sure. We can take it slow if that's what you need."

"Why are you focused on Callie and Lindsey?" Tess asked. "And who spoke to you about them?"

Patricia gave her a slow smile. "Someone's been doing her homework."

"Was it Blake?"

Patricia smoothed the front of her blouse. An expression passed across her face before Tess could place it. Was it surprise?

"You think I should speak with Blake?"

Tess took a seat in the green velvet chair. "I know you already did."

"I'm not worried about him." Patricia clicked the recorder on. "I'd love to hear your perspective on those trips to Block Island. You five went every summer. What were they normally like, and how was the final one different?"

"Who said it was any different?" Tess asked, though the question unnerved her. It *had* felt different. Zoe had seemed distracted all week, more attached to her phone and her fuse shorter than usual. She'd seemed on edge but wouldn't admit it.

"Tell me how it wasn't different, then."

"The trip was normal," Tess said. "Up until the very end when she asked us to leave her behind."

Patricia uncrossed her arms and leaned forward, resting her elbows on her thighs.

"Did that really happen? No other witnesses ever came forward to say they saw her around the island that day."

Tess glanced at the recorder. It seemed alive, listening and waiting to pounce.

"Zoe was spontaneous," Tess said. "I don't know why no one saw her, though. Do you remember every person you see?"

"No, but I might remember a pretty young woman walking around in those sunglasses—wouldn't you?" Patricia waited for a response. Tess shrugged. "So you were honoring her spontaneity by leaving her behind. You were being good friends. Is that how you see it?"

Tess flinched. *Good friends* had a knife's edge to it.

"The rest of us had to get back to the mainland, and Zoe knew that. She didn't want anyone to stay with her. But you know all this."

"Maybe it's the true crime reporter in me, but that detail has always seemed strange. What young woman goes off on her own when she has the option to stay with the pack?"

"She didn't think anything bad would happen. None of us did. It's Block Island, for God's sake."

"Bad things can occur anywhere. What happened next?"

"We got on the ferry and went our separate ways. The next day, we realized no one could reach her. The police organized a search party. Then you got involved and we couldn't go out in public anymore."

Patricia gave Tess a sad smile. "That's not fair. I never barricaded you in that house."

"You might as well have. Did you think about the consequences of making those claims against us? Or were you just thinking about how Zoe's story benefited you? Views and money and now a full-blown career doing this—I bet it feels worth it."

Tess took a breath. She rested her palms against the velvet of the chair cushion to level herself.

Patricia sighed. "I understand why you feel that way. Back then I was just following my instincts, and even I was surprised by the response to her story. The more I talked about it, the more people wanted from me, so I gave it to them. Maybe I was making more out of the sunglasses than I should've, but *something* happened to Zoe. I couldn't stop thinking about what you four might be hiding. What would you have done in my shoes?"

"I don't know, but I would've looked at the whole picture," Tess said. "She had a boyfriend everyone forgot about pretty quickly."

Patricia waved her hand as if batting a fly. "He couldn't make a person disappear."

"And, what? We could?"

Patricia tilted her head. "Four smart women could do a lot of damage if they wanted, don't you think?"

"I personally would be more worried about a single man than four women," Tess said.

"That's fair. Maybe I didn't look at Blake hard enough," Patricia said. "Would it make you feel better if I promised to spend some of my investigation on him?"

Tess thought of seeing Blake at the brewery. How she'd momentarily felt sorry for him, but now she couldn't stop thinking about his insinuation that Zoe hadn't felt genuinely liked by her friends. There was no way to ask Zoe if it was true; Tess would carry it with her forever.

"It's always a good idea to look at the boyfriend again," Tess said. "I never liked him."

"Then I'll do that," Patricia said. "Who else did Zoe spend time with? Did she have any weird friends or exes? Anyone who wouldn't leave her alone?"

"What do you mean? Like a stalker?" Tess asked.

Patricia shrugged one shoulder. "Sure. Or someone she might've ghosted who didn't take kindly to being snubbed."

"She would've told us about something like that."

"So you knew everything about Zoe? You didn't keep anything from each other?"

Tess paused. She'd always thought they didn't have secrets. That had been the impetus of Tess and Zoe's argument on the last night of the trip, the unshakable feeling Tess had had all week that Zoe was hiding something. But she'd never tell that to Patricia.

"I don't think it's possible to know *everything* about another person," Tess said.

"Then you didn't really know Zoe as well as you thought?" Patricia asked.

The question landed like an anchor tossed over the side of a boat, dropping heavy and fast underwater.

"That's harsh," Tess said.

"It's just a question. Who else did she hang around besides you girls?"

Tess reached back in her memory as best she could. She knew Zoe had a full life, running a business and traveling to shows. She was almost always working, her dedication something the rest of them commended her for all the time. And she had a group of friends from college she saw sometimes. But no one Tess would sacrifice to Patricia.

"I don't know," she said finally. "She was always busy with work. When we got together, we were too busy catching up with each other to talk about other people in her life."

Patricia lifted her chin and leaned back. "Didn't you find that strange?"

"No."

"Why didn't you want to know more about her life outside of your little circle?"

Tess blinked at Patricia. This was the very reason why she and Zoe had argued. The very reason why Tess carried so much guilt all these years later. She couldn't respond to Patricia, though. The only answer was that she did want to know. But the next question would inevitably be *Why didn't Zoe trust you enough to tell you, then?*

Patricia gave Tess a cool, level stare.

"Can you just be real with me for one second?" Patricia said. "Did something go wrong on that trip, something unexpected? I'd understand if there was an accident, and the rest of you made an impulsive decision in the name of self-preservation."

Tess's arms rippled with goose bumps. She rubbed them with her hands. "We didn't do anything to Zoe on that trip."

"What about after it? Can you say for certain nothing happened after?"

Tess understood then how Callie must have felt when she gave her own interview. How a question asked in just the right way could poke a tiny pinprick of doubt in the fabric of reality. And how the light let in by that pinprick could be enough to illuminate all the things that had once been undeniably false. Just enough light to wonder *What if?*

She simply didn't know for sure what anyone else did after they'd stepped off the ferry onto the mainland. She didn't know if anyone returned to the island or met up with Zoe later after she came home.

"Well?" Patricia asked.

"All I know is that I didn't do anything to Zoe. I didn't see anyone else do anything to her. I don't know why or how her sunglasses ended up on that beach. That's the truth. I can't give you anything else, Patricia. That's all I have. I can't defend anyone but myself."

"What do you think they'll say about you chatting with me?" Patricia asked. But she turned off the recorder and started to pack her things into her bag. "Off the record. You can be honest."

"I'll just tell them the truth," Tess said. "You told me to do this—or risk being implicated with one of them."

Patricia stood up and slipped her bag onto her shoulder. "Which means you think there's a chance one of them will somehow be implicated. But these are your friends?"

Tess walked to the closet and retrieved Patricia's blazer. The hanger clanged against the door as she shut it.

"At the end of the day, all that matters is being there for my daughter," Tess said. "Five years ago, my friends were the most important people in my life. My priorities have shifted. That's why I talked to you. So you'll take it easy on me when you write whatever you plan to write about us."

"Thanks for your time," Patricia said, draping the blazer over her arm. "By the way, I don't think Callie and Lindsey were truthful about their alibis. So if you can remember what they were really up to and want to make *sure* you're not answering for their mistakes, call me."

Tess walked her to the door without saying a word. She felt ill. Patricia bounded down the front steps and slid into her car. Tess wished she could rewind time and undo the interview, then keep rewinding all the way back five years earlier when they were still on Block Island, during the final day with Zoe, and force her to get on the ferry home. If it were possible to rewrite history, she'd fix whatever had caused Zoe to be so barbed that final week. She'd reach back through time and be the friend Zoe needed.

Chapter Eighteen

Lindsey

Lindsey was floundering without her routine of scrambling to the office only to sit at her desk all day. She now got out of bed hours later than when she'd had a job, and set out on foot around Newport, lamenting the crowds and the heat but also needing to move her body. Sitting in the apartment was suffocating, so she huffed all over the city, meandering the Cliff Walk past gilded mansions and walking quiet neighborhood streets that didn't interest the tourists. Once she felt adequately wringed out, she would park herself at the bar below her apartment and treat herself to a drink.

Lindsey tilted the bottle to her mouth and let the cool liquid run over her tongue, swallowing the last bit of beer. She checked the time on her phone. Fred would pick her up soon, so she waved off the bartender's offer for one more. She counted out some cash and pushed it across the bar.

Lindsey stepped outside to wait for Fred. She was just buzzed enough that the crowds clogging the sidewalks didn't annoy her. Streams of people passed like clouds, drifting and shape-shifting in and out of sight.

She looked up the street for Fred's car, her eyes focused on the next block. No sign of him yet. But before she turned away, her eyes locked on one person in the crowded street, and her brain quickly sobered.

Patricia. A block away, striding purposefully in Lindsey's direction.

Lindsey froze, then frantically reached for the locked doorknob to her apartment stairs. But then, as if time skipped a few beats, Patricia was in front of her before she could fumble for her key and get inside.

"You're impossible to get a hold of," Patricia said as she approached. As if she knew Lindsey's routine, knew she'd be at the bar right now. Patricia pulled her sunglasses off. "Your manager won't even take my calls. And do you ever check your email?"

"I don't work there anymore," Lindsey said thickly. "Because of *you*."

"Can I buy you a drink?" Patricia asked with a nod toward the bar. "As an apology?"

Lindsey dug in her pocket for her house key.

"We really should talk," Patricia said as Lindsey inserted it into the lock. "You deserve a chance to explain some anomalies I've found in your story recently."

The beer in Lindsey's stomach turned.

"Walk with me," Patricia said. "Let's talk."

Lindsey spun around, yanking the key from the lock in the process. "I'm not walking with you. I'm not talking to you. You can go to hell, for all I care."

Patricia blinked. Lindsey felt a surge of power seeing the surprise on her face. People passed on the sidewalk in both directions, jostling Lindsey.

"I just wonder," Patricia said carefully, "if you were actually at your apartment the day Zoe went missing, like you said. Someone told me they remembered seeing you out that night."

"You always thought I was a shitty friend to Zoe," Lindsey cut in. "Just say it. From day one you pegged me as the worst friend, and whatever you heard—it's validating, isn't it? And you love that, don't you?"

Lindsey flexed and balled her hand into a fist a few times. She wasn't sure how Patricia had arrived on the edge of the truth like this, a truth she'd thought had been smoothed over with enough lies to disappear.

Patricia glanced down at Lindsey's fist and raised her brows. "You're not going to swing at me, are you?" she asked.

Behind Patricia, Fred's car rolled up to the curb. Lindsey darted around her and slid inside, slamming the door shut hard. Fred, confused, pulled back onto the road, and she locked eyes with Patricia as they passed.

Patricia seemed puzzled as Lindsey flipped her middle finger.

"What's going on? Who was that?" Fred asked.

"No one. She thought I was somebody else."

"You just gave her the bird," Fred said.

Lindsey leaned her head against the window and let the vent whisper cool air into her face.

"She said something that pissed me off," she said. "But I've never seen her before. She's just a stranger."

Lindsey's nerves calmed when she stepped onto the boat and Fred powered them out of the marina. Nothing but clouds above and the chop of the sea below, a half bowl of sky in one direction and a bottomless valley of ocean in the other. The farther she was from the shoreline and Patricia, the better she felt.

After a while, Fred cut the engine and let the boat drift. He joined her on the bench, a glass of wine in each of their hands. The sun was setting in a melting orange haze beyond the suspension bridge. Their conversation drifted easily, as always, nothing too personal until Fred started to reminisce.

"You wouldn't believe the trouble I used to find," he said. He pointed toward Jamestown. "Right over there, actually."

"What kind of trouble could someone find over there?"

He shook his head. "I knew someone who threw these . . . parties? They were bigger than that. Soirees. So much excess on display. Once, Willie Nelson showed up after the Newport Folk Festival and played a set. *Willie Nelson.*" He took a long sip of wine. "This was a hundred years ago, though."

"Wow," Lindsey said. "Willie Nelson."

"Sometimes they'd do fireworks over the bay, too. You'd always get topped up with a full drink, even if your glass was empty just two seconds before."

"No way," she teased. "They topped off drinks? So wild."

He laughed. "Maybe *wild* is in the eye of the beholder."

"Do you see *wild* when you behold me?"

His eyes traced the contours of her face as he considered this.

"I don't know yet," he said. "I need to get to know you better."

"Pretty sunset tonight," Lindsey said to change the subject. There would be no getting to know her better.

"Very pretty," he said, shifting. "Listen, I have to tell you something. I have a friend who's looking to fill a part-time opening at his company. It's a tech job. Customer service. I referred you for the position; I hope that's okay."

"You referred me?" she asked, bewildered. "Why would you do that?"

The boat swayed and water lapped against the hull.

"Isn't customer service what you did at your last job? He asked me some questions about your work experience, but I didn't know what to tell him," Fred said. "So I looked at your LinkedIn and gave him the basics. I figured if I asked you for the information, you'd say no. But I wanted to help."

Lindsey held up her free hand. "Wait. Hold on. We promised not to do anything like that," she said.

"I know. And I'm sorry, but I thought it would be okay if it got you a job. You seemed worried about it." The boat creaked. "Say something."

"We weren't supposed to look each other up."

She expected they'd eventually run their course, but not so soon. Not when she didn't have any other income.

"Wait. You haven't searched my full name before?" Fred asked. "Just out of curiosity?"

"I don't *know* your full name," she said.

He looked at her quizzically. "Yes, you do. I told you the first day we went out."

"I'm supposed to remember everything everyone tells me?" Lindsey asked.

He ran a hand through his hair. "Of course not, but don't you think it's getting to a point where we can know each other better? Just a little? Are you scared I won't like you if I know you?"

Lindsey laughed, but it was nervousness, not humor, that triggered it. How had he known to press directly on her deepest fear? She had no playbook for this and wished she could call Zoe to ask her for advice. She would've known what to say.

"Yes, actually. I do worry about that. Did you look at anything besides my work history?"

"No," he said. He watched her for a second. "Will you tell me who that woman back there was?"

Lindsey shook her head. He ran his fingers lightly over her arm. She could feel he wanted to ask her why not, why couldn't this be the first thing she opened up about? What he'd witnessed between Lindsey and Patricia would likely nag at him like a pebble in his shoe until he understood it.

"Why do you care who she is?" she asked.

He looked at her like she must be joking. "Are you really asking me that? You were so upset when you got into the car, you were practically radiating. And then you flipped her off. That's a lot of emotion to feel for a stranger." He shrugged. "It worried me. I worry about you a lot, you know. I wonder if you're lonely. I wonder if you have people in your life to lean on. You never mention anyone but your roommate, and she's never really around. Being fired, that's a hard thing to go through alone. Everyone has their shit, you know? I worry yours is heavy sometimes, but you don't like to admit it. Or you just don't want me to know about it."

Lindsey swallowed; it was almost too much to think of someone caring enough to worry about her to this extent or being able to read her so clearly, without judgment.

"That's a lot of emotion to feel for a stranger," she said.

He laughed, but she heard the vulnerability in it. He'd opened up, and here she was, joking. Not exactly responding in kind. But she knew this was the type of situation that called for emotional give-and-take. Honesty.

"She's just . . . someone I have a rough history with."

"So you do know her. Is she a friend?"

"Never a friend, no. Can we leave it there for now? I don't know how to even begin to tell you why I hate that woman."

"I hate her, too," he said, hanging an arm over the side of the boat. "Whoever she is, if you don't like her, that must mean she did something unforgivable."

"Bold of you to assume I'm not the problem in this scenario."

He smiled. "Lindsey, come on. Be serious for a second. You're not the problem."

It was such a small statement, but somehow they were the words she needed to hear more than almost anything else. She leaned in and kissed him, her wineglass slipping from her hand and shattering on the deck.

"Shit," she said.

"Don't worry about it," Fred said, pulling her back in and kissing her again, his hand pressed to her cheek.

In minutes, they were below deck in the boat's only bedroom. They pulled off their clothes urgently. She tripped on her shorts, only to catch herself by tumbling against the wall, and he couldn't get his pants off without shaking his leg to free the fabric tangled around his ankle. But then the edges of reality softened and receded. Lindsey allowed herself to forget it all for a while.

It didn't last long, but once it was over, she rested her cheek on the warm skin of his shoulder.

"If we're going to change what this is," she said, "and make it a *thing*, you deserve honesty. All those things you worry about, you deserve to know. You shouldn't have to wonder."

Fred pressed a finger to her lips. "I agree, but not now. We have time."

The words she wanted to say were just at the edge of her lips: *I'm a horrible person.* She bit down on the inside of her cheeks to push them away, to replace them with something else.

"Hey," she whispered. "Will you come with me to this party I have to go to? It's this weekend on Block Island. An old friend just bought a house out there."

"Oh," he said, eyes still closed. "I'm your plus-one now? Just like that?"

She fished his phone out of his pants pocket and saved Callie's address in his map app. His fingers grazed over her hair, and after a while, his breathing slowed and his eyes shut. Lindsey eased herself out from under his arm, tossed on her shirt, and quietly padded to the bathroom.

When she was done, she stepped into the main cabin, looking for her phone. She couldn't remember when she'd last seen it. She scanned the table, counters, and floor, but didn't see it.

Lindsey glanced back at the closed bedroom door. There was no denying that they had demolished the rules tonight and would have to figure out a way forward to genuinely start knowing each other. She'd never snooped around the boat the other couple of times she'd been on it because it had felt like a violation, but now curiosity pulled her toward the drawers and cabinets she'd never felt she should touch before.

She pulled the first drawer open. Scissors, tape, rubber bands, superglue, a pile of receipts. Painfully ordinary. She wanted something more real. The next drawer held silverware. The third was packed with paper plates. This one surprised her; they were a store brand. Fred shopped at Target?

She shut the drawer and moved to the cabinets—glasses, bowls, plates. Cans of beans and jars of olives.

There was a small bookshelf set above the table and bench. She slid onto the bench and skimmed the titles. Mostly nonfiction books about sailing, local hurricane disasters, shipwrecks. Lindsey pulled the largest book off the shelf, a hefty coffee-table book filled with glossy photos of antique boats. As she shifted the book into her lap, the back cover flopped open, and loose papers spilled out and scattered across the floor.

Lindsey set the book down on the table and crouched to collect the papers but then stopped cold.

Zoe's face looked back at her.

A printed black-and-white version of her Missing poster and an online news article from five years earlier. Lindsey swiftly took in the other pages: more images of Zoe—some in color, some grayscale—all from news articles about her disappearance printed off the internet.

Lindsey's legs quaked. Her hands worked as fast as her mind. What the hell was this? Had he lied about only looking up Lindsey's work history, finding Patricia's stories in the process? He must have printed out the articles to get a better sense of Lindsey. He worried about her; he probably just wanted to understand her past.

She glanced over her shoulder at the closed bedroom door again, setting the papers on the counter. Something with more weight than the papers clanged against the Formica countertop. She flipped the pile over: a paper clip, clamping a real photograph face down onto one of the news articles.

She pulled the clip off and flipped the photograph over.

Zoe, glossy and in color, her hair long and loose, blowing in the wind and partly obscuring her face. Wearing a magenta dress Lindsey recognized instantly. Her head was tilted casually to the side, and she was smiling. But there was something in her expression that seemed off. The smile. It appeared genuine, but someone who knew her well—someone like Lindsey—could see the slack at the corners of her mouth. It wasn't her true smile.

Lindsey felt unsteady, as if the boat was rocking harder against the tide than normal. As if it was about to storm.

In the photo, Zoe was sitting on a boat. A boat that looked like Fred's.

A creak from the bedroom. Lindsey threw the papers back into the book and slammed it shut, slipping it back onto the bookshelf only a second before the bedroom door opened. Fred stepped out in his boxers, blinking in the dim light.

"Wondered where you went. You okay?" he asked.

She nodded quickly. He smiled and then closed himself in the bathroom. She listened to his piss hit the toilet, willing herself to pull it together before he finished. She could just ask him about the photo—there had to be a reasonable explanation for it. The articles, those were easier to explain away. And maybe the picture was, too. She would ask him.

When he came out, he stretched and nodded at the upper deck.

"Should we get dinner?" he asked.

She opened her mouth, but those words she needed to say refused to come out.

"Earlier, you said you only searched my work history. Is that really all you looked at?" she asked instead.

He gazed at her curiously. "Why? What else is there to see?" When she didn't answer him, he said, "Just your work history. I promise."

She wanted off the boat. Either he was lying about how deeply he'd researched her, or he had articles and images of Zoe in his possession for another reason. And neither option felt great.

"You know, I need to pack and run some errands before I leave for that party," she said. "Let's head back, okay?"

"Okay," he agreed slowly.

"But I had a great time tonight," she said.

Fred dressed, planted a kiss on the top of her head, and went up to start the engine a few minutes later. Lindsey quickly put on the rest of her clothes and removed the book from the shelf once more. She unclipped the photograph of Zoe and stuffed it into the zippered pocket of her purse.

She wasn't exactly sure why she took it, except that she couldn't leave it behind.

And if the photo was gone the next time she looked for it in that book, if someday Fred denied there had ever been a picture of Zoe Gilbert on his boat, Lindsey might not believe her own memory of its existence.

Chapter Nineteen

MEG

Cameron Oakes's office was in a historic Newport building on Spring Street. By the look of the sign out front, he was in the financial investment business. Meg walked up the front steps of the porch, which was outfitted with a hanging swing and pots overflowing with vibrant flowers. She let herself into the lobby and told the receptionist she was there for Mr. Oakes.

"Oh yes, he's expecting you," she told Meg, leading her to a closed door down the hall. The antique carpet runner and historic paintings on the walls made the office feel more like someone's outdated great-aunt's house than an office.

The receptionist knocked on the door and a man answered, adjusting the knot of his tie as he greeted them.

"Meghan, come on in. Great to meet you."

He was tall with dark hair lightly flecked with gray. She noticed his posture and how easily he carried himself. An effortless confidence in his stride.

Meg followed him in. "Thank you again for taking the time to see me," she said.

"Oh, it's no problem," he said.

She scanned the office. On one wall, there was a gallery of photos of himself and, presumably, his family. A shelf near the window was stacked with books and several small plants. In the corner was a telescope.

"You do a lot of stargazing?" Meg joked.

Cameron smiled as he dropped into his desk chair.

"Oh, that. Not really. I just needed somewhere to keep it after I downsized to a smaller place." He studied her for a few seconds. "You wanted to talk about your friend. I wish I'd had a chance to get to know her better, but we'd only just met before she disappeared. I could tell she was special, though."

Meg swallowed. "She was special."

He paused, thinking. "She was an artist, right? A jewelry maker? I remember she showed me some of her work. She seemed naturally talented."

"Her jewelry was gorgeous," Meg agreed. "She always knew how she wanted to spend her life. I envied how sure she was about her path."

Cameron gave her a somber smile. "It's a gift to know oneself that well." He tapped the desk. "You know, I've been trying to figure out how you knew to contact me. I wouldn't say I was a key person in Zoe's life."

Meg shifted in her seat. "I have to be honest with you. There's a true crime podcaster named Patricia Adele—do you know her?" He shook his head. "She's writing a book about Zoe's disappearance, and I happened to get my hands on a list of people connected to her project. You're on the list. That's how I found you."

Cameron frowned. "I'm on a list? What kind of book is it?"

Meg explained what she knew. Told him about the opening pages and what angle it seemed Patricia was taking. How she was casting a wide net and reeling in people from all corners of Zoe's life. What Patricia did to them five years earlier, what she was doing now. The sense of safety she had cost them. The trouble she could cause for innocent people if she felt even slightly suspicious of them.

"I was hoping, if you'd already spoken to her about the case, you'd be willing to share with me what you know. But I'm also happy to be the one to tell you not to talk to her when she finally does contact you. Maybe it'll throw a wrench in her plans."

Cameron leaned back in his chair with his fingers laced behind his head. "I like it. You're setting up roadblocks for her. That's good. Slow her down a bit, right?"

"Ideally. She'll probably contact you one way or another," Meg said. "Even if you have nothing to say about Zoe, she's going to want to talk. Just steer clear."

A muscle in his jaw flexed. "I don't know what happened to Zoe. I wouldn't have anything useful to share."

"She's relentless. And hyperfocused on getting what she wants. Don't give her an inch, trust me," Meg said. "You're on her list—but how did you and Zoe know each other, anyway?"

"Oh, we met at a chamber of commerce networking event," he said. "I remember I was about to leave, I was so bored by everyone. But then a mutual friend introduced me to Zoe, and we talked until the event was over and everyone else cleared out." He shrugged. The gesture had an air of defeat about it, like he didn't want to linger too much in a good memory. "We met up a few times here and there to talk about her business, that kind of thing. She was a bright, ambitious young woman, and I was sorry to hear she'd gone missing. It was all over the news."

Meg remembered Zoe complaining about all the networking events she had to attend while her business was up and coming. *Everyone's twice my age, and no one takes me seriously,* she'd said more than once.

"She must've appreciated your interest in her work," Meg said. "Sometimes she struggled with feeling like other business owners thought she was just playing dress-up. That her work was silly or frivolous. But she was incredible at what she did. And so successful for her age."

Cameron smiled. "I was young and scrappy and entrepreneurial myself once. I think she appreciated that I understood her."

Understood her. Meg repeated this to herself, turning the phrase over in her mind. Had she imagined the slanted, almost-romantic way he'd said it?

And how had this man—who knew Zoe enough to understand her—skated under the radar during the initial investigation? Meg would've remembered him if he'd been around back then.

"Did you ever talk to the police?" Meg asked. "If Patricia knows that you knew Zoe, they must have known, too."

"Maybe? No one ever asked," he said, shrugging.

"You followed the news when Zoe went missing," Meg said. "But you didn't go to the police to see if you could help?"

"I hadn't seen Zoe in a while," he said. "It's hard to offer assistance when you have nothing of value to give."

Meg studied his face for any sign of familiarity. "Did you help us search for her? I mean, you knew her. You liked her. You followed her case. I don't recognize you at all, though. Did you come to any of the searches? Am I just forgetting we crossed paths back then?"

Cameron folded his hands on the desk and leaned forward slightly. "I'm embarrassed to say I was nursing an injury that summer and couldn't search even though I wanted to. It bothered me to know a friend was missing and I was laid up, unable to help."

"What kind of injury?" Meg asked. She followed the pointed question with a smile. "If it's not too personal."

"It was stupid," he said. "I dislocated my shoulder moving some furniture and was in a sling for eight weeks. Sometimes I forget I'm not twenty anymore."

"And you last saw Zoe before that injury?" Meg asked. She felt she was collecting pieces that didn't quite fit together but might—if she asked the right questions. If she knew *what* those were.

Cameron laughed. "You sure you're not the one writing a book?"

"No, no," Meg said, shaking her head. "I'm sorry. I'm just trying to understand."

"What do you really want to ask? It sounds like you're tiptoeing around it. You can just ask me."

Meg tensed at his forwardness. "Okay. When did you last see her?" She paused, debating whether she really wanted the answers to all her questions, then finally asked, "And was your relationship with Zoe romantic at all?"

"I wouldn't say it was romantic, exactly," Cameron said with an indecisive wobble of his head. "But I also wouldn't say it didn't have the potential to go there. If things had turned out differently."

"But you had feelings for her," Meg said, surprised by how uncomfortable this revelation made her feel. Not because of Cameron, exactly, but because he represented an aspect of Zoe's life unknown to Meg. A secret Zoe had kept from her. And, quite possibly, not the only one.

"I found her charming and interesting," Cameron said. "And yes, I had some feelings for her. But we both were so busy that summer and hadn't gotten together in a while when she disappeared. At least six weeks, I'd say. We didn't end on a bad note, by any means. It was just . . . unfinished. She seemed to have a lot of things going on that summer. A lot on her mind. She was too busy for me, frankly."

Meg could see why Zoe might've liked this man. He was easy to talk to, warm, seemed to be fairly emotionally intelligent. But why hadn't she told Meg about him?

Maybe she was reading too much into it. Had she told Zoe about every person she interacted with? Maybe he was just someone on the business side of her life, not worth mentioning to her friends.

"Do you think she had feelings for you?" Meg asked.

"I mean, she made the first move when we kissed. What would you say?"

Meg's mouth went dry. Zoe would've told them about him, unless there was something stopping her. Unless she'd stopped trusting her friends long before she ever vanished. If she thought they were only pretending to like her and didn't think they deserved to know.

Meg stood up and held out her hand. She wasn't sure how much more she could hear without feeling like she didn't know Zoe at all.

"Thank you for taking the time to see me," she said as he shook her hand. "And I think you should tell the detectives you knew her. Who knows, maybe there are small details you remember that could help."

He let go of the handshake and studied her. "Is that your way of saying I should tell them I knew Zoe before you do it for me?"

"No, I just mean—"

"I'm joking," he said. "I'll reach out and see if there's anything I can offer. But if that podcaster calls me, I plan on ruining her day."

"Please do," Meg said. "Thanks again."

She saw herself out through the lobby. Before she got into her car, she looked back up at the old house, with its mansard roof and decorative historic swirls around the window frames. She wondered if Zoe had come here to visit Cameron at work, or if all their time together had been spent at other places. Places Meg didn't know about. Because, regardless of what she'd believed for years, it was clear that Zoe hadn't told her everything.

Cameron's face appeared in the window to the left of the front door. He saw Meg standing beside her car parked on the street, staring at the old house. For a long moment, he stared at her without expression; then, as if remembering he should emote, he smiled and lifted a hand to wave goodbye.

The hair on Meg's neck rose despite the heat of the summer afternoon. She raised a hand to wave back and quickly slid into her car and turned on the engine. She didn't look back as she drove away.

Meg didn't sleep that night. Nor did she finish any of her work the next day before it was time to pack her bag and head to the ferry. She was too tangled up in questions about what other secrets Zoe might've had and how deep they might've run.

She tried directing her thoughts to more neutral places. How Zoe's fingers were always stacked with thin silver rings that she'd toy with when nervous. How her nail polish was perpetually chipped from hammering metal and using her fingernails to work small jump rings into place. The feel of those stacked rings as Zoe grabbed Meg's hands one final time before she was gone.

But the redirection never lasted long enough.

An hour before her mother was set to drive her to the harbor, a group text from Callie lit up Meg's phone. She had already texted twice in the last day, confirming and reconfirming they'd be at the housewarming. Finally, everyone had agreed. Tess first, and Meg next because she'd already promised Tess. And finally, Lindsey. Hours later, but still. A confirmation from all.

Callie: Safe travels! Can't wait to see you!

Meg waited for someone else to respond first while she packed a few outfits and her toiletries into a travel bag. Her only options were the clothes she'd brought home from Boston—one work dress, a few casual dresses, and a couple of pairs of shorts and T-shirts—unless she resurrected the clothing from high school still hanging in her closet. She'd intended to help her mother clean out the room one day, but her prior visits home had always been too brief, and she almost never slept in there, preferring the outdated wood-paneled basement to the bedroom full of reminders.

The knickknacks on the bookcase caught Meg's eye. Scrapbooks and photo albums stacked together next to a framed group photo. Meg had gone straight to the drugstore to print pictures after getting off the ferry from that last trip. Hours, maybe minutes, before Zoe went missing. Maybe at the same second, for all she knew. That short, naive span of time before everything changed.

The picture showed their final night together. The sunset had been incredible, blazing the sky with red and orange streaks, and they'd run barefoot to the beach from the rental cottage for the best view of it.

Meg had propped her phone on the edge of a lifeguard chair and set the timer. The flash went off, blotting out the sunset but illuminating the five of them. The sky was gone, but they were there. A globe of bright light held them together like a collective aura.

Callie hadn't asked them to bring contributions for the memorial, which struck Meg as strange, so she snatched the photo albums and frame off the shelf and shoved them into her travel bag.

"Meg! Ready?" her mother's voice called out from across the house.

"Coming!" she yelled back.

Her mother made nervous small talk on the drive to the harbor.

"The weather is supposed to be beautiful tomorrow," she said. "You'll call me when you get there safe and sound, right? I wonder what kind of food she'll serve. I hope you like it. I'd hate to think about you not eating."

"Mom," Meg finally said gently. "I'm going to be fine."

Lucy went quiet. Then she sniffed, and Meg looked over as the car slowed in front of the harbor. She wiped her eyes as she shook her head.

"I *know* you'll be fine," Lucy said. She grabbed Meg's hand and pressed it between her two palms. "But you're going back to the island for the first time, and you're seeing your old group of friends for the first time in a long time, and I just feel all mixed up watching you go. Like it's your first day of camp, only scarier."

Meg smiled. "It's just Callie Sutter's fancy new house. There's nothing scary about it."

"You know what I mean, honey. I can't help but worry that something might happen to you."

"I promise I'll be fine," Meg said. She opened her door and climbed out. "I'll call you as soon as I get off the ferry. Please don't worry about a thing. Love you."

Meg stood on the sidewalk, briefly immobilized by her senses. The smell of low tide hanging over the scent of diesel fuel. Countless indistinct conversations coming from the people lined up at the ticket counter and the entrance to the ferry, voices crisscrossing and blending. Cars beeping on the street and accelerating around jaywalking pedestrians laden with overstuffed duffel bags and coolers.

She spotted Lindsey and Tess already in line to board the boat. She approached the ticket booth and paid for her fare, then made her way over to them. They were distracted, both looking down at their phones.

"Room for one more?" Meg asked as she came up behind them.

Lindsey spun around and grabbed her in a surprise embrace. Meg locked eyes with Tess, who gave her a single-shoulder shrug as if to say she hadn't expected Lindsey's affection, either.

"I'm sorry," Lindsey said as she stepped back. She shook her head, strands of hair falling from a lopsided bun. "I'm just really emotional right now."

"Don't apologize," Meg said. "It's good to see you."

She lifted a strand of Meg's hair from her shoulder. "You changed your hair. I like it."

"Oh, I just stopped dyeing it," Meg said, unprepared for the attention. Not just the attention, but the depth of it, too. How Lindsey remembered something as inconsequential as how Meg used to color her hair, and how much more they had cataloged away about each other.

"You should keep it like that," Tess said. "It brings out the green in your eyes."

"What about that time you let me cut your hair with your mom's kitchen scissors?" Lindsey said. "She was so mad."

Meg laughed, her discomfort beginning to unwind. "She used those for *food*. Of course she was mad. We were always getting into her things and making a mess."

The line shuffled forward into the yawning cavern of the boat. They showed their tickets and stepped inside. Meg held tight to the steel railing as she ascended the stairs. The last time she had stepped onto this boat, she was leaving the island after the search had been called off.

On the top deck, they settled shoulder to shoulder on a bench, their bags nestled between their feet. Meg was pressed in the middle.

"Do you remember the time you and Zoe asked a family to put their little kids on their laps so we could all sit together?" Lindsey asked Meg.

"We didn't actually do that," Meg said. "Did we?"

"You did," Tess said. "Remember? The funeral?"

It came back to Meg in a rush. Meg had been Zoe's backup as she approached a family whose children were sprawled out everywhere, taking up precious seating. *Would you mind if we squeezed in right here? We're traveling to a funeral and would like to sit together,* Zoe said.

The mother had scooped her kids onto her lap immediately. *I'm so sorry for your loss,* she said to them.

"The looks that lady gave us when we forgot we were supposed to be mourning and started talking about which bar to hit first," Tess said.

"I forgot all about that," Meg said. She broke eye contact with Tess, feeling suddenly vulnerable.

The ferry horn blared, and the engines rumbled to life below deck. Meg gripped the strap of her overnight bag, a cold sweat blooming along her hairline. It was too late to turn back. Too late to call her mother and say she wanted to go home.

The ferry slid out of the harbor, and soon they were cruising on the open ocean, pulled toward the island like a hand was reaching out from the past, whisking them back.

Chapter Twenty

CALLIE

Callie was halfway through a bottle of wine by the pool. She recorded the water distorted through her glass, slapped a nostalgic filter on the footage, and captioned it with *Tomorrow . . . come back here for something special xo.* She clicked "Share" and, as if on cue, heard tires crunching down the driveway and car doors slamming shut. She got to her feet but stood rooted in place for a few seconds, momentarily lightheaded. They'd actually come.

She inhaled as deeply as she could, exhaled slowly, let the dizziness pass, and started off to see her old friends.

As she rounded the side yard, they came into view, lit by a radiant glow emanating from the house windows. A surprise sob rose up her throat. They looked ethereal in the near dark, like a shimmering mirage.

Lindsey pulled luggage from the back of the minivan taxi as Tess counted money for the driver. Meg shut the trunk for Lindsey with a loud thud. Together, they thanked their driver and lifted their bags into the crooks of their arms. Lindsey said something to Meg and Tess, pointing up at the house. Their eyes followed her fingertip.

Callie watched them for a few seconds, concealed in a shadow cast by the house, surprised by her reluctance to show herself. It was like standing at the door to their camp cabin for the first time again, unsure how she'd be received by the girls on the other side. If they would love her immediately or think she was annoying—or worse, feel completely ambivalent about her. But she willed herself to step over the threshold and welcome whatever came next.

"You're here," she said as she jogged toward them. They turned in her direction at the sound of her voice, and as soon as she felt their collective gaze upon her, a pebble rolled under the sole of her foot. She stumbled into Lindsey, who caught her before she went down. A flush of embarrassment crept over Callie's face, but she smiled as she corrected her balance.

"Thanks. Sorry. I'm so clumsy," she said.

Lindsey sniffed. "Clumsy? Or is our hostess a little buzzed?"

Callie instinctively slanted herself away from Lindsey. "I had a couple of glasses, but—"

"Thanks for having us, Callie," Tess cut in, reaching for a hug.

Callie accepted the embrace—the only one offered to her—and thanked Tess for coming.

"I'm grateful you're all here," Callie said.

"It's weird to be here," Meg said as her eyes swept across the front of the house. "Your house is beautiful. Where can we put our bags?"

She hitched the strap of bag on her shoulder. A strange look glinted in her eye. Callie remembered then how skeptical Meg had always been. Distrustful of new people, hesitant to take information at face value. Of course she wouldn't arrive with arms wide open. She would need time to feel out the situation. After all, she'd been the last to accept Callie's arrival at camp, refusing to extend her friendship until it was clear Callie wasn't moving to another cabin and everyone else had already welcomed her as part of the group.

"I need to pump," Tess said, wincing slightly. "Okay if I stash breast milk in your fridge this weekend?"

"Of course," Callie said. "Whatever you need, just let me know. I want you to feel completely at home while you're here."

She led them into the house and up to the second floor. At the landing, she stepped aside.

"There are four rooms. They each have a bathroom, so no one has to share like the old days," she said. "We were never good at sharing a single sink and shower."

"I thought we shared just fine," Meg said as she slid into the first room on the left.

"Yellow one's mine," Lindsey said. She tossed her bag inside.

"I'll let you get settled and freshen up," Callie said. It wasn't lost on her that there was one empty room; she wondered if they all noticed it, too. "Snacks and drinks will be waiting by the pool. Come down whenever you're ready."

"Thanks, Cal," Tess said from her doorway. "Be down soon."

Callie gave her a small nod of gratitude. Then they clicked their doors shut, and she stood alone on the landing, doing her best to accept the storm brewing under her ribs.

They were together. Five years of exile seemingly over. Or at least paused.

She just hoped this was real forgiveness, and that she deserved it.

The three women emerged from the house together twenty minutes later. Callie stood from the pool lounge chair and raised a hand, directing them to the fieldstone steps lit by strands of bistro lights.

"Nathan's going to make dinner," she told them as they stepped down to the pool area. "Salmon and veggies. Or we could go out to dinner, just the four of us. Whatever you want. But I put this together for now."

She gestured at an elaborate charcuterie board spilling over with various types of cheeses, meats, fruits, and crackers. Wine and sparkling water were arranged beside it.

Lindsey pulled the cork from a bottle of wine and poured it into four glasses while Tess passed a plate to each of them. Once they each had a glass of wine and some food, Lindsey leveled her gaze at Callie.

"So, what can we expect from this weekend?" she asked.

Callie wasn't ready to tell them everything yet. She pointed across the yard as she spoke.

"We'll have a memorial table set up right over there, and a candlelight vigil, too, once everyone's here tomorrow." She paused and glanced at each of them, still amazed they'd shown up. "Look, I know I had a lot of audacity asking you to come here this weekend. None of you had to say yes, but I think the fact that you did means it was time for us to reunite. We should be together tomorrow. I don't know what it was like for each of you, but the last four anniversaries were torture. I never feel more alone than I do every year on August tenth."

"You're throwing a housewarming party, though," Meg said. "This isn't actually about Zoe or any of us. It's like we were tacked on as an afterthought."

A pit opened in Callie's stomach hearing this, but it wasn't a surprise that Meg saw it this way. She didn't know the entire picture yet.

Tess lowered her glass. "At least we're together."

"Is that a good thing?" Lindsey asked. "The last time we were together, it didn't go so hot."

"I know you still resent me for the interview. I was only trying to help; it just didn't turn out how I thought it would back then. I'm sorry."

"You should've told us before you did it," Meg said. She was watching the wine in her glass as she swirled it by the stem. "What you did changed who we were. Fixing it isn't as simple as throwing a party."

"The interview changed who we were?" Callie asked, a faint laugh underpinning her words. "We weren't already fundamentally altered by Zoe's disappearance? It was all my fault?"

"It was a chain reaction," Lindsey said. "You were one of the links in the chain."

"And you know the truth about how that situation came to be," Callie said to Lindsey, her words thorny.

"What truth?" Meg asked, a note of worry in her question.

"Patricia finagled Callie's interview. And Callie was none the wiser."

Lindsey explained to Meg and Tess what had happened when she'd visited Callie. How Callie's father had let it slip.

"Knowing this might not change anything for you three, but it does for me. I see that whole time differently now," Callie said.

Meg was quiet, thinking. Tess nudged around the food on her plate.

"What a twisted thing to do," Meg finally said. "I don't know what to think anymore."

"Is this weekend going to be a mess?" Lindsey asked. "Like, are we going to survive this party, Cal?"

Callie stared at the water in the pool. The surface hardly moved save for tiny ripples. She could feel them waiting, but she'd said as much as she could for now. To tell them everything might send them running, and she wanted them to stay. To see this reunion through to the very end, come what may.

Somewhere nearby, fireworks shocked the night air. Then another round, and another. They sounded closer with each explosion. Her throat squeezed tight.

"I think Callie did what she thought was best. And I'm sure that's true this weekend, too," Tess said. Callie mouthed *thank you* to her.

"We were a mess before the interview," Callie said. "We were falling apart. And I couldn't just sit back and watch that happen."

"Still, it was the wrong move," Lindsey said. "You miscalculated."

"It *was* the wrong move," Callie said. "You're right. But what options were there? Hope that Patricia might wake up one day, feel bad, and stop making us the focal point of Zoe's disappearance? I had to be proactive. We can go our separate ways after this weekend if that's best. We should've all been part of the interview five years ago, but I can't go back in time and change what happened or how it happened. But I hope this weekend shows you that I'm sorry."

She took a long sip of her wine, suddenly exhausted. Beyond the trees, the lights inside the guesthouse came on. Nathan emerged a few moments later and walked over to the main house. Callie stood up, needing a break.

"I'm sorry, you guys. I need to get some rest," Callie said. "Nathan will have dinner ready soon."

"Callie, no. Stay," Tess said. "There are a million other things we could talk about."

"It's hard to be together and talk about much else," Callie said. "I'll see you in the morning."

She crossed the lawn to the house, her feet wet from evening dew on the grass. After telling Nathan she was going to bed early, Callie ran herself a hot shower and climbed into bed. She snapped an unfiltered selfie, grainy in the low light, fresh faced, with wet hair piled on her head in a towel, and posted it with a short caption: *Keeping it real and baring who I really am. Link in bio for my current skincare holy grails.*

Chapter Twenty-One

LINDSEY

The plush guest room bed had been made up with silky, wrinkle-free sheets spritzed with a lavender linen spray. But instead of falling into a restful sleep, Lindsey stared for hours at the ceiling and its long, shifting shadows.

The photograph of Zoe, tucked in her makeup bag, pulsed from across the room like a beacon that wouldn't quiet. The minutes ticked closer and closer to midnight, until finally, the new day turned over and it was official: A bridge five years long stretched between Lindsey and the last time she saw Zoe's face.

And there was Fred. He would be on the island, at Lindsey's side, in mere hours, and she still couldn't account for why he had the photograph and the news clippings on his boat. Why stash them inside the pages of that book—for safekeeping or to keep them hidden? Did he know Lindsey and Zoe had been friends? Had he accumulated those things years earlier—or in the short time since he and Lindsey had met this summer?

The answer to the last question needled her the most.

She could theoretically excuse the news clippings; he'd looked up her work history, after all. It wouldn't have been hard to dig a little further and find the articles about Zoe with Lindsey's name laced throughout. Anyone with an internet connection could do that.

But the color-print photo of Zoe? It was next to impossible to excuse that away.

Before bed, he'd texted to say he was looking forward to the party, and the only words Lindsey's hands wanted to type in response were *I don't know if I trust you anymore. I don't think I know you at all. Don't come here tomorrow.*

But instead, she'd sent a thumbs-up emoji and plotted her next move. She could either push him away and never speak to him again, or she could keep him close enough to understand what he knew about Zoe. The second Fred realized he'd walked into Zoe Gilbert's memorial, Lindsey would be able to read the truth in his eyes. Either Zoe was a piece of Lindsey's past that Fred had just discovered in a Google search, or Zoe herself was a part of Fred's past.

Or, worse, neither was true and he was someone like Patricia, so eager to embed themselves in a true crime story, they'd pay to spend time with one of the people closest to the case. He'd pushed so hard for honesty the night before on his boat, she couldn't help but wonder about his real motivations.

She tossed and turned, pressed her face into the pillow, flung the sheets off. The house was serene: the pipes silenced after showers had been taken, doors clicked shut, and locks turned tight. Still, sleep wouldn't come.

Lindsey swung her legs out of the bed, riffled through her makeup bag for the photograph, a joint, and her lighter, and started downstairs as quietly as possible. None of the steps creaked underfoot like her childhood home, where certain ones always betrayed. Unlike that house, this one kept its secrets.

In the kitchen, long beams of moonlight streamed through the windows. She let herself out the back door and sat at the patio table.

The air was cool and carried the suggestion of fall coming soon. Another season ending. Another year without Zoe.

She studied the photograph, rubbing one corner with her thumb. She wished there was a way to zoom out and see the entire scene. To press play and watch the next few moments unspool in real time. She imagined Fred behind the camera, cracking a joke to make Zoe smile, then him leaning in to show her the image, to say how beautiful she looked.

The thought made her shudder. Lindsey had deliberately mirrored Zoe in so many ways, from dressing like her to adopting the same faint Rhode Island accent since Lindsey had never naturally developed one of her own. But to have Fred in common? Would Lindsey ever become herself, or was she doomed to always be a lesser copy of Zoe?

A creak from the direction of the house startled her. She quickly slid the photo off the table and into the waistband of her shorts, concealed by her top.

Meg eased the French door shut behind her. "Didn't mean to startle you."

Lindsey exhaled. "I didn't expect anyone else to be awake."

Meg dropped into the chair opposite Lindsey.

"I had a nightmare," she said. "Can't remember it now, though. I hate that. It was so vivid, but as soon as I opened my eyes, all I had left was the awful feeling of it."

Lindsey shifted in her seat and held up the joint. "It's been a while. You still smoke?"

"When the occasion calls for it," Meg said. "I would say this weekend is such an occasion."

Lindsey nodded and lit the joint. They passed it back and forth a few times, listening to the crickets and not speaking. Not exactly a comfortable silence, but a tolerable one. Finally, Meg sighed and lifted her chin.

"The moon was full five years ago," she said. "The last night of our vacation."

"How could you possibly know that?" Lindsey asked.

Meg dropped her ear toward her shoulder, cracking her neck. Then to the other side. Something in her face dimmed.

"I have a good memory." Then, after a few beats, Meg squeezed the bridge of her nose. "I have to tell you something. When Patricia was at my office, I stole a list of names from some paperwork she'd brought with her."

Lindsey raised her brows. "Really? I'm impressed."

Meg rolled her eyes. "I know how to break the rules when I need to. But listen—she also left me the opening pages of her book's manuscript. On purpose. She wanted me to read them."

A charge went through Lindsey's body. "And?"

"I didn't want to look at it," Meg said. "Obviously, she gave it to me for a reason. She wanted me to know what was on those pages. So, on principle alone, I thought I shouldn't read it. But I did."

Lindsey shot her a look. "Did it say something about us?"

"Yeah," Meg said. She took a hit off the joint and handed it to Lindsey. "In particular, that she has some witnesses who contradict your and Callie's stories. I think she plans to write that you both lied about where you went after we left Zoe."

"Why would she say that?"

Meg shook her head. "I talked to some of the people on her list. There's a bartender who says she saw you out when you were supposed to be back at your apartment."

Lindsey's stomach dropped like a boulder off a cliff. Sudden and punishing. Her breath shallowed.

"A bartender saw me somewhere?"

"Apparently. I also talked to Blake, that guy Zoe dated on and off," Meg went on. "And some other guy who knew her through a friend. It's like Patricia is planning to get quotes from any person who ever interacted with Zoe." She sighed. "Honestly, I can see how this will play out. Patricia's going to get her book deal. It'll be full of holes, but people will buy it."

Lindsey hated the sound of defeat in Meg's voice.

"If that happens, we'll just have to make sure we tank her sales." Lindsey tilted her head back and sighed loudly. "Let's write our own book and make sure it's out before hers. You can teach us how it's done. What do we have to do first?"

Meg smiled. "It's nice to be around your fire again."

"Is it fire? Or rage?" Lindsey asked. She cocked her head toward Meg. "I hate being angry, but I forgot how to be anything else."

"I think that's part of your fire," Meg said. "Feeling deeply is your strength. Is that weird to say? It probably is."

It was true Lindsey felt everything to an extreme, but she'd never considered it a strength. She'd always rallied against it, drinking it away or letting her anger dominate so the more complicated feelings would be silent. But Meg saw beyond that. Meg had known Lindsey early enough in life to know there was more to her than just her rage.

"I've always felt taken care of by you," Lindsey said. "You've always understood me. I trusted your instincts, and it was hard to lose that when we stopped talking. Your perspective and your ability to read a situation. Maybe that's why I've floundered so much."

"I never knew that." Meg pressed her thumbs against her eyelids. "Crying in the middle of the night on Callie's back patio while we smoke together. What is this, 2002?"

"I wish," Lindsey said with a small laugh.

They shared a few minutes of silence, now with more ease. But Lindsey was thinking of the bartender, her mind reaching back through time to put a face to this witness. Her memories were nothing but haze, though. Was it possible she'd been seen? That her cover story for that night would be blown?

"Do you know Cameron Oakes or Miles Bell?" Meg asked.

Lindsey searched her memory. "I don't think so. Why?"

"They're on that list," Meg said. "I emailed them. Miles hasn't gotten back to me, but I spoke to Cameron. It sounds like he and Zoe hung out that summer and he had feelings for her, but she ghosted him.

I'm sure he's harmless. Maybe he was just some guy who liked her more than she liked him. But I can't shake the feeling that he wasn't telling me everything."

"You're a stranger to him—of course he wasn't telling you everything," Lindsey said. "I don't think she ever told me about him. I have no memory of her hanging out with someone named Cameron that summer."

"Neither do I," Meg said. "But, in addition to talking to him, Tess and I also sort of ambushed Blake at his job." She blew air through her lips. "He did not like that very much."

"Did he say anything?"

"Nothing helpful. Just some things he thought would upset us. Then we left without paying our bill." Meg smirked. "And we had Tess's baby with us. I'm a bad influence. Anyway, it seems like dead ends right now. I honestly thought that Patricia had legitimate witnesses and you or Callie were hiding something." She tilted her head to look at Lindsey. "Even if you lied about where you were that night, I don't think that means you hurt Zoe."

Lindsey looked away. It was unbearable to hold Meg's gaze while she was right on the doorstep of the truth.

Meg kept talking, filling the empty space Lindsey left between them.

"I just . . . There's so much I wish I could ask Zoe. Sometimes I can't stand that I have no way to talk to her anymore. I thought it would get easier, but it hasn't. Has it gotten easier for you?"

"Not for a second," Lindsey said.

Meg sighed. "Okay, this is getting too heavy. Change of subject. Tell me about your life lately."

"My life lately," Lindsey repeated. "Well, I got fired. But you knew that. I've been seeing someone. It's really new and probably won't last long, but he's coming to the party."

"Oh!" Meg said, brightening. "That's exciting. What's his name? How did you meet?"

Lindsey smiled. "Fred. We met through mutual friends."

"And? What's he like?" Meg asked. "Is he hot?"

Lindsey's cheeks burned. "How about you meet him tomorrow and tell me what you think? Like the good ol' days."

"I was brutal back then," Meg said. "I promise to be nicer when I meet him."

"Don't hold back," Lindsey said. "I need that Meg intuition I've missed so much."

"Deal."

They finished their joint and Lindsey crushed it under her heel on the patio stones. She stretched her arms wide, glancing up at her bedroom window. From the ground, it looked dark. Foreboding.

"Can I sleep in your room?" Lindsey asked. "If you don't mind company?"

"I would love the company," Meg said. "I was dreading waking up in the morning on the anniversary. It'll suck less with you there."

Upstairs, they curled up back-to-back in bed. Lindsey relaxed against the steady cadence of Meg's rising and falling rib cage, and her last thought before she fell asleep was that being with Meg felt like returning home after a long trip. As if she'd spent years in another country unable to speak the language, and finally she was back where she was understood.

Chapter
Twenty-Two

MEG

Meg woke pressed to Lindsey's back, left arm hooked under the pillow with her right wrapped around her waist as if protecting herself. A faint snore emanated from Lindsey's throat. Her long lashes flickered as her closed eyes moved back and forth. She hadn't changed at all in the years they'd been apart—at least not on the surface. Meg was sure there were new sides to Lindsey she'd discover if they stayed in touch after this weekend. Same with Tess and Callie. They'd have to get to know her again, too. She wasn't the same person she'd been before, either.

Meg eased herself out of bed and padded softly over to her suitcase to unpack the photo albums she'd brought for the memorial. Zoe had drawn a heart on the light-blue fabric cover of the first one. The sight of the doodle twisted something deep in Meg's chest. A long-held screw tightened one too many notches, splintering the wood around it.

The moon had been full five years earlier, and its glow had brightened Zoe's face so that Meg could read her reaction clearly. The surprise that flashed in her eyes, the apologetic smile that followed. The smell of the fire and the way the smoke clung to Meg's hair for days afterward like a ghost. The way Zoe had whispered to Meg, "Can you keep a secret?"

Lindsey stirred in the bed, stretched her arms, opened her eyes. A few seconds passed before she seemed to register where she was.

"Tell me I didn't snore," she said in a groggy voice as she shifted herself upright.

"You're asking me to lie to you," Meg said. She held out the album. "Did you bring anything for the memorial? Callie probably won't need them, but I brought some photos anyway."

Lindsey blinked a few times, then rubbed the sleep from her eyes. "I think I might have a picture, yeah. You and Tess would have the most stuff, though. You were always documenting everything. I don't think I ever had any real pictures of my own without you two sharing copies with me."

"Tess documented everything," Meg said. "I just wanted to feel cool, so I bought a camera."

Lindsey sat up a little straighter. "Zoe wasn't big into taking pictures of herself, right? Do you remember?"

Meg thought back. "She liked when we took her picture in the right light; I remember that much. Why?"

"Just curious," Lindsey said as she pulled her knees up and propped her chin on them. "A lot floating to the surface lately. It's almost like the longer she's missing, the less I understand her."

The screw in Meg's chest turned again, tighter. Why was she still clinging to old secrets? She wanted to know Lindsey again and to be known by her, too. To return to the unrestrained honesty they had once shared before everything. It had been easier to be wary of Lindsey from a distance with Patricia's suggestion that perhaps she was hiding something. But in person, it seemed ridiculous to assume the worst of Lindsey. And for Meg to continue keeping her own secrets.

"I never told you this," Meg started, sitting on the edge of the bed with the album in her hands, "but after the rest of you went into the cottage for bed that last night together, I told Zoe I had feelings for her."

Lindsey's mouth fell open. "Wait. What? You and Zoe? You did? Were you two ever . . . ?"

"No, but I was in love with her and had been for a while. I told her that night." The words came out like a ribbon unspooling. There was no winding it back up now. "I thought . . . I don't know, I thought she might've felt the same, but she had just gotten back together with—"

"Blake," Lindsey said, a flatness in her tone that betrayed her distaste. "What did she say?"

Meg pulled gently at a stray thread on her pajama shorts. "That she could see us giving it a shot one day. But I think she felt bad promising me something she couldn't guarantee, you know? My timing wasn't great, but after spending that week together, I felt like I had to say something or I'd die."

Lindsey leaned back against the headboard. "The bond you and Zoe had was always different from the rest of us. I could tell. There was definitely love there. You probably would've worked out eventually."

"I thought so, too. But there was something else she said that night," Meg said carefully. The thread came loose in her fingertips, and she flicked it away. "She asked me to keep a secret for her—I didn't even tell the detective because I thought Zoe would turn up eventually, and the last thing I wanted to do was betray her. Especially if there was a chance for us."

"You held out hope," Lindsey said. "And you wanted that trust to be intact when she came home."

"Exactly. Do you remember the last night together? How Tess kept saying Zoe was acting weird?" Meg asked.

"I remember some of it," Lindsey said. "They were bickering, and Zoe went off on her."

"Tess wasn't wrong. Zoe said she was dealing with a situation that had gotten weird, but she wouldn't say more than that. I got the feeling that whatever it was, it consumed her thoughts that week and that's what Tess noticed."

"She never told me anything like that," Lindsey said. "I was oblivious. I lived with her and completely missed it."

"She was good at keeping things to herself. But she was planning to tell me eventually—and all of us, I'm sure. She said once she figured out how to smooth it out, she was going to tell me and we'd laugh about it. I should have told the police, but there was nothing solid to tell, and the more time that passed, the guiltier I felt not admitting it all up front right away. Part of me wondered if her disappearance was connected to how she was handling the situation. I didn't know how to talk about any of it—my feelings for Zoe, her secret—without drawing suspicion. Patricia would've called me a jilted lover, or she would've said I knew Zoe's secret but was withholding it." Meg took a breath. "I wish I'd handled it differently. I just didn't know how to be honest without causing more trouble."

Lindsey groaned and dropped her chin to her chest. Then she lifted her eyes. "I know what you mean. I messed up pretty bad the day Zoe disappeared, Meg. Unforgivable-level shit. And I never told anyone about it, either."

Meg went still. "Does this have to do with what the bartender saw?"

"I didn't think anyone saw us. I thought it would go away if no one else knew it happened." She squeezed her eyes shut. "I slept with Blake. God. I've never said it out loud. Ever. I hate myself for letting it happen."

Angie the bartender had thought she remembered seeing Lindsey with a man. Blake.

"I don't understand," Meg said, thinking only of Zoe. How she'd turned Meg down because of Blake. "Why? How did that even happen?"

"I'd just gotten home from the ferry, and he showed up at our apartment looking for Zoe," Lindsey started, her voice frail. "I told him she'd stayed on the island, and he said he would wait for her. Parked himself right on our couch without asking. I was trying to unpack and do a week's worth of laundry, but I was so distracted by him. Did you know I liked him first?"

Meg shook her head. "When? In college?"

"Yeah. Before they ever got together, I told her I had a thing for him. But Zoe thought he wasn't my type, and then she started dating him. That's when we went on tour with his band for a little bit." Lindsey paused. "The night they broke up, I drove her home from Buffalo, and it occurred to me that if she could just take whatever she wanted, I could, too. So I started stealing little things from her. How she dressed, how she talked, what she did on the weekends. I think I wanted to be Zoe more than I ever wanted to be myself. I was always trying to be like her, but I never came close."

"Oh, Lindsey," Meg said.

"I was shocked when they got back together," Lindsey said. "One day she came home from her studio and said, 'Guess who I ran into today? The drummer.'"

Meg couldn't stand to hear the details of Zoe rekindling her romance with him. She redirected Lindsey. "So, he came to the apartment looking for her, but she wasn't there."

"Right, yeah. He was sitting there for hours having these flirty conversations with me while I was cleaning. I tried to ignore him, but I did still really like him. I was just praying Zoe would get home and he'd leave. But after a while, he said he was hungry, and since I hadn't eaten anything all day, we went to grab some food. We had more to drink than we should've. I guess the bartender noticed."

"This was when you were supposedly at your apartment, asleep," Meg said. "You told the detectives you didn't hear Zoe come home because you were exhausted and went to bed early."

"I didn't even go back home after that," Lindsey went on. "His place was around the corner, so I followed him back there. I told myself I'd sober up, then go home and make up a story if Zoe asked where I'd been. Blake didn't seem to care whether it was me or Zoe that night, as long as it was a warm body." She paused and held Meg's gaze. "You should have been with her. Not that guy. You."

Meg couldn't entertain that idea without feeling like she'd dissolve. "And then what? You slept together?"

"I thought I deserved to be with him because Zoe had decided for me years earlier that he wasn't my type. But who was she to tell me that? Why could she take the things she wanted but I couldn't?" She sighed. "Afterward, he said I was desperate. I think the exact words were, 'How desperate can you be? I'm dating your best friend.' Like it had all been my fault. And I thought he was right. I ruined everything by being desperate and pathetic, and Zoe would find out, and I'd lose her over a stupid, impulsive, drunk mistake. It was practically morning at that point, so I went home, changed, and went to work. Her door was shut, and I didn't check if she was in bed. I just assumed she was. And I couldn't face her at that point anyway. So I left and never said a word about it."

"And Blake didn't tell anyone, either?" Meg said. "Do you think he told Patricia?"

"He knew how bad it would look for him, too. He told the detectives he was home all night waiting to hear from Zoe, which his roommate backed up. His roommate wasn't even around; he was playing video games in his room the entire time. And no one ever came forward saying they saw us together, so we didn't have to account for anything. Until now, I guess. I remember I was so worried Patricia would find out, I even called the bar to ask if they had security cameras. They did, but they erase every twenty-four hours."

"Would you have told Zoe?" Meg asked. She needed to know how things might have played out in an alternate universe. If Lindsey's confession would've broken up Zoe and Blake, leading her to Meg.

"I honestly don't know," Lindsey said. "Once we realized she was missing, I tried praying. It had been years since I'd gone to church, but I tried bargaining with God in case it worked. If He returned Zoe unharmed, I'd confess everything with Blake. I would change. Become a good, honest person. But would I have told her if she came home that night or the next day and had no idea what we'd done and he kept his mouth shut, too? I don't know." She studied Meg's face. "Do you hate me? I would understand if you do."

"I don't hate you," Meg said. Maybe she would've hated Lindsey for this if she'd learned about it at the time, but not now. She could empathize too much. "You know, you're going to have to decide what to do. It's all circumstantial, but since Patricia already talked to the bartender, she knows you weren't at home all night like you said. She'll imply you could've killed Zoe and lied about that, too. And if you try to be honest about it, Blake will just deny your version of events and you'll look like an even bigger liar."

Lindsey's eyes went glassy. "I know," she said. "It's been easier to lie."

"But you're probably sick of that, too," Meg said.

"I am. I'm sick of all of this." Lindsey swiped at her eyes, angry now. "What I did is bad enough on its own without Patricia turning it into something more. I just don't think she'll be happy until Zoe is found or someone is held accountable." She rested a palm against her chest, as if to calm a racing heart. "I don't want to be that person. I don't want to be blamed for more than I did."

"I know," Meg said. "So we make sure she doesn't find out about any of this. And we hope that in the end, she roots out the truth and leaves us alone."

Lindsey shook her head. "I don't believe that. What she wants most is a good story. Not necessarily the truth."

Chapter Twenty-Three

Tess

The breast pump rhythmically drew and released Tess's nipples from the flanges while the attached bottles filled with milk. She sat on the closed toilet in the bathroom, listening to the pump's mechanical whine morph into a persistent voice, bleating out two-syllable words and phrases. *Mama. Liar. Tell them.*

Tess had been ready the night before to come clean about her interview with Patricia. And she would have if Callie hadn't cut out early. Tess didn't think it had been fair of Meg and Lindsey to give her such a hard time. But now, while her pump murmured to her in the quiet bathroom, she worried they'd give her the same treatment once they knew the truth.

Tess looked down at the bottles and decided that was enough for now. A few ounces in each was better than nothing and relieved the tight, swelling pressure that had woken her up, her body unaccustomed to sleeping long stretches without a single feeding or pump session. She detached herself from the machine, transferred the milk into bags, and washed all the pump parts with hot, soapy water. She set the pieces on a towel to dry.

With the milk bags in hand, she headed downstairs to the kitchen and tucked them into the fridge behind glass bottles of pink kombucha, hopefully concealed enough that no one would mistake them for one of Callie's healthy drinks.

It was early, but the coffeepot was already full, and a hearty breakfast spread was laid out on the kitchen island. Bagels, three types of cream cheese, sliced berries, oranges, organic yogurt and granola, local honey. A small square of card stock propped against the fruit bowl read **GOOD MORNING! HELP YOURSELF! XO, C**, marked with a tiny heart.

Tess piled a plate with food and brought it outside along with a mug of coffee. She settled herself at the patio table and smelled the faintest trace of weed in the air. Lindsey, probably. Tess hadn't smoked in years; the last time she'd gotten high had been a few nights before their trip ended, when Zoe shared her stash with Tess while the others were out.

"I need a night off from the bar," Zoe had said as she rolled the joint on the countertop in the rental cottage. "One morning without a hangover would be nice."

"Look at us, detoxing with weed," Tess said.

They smoked out back where passersby wouldn't see. Soon, Tess felt light enough to ask the question that had been nagging her all week.

"You're hiding something, aren't you?"

Zoe crossed her legs and shifted her body away from Tess. But she also let out a laugh like that was the most ridiculous thing Tess could've said.

"What is it?" Tess asked. "You're not pregnant, are you?"

Zoe fixed her with a cynical expression. "You've watched me drink all week."

"Then what is it?"

"I'm not hiding anything," Zoe insisted.

But Tess had been persistent and confident enough in herself back then to keep pushing. She'd prided herself on how well she knew her friends, and Zoe had seemed off all week in little ways. Quieter than usual. Taking off for walks without telling anyone else. Vacantly staring into the distance like she saw something no one else saw.

"Is it work?" Tess asked. "Your parents okay?"

"Everything is fine, Tess. Stop," Zoe snapped.

So Tess had stopped, jarred by the sharpness of Zoe's response. Later, once Zoe was gone, Tess regretted how easily she'd backed down. She knew in her gut she'd been on the brink of learning why Zoe was acting out of sorts. The regret haunted Tess, how easily she had let a potentially important piece of information go free. She'd told Meg about it once, calling and weeping into the phone. *It's all our fault,* Tess had said. And she truly believed it was; they had been bad friends, caring too little about the heaviness Zoe seemed to carry, too self-absorbed to insist on the truth. *Something was up with her and we ignored it.*

But Meg had been stoic, emotionless. *Stop creating problems where there are none,* she had said before hanging up on Tess.

"You're up early," a voice said. She looked up, shielding her eyes from the sun. Callie's mother pulled out a chair and sat down.

"Mrs. Sutter," Tess said.

"Why do you girls still insist on calling me that? Elizabeth, please."

"Sorry. Old habits," Tess said. "That's a pretty necklace."

Elizabeth touched the strand around her neck. She wore a pale-blue dress and tan wedges, her hair curled loosely and sprayed into place. Tess was impressed that she was up and ready for the day so early.

"Thank you, darling. I've had these forever. Pearls are timeless." She eyed Tess's oversize nightshirt. "What are you thinking of wearing for the party?"

Tess picked up her mug of coffee, holding it like a shield. "I had a baby, and none of my old clothes fit quite the same. And I wasn't sure what I *should* wear today."

Elizabeth gave a gentle shake of her head. "I told my daughter it's confusing for guests when two events are combined, but what do I know? I've only hosted and organized hundreds of parties in my lifetime."

Tess held the mug up to her mouth, unsure what to say.

"Anyhow, are you girls happy to be speaking again? It was a shame losing Zoe caused such a rift."

Tess flinched and set the mug down. "The rift wasn't because of Zoe. It was because of Callie."

Elizabeth maintained a steady smile. "But really, it started with the disappearance."

"I mean, sure. That started it. But Callie's interview was the reason we all stopped speaking," Tess said. "Didn't you know that?"

"Honestly, no. But what a strange reason to have a falling-out," Elizabeth said. She straightened a gold bangle on her wrist, then turned to Tess. "What do you think happened to her? Do you think we'll ever really know?"

Tess swallowed the bitterness in her mouth. Before she could answer, the back door swung open and they both turned toward the sound. Callie stood on the threshold, smiling.

"How's everyone?" she asked, eyeing her mother.

"I was just about to get ready for the day," Tess said, relieved for an excuse to exit the conversation.

"Sweetheart," Elizabeth said as Tess gathered her still-full plate of food and half-drunk mug of coffee, "if you need to borrow an outfit for the party, just come find me in the guesthouse. I have plenty of clothes, and I'm sure some of my looser dresses would work on you. Something nice and flowy will flatter your figure just perfectly."

"Mom," Callie said, a downturn in her voice.

"Thanks, Mrs. Sutter," Tess said. "It's kind of you to offer."

Callie opened the door for her and followed Tess inside.

"God, I'm sorry about her," Callie said. She slumped against the wall and rubbed her neck.

Tess sat at the island and picked at her food, her appetite waning. "I can't believe it's been five years," she said as she nudged a kiwi slice around her plate. "Can you?"

"No." Callie glanced toward the stairs, then, in a low voice, asked, "Do you think Meg and Lindsey will ever let me live down that interview? I mean, have *you*?"

"I understand why you did it. And that the whole situation was more manipulated than we realized," Tess said. "If that counts."

"It counts," Callie said.

Tess cleared her throat. She saw her opening, the chance to admit she'd given Patricia an interview. Out of everyone, Callie would understand why Tess had done it.

"Speaking of that—" Tess started, but footsteps on the stairs made her swallow the admission.

Meg and Lindsey appeared in the kitchen a moment later. They joined Tess at the counter, filling plates with fruit and bagel halves, smearing cream cheese on top. Tess watched them move silently while Callie pretended to be fascinated by her espresso machine.

"What time does the party start?" Lindsey asked.

Callie turned around. "Midafternoon. But you three should go enjoy the morning. We rented mopeds so you could get around easily. Hit the beach or go shopping."

"You're not coming?" Tess asked. She couldn't tell them without Callie, and doing it now wasn't an option. Her nerve was gone.

"I can't," she said. "I've already gotten a call that the photo booth people had an issue getting on the ferry. I need to be here to manage the chaos. But please take the mopeds out. There's no reason for you to be cooped up here for the most boring part of the day." She paused. "I know it's an emotional day for all of us, but I promise we'll have plenty of time to honor Zoe later. She would want you to have some fun in her name this morning."

After breakfast, Tess, Meg, and Lindsey ambled up to their rooms, changed into bathing suits, and packed towels into tote bags. They passed around a bottle of coconut-scented sunscreen and slathered it on before slipping out the front door.

The mopeds were lined up outside the garage. Tess had no idea when they'd been delivered to the house or by whom. Things just *happened* here by magic.

"I'm not wearing that," Lindsey declared, removing the black helmet sitting on the handlebars of her bike and dropping it to the ground. "I look stupid in helmets."

"That's a dumb hill to die on," Meg said as she slid hers onto her head.

Tess clipped on her helmet as well and stuffed her bag into the basket on the front of the moped. "Yeah, today's not the day to crack your skull open."

"Let me have a little fun in Zoe's name." Lindsey revved her moped to life. "Where we going? The bluffs?"

They agreed and kicked their bikes on, too. They buzzed down the driveway and out onto the quiet neighborhood road. Soon they were on Mohegan Trail, where the roadside was dotted with cottages and dense beach shrubbery, and not long after, they arrived at the dirt parking lot atop the bluffs. They left the bikes and started on foot down the dusty path to the staircase.

Their sandals crunched over pebbles along the trail, tall shrubs and trees bordering its edges until they rounded a corner and the view opened like a portal. One hundred and forty-one wooden steps descended from the top of the cliff along the side of the bluffs, waves crashing on the rocks below. The ocean spread into the distance, blurring at the hazy horizon and giving the impression there was nothing else out there but water and sky and this hunk of land floating in the middle of it all.

They paused together at the top of the stairs. Meg and Lindsey had to be thinking the same thought as Tess: The last time they were on this stony beach, Patricia Adele had been by their side.

Beach vines reached for their arms over the wooden rails as they made their way down. Every so often, they stopped to make room for a group huffing their way back to the top. At the bottom of the stairs was a steep, sandy drop buffered by boulders. A skinny rope functioning as a handrail helped them down the rest of the way to the beach.

They found a spot in the sand free of large rocks and people, and they spread out their towels in a row. The beach was littered with stones and boulders of various sizes. There were no lifeguards or bathrooms, just expansive views of the Atlantic and the imposing bluffs. The tide was strong, and waves slammed the shore.

"You know what I thought when Patricia found Zoe's sunglasses?" Tess asked, leaning back on her elbows. She squinted at the ocean, the sun glaring off its surface like a mirror.

"That she seemed like a goddamn kid on Christmas morning?" Lindsey asked. "That she knew she had just scooped the story of the year?"

"I thought it meant the rest of the clues the police needed to solve the case would appear quickly. That within days or weeks it would be over, and Zoe would be home."

"Me too," Meg said. "My expectations were too high. Now I think we'll be lucky if we ever know what happened."

Tess peeled a hangnail off the edge of her thumb. The sting was made worse by the salt on her fingertips, her own sweat betraying her. She thought about Callie back at the house, her question that morning.

"Where do you two stand with Callie?" she asked.

"I'm proceeding with caution," Meg said. "I don't like letting down my guard before I know everything. And I just feel like there's still something she isn't telling us."

"If she pulls anything today, it's over for good," Lindsey said. "It's like she wants us to tell her she's a good person and she did the right thing with that interview, but I just can't. I need more time."

"It was just an interview," Tess said, testing the waters. "Maybe we blew it out of proportion."

Meg lifted her sunglasses and stared at Tess with squinted eyes. "Callie lied to us about where she was going, went on live television to talk about her own alibi, and then basically shrugged when asked if any of us three could've been responsible for Zoe going missing. Do you not remember the way Patricia's fans ran with it afterward? You lost your job."

Tess's stomach fluttered. Of course she remembered. Would they see her interview the same way?

"I don't want to talk about this. Can we swim?" Lindsey asked.

Tess said she'd keep an eye on their things while Lindsey and Meg went in the water. They waded out carefully over the slick rocks and into the surf. They jumped waves and floated on the water's surface while Tess watched, thinking there was no way to tell them what she'd done. Speaking to Patricia had been a mistake, and as soon as she got back home after the weekend, she would contact Patricia and tell her to delete the file holding Tess's interview. Make it go away before it turned into a real problem. There was no need for anyone to know it had ever happened.

After an hour, hot and salty and restless, they made their way up the cliff steps. They sped off on their mopeds and took the long way back, zipping downtown and slicing through the crowds on Water Street by the ferry landing and shops. The smell of fried food and salt water filled the air. Other mopeds sped past. They rounded Dodge Street, swinging through the intersection near the historical society where a farmers market was set up on the lawn.

And then they passed the old Ives campground. Lindsey, at the lead, slowed her bike as the entrance flashed by. She gave it a wave of acknowledgment with one hand, and Tess did the same. The wind rushed between her fingers like she was sieving time in her hands.

They didn't stop, though. There was nothing here for them anymore. It was a place lost to the past, the camp as gone as the summers they'd spent sleeping in its cabins, creating art, finding a pack of girls to call their own. They'd taken what they needed from this place—each other—and lost some of it along the way.

Chapter
Twenty-Four

LINDSEY

The house was teeming with activity when they returned from the beach and parked the mopeds outside the garage. A catering van sat with its doors yawning open as white-shirted caterers hauled covered trays and cardboard boxes of produce into the house. Two men in sweat-spotted shirts loaded a photo booth onto a dolly and began wheeling it away. More men hauled lighting equipment and components of a buildable dance floor from their trucks to the backyard.

Lindsey wiped sweat from her hairline. Meg and Tess unclipped their helmets and tossed them into their moped baskets.

"I wasn't expecting all this," Tess said.

"Who knew we needed a dance floor at a memorial?" Lindsey asked.

Inside, Callie was directing the catering team around the kitchen as they set up.

"Oh, you're back," she said, brushing some loose hair off her face. She was in cutoff jean shorts and a simple gray tank top, her face free of makeup. "Can I grab you three for some help with Zoe's table?"

They followed Callie into the backyard to a long table draped in white linen. A vase of fresh hydrangeas and unlit tea lights littered the surface. Callie set her items down: a stack of flyers detailing Zoe's case and who to contact with tips, photos, sketches of her jewelry designs, beaded bracelets she'd made during the first summer together. The Missing poster sat inside a large black frame, and the words ZOE GILBERT, printed on an expensive-looking banner with the date she went missing, hung above it all. Callie handed out the items and instructed them where to put each one. It took only a minute or two, and Lindsey couldn't help but wonder why Callie had bothered to ask for their help when she didn't need it.

"We should have a moment of silence," Callie said, stepping back from the table and giving them a small shrug. "Right?"

They linked hands and went quiet, but around them the party preparations carried on. Drills whirring, metal cookware clanging, a glass shattering as it fell off the bar. A neighbor's lawnmower kicked on, and Callie's mother called for her from the guesthouse balcony.

Meg leaned over to Lindsey. She thought Meg was about to comment on the absurdity of the situation, but instead she whispered a question.

"You said you brought pictures, right?"

Lindsey's heart paused. All she had was the one picture she'd stolen from Fred's boat, still stashed inside her makeup bag. But she didn't want to be the only one not contributing to the display.

"I only have one picture," she whispered back. "I wish I'd brought more."

"I've got you," Meg said. "I have all those albums upstairs."

They let go of each other's hands as Callie scampered off to help the photo booth crew when Elizabeth called her name from across the yard a second time.

"Let's get ready," Tess said, giving a nod toward the house.

Once she heard Meg's shower turn off, Lindsey left her room wearing the black dress Fred liked.

"Knock, knock," she said as she tapped Meg's bedroom door with her elbow. "Are you decent?"

Tess opened her door across the hall, one towel wrapped on her head and another pulled around her body.

"You getting ready together? Can I come, too?" she asked.

Meg opened her door already in a dress, her damp hair wetting the dark blue of the fabric.

"What are you two wearing?" Meg asked. "What's the vibe?"

"Came to ask the same thing," Tess said as she and Lindsey entered Meg's room.

"The vibe," Lindsey said as she put her makeup bag on the bathroom counter and plugged in her curling iron, "is waterproof mascara and old money."

"A classic theme," Meg said.

"I'm between a maternity dress that's too big or a pre-baby dress that's too small," Tess said as she pulled the towel off her head and roughed her hair with it. "Oh, I almost forgot. Mrs. Sutter offered to let me wear one of her baggy dresses should I need something tentlike for my figure."

"Damn," Lindsey said as she unzipped her makeup bag and slid out the photo of Zoe. "Mrs. Sutter has no filter."

Meg leaned over Lindsey's shoulder and looked at the picture. "She looks incredible. Where was this taken?"

Lindsey leaned close to the mirror as she clamped her eyelash curler around her lashes. She looked into her own eyes.

"I can't remember," she said. "I found it recently."

"I'm going to run our things down to the table now before it gets too busy," Meg said. "You have anything, Tess?"

Tess nodded and pulled a comb through her hair. "Just a box of photos," she said. "It's on my dresser."

Meg left the room to bring their photos downstairs. Tess looked at Lindsey in the mirror.

"I shouldn't have brought so many pictures," she said. "What if someone spills something on the table? Or steals them? You were smart to only bring one."

Lindsey wiggled the mascara brush onto her eyelashes. Would she have even thought to bring anything for the memorial had she not found the picture by chance?

"I wouldn't call it 'smart,'" she said. "Your things will be fine, though. Don't worry."

Lindsey shook out her hair and turned to give herself a look from all angles in the mirror. The dress was a little much for the occasion, but it made her look good. And she wanted to look good for what might well be her last day with Fred.

When Meg returned a few minutes later, she reported that around a dozen guests had already arrived at the party.

"How many people are coming to this thing, anyway?" Lindsey asked.

"Probably too many," Meg said. "I'll be surprised if anyone else at the party even knew Zoe."

Tess set her curling iron down on the vanity counter. "Ouch. I should pump before we go out there. Excuse me."

She left the bathroom abruptly, and Meg gave Lindsey a curious look.

"Are you panicking yet?" Meg asked. "Because I am. And clearly, so is Tess."

Lindsey put her makeup away and unplugged the curler.

"We can handle ourselves," she said. "So the crowd at this party-memorial might be absolutely bizarre. We might have to pretend we're having a good time while we're actually dying inside. But we'll get through it."

Meg gave her a grateful smile in the mirror. "Hope so. Meet you down there in a little bit?"

Lindsey nodded, then went back to her room, where she had a handful of text messages on her phone. She hadn't heard it pinging from next door, but Fred had sent her a few questions over the last hour:

What time should he meet her there? Was there a dress code? Did she want to stay with him on the boat that night?

Lindsey started typing when three dots popped up on the screen indicating that he was also typing.

Just getting here, he said. Where should I meet you?

She typed quickly, hoping he wouldn't wander into the backyard and see the memorial before she got to him.

Out front. I'm coming down now.

Lindsey ran down the stairs and out the front door. Fred leaned against one of the trees that lined the driveway, looking down at his phone. He wore a tan linen suit and breezy white shirt, Ray-Bans over his eyes and a straw Panama hat on his head. She watched him for a moment from the front door, then pulled her shoulders back and straightened her dress and walked toward him.

Her footsteps brought his gaze up from his phone.

"Hey, you," he said, smiling as she approached. He pulled her in for a long embrace, and she willed herself not to go stiff in his arms. He smelled like aftershave and soap.

"This place is great," he murmured into her ear. "And you look incredible."

She pulled out of his arms. "The party's around back."

He studied her face. "Everything okay?"

"Of course," she said. "Come on, let's get a drink."

She took his hand and led him past the row of hydrangea bushes into the backyard. Already at least forty guests were milling around. The bartender was mixing signature cocktails, and the band was setting up their instruments. A breezy playlist came from a Bluetooth speaker while the party warmed up.

Lindsey led Fred through the yard. She tried swallowing, but it felt like there was nothing but cotton on her tongue.

"I think I told you this was a housewarming," Lindsey said.

"Isn't it?" he asked.

They were close to the table. Lindsey could see Zoe's face in the photos, her name on the banner.

"It is," Lindsey said as she stopped in front of the memorial. "But our friend went missing five years ago today, so this is for her, too."

She thought she saw surprise catch at the corner of his mouth like a sneer, but it quickly vanished. He removed his sunglasses and squinted at the memorial, then looked at Lindsey.

"You lost a friend? I'm so sorry. I didn't know."

"I never told you," Lindsey said.

He lifted one of the flyers from the table and kneaded the back of his neck as he read it. As if he'd never heard of Zoe Gilbert or seen her face before.

Lindsey hated the crushing sensation in her chest, how it felt like her heart might truly be snapping. Hated that it meant she actually cared about him but couldn't anymore. He'd lied to her face so easily, she'd never be able to trust him again. Wouldn't even be able to pretend to trust him for the sake of making some money.

When he finished, he set the flyer down and looked at Lindsey. She recognized a change in his eyes, as if he was trying to read her.

"I knew Zoe for a long time," Lindsey said. "We met out here at that art camp I told you about." She wished she could retrieve the few personal details she'd told him. Take back the parts of herself she'd given him. "I loved her so much. We were roommates for a long time, too. I just . . . She was a huge part of my life for a long, long time, and when she went missing, I stopped knowing how to be myself. Or maybe I became more myself, but either way, I hate life without her."

She tilted her head back to stop the tears from falling. Fred put his arm around her and kissed her temple.

"Grief is so hard," he said. "I wish you had told me about her sooner."

This sent Lindsey in a new direction—outrage. How dare he? Standing there acting like this was all-new information. She slithered out of his arm and sifted through the photos on the table until she found hers. His.

"I love this picture of her," she said, putting it into Fred's hands. "Don't you?"

He blinked at the photograph, silent. A few long seconds passed.

"Where did you get this?" he asked quietly. "Were you going through my things?"

"Don't spin this," Lindsey said. "The second you saw this table, you had the chance to tell me you knew who she was, but you didn't. That's the real issue here. Why did you have this picture? And those news articles?"

Fred looked past her, as if he wanted someone to help. He sighed and put the picture back on the table.

"I didn't know her," he said. Lindsey stared a hole through him. He put his hands up. "A friend of mine knew her for a short time, and he was obsessed with the case when she went missing. I helped him with some of the research, but I don't even know where those documents are anymore." He paused. "Clearly, somewhere on the boat."

"Is that true?" she asked, more tears welling in her eyes. But this time she couldn't stop them. "Isn't that your boat she's sitting on?"

"Please don't cry," Fred said. "Please. I understand why you're upset, but we can talk about it more later, okay? We don't have to do this now. I'll answer all your questions, but let's just enjoy the party."

Her face was hot, her eyes burning. Before she could answer him, a voice rang out.

"Oh my goodness, hello!" A moment later, Callie's hand was on Lindsey's back. "Welcome, I'm Callie Sutter." She held her other hand out for Fred to shake. "Can I get you a drink and show you around?"

Fred cleared his throat. "We're sort of in the middle of something."

"You have to try the signature drinks we designed for today," Callie went on. "Linds, you don't mind if I steal your date for a few, do you?"

Lindsey shook her head.

Callie smiled and looped her arm through Fred's and steered him in the other direction, casting a quick look over her shoulder at Lindsey, transmitting so much in one glance. *Take a beat. I've got this.*

Lindsey darted into the house and up to the second floor. She found Meg and Tess on the landing about to head downstairs.

"Hey, what's wrong?" Meg asked worriedly when she saw Lindsey's tear-streaked face.

"Nothing," she said. "The guy I told you about. We had some words."

"Asshole," Tess muttered.

"I just need a minute before I go back out there. I have to fix my face," Lindsey said.

Meg and Tess put their arms around Lindsey's shoulders. She swallowed over the persistent lump in her throat. Now that she was cooling off, she was so embarrassed that she wanted to shrink down to the size of a grain of sand and blow away in the wind. Would it really have been so bad if she'd just asked Fred about the articles and the photo when she first found them? She could've given him the benefit of the doubt instead of assuming her discovery was a sign he'd done something terrible.

But Lindsey's ability to be rational when it came to anything related to Zoe had long since been extinguished. And since there had been no simple explanation for what she'd found on the boat, she'd allowed fear to convince her that something was very wrong. She'd been right in feeling scared in the moment, but maybe it was possible she'd misunderstood the whole situation.

She took a breath to relax her nerves, exhaling slowly while Meg and Tess rubbed her back.

"You want to introduce us so I can tell you if he's even worth your tears?" Meg asked.

Lindsey let out an unexpected laugh. "Yes. But I think he is. I think I overreacted."

She excused herself while Tess and Meg went down to the party. In her bathroom, she stared at her red eyes and splotchy skin. The waterproof mascara had failed her and ran in black rivulets down her face. She dabbed the ruined makeup away with a washcloth and started over, blending and powdering until she was back to normal, her moment of vulnerability covered up.

She did the same with the questions itching her brain. *Later,* she promised herself. After the party, she would let Fred explain. She'd go back to the boat with him, apologize for snooping and questioning him, and tell him everything. But only if he was just as honest with her first.

Chapter
Twenty-Five

CALLIE

Lindsey's date said his name was Fred. He was older than Lindsey and good-looking, with an angular face and a furtive expression in his eyes. Callie had intervened in what seemed like the beginnings of an argument—from across the party, she'd noticed the redness in Lindsey's cheeks. So Callie swept in and pulled Fred away for two reasons: She didn't need anyone making a scene today, and she was, after all, a good friend.

"So, how do you and Lindsey know each other?" Callie asked. She handed him an elderflower-and-gin cocktail.

Fred sipped the drink while his eyes roved the party. "I didn't know I was coming to a Sutter party, but I recognize the telltale signs."

"Oh," Callie said, noting the way he sidestepped her question. "You know my parents?"

"Mostly your father, but I've met your mother a few times. It's been a long time, though."

"Sorry to disappoint," Callie said lightly, "but this party is nothing like one of theirs. They're here somewhere; make sure you say hi. I'm sure they'll be happy to catch up."

"Absolutely," Fred said. "Always nice to reminisce."

"Don't be offended if my father doesn't immediately remember you, though. His memory . . . it's just not what it used to be . . ." Callie's voice trailed off.

He frowned. "Dementia is a thief. I'm sorry your family is battling it."

"It is a thief," Callie said. She swallowed and clasped her hands together. "Anyway, Fred, you'll have to excuse me. I should go finish getting ready. But please, find my parents and catch up. It'll make their day to see you."

He thanked her and headed back in the direction he'd last been with Lindsey. Callie hoped he wouldn't find her until they both had cooled off and could keep their drama to a minimum. Once he was gone, she darted back inside through the crushing heat and bustle of the catering crew in the kitchen and found her father halfway up the stairs to the second floor.

"Dad," she said, surprised to see him. "What are you doing?"

"Trying to get to my bed to rest," he said over his shoulder. He trudged slowly. The papery skin on the back of his neck was dry and sprinkled with age spots, and seeing his imperfections up close made her feel as if she was invading his privacy.

"Come on up," Callie said, skirting around him. "How'd you end up over here instead of in the guesthouse?"

He paused and glanced around.

"It looks the same. Must have gotten confused with all the people everywhere."

"No big deal," Callie said, thinking of Fred's perfectly accurate description of dementia: a thief.

Her father followed her to the third-floor master suite, where he took a seat in a plush armchair by the window.

"I just ran into a friend of yours outside. Do you remember someone named Fred?" Callie asked as she sat at her vanity and picked up the curling iron to finish her hair.

He lifted his chin and looked in her direction. "No. I don't think so."

"Oh," Callie said, but she was determined not to let it bother her. How often had she forgotten former interns' names at MindBalm, for example, even though she'd worked with them on a daily basis for months? It was human for names to slip one's mind.

"It was nice of you and Nathan to invite us today," he said as he stared out the window.

Callie misted hairspray around her head. "Why wouldn't we have invited you?"

A flash of a smile lit the corner of his mouth. "Have you met your mother?"

Callie laughed, and just as quickly, her eyes smarted with tears. As long as he could still crack a joke at Elizabeth's expense, the father Callie knew was still in there somewhere. At least she had that.

He stood up from the chair and stretched his arms.

"You going to be okay getting back?" Callie asked as he headed toward the door.

"I guess we'll find out," he said. "Don't worry, I'll be fine."

He closed the door behind him. Callie went into her bathroom to get changed, making sure her sticky bra was positioned correctly and that the dress, with its low back and braided straps, draped just right. Once she was done, she looked out the window and surveyed the party.

Rental tables overlaid in cream tablecloths were flanked by bamboo folding chairs. Arrangements of summer flowers overflowed from pedestal vases at the center of each table. Waiters crisscrossed the yard with trays of drinks and appetizers balanced on upturned palms.

Callie lifted her phone to snap a picture, then turned the camera on herself.

"Hi, friends! Just want to show you my dress," she said to her reflection in front of the full-length mirror. "Unfortunately, I can't link it because it's from a local boutique, but the shoes are from an incredible Portuguese brand, so swipe for those details. Every dollar you spend today on any of my links will go to a very good cause." She posted the video and started a new clip. "My dear friend Zoe Gilbert has been missing for five years as of today. When I moved to Block Island, I knew I wanted to throw a housewarming party. Entertaining is just in my blood. But then I had the idea to give my simple party a real purpose. Instead of just inviting some friends and family over to see our beautiful new home, why not invite them—and all of you—over to see our beautiful new home *and* bring fresh eyes to Zoe's case. Please click the link in my bio to read about Zoe. I've been working on revamping her website to give you the latest information straight from the source. If you or someone you know has any information that might help find her, you can contact our tip line or message me directly." She posted the clip and started one final video. "Check in here throughout the day. It'll be like you're all right here alongside us. Love to you all."

Just as she wrapped up, Nathan opened the bedroom door. He was in the outfit she'd selected for him—a white gauzy top with the sleeves pushed up to his elbows and relaxed faded-red shorts. Coastal, summery, classic.

"I was just on my way to find you," she said.

"They're here," he said, slightly winded, like he'd been sprinting around looking for her. "They're in the office downstairs right now."

Callie's heart quickened. "Already? Okay. Not a problem. Thanks for telling me. Can you keep them inside for a few while I find the girls and tell them?"

Nathan nodded, then left just as quickly as he'd appeared.

Her friends were seated on the outdoor sectional by the stone wall. A large oak tree beside it stretched leafy branches overhead, shading them from the sun.

"You all look so beautiful," Callie said as she perched beside Meg on the arm of the sectional. Lindsey's dress was a little heavy on the cleavage, and Tess didn't look completely comfortable, but at least she hadn't borrowed clothes from Elizabeth. "So, listen. I have a little bit of a surprise."

"A surprise?" Meg asked. "I had a feeling."

"You did?" Callie asked, confused. She was positive Nathan had been able to keep the surprise guests out of sight.

"Just let her finish what she was saying," Tess said.

"What is it?" Meg asked, ignoring Tess. "Is it another interview? For the anniversary? Or are you going to tell us where you really were after we left Zoe on the island?"

Callie laughed. "Wait. What are you talking about? Are you kidding?"

"An interview would make sense," Meg said stiffly. "Patricia shared the first pages of her book with me. She has an eyewitness who contradicts what you said you did after we went home. Maybe you're trying to spin that story in your favor like before."

Callie balked. "Sorry, what? I have no idea what you're talking about. Whoever Patricia's witness is, they're lying."

"I just assumed—"

"That I was doing the same shit all over again?" Callie gave a slow headshake. "That hurts, Meg."

"Did you see if Fred left?" Lindsey asked, as if she hadn't heard the discussion happening in front of her.

"No, he's here somewhere," Callie said with a flap of her hand. "What were you two arguing about, anyway? Can you keep it under control until the party's over?"

Lindsey's eyes flicked back to Callie's. "What's the surprise?"

"It's not an interview. I hope you know I wouldn't do something like that again unless we did it together."

Before she could say more, Tess gasped.

"Zoe's parents," she said as she got to her feet.

Callie sighed. "That's the surprise."

"Why didn't you tell us you were still in touch with the Gilberts?" Meg asked.

Callie furrowed her brow. "I didn't know you weren't. I check in on them a few times a year. None of you keep in touch with them?"

"I thought they didn't want to talk to us," Lindsey said. "I thought . . ."

"That they blamed us for leaving her by herself," Tess said in a hushed voice. "I thought so, too."

"Well, they don't. They never even implied that," Callie said. "I think they were just consumed by grief when Zoe wasn't found, but there's no reason to think they blamed us. I thought it would be special to have them by our sides today."

A quiet moment followed as Nathan and the Gilberts made their way over. Callie worried she'd miscalculated. She'd invited the Gilberts on the assumption that her friends still had some contact with Zoe's parents and would be happy to see them. But now she realized she was the only one who hadn't pulled away from them out of guilt.

"Look who I found!" Nathan said as he approached.

"I'm so happy you could make it," Callie said, giving Zoe's mother, Pearl, a hug first. She smelled warm, like vanilla and home. Pearl and John Gilbert were tall and graceful, with heads of dark hair and deep-blue eyes just like Zoe. She'd practically been a clone of them. Even as an adult, people often confused them for three siblings.

Pearl withdrew a bottle of wine from her bag. "Here, before I forget. Happy housewarming to you two. Your home is incredible." She stepped away from Callie as if pulled by an invisible force to Meg, Tess, and Lindsey. "Oh, I've missed you girls."

She gave them each a long embrace. When it was Tess's turn, Callie watched her squeeze her eyes shut tight, as if this reunion was too much and she might spill over. Lindsey seemed the most nervous to greet them; her shoulders pulled forward into a posture that shrank her. Meg smiled placidly when it was her turn, her eyes locking with Callie's as she hugged Pearl.

John Gilbert straightened the collar of his shirt. "How nice to see the old gang back together."

"Doesn't happen often," Callie said. "But today's an important day."

"You always were so good with rallying the troops," Pearl said. "I'll never forget how helpful you were when we were first looking for Zoe."

"We all did our best to help," Callie said.

She didn't want to take all the credit, but she *had* been the only one to do anything practical in the first hours after they realized Zoe was missing. Printing the Missing flyers, calling the ferry terminal to ask about security cameras in the area, hiring the most successful search-party organizer in the region. All of it for nothing, but still. She had tried. It was more than she could say for her friends. Meg had been paralyzed by panic, while Tess had convinced herself that if she only called Zoe's phone enough times, she'd eventually answer and tell them where she was. Not to mention Lindsey's refusal to make phone calls to Zoe's colleagues and the guy she was dating. *Give me another job,* she'd demanded, as if Callie were the overseer of finding Zoe, responsible for everything while the rest of them could hardly think for themselves.

"We're so grateful for what you're doing here," Pearl said, gesturing around. "Bringing people together today, using your platform for our benefit."

"Your platform?" Meg asked.

Callie met Meg's distrustful tone with a smile. "Yes, my platform. I was going to tell you last night, but the timing wasn't right. You were still . . . settling in. But the reason I combined the housewarming and memorial is *for* Zoe. We have guests coming from every corner of every industry today. People with a lot of collective influence and money. If we want to control the eyes on Zoe's case, and if we want to be in charge of the story, what better way than to gather influential people together in one place and tell them about Zoe? There are millions of people who will see the party today, between all the guests and their collective followers. Millions more than Patricia ever reached on her own. We'll flood social media with Zoe's story via the people I've chosen to invite here today. Instead of her story revolving around what someone thinks the four of us did, it'll revolve around her. The way it always should have."

"This party is so important that people will care about a cold case?" Lindsey asked. "Why didn't they care before? Do they only care if they're impressed enough by how much money you spend on entertaining them?"

Callie felt the swift kick of shame she'd experienced numerous times around Lindsey growing up. Their financial differences pitted them against one another despite how well they got along in other areas of life. Apparently, that aspect of their dynamic hadn't changed.

Pearl reached out and squeezed Lindsey's arm. "I know how you feel. It's hard to accept that people need to be persuaded to care. But a few months ago, one of the parents in our missing-children support group had her daughter's case solved after a video about it went viral," Pearl said, glancing at each of them in turn as she spoke. She smiled nervously. "Maybe it's silly, but it gave us hope. If her child could be found, then why not ours?"

John nodded. "When Callie called us to share the good news about her new home, we told her about the viral video, and she offered to host the memorial here, today. In the hopes that Zoe's case gets traction online, too."

"But her case *had* traction online before," Meg said.

"This is different," Callie said. "These people aren't random nobodies like Patricia. These are trustworthy people in their industries with loyal followings. And we're in control of the narrative because we're inviting them into *our* memorial. And so much has changed online in the last five years. To have her story go viral now is worlds different than when it first went viral. And the people who will see it are different than the people following Patricia. They never wanted to truly find Zoe. They just wanted to play detective."

Callie glanced around the circle. This time, her attempt to do the right thing included all of them. Couldn't they see she was making amends?

Lindsey glowered. "Why didn't you tell us any of this before now?"

Callie held Lindsey's gaze. Lindsey, always pushing back. Always challenging for the hell of it. Some things never changed.

"Because I thought you'd question my intentions if I came out of left field one day with this idea," Callie said. "I didn't think you'd be receptive to anything besides a memorial for Zoe."

"For what it's worth, we think this is a great idea," John said. "Patricia reached out to us about the book. We told her we didn't agree with how she treated you four, and we wouldn't support her work unless she promised new leads and angles. *Legitimate* ones. But we think using social media will be a better way to gather new leads and spread the word."

"We're still undecided about being involved in the book," Pearl said. "Are any of you . . . ?"

"Never," Lindsey said. "We'd never help her. We can't trust her."

"Trust is important," Pearl said. "I always told Zoe, if you have your integrity, you have everything you need."

"Even if she says she's changed, it's hard to take her at her word," Meg said.

"Right," Callie agreed. But even as she said it, a knot of discontent in her stomach pulled tight and transformed into something heavier, darker, like a sinkhole opening. She was thrust back to the days after her interview, misunderstood on a fundamental level by the three people she cared about most in the world. More than her own family, even. Though she wasn't sure she'd ever told her friends outright the depth of her love for them, how crucial they were to her entire existence. She'd always assumed it went without saying that they simply *knew*. But then they were all gone from her life, and Callie realized she had needed them more than they needed her.

"I hate to cut this short," Nathan interjected, "but Callie and I should start making the rounds and say hi to everyone. Would you all excuse us?"

He took her hand and she followed, grateful for once to be led and not have to act for herself.

"Thank you," she said. He gave her a knowing look.

"Let them process everything for a little while," he said.

They made their way around the party, greeted old friends and colleagues from New York whom they hadn't seen in months, chatted with relatives who'd made the trip to scope out their new life. Even some of the neighbors had meandered over.

Soon the hors d'oeuvres ran out and dinner was served; salmon, scallops, and roasted summer vegetables. The caterers assembled a raw bar with five varieties of local oysters nestled in a bed of chipped ice. Guests topped the oysters with cocktail sauce and grated horseradish before sucking them back. Callie joined in and let the slippery, brackish bivalves slide down her throat like a thick mouthful of ocean water. The taste was that of every summer she'd spent on the island. Nostalgic and sharp—the flavor of the past meeting the present.

Dinner wound down, and the sky turned a deep pink and pale blue. Callie slipped away from her table to distribute candles and MindBalm-branded matchbooks for the vigil. Once every guest had a candle in hand, she borrowed the microphone from the band and motioned for the Gilberts and Tess, Meg, and Lindsey to stand with her. They made their way to where she stood at the front of the party, and she handed her phone over to Nathan to live stream her speech to her followers.

"Good evening, everyone," she said into the microphone. "I know we billed this party as a housewarming, but I have a confession. I have another intention for gathering you all here today. You probably noticed the memorial table for our dear friend Zoe Gilbert. Whether you knew her personally or not, her story likely touched you when it first broke five years ago. And maybe you remember how cruelly we—Zoe's best friends—were treated by some in the media following her disappearance, and the wildfire of rumors that spread online. You might even remember my interview and how clumsily I handled it." She paused to smile into the crowd before she said the next part. "Maybe some of you have even wondered if any of the rumors about us were true. Honestly, I would've wondered, too. Here's the truth: The only thing we were guilty of was loving Zoe and not knowing how to carry on without her. That's why, today, we've come together with John and Pearl Gilbert for the first time since Zoe went missing, to ask for your help in finally bringing resolution to her case."

She looked over her shoulder at one of the lighting technicians and gave him a nod. On a white screen behind the drum set, a projected video started to play.

"Please enjoy this short video," Callie said.

The video spliced together a few minutes of VHS home movie clips the Gilberts had provided, plus still images of Zoe through the years and snippets of the news stories that covered her case. There were photos from camp, from their summer trips to the island as adults. A story about Zoe Gilbert that included the people who loved her. All of it played over soft piano renditions of Zoe's favorite songs. At the end, the video listed various ways to contribute financially to her search. A website dedicated to Zoe flashed on the screen.

Callie watched her friends and the Gilberts as the video rolled, their faces lit by light bouncing off the projector screen. Pearl and John had known that she was working on something, but not that it would be a video shown at the party. And her friends, they looked as surprised as Callie hoped they'd be. This was her apology to them. Standing together in front of all these people, in front of Callie's one hundred thousand followers, proclaiming their innocence and showing the world how deeply they *all* wanted answers.

It was what she'd thought she was accomplishing five years earlier.

When the video ended, Callie lit a match and brought the flame to the wick of a candle. She picked up the microphone in her other hand and nodded at her guests. They began lighting their candles, too.

"I'm sure you all know from television shows and true crime podcasts, one of the best ways to revive a cold case is with money and leads," Callie said. "Think of the candle you're holding in your hand as one of those two things. Individually, it seems like nothing much. But if we put all our candles together, we might make a light bright enough to solve this case. Ask yourself how you can help. Do you have a platform we can use to spread the word? Can you circulate this video and help Zoe's case go viral for the right reasons? Do you have a tip that might assist detectives? Or can you generously donate money to the reward fund? Spend some time at Zoe's table tonight. It's right over there; you can't miss it. Take a flyer, take pictures of everything, share with your followers, and take action before you get on the ferry to go home. We can have a good time at this housewarming while also doing some good in the world, right?" She smiled again at her guests. "Okay, that's enough from me. I'll let someone else talk now."

Pearl took the microphone. "Thank you, Callie. Thank you, everyone, for being here. This means the world to us, really. We miss our girl every day and we just—" Pearl stopped short, shook her head. She pursed her lips together. John took the microphone with one hand and, with his other, rubbed small circles on his wife's back.

"We're grateful Zoe had a friend like Callie," he said, then quickly motioned at the others. "And all of you. She was an only child by birth—something she never forgave us for—but you four were her sisters in every sense of the word. Thank you again for being here, everyone."

Callie took the microphone back in hand. She held it out for her friends, but they all shook their heads. She raised her brows, insisting. But still, they made no move to take the microphone. Instead, they were distracted by something in the yard. Callie followed their line of sight, but the professional lighting was trained in Callie's direction, making it difficult to see beyond the glare.

"Okay," Callie said, regrouping. "Let's take a moment of quiet reflection for Zoe. Then let's celebrate her beautiful legacy."

The guitarist took his cue and began to strum a wistful tune. Callie replaced the microphone on its stand and slid beside Lindsey.

"What are you looking at?" she whispered into Lindsey's ear.

"She's here," Lindsey said in a barely audible voice.

Then Callie saw what Lindsey saw, a sight she couldn't believe was real. After all these years, there she was. In the flesh, back with them where it all began.

The guitarist came to the end of the song, and silence settled over the party. Guests looked to one another and then to Callie for what to do next, no one wanting to be the first to blow out their candle.

Callie cued the band. "Play something happy," she commanded and walked off.

A new song filled the air as she stalked across the yard to the memorial table.

"I don't remember inviting you," Callie said with a steady voice.

Patricia closed a photo album she'd been looking through. "Great speech. I think what you're doing is admirable."

"Why are you here?"

"To see if we can talk," Patricia said.

They stared each other down for a few seconds before other guests approached the memorial table as Callie had requested.

"Can we take this somewhere else?" Callie asked.

"Of course," Patricia said.

Callie led her to the outdoor sectional where her friends and the Gilberts had gathered. Patricia halted next to Callie.

"John. Pearl," she said, a trace of an almost-apology in her tone. "I didn't realize you'd be here."

"Patricia," Pearl said with a downturn in her voice. "Please tell me you're not here to harass the girls."

Patricia stepped forward. "No, of course not. But I'm writing your daughter's story. Shouldn't I be here?"

"Not like this," John said. "Not uninvited. Please. Move on. If you're going to do this work, do it properly. Give us something concrete. Leave these four alone."

Patricia's face hardened. "I *am* doing it properly. I'm working on some very concrete angles, but I still have questions for them. What am I supposed to do if I have witnesses who contradict some of the stories your daughter's friends have told me? There are inconsistencies in the timeline that might be nothing—or they might be everything. It's not my fault that those inconsistencies exist. I can't write a book without tying off loose ends."

"Don't you understand that your behavior alienated Zoe's best friends?" Pearl asked. "Can you blame them for not wanting to have anything to do with you? You could've had their help if you'd approached this differently from day one."

Patricia paused and glanced at Tess. "You didn't tell them?"

"I—" Tess started.

"They don't know?" Patricia asked. "About your interview? It's not that *none* of them will answer my questions. It's that only one of them will, but she doesn't have the answers I need."

"What's she talking about?" Callie asked.

Meg swung her head toward Tess. "When?"

"Just the other day," Patricia said. "She was willing to sit down with me at her house. I thought you'd at least tell them about it."

Callie pressed a hand to her collarbone, her pulse thudding under her palm. "Just stop."

"Patricia, it's time to leave," Pearl said, holding her hands together. "We'll revisit this later. Today is the wrong day."

"I just want to know why Lindsey and Callie lied about their whereabouts the day Zoe went missing," Patricia said, a desperate twinge in her voice. "I can't move on until I understand."

"Get out right now," Callie said, enraged. "I'll call the police."

"She's leaving," John said as he took Patricia by the elbow and pulled her away. Pearl apologized and ran to follow her husband, the three of them vanishing into the shadows along the side of the house.

"Did you really talk to her?" Lindsey asked Tess. "After everything, you talked to *Patricia*?"

"Behind our backs," Meg said flatly.

"There's so much more to it. I don't know— I need to pump," Tess said. "I'm so sorry."

"Tess, wait," Callie started to say, but Tess was already rushing off in the opposite direction of Patricia and the Gilberts, soon swallowed up by the party.

"Did you know?" Meg asked Callie, more of an accusation than a true question.

"Does it matter?" Callie said icily. "Instead of immediately punishing her, can you consider for one second why she might've felt compelled to do it? Give her the benefit of the doubt? Not that you were ever very good at that."

"Come on," Meg said to Lindsey, turning and walking off.

The band was in the middle of a buoyant pop song, something sunny and carefree. Lindsey hesitated, her eyes locked on Callie's, and Callie hoped that maybe she'd gotten through to her.

But then Lindsey followed after Meg. And Callie was once again abandoned in the wake Patricia Adele.

Chapter
Twenty-Six

TESS

Tess's vision blurred as she elbowed her way through the crowd. The band was playing some sickly-sweet song about love, and it only made her feel worse. She moved swiftly in case anyone was following; even if Callie stopped her, she wouldn't be able to explain herself. The humiliation ran too deep for words.

She slipped into the house via the kitchen, hurried past the clanging of pots and running water as the caterers cleaned up from dinner, and went straight out the front door without even considering going upstairs first.

Their voices came from the far end of the front yard. John and Pearl arguing with each other, just the two of them. Patricia was gone, but Tess couldn't face them, couldn't apologize enough for the years she'd cowardly avoided them, thinking they hated her.

A queasy sensation roiled through her stomach, and her mouth filled with saliva. She needed to get away. The party was too loud, too invasive. Everything was too much.

Tess ran down the driveway, her sandals slapping her feet. She ripped them off and threw them aside, then ran faster, barefoot, until she reached the road. The neighborhood was eerie in its stillness. The sun had nearly set, casting long shadows against the shingled houses and wavering sea grasses.

She heard crunching behind her and wheeled around.

"Hey, calm down," Patricia said.

"What are you doing?"

"I'm waiting for a ride," she said, looking down at Tess's bare feet. "What's going on there?"

Tess ignored her. "I rescind my words. The whole thing. I know you just want the part that implies I don't trust them, but I don't want you to use any of it. You don't have my permission." Patricia was unreadable in the darkness. Tess couldn't stand being near her another second. "You hear me? I don't care if you take me down with them. I shouldn't have let you scare me into talking to you the first place."

And then she ran.

She ran until her lungs felt like they might burst. Her legs quivered under her, and she eventually slowed to a walk, all the muscles in her body rebelling against the unexpected burst of activity. Her breasts ached; she needed to pump soon, but going back to the house wasn't an option. She couldn't face them—she'd deal with discomfort instead.

Tess followed the curve of the quiet road, passing a single moped parked on the shoulder. The driver stood in the scrubby overgrowth, photographing the setting sun, and didn't notice Tess pass by.

Up ahead she saw the turnoff for the Mohegan Bluffs and took off jogging again, breathing through the fire in her lungs and the soreness in her feet. The small parking area was empty. No mopeds or bikes, no signs of life. Tess ran down the path to the top of the stairs, where the trail opened high atop jagged cliffs and the swelling ocean. The sun had set over the far lip of the bluffs in a final burst of color against the dark sky. The uppermost portion of the meandering staircase was faintly illuminated, but the lower half and the stony beach below were dark. From up high, Tess couldn't tell which way the ocean was moving, whether she was entering a rising or falling tide, but she started down the steps regardless.

She paced herself but quickly felt the momentum created with each drop of her foot. Like dominos falling. Like all the pieces that knocked into place following a single choice, then another, and another. Down, down, down. Zoe staying behind. No one knowing where she was. Patricia obsessing about the mystery of it all. One thing after another, a knotted string of circumstances. But every string had an end. She hoped this one did, too.

At the bottom, Tess paused. Earlier, in the daylight, while wearing shoes, the sand and boulders had been difficult enough to contend with. But barefoot in the dark? She would just take her time.

Waves crashed and receded at a steady cadence. Tess gripped the timber railing. With a clap of despair, she remembered a night at camp when they'd snuck away and sprawled out on the dewy grass down the street at the Southeast Lighthouse. They'd passed around warm bottles of beer stolen from a stranger's beach cooler earlier that afternoon. Lindsey rolled a joint. In general, an unremarkable night. And yet, the memory of it endured like other details that struck Tess out of nowhere, these glimmers of the past. The perfect white crescents at the base of Zoe's nails. Her hair dark and thick as a moonless night. The slice of stomach always on display in her cropped shirts. Her teeth a little crooked. Everything about her slightly off-kilter, perfectly tilted in its own way.

Tess slinked down the platform and onto the steep path, her feet scrambling for purchase against the slick ground. She realized too late she'd made a mistake.

She slid, all sense of balance gone. Her body momentarily felt like it belonged to someone else as she fell through the air. She aimed for the ground with her feet but came down too fast, too awkwardly. A sharp fire in her foot and then her ankle rolling away from the pain, only for it to twist unnaturally, overextended in the wrong direction.

She tried to move, but the pain shot up her leg and burst like electricity. She angled her leg and foot the other way and saw a dark streak against the pale skin of her foot, a gash from a shard of glass now winking at her in the dark. And the ache inside her ankle bone throbbing a warning not to even try to put pressure on it.

The pain brought tears to her eyes. A sob was lodged so deep inside, it seemed impossible it would ever make its way out. But then Tess opened her mouth and released something primal, the wounded animal inside her finally snapping. Screaming.

At the shard of glass in the sand, danger hidden in plain sight.

At Patricia for commodifying their loss.

But mostly at herself, for losing her friends all over again.

Tess pulled her good leg up so she could rest her forehead on her sandy knee. She listened to the tide washing up on the beach and accepted that, eventually, it might come up high enough to snatch her. She had walked right into its grasp, after all, and would have to spend the night out there alone, unable to make it back up the stairs unless she went on her hands and knees. And even then, she risked falling or injuring herself further. The smartest thing to do would be to stay and wave down the first beachgoers who descended the staircase once the sun rose again. But right now, she had nothing. No cell phone or way to call for help. Just her pain and a hungry tide.

Chapter Twenty-Seven

MEG

"He must have left," Lindsey said. "Or he's here and avoiding me. Not sure which is worse."

Meg and Lindsey had been sitting at a table littered with empty cocktail glasses and abandoned handbags for what felt like hours, but really, it had only been thirty minutes. It was almost nine and the party hadn't thinned. The dance floor was choked with guests, the bartender still pushing out drinks. The band hadn't stopped playing, and now Callie floated around the party, smiling as though nothing had happened.

"Did you try calling him?" Meg asked.

Lindsey wrinkled her nose. "God, no. You know, it's probably for the best. A clean break is easier."

But Lindsey scanned the party expectantly even as she said this.

"Linds, what happened?"

"It was stupid." She shifted in her chair opposite Meg. "How long does it take Tess to pump?"

"She's not still pumping," Meg said. "Would *you* want to face us right now if you were her?"

"Hard to say. I wouldn't have done what she did," Lindsey said.

Meg leaned back in her chair and crossed her arms. She still couldn't believe it was Tess who'd gone behind their backs to give an interview this time. Tess, who had invited Meg to her house and been her wingwoman in confronting Blake. Tess, who'd sat with her and Lindsey for an hour on the ferry, and who'd spent that very morning on the beach with them.

"I don't know," Meg said. "We should check on her. Make sure she's okay."

The band kicked off another song as the lead singer passed props into the crowd. Feather boas, top hats, plastic instruments. Callie reached for a maraca and shook it overhead, swiveling her hips to the music.

"Why didn't she tell us about it?" Lindsey asked. "This is what happened: Callie's interview saved her from the same level of shit the rest of us received, and Tess wanted to save her own ass the same way this time around." She took a long sip, finishing her drink. "I'm not necessarily saying I blame her, since she's got a kid to think about now, but at least be honest, you know?"

Meg felt a dull ache behind her eyes and forehead. She kneaded the muscles of her shoulder with her hand to free some of the tension gathering in her body. Lindsey had a good point. Self-preservation could be a powerful motivator. Lying might've been a small price for Tess to pay if it meant she and her family could dodge public scrutiny.

A courtesy they never gave to Callie when she'd made the same choice. Meg sighed. Maybe they were hypocrites.

Lindsey uncrossed her legs and dropped the empty glass from her hand. It thudded against the tabletop and rolled to its side.

"He didn't leave," she said. "Oh God. He's coming over here. Don't look; he'll know I'm talking about him."

Meg couldn't help but smile. "But you are. You really like him, don't you?"

Lindsey gave her a withering look. "I know he's about to dump me. Stay with me, please."

"I'm not going anywhere," Meg said.

She watched Lindsey track Fred's movements through the yard. After a few moments, Meg felt his presence behind her.

"Lindsey," a man's voice said. "Can we talk a minute?"

A chill spilled over Meg's body. She knew that voice. It was familiar, yet not. She turned, her eyes falling on Fred's face.

"Cameron? What are you doing here?" Meg asked.

She must be mistaken. Or he had a twin brother named Fred that Lindsey somehow knew. But Meg quickly brushed that idea aside; he was without a doubt Cameron.

His posture stiffened. "It's Fred," he said, barely glancing at her.

Meg whipped her head back to Lindsey. "He's the guy on Patricia's list, the one I met with. He told me his name is Cameron Oakes."

Lindsey opened her mouth, but Fred cut in before she could say anything.

"Okay, hold on," he said. "My full name is Cameron Frederick Oakes, but I go by Fred with everyone in my life. Since you emailed looking for Cameron, it was easier to go by my first name than explain the nuances of my nickname to a stranger."

"He knew Zoe," Meg said in a voice meant only for Lindsey. "Did he tell you that?"

"You *knew* her, or you knew *of* her?" Lindsey asked him. The question sounded like a kind of crossroad.

"Can we talk privately?" he asked.

"Answer the question." Lindsey's chin quivered, and Meg watched her ward off tears with anger. "Fine, don't answer me. But I guarantee you we're going to compare stories, and the second those stories don't match, I'll know you're full of shit. Was anything you ever said true?"

His shoulders dropped. "Lindsey, please. Let's have an adult conversation about this."

"About what, exactly?" She laughed humorlessly. "You weren't helping a friend keep up with Zoe's case, were you? You knew her."

Meg felt the situation slipping out of control.

"Lindsey, let's go inside," she said.

Fred stepped closer to Lindsey and lowered his voice. "I had no idea you two were friends until I looked into your work history and found the articles about her case. I printed out a few to read, and put them in a book to get them out of the way before you came by one night. At that point, I thought you'd be embarrassed or mad at me, so I pretended I didn't know." He shook his head. "I wasn't exactly expecting any of this today; otherwise I would've told you sooner."

"Where did the picture of Zoe come from, then?" Lindsey asked.

"What picture?" Meg asked. But as soon as the words left her mouth, she understood—the lone photo Lindsey had in her possession for the memorial. A photo Meg had no memory of ever seeing before. She tried to recall the details now, but she couldn't conjure much. She'd need to find it and take a better look.

"She gave it to me," Fred said. "But it was a long time ago."

"You kept it," Lindsey said. "You must have really liked her. Or did you love her?"

Meg held her breath at this question. Zoe had never once said the name Cameron *or* Fred to her. Was it possible Zoe could've been in love with him?

"What do you want me to say? I apologize for having feelings for someone before I met you?" Fred said. "This wasn't even supposed to go this far between you and me."

Meg wanted to slap the non-apology off his lips. Lindsey looked at Meg, a flick of her brows telling Meg she needed help.

"He lied to you," Meg said. "So, for the record, no, I don't think he was worth your tears."

Fred made a sound of impatience. "I'm leaving unless you want to talk."

Lindsey stood up. "You have two minutes."

"I'll find you," Meg said. A promise that Lindsey wouldn't be alone. "I'm going to check on Tess, but I'm coming right back out here. Don't go far."

Meg watched Lindsey follow Fred until she lost sight of them in the midst of the crowd. Lindsey could absolutely handle herself, but worry coursed through Meg's stomach once she was gone.

She stopped at the memorial table to find the photo, a small part of her hoping she would see an answer in that small rectangle. Two girls, much younger than Meg, stood in front of the table, taking selfies with their phones.

"Post it with the Zoe hashtags so you get more engagement," one of them said to the other before they wandered away.

Meg's hands shuffled the papers and pictures spread on the table until she found the one Lindsey had brought. It was better quality than a cell phone offered. Sharper, brighter. Taken with a real camera. Zoe had liked him enough to give him this photo of her. He'd liked her enough to hold on to it for at least the last five years.

Meg hated feeling jealousy, but there it was. Licking at her heart like a tiger lapping at its paws.

She turned, head swimming, and went into the house to find Tess. The din from the party was blissfully muted as soon as the door closed behind her. The kitchen was empty and spotless, all traces of the catering company gone. Meg bounded up the stairs to the second floor, calling Tess's name as she went.

"Can I come in?" Meg asked the closed door to Tess's room. No response. She knocked again. "Tess? It's just me."

Silence.

Meg tried the doorknob, expecting it to be locked, but it gave way as she turned it. The door swung inward, revealing a room lit only by light coming from the party outside. The bed was neatly made but empty. Tess's wallet sat on the dresser. Meg peered into the attached bathroom, dropping the photo on the vanity as she bent to inspect the components of Tess's breast pump set out on a towel. Meg looked closely, but there was no sign of moisture. The pump hadn't been used or cleaned in a while.

Meg went back to the hallway and pulled her own bedroom door open. Dark and empty, as she'd left it. Then she entered Lindsey's room, to the same end. She peeked into the empty fourth room. No sign of life.

Meg stood at the bottom of the stairs to the third-floor suite and called up into the dark.

"Are you up there? Tess?"

No response. Meg went back to her room and pulled her phone from the charging cable to call Tess. A moment later, a tinkling chime came from the next room over. She followed the sound and found the ringing phone under a shirt on the bathroom floor.

When Meg ended the call on her phone, the ringing stopped. The silence that followed had a frightening, familiar quality to it. Tess hadn't come up to her room. She had to be somewhere—just not here.

Back outside, the band was playing a slow song, and couples were turning on the dance floor, bodies pressed close. Callie and Nathan swayed together, unbothered. John and Pearl were out there, too. Her head rested on her husband's shoulder, their clasped hands by her chest.

Meg passed them all and went in the direction she'd seen Lindsey go with Fred, past the memorial table and the pool, around the side of the house. They were sitting on the front steps, the lantern overhead illuminating them.

"Hey," Meg said pointedly. "I need you, Linds."

Lindsey stood up, brushed the back of her dress, and left Fred without another word. He went inside through the front door.

"Are you okay?" Meg asked. "What happened?"

Lindsey waved a hand. "He apologized up and down. Not just for the name thing—which is kind of my fault, I guess—but everything."

"None of this is your fault."

"He told me his last name the first time we met," Lindsey said. "I forgot, and honestly, I didn't care. We weren't supposed to want to know things like that."

"Was he ever planning to tell you he knew Zoe?" Meg asked.

Lindsey sighed deeply. "He said he didn't know how to bring it up after he made the connection between me and Zoe, and he was really caught off guard when he found out this was her memorial. I think eventually he was going to tell me."

"They were dating, weren't they?" Meg asked. "When I met with him, he made it sound casual. But it was more serious, wasn't it?"

"He said it started off casual and got more serious, but she pulled away from him a few weeks before she disappeared. He didn't know why."

"The situation she told me she was worried about," Meg said. "He didn't know what it was, either?"

"He didn't know what I was talking about." Lindsey looked straight at Meg. "I want to believe this was just a huge misunderstanding and he's genuinely sorry about lying to me. But I need you to tell me if that's stupid. Be honest."

"I think you need to trust your own instincts on this one," Meg said.

Lindsey groaned. "I don't know how to." She nodded toward the house. "What's Tess doing in there?"

Meg wanted to understand Lindsey's relationship with Fred and had so many questions for her, but not now.

"She's not in the house."

"Where is she?" Lindsey asked.

"Don't know."

"Maybe she left?" Lindsey pulled her phone out of her small handbag and tapped the screen. "I'll text her."

"If she left, she went without her phone and wallet," Meg said. "Everything's still in her room except her. Even her pump."

Lindsey's finger went still. "Okay. That's weird. But we're on an island; she can't just disappear—" She stopped short, her face paling. "I didn't mean to say that."

"We should have Callie get on the mic and ask if anyone knows where she went."

"Tess would hate all that attention," Lindsey said. "She's around here somewhere."

They combed through the party, searching the dance floor and the pool and bar. Lindsey climbed over the stone wall and poked around the neighbor's yard, and Meg knocked on the guesthouse door, but no one answered.

They made their way back around to the front and down the driveway this time, calling Tess's name.

"What's that?" Meg asked, pointing to something on the ground ahead of them. It was flat, with a shimmer to it.

As they drew closer, the object took form: a pair of sandals.

"Are these hers?" Meg asked as she picked them up. Small gems across the top glinted.

"Pretty sure they are," Lindsey said. She walked to the end of the driveway and looked one way up the street, then turned her head the other way. "What are *you* doing out here?"

"Is she okay?" Meg asked as she jogged over to Lindsey.

But Lindsey wasn't talking to Tess.

"I'm waiting for a taxi to drive by. Is that okay with you?" Patricia asked. She was sitting on the grass by the side of the road, her phone resting on her thigh. "My battery died. I can't even call for a ride, and since I was *kicked out*, I can't exactly ask to borrow a phone."

"Have you seen Tess?" Meg asked.

"Can I borrow your phone?" Patricia asked.

Meg heard an offer in the question. A phone call in exchange for information. Which meant she had something to give—and had probably seen Tess.

"Which way did she go?" Meg asked as she handed her phone to Patricia.

Patricia dialed a number and, as it rang, gestured down the road out of the neighborhood.

"Yeah, hi. Can I get a taxi, please?" Patricia said into the phone. Once she'd arranged the ride, she hung up and gave the phone back to Meg.

"We need the mopeds; we should look around, and it'll be faster on wheels," Meg said to Lindsey. They ran back up to the house. "I'll get Callie. You get the keys."

Lindsey agreed, and they split up.

Around back, Callie was holding court by the pool, a group of people laughing at something she had just said.

"Callie, sorry," Meg said, offering a tepid smile to the people staring at her with displeased expressions. "Can I steal you for a minute?"

"Not right now," Callie said.

"It's important."

Her tone caught Callie's attention. She excused herself and followed Meg to the front yard, where Lindsey was returning from inside the house with moped keys in hand.

They explained the situation to her. Callie listened, and when they were done, she clipped a helmet on her head. Meg and Lindsey climbed onto their bikes and started them up. The motor thrummed under Meg's thighs as she left the driveway and turned onto the road behind Lindsey and Callie. Their headlights sliced the darkness ahead.

Callie led them through her neighborhood, the trio pausing every so often to call Tess's name. After a few minutes combing the residential streets, they pulled over.

"How far could she have gone?" Callie asked. "Should we just keep going until we find her? Should we ask around?"

"We should keep going," Meg said.

They rode downtown, slowing as they hit the main drag and pulled into the ferry landing parking lot. They split up on foot to check inside the restaurants that were still open, holding up their phones to show a photo of Tess from earlier in the evening.

"Have you seen this woman?" Meg asked nearly every person she passed, but no one recognized Tess, and no one claimed to have seen her.

They regrouped again at their bikes and rode toward the other side of the island. The road took them past the old Ives Art Camp entrance, where they stopped, idling in the middle of the desolate, unlit road.

"She wouldn't have come here," Lindsey said.

"You're right," Callie said. "It's too far from the house on foot. Where else would she go, though? Did she get a ride?"

Meg shut her eyes, conjuring all the old nooks and crannies of the island, places she hadn't thought about in years. Her mind brought her back to earlier that morning—the bluffs. The lighthouse. Two places walkable from Callie's house, a short bike ride from the camp. She gave the idea to Lindsey and Callie.

"That seems dangerous," Callie said. "I can't see Tess going to the bluffs alone at night."

"We used to go all the time at night," Lindsey said.

They weren't supposed to leave the camp at night, but that never stopped their teenage recklessness. They'd been unafraid of danger catching them as they ran down the rambling staircase and swam against the dark riptides.

Leaving the camp behind, Callie and Lindsey seemed like shadows of the kids they had once been. Meg could still imagine them as teenagers. And if she tried hard enough, she could almost convince herself they were all still together. Sixteen, seventeen years old again, searching for trouble, hungry for adventure. The way one half-baked idea to see if the lighthouse was haunted snowballed fast between the five of them until they were at the bottom of the bluffs, swimming in dark, choppy water, the feeling of invincibility coursing through them.

Reality tilted. Time was untenable. They were adults, but somehow still those girls, too. They were teenagers meeting for the first time in an old wooden cabin, Callie's face a puffy mess as she crashed into their lives. They were twenty, separated by college, making a pact to spend a week on the island together every summer. They were twenty-nine, searching for Zoe, watching Patricia Adele lift a pair of heart-shaped sunglasses from the sand, the catalyst for everything.

The thick summer air and dark, gauzy sky wrapped around them tonight just as it had countless times before. Just as it had when Zoe vanished. Just as it would in the future.

Meg swallowed as they neared the bluffs, a familiar, old fear flooding her body. History never repeated itself exactly the same way twice, did it? Especially not in the same place, with the same people. This time had to be different—she didn't have the heart to imagine it any other way.

Chapter
Twenty-Eight

LINDSEY

The moped shuddered as Lindsey jerked it to a stop. Meg and Callie slowed on either side of her in the small dirt lot and killed their engines, too. They listened to the night, but the only sound was the roar of the waves below the bluffs.

They left the mopeds and walked the darkened trail to the staircase. The brush along the edges of the path seemed too still, too dense. Lindsey's eyes had adjusted to the low light but still played tricks, the corners of her vision telling her there was movement just out of range. She heard a stick snap.

"Are there coyotes on the island?" she asked.

"No," Meg replied. "I don't think so."

"I can't believe the things we used to do," Lindsey said. "We had no concept of danger."

"We didn't know any better," Callie said. "We had to grow into our fear."

At the top of the staircase, they called out for Tess. Waves battered the rocks below, rhythmic as a heartbeat. They tried again, louder this time. Still no response but the wind and water.

"What do we do now?" Meg asked. "Go back to the house and wait?"

Lindsey felt something she couldn't explain, a disturbance carried on the air. Not quite the same as the fear she'd felt walking the dark trail, thinking unseen danger lurked nearby. But an uncanny awareness that they weren't done yet. The only other time she'd had such a prominent feeling had been when they were searching for Zoe. She'd known in her bones they hadn't looked hard enough.

"Not yet," she said. "We should check the beach."

"It wouldn't make sense for her to go down there," Callie said. "It's so dark."

"I won't sleep if I don't check the beach. You can stay here if you want, but I'm going," Lindsey said.

Meg looked up at the sky; Lindsey knew what she was thinking. The full moon five years earlier, the final night with Zoe. The way the island had been their sanctuary for half their lives, until suddenly it wasn't. And now they were in the same position they'd been in when they last left this place together: down by one, worried, searching.

"No, you're right. We should check," Meg said. "And if she's not down there, we'll go back to the house and get some help. But we should check first."

Lindsey descended the stairs quickly, her cheap sandals barely padding her footfalls. Each step echoed through her knees. Meg and Callie followed behind.

Lindsey reached the bottom and called Tess's name, breathing heavy, squinting into the night.

All at once, they caught sight of something. A silhouetted figure sitting upright on a rock.

"Right there," Lindsey said as relief flooded through her. Relief at finding Tess, but also relief that she had trusted her instinct and it had been right.

They scaled the sloping ground carefully, one at a time, scrambling to Tess's side, calling to her as they approached. She didn't look over her shoulder at the sound of them. Just sat facing the ocean, one leg stretched out long and the other bent so her chin rested on her knee.

Callie crouched in front of Tess and took her face in her hands and turned her head side to side.

"Are you okay?" Callie asked.

"I'm fine," Tess said.

"Oh my God, is that blood?" Lindsey asked. She bent down for a closer look at a dark streak on the rock. "Did you hurt yourself?"

Meg fumbled with her cell phone, holding it above her head. "I don't have any service down here," she said. "Shit."

"Tess," Lindsey said firmly. "I asked you a question."

"I said I'm fine," Tess repeated. Callie let go of Tess's face and shot Lindsey a look that something was wrong.

"Her foot is bleeding," Callie said. She stood up and tore a thick strip of material off the bottom of her dress. "Here, Lindsey, wrap that around the cut as tight as you can."

Lindsey took Tess's injured foot into her lap. The blood was tacky, the cut angry and sandy. She swallowed and quickly wrapped the fabric around the slice in Tess's foot.

"Stop helping me. You didn't have to look for me," Tess said, pulling her foot away from Lindsey.

"Are you for real?" Lindsey asked, gesturing at Tess's foot. "It's a damn-good thing we looked for you. What exactly was your plan?"

Tess's face went slack. Her voice cracked. "Just go back to the party."

Callie softened her tone. "Tess, stop. Did you hurt anything else besides your foot? Did you hit your head? Because if you did, we need to get you to the medical center."

"It's just my foot," Tess said.

"We went all over looking for you. You have no phone. You're not even wearing shoes," Lindsey said, disbelief outweighing her concern. "What were you thinking?"

Tess bowed her head and covered her face with her hands. Her hair fell like a curtain around her cheeks.

"We were just worried," Callie said softly. "What happened?"

"You could've just told us the truth," Meg said. "So you gave Patricia an interview. Okay. Lindsey and I should've given you a chance to explain. Right?"

Meg raised her eyebrows at Lindsey.

"Right," Lindsey said.

"She should see a doctor in case that cut needs stitches. It might get infected. You'll need a tetanus shot," Callie said.

"We should've given you the chance to explain, too," Lindsey said to Callie. "You and Tess were afraid of what would happen if you didn't talk. Can we all agree on that?"

They each murmured their agreement.

"Can you get up?" Lindsey said as she held out a hand for Tess.

Tess hesitated, then shifted her body. She gasped.

"I can't put much weight on my foot," she said. "I twisted my ankle when I stepped on the glass."

Lindsey grasped Tess by the hand and forearm. Callie hooked her arm under Tess's other side. They helped her up onto her good foot. Her other leg was bent at the knee as she hopped, with their help, to the base of the stairs.

"Meg, follow us up in case she needs support from behind. Go slow. If anyone needs a break, just say so," Callie ordered.

Together they moved as one, negotiating the stairs methodically. Tess hopped in step with their support.

"Today's been a disaster," Callie said after a few slow minutes. "I should've told you the Gilberts were coming. And that I was going to use the party as a way to amplify Zoe's case. I just didn't want any of you to be scared off. We had to do it together this time. I should have told you sooner, though." She paused and glanced at Lindsey. "Did you ever find Fred?"

"Yeah. *Fred*," Lindsey muttered as they started up the next step, carefully balancing Tess between them. "Funny story. Meg met him the other day as *Cameron*."

Meg explained the list of names, how she'd gotten a hold of it and reached out to some people, including Fred; how she and Tess had even hunted down Blake.

"God, Blake," Callie muttered. "I always thought there was something off with that guy. Why's Fred on a list with Blake, though? Zoe knew him, too?"

"Apparently," Lindsey said. "They were together that summer. He says he hadn't seen her in weeks before she went missing, though."

"*Together* like . . . dating?" Callie asked. "I thought she was back together with Blake."

"I think there was some overlap," Lindsey said. "I think she withdrew from Fred when she got with Blake."

"So you both dated this Fred guy," Tess said. "What are the odds of that?"

"Listen," Lindsey went on, "I need to get something off my chest about Blake. Please don't judge me for this."

She told them the same story she'd confessed to Meg that morning. Her longtime, ill-fated crush on him, drinking too much that first night back, going to his place afterward.

"Then you weren't even at your apartment that night," Callie said. "You said you didn't know if Zoe came home because you were sleeping—but you weren't even there?"

"I wasn't."

"So maybe she did go back to the apartment," Tess said, a trace of betrayal in her voice. "She could have gone home, packed some things, and left on her own, and we'd never know for sure."

"I guess," Lindsey said faintly, feeling exposed and vulnerable. Even if they hated her for it, at least they knew the truth and she could stop carrying the weight of her deceit. "I don't think she came home, though. In my heart, I don't think she ever left this island."

"I think you're right," Callie said softly. "Well, we're on a roll. What else needs confessing tonight?"

"Tell us why Patricia says she has a witness who claims you're lying about where you were," Meg said. "She has a real witness who saw Lindsey out that night with Blake. So your witness is probably legitimate, too. Where were you, really?"

Callie stopped, jarring Tess and, in turn, Lindsey.

"I wasn't lying about where I went after we left the island," Callie said. "Do you really not believe me?"

Tess glanced at Lindsey. Lindsey shrugged.

"If you say you told us the truth about where you were, then we believe you," Lindsey said.

"I swear," Callie said. "I'll find out who her witness is supposed to be. Either Patricia's lying, or they're wrong. Either way, she has no right to publish anything like that about me."

"Sorry to bring the mood down," Meg said. "I had to ask."

"Your turn to tell us something," Tess said to Meg over her shoulder. "Make it good."

"I was in love with Zoe," Meg said without hesitation. Tess and Callie gasped. "And we might've had a chance if . . . everything had been different."

"I knew it," Tess said. "Remind me to show you the pictures from six or seven summers ago. I have them in my box back at the house. In every picture of you and Zoe, you both look so content when you're together. I just knew it."

"But we weren't—"

"She loved you," Callie said, cutting Meg off. "I always saw it, too."

"We were both always dating other people," Meg said. "The timing never worked out for us."

"You still had her love," Callie said. "Even if the timing was off."

After this, Lindsey lost her sense of time as they ascended the bluffs. When they reached the top, they guided Tess down the dirt pathway to their waiting mopeds. She climbed onto the middle bike, and Lindsey put her helmet on Tess's head.

"I wasn't going to wear this anyway," she said. "But you seem pretty accident-prone tonight."

"Thank you," Tess said. "And sorry for causing so much trouble. I wasn't thinking. I just had to get away."

"We're just relieved you're okay." Callie clipped on her helmet and started her bike. "I have a few doctors back at the party who can check your foot."

"I'll be fine tonight," Tess assured her. "Let's go back and enjoy the rest of your housewarming. Zoe would've wanted us to celebrate her before the day ends."

"I wonder what she'd think about all this," Meg said as she started up her bike.

"She'd tell us we were idiots but that she loves us," Lindsey said. "I can practically hear her voice."

"Me too," Meg said.

Meg and Callie took off first, leaving a cloud of dust in their wake. Tess wrapped her arms around Lindsey's waist, her head resting in the dip between her shoulder blades. The tender spot where Fred had kissed her the night on his boat. Her stomach lurched at the memory. *You let it go too far,* Zoe would have told her.

As Lindsey carefully guided the moped onto the road, she wondered what else Zoe might've said about Fred. What kind of joke she'd make about them being drawn to the same men over and over. She'd probably suggest they become sister wives. *We already share the household chores; why not add a husband to the mix?*

But she would never know for sure. Zoe was still gone, and eventually Lindsey would have to make peace with never knowing what had happened. But not tonight.

Instead, she focused her attention on what was still real and tangible: Tess's grip around her waist and the rush of wind in her ears as they sped home.

Lindsey parked the moped in front of the garage, where Callie and Meg were waiting. The party sounded like it hadn't waned. The band was in the middle of a song that vibrated the night air. Voices and laughter laced around the music as if the other guests hadn't even realized their host had left the party.

Together they helped Tess upstairs to her bedroom. Lindsey ran warm water in the tub while Callie went in search of her first aid kit. Meg helped Tess sit on the lip of the tub and set her foot inside. She winced and sucked in a sharp breath as her foot met the water. The water went murky with dirt and grains of sand.

Lindsey lathered soap in a washcloth that felt too expensive to get dirty. She sat on the edge of the tub next to Tess and motioned for her to lift her foot.

"This is going to hurt," Lindsey said. "Don't hate me."

She dabbed the remaining dirt off the cut and gently cleaned it while Tess clenched her eyes shut. Callie returned with bandages and ointment and a pair of crutches.

"How are you always prepared for everything?" Lindsey asked, eyeing the crutches. Twenty-four hours earlier, the question would've been tinged with annoyance. Callie Sutter to the rescue again. But now, Lindsey saw it differently. Being prepared—and coming to their aid— was her way of caring.

"They're not mine. The previous owners were doctors," Callie said. "Lucky us, they left a garage full of medical supplies."

"Luck always finds you," Lindsey said.

Once Lindsey was done, she switched spots with Callie, who pulled Tess's foot into her lap, wrapping it in a towel. She patted it dry and bandaged it up. She then wrapped a brace around Tess's ankle and shook to life an emergency ice pack.

"Good as new," Callie said as Tess propped herself up on the crutches and tested them out around the bathroom.

"How do I go back to my normal life after this?" Tess asked, gesturing at the crutches.

"I'll come over and help with the baby when James is at work," Lindsey said. "I have some free time on my hands now."

Tess blinked at her.

"What?" Lindsey asked. "Don't cry. What did I say?"

"Nothing," Tess said. "It's just . . . that's exactly what I need. Help from a friend. You don't even know."

"Don't get excited," Lindsey said as she drained the tub. "I'll probably just be in your way. But at least it's an extra set of hands while yours are holding crutches."

Lindsey wiped down the floor and dropped the dirty towels into a wicker laundry basket, then washed her hands in the sink. On the counter, half covered by a hand towel, was Fred's photo of Zoe.

"Why is this in here?" she asked, frozen by the sight of it. "Who put this here?"

"What?" Callie asked as she picked up the first aid kit and zipped it closed. "That picture?"

Lindsey dried her hands as Callie lifted the photo and stared at it.

"It's Fred's," Lindsey said. "That's why we were arguing earlier. I found it on his boat."

"I must've dropped it," Meg said. "I had it when I was looking around for Tess earlier."

"When was this taken?" Callie asked. Her eyes flitted over the image, and then she looked at Lindsey. "When? That summer?"

"I guess so," Lindsey said. "He said she gave it to—"

"Zoe did?" Callie asked.

"I mean, that's what he said. Right?"

Meg faltered. "I think so?"

"I don't understand," Callie said, her eyes focused tight on the picture. "The cushion, my mother imported that fabric from Italy. This picture was taken on my parents' old boat."

Chapter Twenty-Nine

CALLIE

"That makes no sense," Lindsey said, reaching for the photo.

Callie let her take it. She leaned against the edge of the vanity and willed herself to remember taking the picture of Zoe, of being on her parents' boat together that summer. Because she must've been the one to take it. It was the only logical explanation.

"I must have taken it in June or July," Callie said, more to herself than the rest of them. "I must have been home for a weekend and taken her out on the boat and don't remember."

"And you didn't invite any of us?" Lindsey asked.

Callie looked up at her, hearing the broader question in her tone: *Does* that *make any sense?* Back then, they did as much together as they could. Callie knew Lindsey was right. What were the chances only two out of the five of them could make it that day? Or that none of them could even remember the invitation now?

"I don't know," Callie said. "Maybe you were all busy."

"You never took us on the boat," Meg said. "Maybe once or twice, but that was back in high school or college, right?"

"I don't think I ever went on the boat," Tess offered.

"I could've sworn you didn't come home that summer until we went on our trip to Block Island," Lindsey said. "Zoe and I went out to New York to visit you around the Fourth of July, right? But we didn't see much of you otherwise. So when would you have taken Zoe on the boat?"

"Okay, so what, then?" Callie asked. "She was on the boat with my parents? When I wasn't here?" But she felt the impossibility of that idea as soon as she suggested it. "That makes less sense than I came home one weekend and just don't remember it."

"Why don't we just ask them?" Meg suggested.

Callie agreed. She grabbed the photo, and together they made their way back downstairs, this time faster with Tess guiding herself on the crutches. Outside, the dance floor pulsed and the band played a Jimmy Buffett song. The bartender wore a weary expression as he continued to fill glasses. Nathan was at the helm of the gourmet s'mores station as people skewered marshmallows and toasted them over a smokeless flame. Even Zoe's table was still well attended, with guests milling around and taking pictures on their phones or flipping through the photo albums.

"They're probably getting ready for bed," Callie said over her shoulder to her friends. They wove through the party, crossed the lawn, and climbed the stairs to the guesthouse. She knocked once, twice, then a third time before her mother answered. Her face was washed clean of makeup and her hair pushed back with a headband. She wore a black pajama set with house shoes on her feet.

"What's wrong?" she asked, eyeing the girls as she tied a fluid silk robe around her body.

"I need your help with something," Callie said, nudging past her mother and creating a path for the others to follow her inside.

The main room was lit only by a single lamp on a side table. It threw a faint net of light onto the couch and floor.

"Don't you think it's a little late to ask for my help?" Elizabeth asked as she shut the door. "The party's practically over. But I have to say, even though I had my doubts, it turned out better than I expected. All things considered."

Callie held out the photo of Zoe. "I need your help remembering when Zoe was on your boat. When did we take this picture?"

Elizabeth squinted at the photo, then patted her robe pockets and pulled out a pair of reading glasses. She looked again and shook her head. She handed the photo back to Callie and glanced at the hem of her dress.

"Why is your dress torn? And why was that reporter here earlier? She was skulking around a little while ago and writing in an impossibly tiny notebook."

"She's always skulking around," Callie said. "Forget about her. When did we take Zoe on the boat?"

"Darling, I don't believe we did. It's probably not our boat," Elizabeth said.

"But the cushions," Callie said. "You special ordered that fabric."

Her mother eyed the picture again. But this time, something in her demeanor shifted. A minute refinement of her expression, almost imperceptible. But Callie caught it, having spent a lifetime learning to read and understand her mother. At the same time, in the sliver of silence while her mother considered what to say, Callie felt something bleak and unnameable galvanize inside her. She pushed it aside for the moment, needing to know she wasn't losing her mind.

"It could be any print. You can't really see the full cushion," Elizabeth finally said, crossing her arms. "May I go to bed now? I'm exhausted."

"Where's Dad?" Callie asked, hating that she felt like a child again, begging her mother to listen to her.

"He's resting. You know nighttime is his worst time. After a full day of socializing, he was absolutely drained and not thinking clearly. Talk to him in the morning, when he's clearheaded again."

Callie called down the hallway for him, ignoring her mother.

"I'm not going to feel right until I talk to him," Callie said.

"I said no. He's resting."

Callie shot her mother a pointed look. "Why can't I just talk to him for a minute?"

"What's happening?" Ben asked, shuffling into the room. "Callie. It's late, you should be asleep."

Callie took him by the arm and led him to the couch. He sat down with a groan. Callie knelt beside him.

"Why are you still up?" he asked her.

She studied his face and put the photo into her father's hands. Elizabeth scoffed.

"Callie, honestly," her mother said. Then, as if registering the other girls for the first time, she shot her finger in the direction of the door. "Can you give us some space? Go wait outside. We're in our pajamas, for goodness' sake. This is invasive."

"They're staying," Callie said. "We'll get out of your hair as soon as we make sense of this picture."

Ben lifted the photo and tilted it in the direction of the lamp.

"Do you remember my friend Zoe ever being on your boat?" Callie asked him. "Who took this picture? Did I take it? Do you remember?"

He studied it for a few moments. The room was still, expectant.

"Where did this come from?" he asked. "Is that our boat?"

Callie gestured toward her friends. "Lindsey—you know Lindsey, she's right there—she got this from Fred. Did you see him tonight?"

"Cameron Oakes," Meg said. "You might know him by that name. He goes by both."

Ben laughed gruffly. "Oh, I know Cameron. I think I saw him today, didn't I? We talked for a while about . . ." He looked at Callie, his eyes tired but searching. Trying. "This isn't his picture, though. It's mine."

Callie put her hand on his knee. "What do you mean it's yours?"

"You're a confused man," Elizabeth said. "Stop talking."

"You stop talking," he shot back. "I'm not confused—you don't know anything."

And then Lindsey crouched beside Callie, her voice gentle as she asked, "Mr. Sutter, were you ever on your boat alone with Zoe?"

Callie reeled back, her eyes on Lindsey as the question hung in the room like a phantom. Callie's ribs tightened, her eyes and cheeks flaming. The unnameable feeling's shape finally materialized: shame.

"Stop!" Elizabeth's face blanched. "You horrible girls, you're driving him to say things he doesn't mean. You're putting thoughts in his head. Get out!"

"Give him a chance to speak," Callie said. "Did Zoe go on your boat with you, Dad?"

"Enough," her mother hissed. She snatched the photo out of Ben's hand and tore it in half.

Ben rubbed his forehead. He gave Callie an insistent look. "I need to tell her to stay off the bow of the boat. She went on there once, but it's not safe."

"You don't have that boat anymore," Callie said. "You haven't had your boat in years."

He laughed but Callie saw faint confusion in his smile. "We were just on it."

"You're thinking of the ferry. We got rid of our boat," Elizabeth said in a thin voice. "Labor Day weekend, five years ago. You said it was getting to be too much for you. You wanted it gone."

"It's not too much—" he started. "I was just on it. Yes, with Zoe. We went out a few times and talked business. That grant we were going to award a small business, your mother and I had decided it would go to your friend, for her jewelry, but—"

"She went missing," Elizabeth finished for him.

"No," Ben said, shaking his head persistently. "No, no. She's not missing. I remember telling her the grant was hers. I remember—"

The room tilted. Confusion, that was it. Her father was confused. Lindsey wrapped her hand around Callie's forearm, and Callie was grateful for the stabilizing force of her friend's touch.

"Zoe went on the boat with you more than once?" Callie asked, humiliated. "Why would you take *my friend* out, alone, on the boat and not tell me?"

"Oh, for God's sake, Callie. Don't be dim. You know him. You know why," Elizabeth said.

For the first time in her life, Callie heard defeat in her mother's tone. A sad resignation. This chilled Callie. The coldness spilled through her body; it didn't mean anything good if her mother would allow herself to be seen and heard this way.

"I'm tired, Ben," Elizabeth went on. "Tired of coddling you. Tired of trying to convince myself you're a better man than you really are. What kind of life is this for me? Watching you like a hawk so you don't say things like *this*? So you don't inadvertently dredge up your indiscretions and mortify me in front of our daughter? I just can't do it anymore. And you even took photos while you were cheating? Why? To hurt me? To hurt Callie?"

"You always make mountains out of molehills," Ben said. He pushed himself off the couch. Callie and Lindsey scrambled to their feet. "She's looking for ways to grow her business. She said it's not doing well. Sales are down. What do you expect? I know business, and we had the money set aside for a grant. I offered it to her—she's Callie's friend; she's running a small business. Nothing beyond that happened."

Callie felt her skin crawling. She didn't believe him, not entirely.

"Zoe's business was doing great," Callie said. "I'm sorry, but I think you're extremely confused, Dad."

He shook his head. "No, I remember that clear as day because it reminded me of a time when I was starting out and nearly had to close my first business. She's in a bad spot, and I want to help."

Callie locked eyes with Lindsey. "That's not true, is it?"

"That's not the impression she gave us," Lindsey said. "But I don't know, Callie. Maybe she wasn't telling us everything."

"No. We told each other everything," Callie said. At least, *she'd* told Zoe everything. There was no one she trusted more out of the group. But was it possible Zoe hadn't felt the same about her? Callie tried to imagine Zoe on the Sutter boat but never mentioning it to Callie. There were only so many reasons she'd keep that secret. Callie's stomach lurched.

"Why do you want her to stay off the bow of your boat?" she asked her father. In the present tense. Because she believed, in his mind, he was five years in the past and Zoe was still around.

Her father blinked at this question. "It's not safe; she might fall. It's happened before."

"With her?" Lindsey asked.

"Ben, stop talking," Elizabeth said.

"Yes, with her," Ben said, impatient. "Why are you looking at me like that? She fell once. It's not safe on the bow." He turned to Elizabeth. "We need to get the grant money to her soon. She's tired of waiting. You were supposed to meet with her about this already, but you keep putting it off."

"She's *gone*," Elizabeth said, her words barbed. "Did you pull her back on board, Ben? Jesus, tell me you did. Tell me you didn't leave her out there in the water. Tell me she went missing for any other reason, but not because of you. Please."

Callie felt an internal collapse, as if her heart had splintered into dust. She stumbled back, away from her father. Images flashed in her mind: Zoe on the boat, her father steering them out into the ocean, Zoe in the water. Callie tried to fill in the moments before that. Tried to will herself to imagine how Zoe could've fallen, *why* she would've been near the edge to begin with, but her mind wouldn't allow her to go there.

"Did you push her?" she asked. "Or did she slip?"

"Push her? No, no." Ben rubbed his forehead with one hand and held up the other signaling to give him a minute. "Everyone, slow down. Just slow down."

"It's why you got rid of the boat," Elizabeth said. "You thought if it was gone, you'd be able to forget about what you did. Is that it? Ben. The girl had a photo of herself on that boat."

He reached over to the side table and picked up the landline left behind by the last owner. Callie and Nathan had never paid to have it connected, but Ben started punching numbers.

"Let's call her. Clear this all up right now. Don't accuse me of leaving someone to drown, Elizabeth. You're my wife." He took a few steps toward Callie. "You don't believe this, do you? Talk to her. Talk to Zoe."

He thrust the phone in Callie's direction, but she recoiled alongside Lindsey, bumping into Meg and Tess.

"There's no way to call her," Callie said. "She fell? She really fell and you didn't help her? And you never told anyone?"

"Stop saying that!" he hollered. "There was nothing to tell. She fell, but I'm sure she was fine. She was fine."

"In the goddamn ocean?" Meg asked, emerging from behind Callie and Lindsey. "You think she was fine after falling into the *ocean*? Why was she even with you in the first place?"

"I don't have to explain myself to you," he said. "Or anyone. Get out of my house. All of you. Get the hell out of here."

"This is my house," Callie said. Her body trembled as her disbelief flared into hatred. "*My* house. You're disgusting. I've always known it, but I never wanted to admit it completely. But you're a horrible person. I never want to see you again. You're a monster."

Callie barely registered the next few moments. Her mother was breathing raggedly, a hand over her mouth. Her father glared, a fury behind his eyes that told Callie she was right. He was a monster, and even if it was an accident, he'd left Zoe to die.

Someone pulled Callie by the arm out of the guesthouse. Her friends spoke rapidly from all sides, but none of their words were clear. Callie wrapped her arm across her stomach, tried to breathe. Her vision swam with vertigo.

An interior door slammed in the guesthouse. They bounded down the stairs, cutting through a quiet section of the party. Callie wasn't sure she would've been able to get herself into the house if she'd been alone. But together, they moved like a singular entity. She was carried by their presence.

Then they stopped short. Callie was jolted back into her body, back into the ugly present moment.

"Why is she still here?" Lindsey asked. Callie followed Lindsey's gaze.

Patricia leaned against the house by the memorial table, her eyes downcast on her phone.

"Hey!" Lindsey yelled sharply at her. Patricia started, nearly dropping her phone. "I thought your battery was dead."

Patricia pushed off the house and walked toward them. She looked at the crutches, at Tess's injured foot, at Meg's tear-streaked face. Callie wasn't sure how stricken she looked, how much pain she radiated, but noted the moment Patricia realized something was off. Awareness lit her eyes.

"What happened?" Patricia asked. When no one responded, she sighed. "Look. I apologize for crashing the party. But this was the only way I could find the four of you in one place, and I think we should sit down and talk about some anomalies I've found in your stories."

"We don't have time for this right now," Meg said.

"I'm trying, here," Patricia said. "If you don't take the time to explain to me why I have two witnesses who claim to refute Callie and Lindsey's stories, I'll have to move forward with what I have." She leveled her gaze at Callie. "I know you want nothing to do with me, but this is my last olive branch. I'm not going to keep begging you four to do your part to find Zoe. I shouldn't have to. So, without your help, I can only draw the conclusion that you're hiding something."

"Your witness lied," Callie said. "And your book's not going to happen, Patricia. It's over."

"Miles Bell works at a marina on Block Island and spoke to your father five years ago today. Why would Miles lie about that? How does it benefit him to lie about your father waiting for you at that marina?" Patricia asked. Her eyes searched Callie's face, but Callie bit down on her tongue to keep herself from dissolving.

"He wasn't waiting for me," Callie said.

"Miles saw you get onto the boat," Patricia said, a plea in her voice. "Help me make sense of it. Your father said he was waiting for you, then you got onto his boat when you allegedly were on the ferry back to the mainland. How could you be in two places at once?"

"I wasn't," Callie said. Her voice was hoarse, as if her body didn't want her to say anything more.

"It's been five years, and he's only now coming forward?" Lindsey asked.

"Well, no," Patricia said. "He told me this five years ago, but I had no proof. I just knew it felt off, especially when combined with your behavior around the sunglasses. You know I have a bartender who puts you out all night with a man when you said you were home, right? Do you want me to publish that? And let my readers draw their own conclusions? Or would you like to take a minute and explain?"

"That was Blake, and I don't give a shit what you publish," Lindsey said.

Patricia's expression froze. "Zoe's Blake?"

"He lied, too, but you only care when we do it," Lindsey said. "Your story is only good when it turns Zoe's friends into villains, right?"

"All I've ever wanted is the truth," Patricia said. "Now I understand yours—but, Callie, I still don't get it. Why'd you lie about taking the ferry back?"

Callie wasn't sure she'd ever be able to take a full breath again. Her lungs felt impossibly small. She imagined Zoe walking from the ferry terminal after the rest of them had left. Ben lying about who he was waiting for. Miles Bell, whoever he was, seeing a young woman climb aboard Ben's boat not long after he'd said he was waiting for his daughter. Deceptions that, when slanted a certain way, looked like truths.

"You don't have to answer that," Meg said, pulling Callie gently toward the house.

"What are you hiding?" Patricia shouted after them.

It caught the attention of some guests near the bar. Suddenly, Callie worried about Patricia causing a scene, as if the party still mattered. As if anything did.

Callie spun around, her strides long and furious.

"You've always been wrong about us, about Zoe—everything," Callie said. "Everything you've suggested about what happened to Zoe is wrong. And I can say that because we do know what happened to her, but we're not going to tell you. You can find out with the rest of the world."

Callie's pulse thrummed in her neck, and adrenaline coursed through her body. She should've done this years ago. Shutting Patricia down—it would have gone so much further than her interview ever did.

Patricia's jaw went slack. She blinked at Callie as if seeing her for the first time. "You know what happened to her?"

"I want you to leave," Callie said.

Patricia hesitated. She stepped closer to Callie and reached out a hand. Callie drew back.

"Don't touch me, just leave," she said to Patricia.

"Please tell me what happened," Patricia said.

Callie considered the satisfaction in watching Patricia beg. For the first time, she had the upper hand, the control. Instead, she turned and walked back to Meg, Lindsey, and Tess. She was done with Patricia Adele.

Once they were alone inside the house, Callie turned to her friends. There was a question she needed to ask while she still had her nerve. Before reality caught up with her.

"Do you think Zoe was . . . Do you think she and my father . . . ?"

"No," Tess said. "He was talking about a grant, right? That has to be what was going on."

"Right," Callie said, though that didn't make her feel any better. The pieces still didn't fit together quite right. "Why didn't she ever tell me? Or any of us? And why did she lie about how her business was doing?"

"With Fred . . . there's a transaction," Lindsey said. "We go out, he pays for my time. I'm pretty sure that was the situation with Zoe and Fred. So it's possible maybe your father did that, too. But I don't believe she would do that to you. I agree with Tess. It had to be about that grant, especially if her business was actually struggling. That makes sense."

"Zoe knew why I ended up at camp the summer I met you four," Callie said. "Because my father cheated and I told my mother about it, and she wanted me gone. My mother acted like it was my fault my father was unfaithful to her. I hated myself for so long because of that. Zoe knew that was a sore spot for me, my father's infidelity."

"She wouldn't have done anything to cause more of that pain for you," Tess said.

Tess was right, but it didn't ease the relentless ache beneath Callie's ribs. The ache clawed at her lungs and heart like it was looking for a way out. There was no way out, though. She'd have to somehow learn to live with it.

"The Gilberts," Callie said. "Are they still here? Should someone tell them? Should I?"

Her legs felt unreliably weak at the thought of this. She pulled out a chair and sat before they gave out. She had no idea how she would ever face them again.

"I'm sure they're back at their hotel by now," Tess said. "And you shouldn't have to be the one to explain this to them. One of us will do it."

"Or the police?" Callie asked. "Do we call them?"

"Well, do you believe what we just heard from your father?" Meg asked. "Do you want me to call the detective?"

Callie hadn't considered *not* believing. But she understood what Meg meant. There was still time to rewrite the story, to brush it off as just a misunderstanding. To excuse her father's story as nothing more than a false memory. Confusion. The Sutters would be more than happy to never speak of tonight again.

"How could I live with myself if I didn't believe it?" Callie asked. "We all heard the same thing. We all heard him say she fell off the boat. Didn't we? How else can we interpret that?"

Meg nodded. "No, you're right. We all heard the same thing."

"Make the call," Callie said. Pure grief welled up in her chest. "How could we go on looking for Zoe after what we just heard? I'm not like them. I can't lie to myself like my parents can. And I would never expect any of you to do that, either."

They walked down the hall to the den. Meg called the detective and explained to him in a low voice what had just happened. Callie climbed onto the sectional couch between Lindsey and Tess. She took a few long, slow breaths, but her body refused to calm. Her hands trembled in her lap. Her heartbeat wouldn't steady. She could smell the sweat that had dried on her skin and the faint hint of salt air they'd carried back from the bluffs. She listened to her friends' breathing and took small comfort in their closeness, but her world was completely off-balance.

Her first night at Ives Art Camp had been much the same: the five of them packed into a small cabin, the scents of Block Island summertime already imprinted on their skin. The cadence of their inhales and exhales as they fell asleep in their bunks. Callie had lain awake long after, staving off her tears and thanking the God she didn't believe in for her bunkmates, the four strangers who had pulled her in when she felt her most lost.

Callie closed her eyes. "What now?"

She was afraid to look at them. They all knew whatever happened next wouldn't be good.

"The police will be here soon," Meg said. "I assume it'll be like last time, when they had us give statements about Zoe's disappearance. We'll tell them exactly what just happened and let them sort out the rest. Let's just focus on tonight, okay? Don't think too far ahead. One thing at a time."

"You're not going to have to do any of this alone," Tess said.

Callie couldn't help thinking ahead, though. She imagined her father in a prison jumpsuit, the fabric hanging off his thin shoulders. Her father sitting in a courtroom with the best, most expensive lawyers in the country by his side. His memory only growing worse until he had no idea what had happened. Was it justice even if he wasn't sure what he had done?

The doorbell echoed through the house, startling everyone. Callie gasped, her nervous system like a fuse shorting out. It was the first time she'd heard the doorbell ring in the new house. It would never sound like anything but a death knell after tonight.

Meg jumped to her feet and ran to answer it. Callie was grateful someone else was taking charge.

What followed was a blur. Two officers from the local department stepped inside the house and guided Callie into the home office, where they shut the door and flipped open their notepads.

"Start at the beginning," they said. "What was happening here? Some kind of cookout?"

"It's my housewarming party," Callie said, then told them everything that followed.

Her voice shook as her words left her mouth. Retelling the night made it all the more real yet even harder to believe. But they nodded as she spoke, as if they believed her.

Callie gave the ripped photograph of Zoe to the officers. They spoke to Fred privately, and afterward, he explained the photo to Callie and the others in the den. His eyes never left Lindsey as he spoke.

"Zoe gave it to me one of the last times I saw her," he said. "A few weeks before she went missing. The boat in the photo looks similar to mine, and she thought I'd find it funny." He paused. A despondent expression moved across his eyes. "It was the only picture of her that I had. I didn't want to forget her. I still don't."

"No one does," Lindsey said as she went to Fred's side. She wrapped her arms around his waist and rested her head on his chest.

When they were done inside, the two officers tramped across the yard to speak with Ben Sutter in the guesthouse. The mainland detectives would arrive in the morning to have their own conversation with him, but Ben was ordered to remain on the island and inside the guesthouse until then.

Callie retreated to the quiet of the den with her friends once the police left for the night. Nathan made a pot of coffee, and they filled their mugs and sat close to each other on the couch. Callie brought the lip of the mug to her mouth, and her stomach immediately turned. She set it down on the table; how would she ever eat or drink or sleep again?

"You didn't deserve this," Lindsey said to Callie. "Whatever you're thinking, it's not your fault."

"I don't know what I'm thinking," Callie admitted. "I just feel . . . empty."

But what she did know was that she wouldn't have to wade alone into the murky days, weeks, years to come. For that, Callie thanked whatever wise fates had tossed her into the right camp cabin as a teenager, giving her friends who would become her sanctuary through the best and worst of what life could offer.

Chapter Thirty

ZOE

Five years earlier, August 2014

Zoe Gilbert had secrets.

Some were inconsequential, like borrowing Lindsey's favorite boots without asking. But she was always careful to wipe the leather clean before returning them to the closet.

Others were weightier and knocked around like stones in her pocket. Secrets that had somehow gone past the acceptable point of being confessable. For one, her jewelry business was struggling, but everyone in her life believed she was an entrepreneurial success. That her pieces sold well and her bank account was healthily fat. Her parents, her best friends, her studio colleagues. They bragged about her accomplishments and persistence. Because she'd let them think for too long that everything was fine, the thought of admitting she'd been misleading them—and herself—made her sick. So she didn't.

And then there was secret number two: Ben Sutter.

On her way to dinner one night in Newport with Fred, Ben had walked past. The three of them stopped to talk, Ben and Fred apparently old friends: *How many years has it been? Those parties were out of control. Let me introduce you to my date this evening.*

"No need," Zoe said, reaching out to shake Ben's hand. "We go way back."

But there'd been no recognition behind Ben's eyes. A few too many beats of silence while he tried to place her, a silence so awkward that Zoe laughed to fill it.

"Mr. Sutter, it's Zoe. I'm Callie's friend."

"Oh, that's it," he said, the expression of mild alarm vanishing from his face. "I completely forgot."

A strange thing to forget, but then again, Callie had rarely had the girls over to her house growing up. And Ben Sutter seemed to be the type of man who only remembered people he deemed important. People like Fred. People with money.

"What are you doing for work?" Ben asked her, though Zoe got the feeling he was only making polite conversation because his friend was there.

"I run a small business," she said. "It's very small. Just me; no employees yet. Turns out running a full business alone is harder than it looks."

"It takes time," Fred said, putting a reassuring arm around her shoulders. "You're smart and creative. It'll come."

They'd been going out for a month, a perfectly casual situation where he paid for dinner and her time. But lately, she worried he was tripping into stronger feelings for her, that his heart would ruin a good thing.

"Elizabeth and I have been working on a nonprofit to help up-and-coming small businesses, actually," Ben said. He dug into his pocket and pulled out a card. "Give me a call, and we can set up a time to discuss it. Sounds like you'd be a good fit for our grant."

"You should do it," Fred told her later over dinner. "Why not? The guy's loaded, and if he's funding a grant, you'd be set for a while."

But what had Zoe gotten when she'd arranged that meeting with the Sutters? An invitation to join them for dinner at a nice restaurant in Providence—only, when Zoe arrived, Mrs. Sutter was absent.

"She had a last-minute scheduling hiccup," Ben had said. "Do you still want to discuss the grant? I told Elizabeth I'd go over everything with her later. She's the one spearheading the nonprofit."

It seemed strange, but not enough for Zoe to leave. They ate and discussed her business plan, and at the end she'd asked for a time to meet with Mrs. Sutter.

Ben thought for a few seconds, then said, "We take the boat out on weekends. Join us Sunday. Elizabeth can talk to you about the nonprofit then."

He'd given her the name of the marina in Jamestown where they kept the boat and a time to meet them. While a valet driver retrieved her car, Zoe stood on the sidewalk outside the restaurant with her phone in hand, debating whether she should text Callie that she'd had dinner with her father. If both Sutters had been there, sure. But since it was just Ben? The valet pulled up with her car, and she put her phone back into her bag. She felt odd about the situation, and Callie probably would, too.

But then Sunday came. She arrived at the marina in Jamestown and found their boat lilting gently in the water.

"Unfortunately, Elizabeth is running late from an appointment," Ben said from the stern of the boat. "Should we cruise for a bit until she gets here?"

Zoe stood momentarily frozen on the wooden platform beside the boat slip, a strange doubt itching the back of her brain. But why would he lie about something like that? He was Callie's dad, after all. If he were a stranger, she'd turn around and walk away. But she knew him. And there was real money on the line. So Zoe had boarded the boat, only expecting a short ride in the surrounding bay while they waited for Mrs. Sutter.

But instead, Ben had cruised out into open ocean, the whole time talking about his own businesses, his own success. Bragging, almost. Showing off like he was trying to impress her. Like she wasn't his daughter's friend. He rambled on and on, sometimes calling her Zoe, sometimes blinking at her until she reminded him of her name. He showed her the expensive Leica he kept on board, as if he wanted her to know he wasn't worried about the possibility of a three-thousand-dollar camera getting stolen or falling into the water.

"Smile," he'd said, holding it up.

She'd smiled. Her instinct was to pretend everything was fine until she was back on solid ground, then she'd call Callie and ask her what the hell was up with her father. Was something wrong with him? Was there even a grant?

But when they returned to the marina and there was no sign of Mrs. Sutter, he looked genuinely crestfallen.

"Maybe she got held up longer than expected," he'd said. "Let me get you a drink. Wine? Beer?"

"I should get going," Zoe said, climbing off the boat before he could fill a glass for her. "Have Mrs. Sutter call me."

She started to walk away when he said, "We should do this again."

The words slithered cold down the back of her neck. She kept walking, hoping no response was enough of one for him to take the hint. Then he'd mailed the picture he'd taken of her on the boat to her studio. It sat among her mail, his handwriting on the envelope tidy and straight. She pawned the photo off on Fred, unnerved at the thought of keeping it.

"Isn't it funny that it looks like your boat?" she'd said, though he'd gotten quiet. A little jealous. "It's my friend Callie's boat. I just thought you'd like to have a picture of me."

And now, several weeks later, she was thinking about Ben Sutter's persistence while his daughter's voice carried over the bonfire in front of Zoe. How he'd called and left her a message the day before while she was on the beach with her friends. *Call me when you get this. Grant money is secured, no application needed. Just need to arrange a time to meet and transfer it to you.* How easy it would've been to ignore him. But after a week on Block Island, her bank account was suffering more than usual.

"I'm just saying," Callie said, "next year, we should go somewhere else. Bermuda is great in the summer."

"Bermuda," Lindsey laughed. "Sounds expensive."

She was drunk. Zoe could hear it in the way Lindsey dragged out the *r* in *Bermuda*, only a beer or two away from saying or doing something she'd regret in the morning. Like the night before, when they'd bickered about Blake, both of them too foggy on the details of the argument to smooth it over properly when they woke up in the morning. But Zoe did recall the way Lindsey's face soured upon hearing his name. *Remember the time you stole him from me?* Lindsey had said, then faked a smile. *Good times.*

It had taken everything in Zoe not to shoot back with *Yeah? And Blake tells me all the time he thinks you're fake and don't actually like me at all.*

"Your turn to set the alarm, Linds." Zoe pointed at the bottle in her hands. "Or are you too inebriated for that much responsibility right now?"

Lindsey rolled her eyes and swallowed the rest of her drink in one go.

"Don't worry, Mother," she said with a hazy smile. "I'll set it. What time?"

"No later than eight," Callie said. "Gives us a chance to grab coffee before our ferry. You guys," she whined, "I can't believe our week together is already over. I wish this didn't have to ever end."

"We'll do it again," Meg said. "We always do."

"And we don't have to come to Block Island every summer," Callie said.

"But we do," Tess said. "Someone back me up here."

Zoe's gaze wandered to each of them, then to the bonfire crackling in the center of it all. They'd stayed together at the same cottage for one week every summer for years, and this was the first time Zoe was beginning to feel over it. Maybe she was aging out of long group trips. Or maybe she was more embarrassed than she could stand to admit, and looking Callie in the eye all week had taken a toll. Every time Callie spoke, Zoe felt awkward. She hadn't done anything wrong besides *not* tell Callie that Ben had tricked her twice into spending time with him alone. That she'd fallen for it because her business was close to failing and she was desperate. That she'd sensed something off about her interactions with Ben, and saying so might hurt Callie's feelings or force her to defend him. It was too messy for Zoe to untangle.

"Zoe, you love it here," Tess said. "Tell them we can't break tradition."

"I don't care. Whatever you guys want is fine with me," Zoe said.

Tess stared at her. "Seriously?"

"Yeah, seriously."

Tess cocked her head and laughed. "Of course you don't care. You've been too distracted all week to care. You were the one who started this tradition in the first place. You were, like, the queen of keeping us together. Now it's like you're on another planet."

Zoe rolled her head back. "God, Tess. Give me a break. Please."

"Am I wrong? You've said maybe ten words to us all day. What's going on with you?"

Lindsey and Callie stared into the fire, staying out of this one. Meg glanced between Zoe and Tess as if trying to decide what to say to defuse the situation, but she came up with nothing.

"What's going on with *you*?" Zoe asked. "Do you need to know every detail of my life? You sound like you're obsessed with me."

"I'm not obsessed. But you're acting shady," Tess said, her voice rising. "We all think so."

"Talking about me behind my back?" Zoe asked. "Great. Thanks, guys."

"How many times have you left the cottage this week without telling us?" Tess went on, undeterred. "You can't take off like that and expect us to not wonder. You can't just come and go as you please."

"You do wander off a lot," Lindsey said.

"I can't take a walk alone without my friends talking about me?" Zoe asked. "How about you install a tracking device on me so you know where I am at all times?"

Most of her walks that week had been to clear her head and wring out her anxiety. But one had been for some privacy while she returned Ben's call, confirming he was serious about the grant money and to schedule a time to meet the next day. She couldn't risk one of them overhearing.

"You're being so dramatic," Tess said. "I can feel that something is off, and it's insulting that you won't let us in."

"Maybe I would if you weren't being a nosy bitch about it," Zoe shot back.

As soon as she said it, she knew she'd gone too far, had channeled too much of her own frustration into the words she spat at Tess.

"Oh?" Tess said. "Maybe I'm a nosy bitch, but at least I'm not completely self-absorbed. At least I care about other people."

Zoe stared into the fire, tamping down the urge to defend herself. She wanted to shoot back that she wasn't self-absorbed, just distracted. But then Tess would ask more questions and demand details.

"Nothing to say to that?" Tess asked. "You're just going to sit there with those tacky sunglasses on and ignore us some more?"

Zoe yanked the heart-shaped sunglasses from the top of her head and tossed them into Tess's lap.

"Better?" Zoe asked.

"Can you two grow up?" Lindsey muttered.

Tess slumped in her chair and diverted her gaze. The fire snapped inside its stone pit. Zoe pressed her lips tight. What if she just told them? Would it be that bad? They were her best friends; surely they'd understand why she had pretended business was fine when it wasn't. They would appreciate that she was simply embarrassed to say she was failing, to let down everyone who believed in her so wholeheartedly. But also, how to tell them everything would be fine because Ben Sutter—who had made her skin crawl a few times—promised her vague grant money when she'd gone out with him alone. Twice. Without telling Callie.

"I'm going in," Tess said, breaking Zoe's rumination. "And for the record, I'm not nosy. I just feel like you're pulling away. Sorry I give a shit."

Tess dropped the sunglasses back into Zoe's lap, then dumped the remainder of her beer into the fire. It sizzled as she stalked into the cottage, slamming the door behind her.

"Woof," Lindsey muttered.

"She'll cool off by morning," Meg said. "Don't take it personally."

"But it was kind of personal," Callie said. "You know how important these trips are to her."

Zoe studied Callie as she spoke. Callie, the weepy girl she'd first taken pity on at camp, had always claimed they could tell each other anything. But *anything* had its limits.

"I'm calling it," Lindsey said as she stood up from her chair and wobbled a few steps. "Night, bitches."

"Wait for me," Callie said as she followed Lindsey inside.

The fire smoked and waned, but the moon was full and threw enough light that Zoe could see Meg's face across the pit.

"Do you think I was too harsh?" she asked.

Meg groaned as she stood up to switch seats and sit beside Zoe.

"I wouldn't call it harsh," Meg said. "You're both strong-willed when you feel passionate about something. Sometimes that's an explosive combination. It's not like it's the first or last time that will happen with you two."

Zoe bounced her leg and pressed her fingers against her eyelids. She thought about having enough funds to move out of her musty studio and into a sunny brick-and-mortar space in Newport with a studio built in, to hire a real web designer and an employee to work the jewelry counter in her new shop.

"I thought this week would be different," Meg said as she poked the dying fire with a stick.

It had been a standard week on the island: They drank and went out to eat and fell asleep on the beach most days. Trudged up and down the bluffs, rode mopeds to every corner of the island. Bickered. Slung passive-aggressive comments back and forth. Laughed over everything and nothing. Read a few pages of the tattered paperbacks stuffed on a shelf in the cottage.

"I just . . ." Meg started. She set her beer on the ground. The bottle tipped and spilled on her foot. "Shit. Listen. Before I lose my nerve, let me say this."

"Okay," Zoe said, watching her with amusement. "You good?"

"You don't have to respond. But I've been trying to figure out how to say this, and if I don't do it now, I'm going to regret it."

"Just say it," Zoe said. The air between them seemed to waver; she knew what she was about to hear.

"If this makes you uncomfortable, just tell me and I'll shut up. I thought about this for a long time, and I think I love you? No, that's not— I *know* I do. And I have for a while; I just never knew how to tell you. Or if it would ruin our friendship, which is the most important thing in the world to me. I had to say it before we go back to real life tomorrow. I can't keep stuffing this down, or it'll eat me alive. So there it is. It feels good to get it out. Are you . . . What do you think? Actually, no. You don't have to say anything."

Her ears went hot. Zoe wasn't surprised; it was something she'd long suspected was hovering between them. She was buoyed by the confession and wanted that for herself—the ability to be vulnerable and open. No longer carrying anything heavy.

"Wow," Zoe finally said. "I always thought there was a chance we'd end up here, to be honest. For a long time, actually."

"Really?" Meg asked.

Zoe cleared her throat. "It's just that right now I'm seeing—"

"Oh, I'm not asking you to break up with Blake for me," Meg said quickly. "For the record, I would never expect that."

"I know," Zoe said. "Everything is so complicated right now. Can we talk about this again someday? When my life is a little less messy? Hopefully soon?"

Meg tilted her head slightly. "What's so messy about it?"

Zoe held Meg's steady gaze. She could tell Meg everything right now and unburden herself. Blake was part of it, yes. Especially now that she knew Lindsey had been annoyed for years about Zoe dating him first. But the messiness was bigger than him.

"Can you keep a secret?" Zoe asked.

"Of course."

"That stuff Tess said earlier? She isn't wrong. I have some stuff going on . . . It's got nothing to do with Blake, though. He's . . . I don't know. That probably won't last long, which is fine. We didn't work out last time, and I feel like Lindsey hates that I'm back with him. It'll run its course."

"That's the secret?" Meg asked with a teasing smile.

"Shut up," Zoe laughed. "No, that's not it. I'm saying Tess isn't imagining anything. I just don't want to share what's going on yet. I have to figure some things out, and then I'll be ready." Zoe tried to read Meg's reaction, if there was any hurt or confusion in her eyes. But there was none. "There's a situation that has gotten weird for me. I just want to be in a good place before we talk about how we feel again. Is that okay?"

"Of course it's okay," Meg said. "Are you in any kind of trouble?"

"I don't think so," Zoe said. "The situation is complicated, not dangerous. But I want to tell you about it when I can. You'll be the first one to know."

They dumped a bucket of water on the fire embers and went inside the darkened cottage. Tess was asleep on the pull-out couch bed, and Lindsey and Callie were shut in the room with the queen bed and twin cot. It was Zoe and Tess's night to share the pullout. Tess was already asleep when Zoe climbed onto her side of the flat mattress, saving them both from exchanging awkward good nights. Metal springs pressed into her hip, but she could tolerate it for a few hours. And in the morning, she'd smooth things over with Tess if they were both still mad.

She gave her phone a final glance before she tossed it aside and fell hard and fast to sleep.

"Wake *up*. God, you sleep like the dead."

Tess's voice was loud and close and irritated. Zoe cracked her eyes open and pushed up onto her elbows.

"The alarm didn't go off," Tess said. "Lindsey 'definitely' set it." She made quotation marks with her fingers.

"Wonderful," Zoe said as she heaved herself out of the bed. She felt as if cement had replaced her muscles.

Lindsey flew into the living room, her hair piled into a lopsided, unraveling bun on her head.

"I'm sorry I'm sorry I'm sorry," she said as she scooped a makeup bag off the coffee table and a pair of dirty sneakers from the mat by the front door. "I swear I set the alarm for eight o'clock!"

"You set it to p.m.," Callie called from the bedroom.

"Someone came in and changed it in the middle of the night," Lindsey said as she shoved her rumpled clothes into her bag.

Meg poked her head out of the bathroom. "Who has the red bikini and who has the blue one?"

"Red," Zoe said. Meg tossed it over Callie's head to her. The material was still damp and smelled of mildew, having never fully dried in the humid bathroom. She stuffed it into her bag along with her pile of clothes on the floor by the couch.

"Blue's mine," Tess said before catching the bundle Meg threw her way.

They rushed around for the next fifteen minutes, washing dishes, stripping bedding, calling out when they found wayward items. A black thong in the bathroom. White sports bra under the table. Hairbrush on the television console.

Callie carried their bag of trash and recycling outside while Meg ran the vacuum around to suck up the unfathomable amount of sand they'd trekked inside over the past week. Zoe accordioned the couch bed back into itself and gave the cottage one last visual sweep.

She glanced at Meg zipping her bag closed by the door and thought about their conversation the night before. About meeting the Sutters on their boat today after her friends left on the ferry and soon being able to tell Meg everything. If anyone could help Zoe make sense of her life, it was Meg.

"Until next time," Callie said as they all filtered out the front door with their luggage. She gave the door a firm tug and checked that it was locked, and they started for the ferry.

Their walk up the side street took them by shingle-sided houses and overflowing gardens. The morning was iron hot and too bright, but the humidity that had plagued them the previous week had dissipated; it felt like a fresh beginning.

On the main drag, they wove through the crowded street and down to the ferry landing. One boat had disembarked, and the lines for the restroom and rental lockers snaked around the small building.

Once they were in line for their ferry, Zoe spoke.

"I'm actually going to catch a later boat; you guys go ahead without me."

"You're not coming with us?" Lindsey asked.

"I'm not in a rush to get home, and I could use a solo beach day."

Callie and Lindsey glanced at each other, a wordless negotiation passing between them as they silently planned who would stay behind with her.

"Don't do that," Zoe said. "I don't need a chaperone."

Tess sighed. "Is this because of me? I'm sorry, okay? I didn't mean to annoy you."

Zoe smiled to put them at ease. "I'm completely over it. Water under the bridge. You could never annoy me, Tess. Promise."

"You sure you don't want anyone to stay with you?" Meg asked. "The weather's supposed to turn later."

Zoe paused. "I mean, I know you all have things to do today to get ready for work tomorrow. And I promise to be home before it gets stormy."

"Fine, but text us updates," Callie said as she shuffled through her tote bag. She withdrew two protein bars and a tube of sunscreen and handed them to Zoe. "There should be enough in here for you, but you might need to buy a backup bottle. And seriously, keep an eye on the weather. It's supposed to be gross later today and tomorrow."

"You're the best, thank you," Zoe said as she slid the provisions into her bag. "I'll see you at home later, Linds."

She hugged each of them goodbye, stealing a few extra seconds with Meg. Then Zoe stepped out of line as they boarded the boat without her. She shielded her eyes from the sun, her heart-shaped sunglasses more for style than function, and waited for them to emerge on the top deck.

The ferry horn blared. First, she saw Callie, her blond hair radiant in the sunlight. Then Lindsey came up behind her, chugging a bottle of water she must've grabbed at the concession counter below deck. Meg and Tess leaned against the railing side by side, spotted Zoe, and waved.

The sun glittered off the water, casting a golden glow around them. She held her phone up and zoomed in, taking a grainy photo that didn't do justice to how ethereal they appeared. Maybe she wasn't outgrowing anything after all. Maybe these trips would become fewer and farther between as life became more complicated; maybe they would switch up the destination at some point against Tess's will. Maybe next time, she and Meg would be something more than they were today. Maybe by then, they'd all know how Zoe had secretly struggled but ultimately found massive success with her jewelry. Maybe people everywhere would know her name.

Zoe felt better already about that particular day, her luck, the future. That sunlight felt auspicious. It was right that she was on Block Island when she started to feel this turn in her fortune. It was the place that had given her everything, after all.

She waved to the girls once more. The ferry called out a single, low bellow as it left the shallows.

Zoe walked from the ferry landing in the direction of the marina, buoyed by thoughts of the good changes to come. And then she thought of the history she had with this island, her friends. The strange magic that had tethered her to these women in their girlhood, when they were fearless and bold and wholly themselves.

How had so many years dissipated since she'd first set foot out here? Time was slippery. Her mother loved to say that it took and took and took and never gave anything back. Time could feel like a shadowy path into a moonlit sea, but today more than ever, Zoe trusted in the promise of whatever came next.

Acknowledgments

First and foremost, many thanks to my incredible agent, Tia Ikemoto. You believed in this book from the very beginning, and I could tell from our first conversation how lucky I'd be to work with you. I was right. You helped shape this book into something better than I could've dreamed up on my own, all while preserving the true heart of the story. I'm so grateful for our marathon storyboarding sessions, your wise editorial feedback, and the endless support you've given me. Thank you for helping me realize my lifelong dream of publishing a novel. Let's do it again!

Endless gratitude to my editor, Liz Pearsons, for giving my book an incredible home at Thomas & Mercer. Thank you for your support and enthusiasm and for helping me bring this story to the next level. I'm so grateful my debut novel is with you.

Thank you, a million times over, to developmental editor Charlotte Herscher, for your brilliant feedback, keen eye for detail, and incredibly helpful edits. I'm so fortunate to have had your help with this novel! Also, a big thank-you to Scott C. and Rachel N. for your meticulous copyedit and proofread of this book. I had no idea I was taking so many creative liberties with commas! I appreciate your work so much.

Thank you to Steph VanderMeulen and Heather Debling, my earliest readers, for your genius feedback on this and every piece of writing I've shared with you over the years—and for your steadfast friendship. I couldn't have written this book without you.

To some of my nearest and dearest—Kali Pezzi, Sara Mouchon, Sara Smith, and Samantha Williams—thank you from the bottom of my heart for the decades of friendship and your constant support and excitement about this novel. You've each taught me so many special things about long-term friendship, and I hope you always know how much I treasure you! You're the friends who became family.

A massive thank-you to Lindsey Noel Smith, my writing soulmate and dear friend, for walking with me through the long process of writing, revising, querying, revising again, going on sub, and eventually selling this book. I know for certain I couldn't have done this without you, at least not with my sanity intact. There aren't enough words to express how much I admire you and how thankful I am to call you my friend. I will be forever grateful that our paths crossed when they did and we found each other in this life! Vague vague art art forever.

Thank you to my parents, Carolyn and Tony Costa, for always encouraging my love of reading and writing. Because of you and my grandparents, Lucy and Michael Kroian, I grew up believing in myself and my passions. I'm grateful for the support you all gave me as I applied for MFA programs at the height of a recession when I was just an English-major undergrad who had no idea what to do after college. You all agreed that pursuing creative writing was a good decision, and you were right. Your support has carried me through the ups and downs of the writing journey!

A huge thank-you to the rest of my beloved family—Mary and Anthony Offiler, Lisa Offiler, Andrew Offiler, Tim Offiler, Sarah Costa, Andrew Costa, and Nick Costa, as well as my niece, Kathleen, and nephews, Henry and Adrian, for the endless support and encouragement as I chipped away at this book over the years. I don't know what I did to deserve an extended family as wonderful as ours, but I'm so grateful for all of you every single day.

Mia and Josie, thank you for napping by my side while I wrote and edited this book.

To Matt and Everett, my two loves and my whole world, thank you for always making sure I have the time and space to write. Matt, thank you for asking to read my short stories from the other side of the world when we first met. You were supportive of my writing from the very beginning, and I don't think I'll ever be able to thank you enough for that. Everett, thank you for being you. I'm so grateful for all the times you've cheered me on as I worked on this book (which I started when you were one!) and how excited you were when I told you it was finally going to be published. You're the most inspiring, creative person I know, and I love being your mama!

And thank you, reader, for taking a chance on a debut author and picking up this novel. I worked on this book for many years with you in mind, and I hope you found something to love in these pages. Thank you, thank you, thank you for reading!

About the Author

Kristin Offiler holds an MFA from Lesley University. Her short fiction has appeared in the *Raleigh Review*, *Waccamaw Journal*, *The Bookends Review*, and *The Bookends Review Best of 2020* print anthology. When she's not writing, she can be found reading on the porch of her 130-year-old house or exploring charming corners of New England. She lives in Rhode Island with her husband, son, and dog. For more information, visit www.kristinoffiler.com.